Praise for Susan Wiggs
and The Lakeshore Chronicles

"Superb. Wonderfully evoked characters,
a spellbinding story line, and insights into
the human condition will appeal to every reader."
—*Booklist* on *Summer at Willow Lake*

"With the ease of a master, Wiggs introduces complicated
flesh-and-blood characters…a refreshingly honest romance."
—*Publishers Weekly* on *The Winter Lodge*

"Rich with life lessons, nod-along moments and characters
with whom readers can easily relate…. Delightful and wise,
Wiggs's latest shines."
—*Publishers Weekly* on *Dockside*

"Wiggs is at the top of her game here, combining a charming
setting with subtly shaded characters and more than a touch
of humor. This is the kind of book a reader doesn't want to see
end but can't help devouring as quickly as possible."
—*Publishers Weekly* on *Snowfall at Willow Lake*

"Worth a look for the often-hilarious dialogue alone,
the latest installment of her beloved Lakeshore Chronicles
showcases Wiggs's justly renowned gifts for storytelling
and characterization. A keeper."
—*RT Book Reviews* on *Fireside*

"Wiggs hits all the right notes in this delightful, sometimes
funny, sometimes poignant Christmas treat, which will please
Lakeshore Chronicles fans as well as garner new ones."
—*Library Journal* on *Lakeshore Christmas*

"Wiggs delights with this Christmas-themed installment in
her Lakeshore Chronicles series…the evolution of Darcy and
Logan's relationship makes enduring love believable."
—*Publishers Weekly* on *Candlelight Christmas*

Look for Susan Wiggs's next novel
THE BEEKEEPER'S BALL
available soon from Harlequin MIRA

SUSAN WIGGS

The Summer Hideaway

THE Lakeshore Chronicles

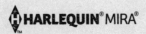

Recycling programs
for this product may
not exist in your area.

ISBN-13: 978-0-7783-1700-5

THE SUMMER HIDEAWAY

Copyright © 2010 by Susan Wiggs

For questions and comments about the quality of this book, please contact us at
CustomerService@Harlequin.com.

Printed in U.S.A.

I wish to thank the Jacobi family for their support of P.A.W.S. and for providing inspiration for the fictional pets in this book.

The Summer Hideaway

Seeking: Private Duty Nurse (Upstate New York)

PostingID: 146002215 *Avoid scams by dealing locally*
Reply to godfrey@georgebellamy.com

Senior accomplished gentleman seeks end-of-life nursing care, full-time, days and nights.

Qualifications:
- age twenty-five to thirty-five
- female (not negotiable)
- must have a positive attitude and a sense of adventure
- must love children of all ages
- must be open to relocation
- no emotional baggage
- nursing skills and valid state certification a plus

Benefits:
- medical, dental, vision, 401(k)
- weekly paychecks with direct deposit

Rustic accommodations provided on Willow Lake in the Catskills Wilderness.

Prologue

Korengal Valley, Kunar province, Afghanistan

His breakfast consisted of shoestring potatoes that actually did look and taste like shoestrings, along with reconstituted eggs, staring up at him from a compartmentalized tray in the noisy chow hall. His cup was full of a coffeelike substance, lightened by a whitish powder.

At the end of a two-year tour of duty, Ross Bellamy had a hard time looking at morning chow. He'd reached his limit. Fortunately for him, this was his last day of deployment. It seemed like any other day—tedious, yet tense with the constant and ominous hum of imminent threat. Radio static crackled along with the sound of clacking utensils, so familiar to him by now that he barely heard it. At a comm station, an ops guy for the Dustoff unit was on alert, awaiting the next call for a medical evacuation.

There was always a next call. An air medic crew like Ross's faced them daily, even hourly.

When the walkie-talkie clipped to his pocket went

off, he put aside the mess without a second glance. The call was a signal for the on-duty crew to drop everything—a fork poised to carry a morsel of mystery meat to a mouth. A game of Spades, even if you were winning. A letter to a sweetheart, chopped off in the middle of a sentence that might never be finished. A dream of home in the head of someone dead asleep. A guy in the middle of saying a prayer, or one with only half his face shaved.

The medevac units prided themselves on their reaction time—five or six minutes from call to launch. Men and women burst into action, still chewing food or drying off from the shower as they fell into roles as hard and familiar as their steel-toed boots.

Ross gritted his teeth, wondering what the day had in store for him, and hoping he'd make it through without getting himself killed. He needed this discharge, and he needed it now. Back home, his grandfather was sick— had been sick for a while, and Ross suspected it was a lot more serious than the family let on. It was hard to imagine his grandfather sick. Granddad had always been larger-than-life, from his passion for travel to his trademark belly laugh, the one that could make a whole roomful of people smile. He was more than a grandparent to Ross. Circumstances in his youth had drawn the two of them close in a bond that defined their relationship even now.

On impulse, he grabbed his grandfather's most recent letter and stuck it into the breast pocket of his flight jacket, next to his heart. The fact that he'd even felt the urge to do so made him feel a gut-twist of worry.

"Let's go, Leroy," said Nemo, the unit's crew chief. Then, as he always did, he sang the first few lines of "Get Up Offa That Thang."

In the convoluted way of the army, Ross had been given the nickname Leroy. It had started when some of the platoon had learned a little—way too little—about his silver-spoon-in-mouth background. The fancy schools, the Ivy League education, the socially prominent family, had all made him fodder for teasing. Nemo had dubbed him Little Lord Fauntleroy. That had been shortened to Leroy, and the name had stuck.

"I'm on it," Ross said, striding toward the helipad. He and Ranger would be piloting the bird today.

"Good luck with the FNG."

FNG stood for Fucking New Guy, meaning Ross would have a mission virgin on board. He vowed to be nice. After all, if it weren't for new guys, Ross would be here forever. According to the order packet he'd received, his *forever* was about to end. In a matter of days, he'd be stateside again, assuming he didn't get himself greased today.

The FNG turned out to be a girl, a flight medic named Florence Kennedy, from Newark, New Jersey. She had that baby-faced determination common to newbies, worn as a thin mask over abject, bowel-melting fear.

"What the fuck are you waiting for?" demanded Nemo, striding past her. "Get your ass over to the LZ."

She seemed frozen, her face pale with resentment. She made no move to follow Nemo.

Ross nailed her with a glare. "Well? What the hell is it?"

"Sir, I… Not fond of the f-word, sir."

Ross let out a short blast of laughter. "You're about to fly into a battle zone and you're worried about that? Soldiers swear. Get used to it. Nobody on earth swears as much as a soldier—and nobody prays as hard. And I don't know about you, but I see no conflict there. Pretty soon, you won't, either."

She looked as though she might cry. He tried to think of something to say to reassure her, but could come up with nothing. When had he stopped knowing how to speak kindly?

When he'd grown too numb to feel anything.

"Let's go," he said simply, and strode away without looking back.

The ground crew chief barked out a checklist. Everyone climbed aboard. Armor and helmets would be donned on the chopper to shave off run time.

Ross received the details through his earpiece while he consulted his lap charts. The call was the type they feared most—victims both military and civilian, *enemy still in the area.* Apache gunships would escort the medical birds because the red crosses on the nose, underbelly and each cargo door of the ship meant nothing to the enemy. The crew couldn't let that matter; they had to roll fast. When a soldier on the ground was wounded, he needed to hear one key phrase: *Dustoff is inbound.* For some guy bleeding out in the field, the flying ambulance was his only hope of survival.

Within minutes, they were beating it northward over the evergreen-covered mountains of Kunar province. Flying at full speed across the landscape of craggy peaks, majestic forests and silvery rivers, Ross felt tense and jittery, on edge. The constant din of flight ops, along with strict regulations, kept conversation confined to essential matters only over the headsets. The rush into unknown danger was an everyday ordeal, yet he never got used to it. Last mission, he told himself. This is your last mission. Don't blow it.

The Korengal Valley was one of the most beautiful places on earth. Also one of the most treacherous. Sometimes the helos encountered surface-to-air missiles, cannonade or tripwires strung between mountain peaks to snag the aircraft. At the moment, the gorgeous landscape erupted with lightning bolts of gunfire and ominous plumes of smoke. Each represented a deadly weapon aimed at the birds.

Ross's heart had memorized the interval of delay between spotting the flash and taking the hit—one, two, three beats of the heart and something could be taken out.

The gunships broke off to fire on the areas blooming with muzzle flashes. The diversion created a lull so the medical choppers could circle down.

Ross and Ranger, the other pilot, focused on closing the distance between the bird and the other end of the radio call. Despite the information given, they never knew what might be waiting for them. Half of their flights were for evacuating Afghan civilians and security personnel. The country had lousy medical infrastructure, so sometimes a pickup was for patient transport, combat injuries, accidents, even dog bites. Ross's unit had seen everyone's horrors and ill luck. But judging by the destination, this was not going to be a simple patient transport to Bagram Air Base. This region was the deadliest of Taliban havens, patrolled on foot and referred to as the Valley of Death.

The chopper neared the pickup point and descended. The tops of the majestic pine trees swayed back and forth, beaten by the wind under the main rotors, offering fleeting glimpses of the terrain. Wedged between the walls of the valley lay a cluster of huts with rooftops of baked earth. He saw scurrying civilians and troops, some fanning out in search of the enemy, others guarding their wounded as they waited for help to arrive.

Muzzle flashes lit the hillsides on both ends of the valley. Ross knew immediately that there was too much small-arms fire below. The gunships were spread too thin.

The risk of drawing enemy fire was huge, and as pilot, he had to make the call. Bail now and protect the crew, or go in for the rescue and save the lives below. As always, it was an agonizing choice, but one made swiftly and followed by steel resolve. No time for a debate.

He took the bird in, hovering as close to the mark as he dared, but couldn't land. The other pilot shook his head vigorously. The terrain was too rough. They'd have to lower a litter.

The crew chief hung out the cargo bay door, letting the penetrator cable slide through his gloved hand. A Stokes litter was lowered and the first soldier—the one most seriously wounded, was placed in the basket. Ross lifted off, hearing "Breaking ground, sir," over his headset as the winch began its fast rewind.

The basket was nearly in the bird when Ross spotted a fresh plume of smoke—a rocket launcher. At an altitude of only fifty feet, he had no time to take evasive action. The miniature SAM slammed into the aircraft.

A flash of white lightning whipped through the ship. Everything showered down—shrapnel, gear, chips of paint, and an eerie flurry of dried blood from past sorties, flaking off the cargo area and blowing around. Then a burst of fire raked the chopper, slugs stitching holes in the bird. It bucked and vibrated, throwing off webbing, random bits of aluminum, broken equipment, including a couple of radios, right in the middle of Ross's first Mayday call to the ops guys at base who were managing the mission. A ruptured fuel line hosed the flight deck.

He felt slugs smacking into his armored chair, the plates in front of his face, the overhead bubble window. Something thumped him in the back, knocking the wind out of him. *Don't die,* he told himself. *Don't you fucking die.* He stayed alive because if he got himself killed, he'd take down everybody with him. It was as good a reason as he knew to keep going.

He had landed a pranged chopper before, but not in these conditions. There was no water to hit. He hoped like hell he could set it down with everybody intact. He couldn't tell if the crew had reeled the basket in. Couldn't let himself think about that—a wounded soldier twisting and dangling from the bird.

Ranger tried another radio. The red trail of a smoke grenade bloomed, and then the wind swept it away. Ross spotted a patch of ground just as another hail of fire hit. Decking flew up, pieces glancing off his shoulder, his helmet. The ship whirled as though thrown into a giant blender, completely out of his control. There was no lift, nothing at all. The whistles and whines of the dying ship filled his head.

As the earth raced up to meet them, he found himself focusing on random sights on the ground—a tattered billboard for baby milk, a mangled soccer goal. The chopper roared as it hit, throwing up more steel decking. The jolt slammed through every bone of his body. His back teeth crunched together. A stray rotor slung free, mowing down everything in sight. Ross was in motion even before the thing settled. The reek of JP4 fuel choked him. He flung out a hand, grabbing Ranger's shoulder, thanking God the other pilot was looking lively.

Nemo was struggling with his monkey strap, the rig used to hold him in the chopper during ops. The straps had tangled, and he was still tethered to a tie-down clamp attached to the ripped-up deck. Ranger went to help him, and the two of them dragged away the wounded guy in the litter, which, thankfully, had been hoisted into the cargo bay before the crash.

"Kennedy!" Ross dropped to his knees beside her. She lay eerily still, on her side. "Hey, Kennedy," he said, "Move your ass. Move your fucking ass! We need to get out."

Don't be dead, he thought. Please don't be dead. Damn, he hated this. Too many times, he'd turned a soldier over to find him—or her—too far gone, floating in root reflexes.

"Ken—"

"Fuck." The FNG threw off his hand, hauling herself to her feet while uttering a stream of profanities. Then, just for a second, she focused on Ross. The soft-cheeked newness was already gone from her face, replaced by flinty-eyed determination. "Quit wasting time, Chief," she said. "Let's get the fuck out of here."

The four of them crouched low against the curve of the chopper's battered hull. Bullet holes riddled the starkly painted red cross and pockmarked the tail boom. The floor was covered with loose AK-47 rounds.

The Apache gunships had broken off and gone into hunter-killer mode, searching out the enemy on the ground, firing at the muzzle flashes on the mountainsides and producing a much-prayed-for lull. The other chopper had escaped and was no doubt sending out distress calls on the unit's behalf. Pillars of black smoke from mortar rounds rose up everywhere.

With no means of evacuation, the crew had to take cover wherever they could. Heads down, in a hail of debris, they carried the litter toward the nearest house. Through a cloud of dust and smoke, Ross spotted an enemy soldier, hunched and watchful, armed with an AK-47, approaching the same house from the opposite direction.

"I got this," he signaled to Nemo, nudging him.

Unarmed against a hot weapon, Ross knew he had only seconds to act or he'd lose the element of surprise. That was where the army's training kicked in. Approaching from behind, he stooped low, grabbed the guy by both ankles and yanked back, causing the gunman to fall flat on his face. Even as the air rushed from the surprised victim's chest, Ross dispatched him quickly—eyes, neck, groin—in that order. The guy never knew what hit him. Within seconds, Ross had bound his wrists with zip ties, confiscated the weapon and dragged the enemy soldier into the house.

There, they found a host of beleaguered U.S. and Afghan soldiers. "Dustoff 91," Ranger said by way of introduction. "And unfortunately, you're going to have to wait for another ride."

The captured soldier groaned and shuddered on the floor.

"Jesus, where'd you learn that move?" one of the U.S. soldiers demanded.

"Unarmed combat—a medevac's specialty," said Nemo, giving Ross a hand.

A babble of Pashto and English erupted. "We're toast," said a dazed and exhausted soldier. Like his comrades, he looked as if he hadn't bathed in weeks, and he wore a dog's flea collar around his middle; life at the outposts was crude as hell. The guy—still round-cheeked with youth, but with haunted eyes—related the action in dull shell-shocked tones. A part of this kid wasn't even there anymore. When Ross met a soldier in such a state, he often found himself wondering if the missing part would ever be restored.

"Let's have a look at the wounded," Kennedy suggested. She seemed desperate to do something, anything. The soldier took her to a row of supine people on the floor—an Afghan teenager holding an iPhone and keening what sounded like a prayer, a guy moaning and clutching his shredded leg, several lying unconscious. Kennedy checked their vitals and looked around, lost. "I need something to write on."

Ross grabbed a Sharpie marker from her kit. "Right there," he said, indicating the teenager's bare chest.

She hesitated, then started to write on the boy's skin. More gunfire slapped the ground outside. After what seemed like an eternity, but was probably only twenty minutes, another Dustoff unit arrived, lowered a medic on a winch line and then beat away in search of a place to land. Inside the hut, the triage continued, with everyone aiding the medics.

Ross moved past a pair of soldiers who were obviously dead. He felt nothing. He wouldn't let himself. The nightmares would come later.

"See if you can stop that bleeding," the new medic said, indicating another victim. "Just hold something on it."

Ross ripped off a sleeve to staunch a bleeding wound. Only after he'd pressed the fabric into an arm did he see that it was attached to an old guy who was being held by a boy singing softly into the man's ear. It seemed to calm the wounded guy, Ross observed.

He needed to find the part of him that could still feel. He needed what he saw in the way the boy's hand caressed the old man's cheek. *Family.* It gave life its meaning. When everything was stripped away, family was the only thing that mattered, the only thing that kept a person tethered to the ground. Other than his grandfather, Ross was lacking in that department. He hated feeling so hollow and numb.

Fire from the insurgents subsided. Two more chopper crews arrived with litters, racing across open ground to reach the others. Everyone burst into action, taking advantage of the lull. The wounded were loaded on litters, pulled along on ponchos, carried in straining arms. Those who were ambulatory piled in, creating chaos. The first bird took off, chugging with its burden, then swung like a carnival ride.

Ross was in the second one, the last to board, grasping a cleat for a handhold. The firing started up again, pinging off the skids. The flight passed in a blur of noise and dust and smoke, but finally—thank God, finally—he could see an ops guy mouth the magic words everyone had been waiting—hoping, praying—for: *Dustoff is inbound.*

They reached the LZ with the last of their fuel, and the ground personnel took over. Ross found somebody in medical to give him some betadine and a couple of bandages. Then he walked out into the compound, the sun beating down on his bare arm where he'd ripped his sleeve off. He was light-headed with the feeling that he'd been to hell and back.

It was barely noon.

Renowned for its swiftness and efficiency, his Dustoff unit had saved a lot of lives. Twenty-five minutes from battlefield to trauma ward was the norm. It was something he'd look back at with pride, but it was time to move on. He was so damn ready to move on.

Guys were milling around the mess tent. Two more air crews were preparing to head out again.

"Hey, Leroy, Christmas came early for you this year," said Nemo, wolfing down a folded-over piece of pizza from the Pizza Hut tent. "I hear your discharge orders came through."

Ross nodded. A wave of something—not quite relief—surged through him. It was really happening. At last, he was going home.

"What're you going to do with yourself once you're stateside?" Nemo asked.

Start over, thought Ross. Get it right this time around. "I got big plans," he said.

"Right," Nemo said with a chuckle, heading for the showers. "Don't we all."

When you were in the middle of something like this, Ross thought, you didn't plan anything except how not to die in the next few minutes. It was a total mind trip to realize he'd have to think past that now.

He spotted Florence Kennedy hunkered down in the shade, sipping from a canteen and quietly crying.

"Hey, sorry about the way I screamed at you out there," he said.

She gazed up at him, red eyes swimming. "You saved my ass today."

"It's a pretty nice ass."

"Careful how you talk to me, Chief. That mouth of yours could get you in a world of shit." She grinned through her tears. "I owe you."

"Just doing my job, ma'am."

"Sounds like you're heading home."

"Yep."

She dug in her pocket, took out a card and scribbled an e-mail address on it. "Maybe we'll keep in touch."

"Maybe." It didn't work that way, but she was too new to know.

He turned the card over to the printed side. "Tyrone Kennedy. The state prosecutor's office of New Jersey," he said. "Does this mean I'm in trouble?"

"No. But if you ever get *your* ass in trouble in New Jersey, try calling my dad. He's got connections."

"And yet here you are." He gestured around the dusty compound. Maybe she was like he'd been—aimless, needing to do something that mattered.

She gave a shrug. "I'm just saying, sir. Anywhere, anytime you need something from me, it's yours." She put the cap back on her canteen and headed into the mess, clearly a different person from the newbie he'd met just a few hours before.

He was surprised to see his hand shaking as he tucked the card into his pocket. Other than a few nicks and bruises, he wasn't wounded, yet everything hurt. His nerve endings had nerve endings. After twenty-three months of numbing himself to all kinds of pain, he was starting to feel everything again.

One

Ulster County, New York

For a dying man, George Bellamy struck Claire as a fairly cheerful old guy. The dumbest show she'd ever heard was playing on the car radio, a chat hour called "Hootenanny," and George found it hilarious. He had a distinctive, infectious laugh that seemed to emanate from an invisible center and radiate outward. It started as a soft vibration, then crescendoed to a sound of pure happiness. And it wasn't just the radio show. George had recently received word that his grandson was coming home from the war in Afghanistan, and that added to his cheerfulness. He anticipated a reunion any day now.

Very soon, she hoped, for both their sakes.

"I can't wait to see Ross," said George. "He's my grandson. He's just been discharged from the army, and he's supposed to be on his way back."

"I'm sure he'll come to see you straightaway," she assured him, pretending he had not just told her this an hour ago.

The springtime foliage blurred past in a smear of color—the pale green of leaves unfurling, the yellow trumpets of daffodils, the lavish purples and pinks of roadside wildflowers.

She wondered if he was thinking about the fact that this would be his last springtime. Sometimes her patients' sadness over such things, the finality of it all, was unbearable. For now, George's expression was free of pain or stress. Although they'd only just met, she sensed he was going to be one of her more pleasant patients.

In his stylish pressed slacks and golf shirt, he looked like any well-heeled gentleman heading away from the city for a few weeks. Now that he'd ceased all treatment, his hair was coming back in a glossy snow-white. At the moment, his coloring was very good.

As a private-duty nurse specializing in palliative care for the terminally ill, she met all kinds of people—and their families. Though her focus was the patient, he always came with a whole host of relatives. She hadn't met any of George's family yet; his sons and their families lived far away. For the time being, it was just her and George.

He seemed very focused and determined at the moment. And thus far, he reported that he was pain free.

She indicated the notebook he held in his lap, its pages covered with old-fashioned spidery handwriting. "You've been busy."

"I've been making a list of things to do. Is that a good idea?" he asked her.

"I think it's a great idea, George. Everybody keeps a list of things they need to do, but most of us just keep it up here." She tapped her temple.

"I don't trust my own head these days," he admitted,

an oblique reference to his condition—glioblastoma multiforme, a heartlessly fatal cancer. "So I've taken to writing everything down." He flipped through the pages of the book. "It's a long list," he said, almost apologetically. "We might not get to everything."

"All we can do is the best we can. I'll help you," she said. "That's what I'm here for." She scanned the road ahead, unused to rural highways. To a girl from the exhausted midurban places of Jersey and the sooty bustle of Manhattan, the forest-clad hills and rocky ridges of the Ulster County highlands resembled an alien landscape. "It's not such a bad idea to have too many things to do," she added. "That way, you'll never get bored."

He chuckled. "In that case, we're in for a busy summer."

"We're in for whatever summer you want."

He sighed, flipping the pages. "I wish I'd thought about these things before I knew I was dying."

"We're all dying," she reminded him.

"And how the devil did I luck into a home health care worker with such a sunny disposition?"

"I bet a sunny disposition would drive you crazy." Although she and George were new to each other, she had a gift for reading people quickly. For her, it was a key survival skill. Misreading a person had once forced Claire to change every aspect of her life.

George Bellamy struck her as circumspect and well-read. Yet he had an air of loneliness, and he was seeking…something. She hadn't discovered precisely what it was. She didn't know a lot about him yet. He was a retired international news correspondent of some renown. He'd spent most of his adult years living in Paris and traveling the globe. Yet now at the end of his life, he wanted to journey to a place far different from the world's capitals.

Lives came to an end with as much variety as they were lived—some quietly, some with drama and fanfare, some with a sense of closure, and far too many with regrets. They were the slow poison that killed the things that brought a person joy. It was amazing to her to observe the way a generally happy, successful life could be taken apart by a few regrets. She hoped George's searching journey would be to a place of acceptance.

Those who were uninitiated in her area of care seemed to think that the dying knew the answers to the big questions, that they were wiser or more spiritual or somehow deeper than the living. This, Claire had learned, was a myth. Terminally ill patients came in all stripes—wise, foolish, filled with happiness or despair, logical, loony, fearful…in fact, the dying were very much like the living. They just had a shorter expiration date. And more physical challenges.

The countryside turned even prettier and more bucolic as they wended their way northwest toward the Catskills Wilderness, a vast preserve of river-fed hills and forests. After a time, they approached their target destination, marked by a rustic sign that read, Welcome To Avalon. A Small Town With A Big Heart.

Her grip tightened almost imperceptibly on the steering wheel. She'd never lived in a small town before. The idea of joining an intimate, close-knit community— even temporarily—made Claire feel exposed and vulnerable. Not that she was paranoid, or—wait, she was. But she had her reasons.

There was no place that ever felt truly safe to her. The

early days with her mother, even before all the trouble started, had been fraught with unpredictability and insecurity. Her mother had been a teenage runaway. She wasn't a bad person, but a bad addict, shot during a drug deal gone wrong on Newark's South Orange Avenue and leaving behind a quiet ten-year-old daughter.

Her life was transformed by the foster care system. Not many would say that, but in this instance, it was entirely true. Her caseworker, Sherri Burke, made sure she was placed with the best foster families in the system. Experiencing family life for the first time, she inhaled the lessons of life from people who cared. She learned what it was like to be a part of something larger and deeper than herself.

To appreciate the blessings of a family, all she had to do was watch. It was everywhere—in the look in a woman's eyes when her husband walked through the door. In the touch of a mother's hand on a child's feverish brow. In the laughter of sisters, sharing a joke, or the protective stance of a brother, watching out for his siblings. A family was a safety net, cushioning a fall. An invisible shield, softening a blow.

She dared to dream of a better life—a love of her own, a family. Kids. A life filled with all the things that made people smile and feel a cushion of comfort when they were sad or hurting or afraid.

This can be yours was the promise of the system, when it was working as it should.

Then, at the age of seventeen, everything changed. She had witnessed a crime that forced her into hiding—from someone she had once trusted with her life. If that wasn't a rationale for paranoia, she didn't know what was.

A small town like this could be a dangerous place, especially for a person with something to hide. Anyone who read Stephen King novels knew that.

If worse came to worst, then she would simply disappear again. She was good at that.

She'd learned long ago that the witness protection programs depicted in the movies were pure fiction. A simple murder was not a federal case, so the federal witness protection program—WITSEC—was not an option for her. This was unfortunate, because the federal program, expertly administered and well-funded by the U.S. marshals, had a track record of effectively protecting witnesses without incident.

State and local programs were a different story. They were invariably underfunded. Taxpayers didn't relish spending their money on these programs. The majority of informants and witnesses were criminals themselves, trading information for immunity from prosecution. The total innocents, such as Claire had been, were a rarity. Often, witness protection consisted of a one-way bus ticket and a few weeks in a motor court. After that, the witness was on her own. And for a witness like Claire, whose situation was so dangerous she couldn't even trust the police, sometimes the only ally was luck.

Now the families she had been a part of so briefly seemed like a dream, or a life that had happened to someone else. She used to believe she'd have a family of her own one day, but now that was out of her reach. Yes, she could fall in love, have a relationship, kids, even. But why would she do that? Why would she create something in her life to love, only to expose it to the threat of being found out? So here she was, trapped into an existence on the fringes of other people's families. She tried so hard to make it work for her, and sometimes it did. Other times, she felt as though she was drifting away, like a leaf on the wind.

"Almost there," she said to George, noting the distance tracker on the GPS.

"Excellent. The journey is so much shorter than it seemed to me when I was a boy. Back then, everyone took the train."

George had not explained to her exactly why he had decided to spend his final time in this particular place, nor had he told her why he was making the trip alone. She knew he would reveal it in due course.

People's end-of-life experiences often involved a journey, and it was usually to a place they were intimately connected with. Sometimes it was where their story began, or where a turning point in life occurred. It might be a search for comfort and safety. Other times it was just the opposite; a place where there was unfinished business to be dealt with. What this sleepy town by Willow Lake was to George Bellamy remained to be seen.

The road followed the contours of a burbling tree-shaded stream marked the Schuyler River, its old Dutch spelling as quaint as the covered bridge she could see in the distance. "I can't believe there's a covered bridge. I've never seen one before, except in pictures."

"It's been there for as long as I can remember," George said, leaning slightly forward.

Claire studied the structure, simple and nostalgic as an old song, with its barn-red paint and wood-shingled roof. She accelerated, curious about the town that seemed to mean so much to her client. This might turn out to be a good assignment for her. It might even be a place that actually felt safe for once.

No sooner had the thought occurred to her than a blue-white flash of light battered the van's rearview mirror. A split second later came the warning *blip* of a siren.

Claire felt a sudden frost come over her. The tips of her fingernails chilled and all the color drained from her face; she could feel the old terror coming on with sudden swiftness. She battled a mad impulse to floor the accelerator and race away in the cumbersome van.

George must have read her mind—or her body language. "A car chase is not on my list," he said.

"What?" Flushed and sweating, she eased her foot off the accelerator.

"A car chase," he said, enunciating clearly. "Not on my list. I can die happy without the car chase."

"I'm totally pulling over," she said. "Do you see me pulling over?" She hoped he couldn't detect the tremor in her voice.

"There's a tremor in your voice," he said.

"Getting pulled over makes me nervous," she said. Understatement. Her throat and chest felt tight; her heart was racing. She knew the clinical term for her condition, but it was the layman's expression she offered George. "Kind of freaks me out." She stopped on the gravel verge and put the van in Park.

"I can see that." George calmly drew a monogrammed gold money clip from his pocket. It was filled with neatly folded bills.

"What are you doing?" she demanded, momentarily forgetting her anxiety.

"I suspect he'll be looking for a bribe. Common practice in third world countries."

"We're not in a third world country. I know it might not seem like it, but we're still in New York."

The patrol car, black and shiny as a jelly bean, kept its lights running, signaling to all passersby that a criminal was being apprehended.

"Put that away," she ordered George.

He did so with a shrug. "I could call my lawyer," he suggested.

"I'd say that's premature." She studied the police car through the van's side mirror. "What is taking so long?"

"He—or she—is looking up the vehicle records to see if there's been an alert on it."

"And why would there be an alert?" she asked. The van had been leased in George's name with Claire listed as an authorized driver.

Yet something about his expression put her on edge. She glanced from the mirror to her passenger. "George," she said in a warning voice.

"Let's just hear the officer out," he said. "Then you can yell at me."

The approaching cop, even viewed through the side mirror, stirred a peculiar dread in Claire. The crisp uniform and silvered sunglass lenses, the clean-shaven square jaw and polished boots all made her want to cringe.

"License and registration," he said. It was not a barked order but a calm imperative.

Her fingers felt bloodless as she handed over her driver's license. Although it was entirely legitimate, even down to the reflective watermark and the organ donor information on the back, she held her breath as the cop scrutinized it. He wore a badge identifying him as Rayburn Tolley, Avalon PD. George passed her the folder containing the van's rental documents, and she handed that over, too.

Claire bit the inside of her lip and wished she hadn't come here. This was a mistake.

"What's the trouble?" she asked Officer Tolley, dismayed by the nervousness in her voice. No matter how much time had passed, no matter how often she exposed herself to cops, she could never get past her fear of them. Sometimes even a school crossing guard struck terror in her.

He scowled pointedly at her hand, which was trembling. "You tell me."

"I'm nervous," she admitted. She had learned over the years to tell the truth whenever possible. It made the lies easier. "Call me crazy, but it makes me nervous when I get pulled over."

"Ma'am, you were speeding."

"Was I? Sorry, Officer. I didn't notice."

"Where are you headed?" he demanded.

"To a place called Camp Kioga, on Willow Lake," said George, "and if she was speeding, the fault is mine. I'm impatient, not to mention a distraction."

Officer Tolley bent slightly and peered across the front seat to the passenger side. "And you are…?"

"Beginning to feel harassed by you." George sounded righteously indignant.

"You wouldn't happen to be George Bellamy, would you?" asked Tolley.

"Indeed I am," George said, "but how did you—"

"In that case, ma'am," the cop said, returning his attention to Claire, "I need to ask you to step out of the vehicle. Keep your hands where I can see them."

Her heart seized up. It was a moment she had dreaded since the day she'd realized she was a hunted woman. The beginning of the end. Her mind raced, although she moved like a mechanical wooden doll. Should she submit to him? Make a break for it?

"See here now," George said. "I would like to know why you're so preoccupied with us."

"George, the man's doing his job," said Claire, hoping that would mollify the cop. She motioned for him to sit tight and did as she was told, stepping down awkwardly, using the door handle to steady herself.

Tolley didn't seem put off by George's question. "There was a call to the station about you and Miss…" He consulted the license, which was still clipped to his board. "Turner. The call was from a family member." He glanced at a printout the size of a cash register receipt on the clipboard. "Alice Bellamy," he said.

Claire looked over her shoulder at George, a question in her eyes.

"One of my daughters-in-law," he said, a note of apology in his voice.

"Sir, your family is extremely worried about you," said the cop. He stared at Claire. She couldn't discern his eyes behind the lenses, but could see her own reflection clearly, in twin, convex detail. Medium-length dark hair. Large dark eyes. A plain, she hoped, ordinary, nondescript face. That was always the goal. To blend in. To be forgettable. *Forgotten.*

She forced herself to keep her chin up, to pretend everything was fine. "Is that a crime around here?" she asked. "To have a worried family?"

"It's more than worry." Officer Tolley rested his right hand atop the holster carrying his service revolver. She could see that he'd released the safety strap. "Mr. Bellamy's family has some serious concerns about you."

She swallowed hard. The Bellamys were made of money. Maybe the daughter-in-law had ordered a deep and thorough background check. Maybe that check had uncovered some irregularity, something about Claire's past that didn't quite add up.

"What kind of concerns?" she asked, dry-mouthed, consumed by terror now.

"Oh, let me guess," George suggested with a blast of laughter. "My family thinks I've been kidnapped."

Two

KAIA *(Kabul Afghanistan International Airport)*

"**S**he did what?" Ross practically shouted into the borrowed mobile phone.

"Sorry, we have a terrible connection," said his cousin Ivy, speaking to him from her home in Santa Barbara, where it was eleven and a half hours earlier. "She kidnapped Granddad."

Ross rotated his shoulders, which felt curiously light. For the past two years, he'd been burdened by twenty pounds of individual body armor plates, a Kevlar helmet and vest. Now that he was headed home, the weight was gone. He'd turned in the IBA plates, shedding them like a molting beetle.

Yet according to his cousin, the civilian life had its own kind of perils.

"Kidnapped?" The loaded word snagged the attention of the others in the waiting room. He waved his hand, a nonverbal signal that all was well, and turned away from the prying eyes.

"You heard me," Ivy said. "According to my mother, he hired some sketchy home health care worker off of Craigslist, and she kidnapped him and took him to some remote mountain hideaway up in Ulster County."

"That's nuts," he said. "That's completely nuts." Or was it? In this part of the world, kidnappings were common. And they rarely had a good outcome.

"What can I say?" Ivy sounded almost apologetic. "It's my mom at her most dramatic."

Growing up, first cousins Ross and Ivy had bonded over their drama-queen mothers. A few years younger than Ross, Ivy lived in Santa Barbara, where she created avant garde sculpture and wrote long, angsty e-mails to her cousin overseas.

"And you're certain Aunt Alice's overreacting? There's no chance she might be on to something?"

"There's always a chance. That's how my mom operates—within the realm of possibility. She thinks Granddad is losing it. Everybody knows brain tumors make people do crazy things. When can you get to New York?" asked Ivy. "We really need you, Ross. Granddad needs you. You're the only one he listens to. Where the hell are you, anyway?"

Ross looked around the foreign airport, jammed with soldiers in desert fatigues, trading stories of firefights, suicide bombers, roadside ambushes. Transport here had been his last movement on the ground. He remembered thinking, please don't let anything happen now. He didn't want to be one of those depressing items you read about in hometown newspapers—*On his last day of deployment, he died in a convoy attack....*

He pictured Ivy in her bohemian guest house on the

bluffs above Hendry's Beach. He could hear a Cream album playing in the background. She was probably making coffee in her French press and watching the surfers paddle to the beach-break for an early morning ride.

"I'm on my way," he said. The homeward-bound soldiers had all been sitting at KAIA for hours. Time dragged at the pace of a glacier. Originally their flight was supposed to leave at 1400, but that had been delayed to 2145. They'd been ordered back to the departure tent and subjected to mandatory lockdown, which meant sitting in an airless tent with nothing to do until it was time to board: 2145 had come and gone, the delay surprising no one.

"Ross?" His cousin's voice prodded him. "How much longer before you're home?"

"Working on it," he said to her. At the moment, he might as well be on a different planet; he felt that far away. "What's going on with Granddad?"

"Here's what I know. He's been in treatment at the Mayo Clinic. I guess they told him then…" She paused, and a sob pulsed through the phone. "They told him it was the worst possible news."

"Ivy—"

"It's inoperable. I don't think even my mother would exaggerate that. He's going to die, Ross."

Ross felt sucker-punched by the words. For a few seconds, he couldn't breathe or see straight. There had to be some mistake. A month ago, Ross had received the usual communiqué from his grandfather. George Bellamy had a curiously old-fashioned style of writing, even with e-mail, starting each message with a proper heading and salutation. He had mentioned the Mayo Clinic—"nothing to worry about." Ross had failed to read between the lines. He hadn't let himself go there, even though he knew damn well a guy didn't go to the Mayo Clinic for a hangnail. He hadn't let himself think about…sweet Jesus…a terminal prognosis.

Granddad's sign-off was always the same: *Keep Calm and Carry On.*

And that, in essence, was the way George Bellamy lived. Apparently it was the way he was going to die.

"He finally told my dad," Ivy was saying. There was still a catch in her voice. "He said he wasn't going to pursue further treatment."

"Is he scared?" Ross asked. "Is he in pain?"

"He's just…Granddad. He claimed he had to go to some little town in the Catskills to see his brother. That was the first I'd heard of any brother. Did you know anything about that?"

"Wait a minute, what? Granddad has a *brother?*"

The connection crackled ominously, and he missed the first part of her reply. "…anyway, when my mother heard what he was planning, she went, like, totally ballistic."

Fighting the poor connection and the ambient din of the airport, Ross listened as his cousin filled him in further. Their grandfather had called each of his three sons—Trevor, Gerard and Louis—and he'd calmly informed them of the diagnosis. Then, like a follow-up punch, George had announced his intention to leave his Manhattan penthouse and head for a backwater town upstate to see his brother, some guy named Charles Bellamy. Like Ivy and Ross, most people in the family didn't even know he had a long-lost brother. How could he have a brother nobody knew about? Was he some guy hidden away in an asylum somewhere, like in the movie

Rain Man? Or was he a figment of Granddad's increasingly unreliable imagination?

"So you are telling me he's headed upstate with some sketchy woman who is…who, again?" he asked.

"Her name is Claire Turner. Claims to be some kind of nurse or home health worker. My mom—and yours, too, I'm sure—thinks she's after his money."

That would always be the first concern of Aunt Alice and of his mother, Ross reflected. Though Bellamys only by marriage, they claimed to love George like a father. And maybe they did, but Ross suspected Alice's tantrum was less about losing her father-in-law than it was about splitting her inheritance. He also had no doubt his mother felt the same way. But that was a whole other conversation.

"And they called the police to stop her," Ivy added.

"The police?" Ross shoved a hand through his close-cropped hair. He realized he'd raised his voice again and turned away. "They called the police?" Holy crap. Apparently his mother and aunt had managed to persuade the local authorities that George was with a stranger who meant him harm.

"They didn't know what else to do," said Ivy. "Listen, Ross. I'm so worried about Granddad. I'm scared. I don't want him to suffer. I don't want him to die. Please come home, Ross. Please—"

"I requested an expedited discharge," he assured her. So far, the promised outprocessing hadn't given him much of a head start.

His cousin acted as though his homecoming was going to bring about a miraculous cure for their grandfather. Ross already knew miracles weren't reliable.

"When are you flying to New York?" he asked, but by then he was speaking to empty air; the connection had been lost. He shut the mobile phone and brought it over to Manny Shiraz, a fellow chief warrant officer who had lent it to him when Ross's phone had failed.

"Trouble at home?" Manny asked. It was the kind of question that came up for guys on deployment, again and again.

Ross nodded. "God forbid I should go home and find everything is fine."

"Welcome to the club, Chief."

The idyllic homefront was usually a myth, yet everybody in the waiting area was amped up about going back. There were men and women who hadn't seen their families in a year, some even longer than that. Babies had been born, toddlers had taken their first steps, marriages had crumbled, holidays had passed, loved ones had died, birthdays had been celebrated. Everyone was eager to get back to their lives.

Ross was eager, too—but he didn't have much of a life. No wife and kids counting the hours to his return. Just his mother, Winifred, a flighty and self-absorbed woman…and Granddad.

George Bellamy had been the touchstone of Ross's life since the moment a Casualty Assistance Calls Officer had knocked at the door, arriving in person to tell Winifred Bellamy and her son that Pierce Bellamy had been killed during Operation Desert Storm in 1994.

Granddad had flown to New York from Paris on the Concorde, which was still operating in those days. He had traveled faster than the speed of sound to be with Ross. He'd pulled his grandson into his arms, and the two of them had cried together, and Granddad had made a promise that day: *I will always be here for you.*

They had clung to each other like survivors of a tsunami. Ross's mother all but disappeared into a whirlwind of panicked grief that culminated in a feverish round of dating. Winifred recovered from her loss quickly and decisively, sealing the deal by remarrying and adopting two stepkids, Donnie and Denise. Ross had been shipped off to school in Switzerland because he had difficulty "accepting" his stepfather and his charming stepbrother and stepsister. The American School in Switzerland offered a comprehensive residential educational program. His mother convinced herself that the venerable institution would do a better job raising her son than she herself ever could.

Ross's grief had been so raw and painful he couldn't see straight. Sometimes he wanted to ask her, "In what world is it okay to look at a kid who'd just lost his father and say to him, 'Boarding school! It's just the thing for you!'?"

Then again, maybe her instincts had been right. There were students at TASIS who thrived on the experience—a residential school as magical in its way as Hogwarts itself. He hadn't known it back then, but maybe the long separations and periods of isolation had helped prepare him for deployment.

Being sent an ocean away after losing his dad could have pushed him over the edge, but there was one saving grace in his situation—Granddad. He'd been living and working in Paris and he visited Ross at school in Lugano nearly every single weekend, a lifeline of compassion. Granddad probably didn't realize it, but he'd saved Ross from drowning. He shut his eyes, picturing his grandfather—impressively tall, with abundant white hair. He'd never seemed old to Ross, though.

On the eve of his deployment, Ross had made a promise to his grandfather. "I'm coming back."

Granddad had not had the expected reaction. He'd turned his eyes away and said, "That's what your father told me." It was a negative thing to say, especially for Granddad. Ross knew the words came from fear that he'd never make it home.

He paced, feeling constrained by the interminable waiting. Waiting was a way of life in the army; he'd known that going in but he'd never grown used to it. When he'd announced his intention to serve his country, Ross had known the news would hit his grandfather hard, bringing back the hammer-blows of shock and relentless grief of losing Pierce. But it was something Ross had to do. He'd tried to talk himself out of it. Ultimately he felt compelled to go, as though to complete his father's journey.

Ross had started adulthood as a spoiled, self-indulgent, overgrown kid with no strong sense of direction. Things came easily to him—grades, women, friends—perhaps too easily. After college, he'd drifted, unable to find his place. He'd attained a pilot's license. Seduced too many women. Finally realized he'd better find a vocation that actually meant something. At the age of twenty-eight, he walked into a recruitment office. His age raised eyebrows but they'd given him no trouble; he was licensed to fly several types of aircraft and spoke three languages. The army had given him more of a life than he'd found on his own. Flying a helo was the hardest thing in the world, and for that reason, he loved it. But he couldn't honestly say it had brought him any closer to his father.

* * *

Eventually the first wave of soldiers was taken to the plane. Another hour passed before the bus came back for the rest. Walking onto the transport plane, Ross felt no jubilation; pallets laden with black boxes and duffel bags were still sitting on the tarmac, not yet loaded. This ate up another hour.

A navy LCDR boarded, settling in across from Ross. She flashed him a smile, then pulled out a glossy fashion magazine stuffed with articles about makeup. Ross tried to focus on his copy of *Rolling Stone,* but his mind kept straying.

About an hour into the flight, the LCDR leaned forward to look out the window, cupping her hands around her eyes. "We're not in Afghanistan anymore."

It was too dark to see the ground, but the portal framed a perfect view of the Big Dipper. Ross's grandfather had taught him about the stars. When Ross was about six or seven, Granddad had taken him boating in Long Island Sound. It had been just the two of them in a sleek catboat. Ross had just earned his Bobcat badge in Cub Scouts, and Granddad wanted to celebrate. They had dined on lobster rolls, hot French fries in paper cones and root beer floats from a busy concession stand. Then they'd sailed all evening, until it was nearly dark. "Is that where heaven is?" Ross had asked him, pointing to the sparkling swath of the Milky Way.

And Granddad had reached over, squeezed his hand and said, "Heaven's right here, my boy. With you."

There was a stopover in Manas Air Base in Kyrgyz-stan, where the air was cool and smelled of grass. During the three-hour wait for bags, he tried calling his grandfather, then Ivy, then his mother, with no luck, so he headed to the chow hall to get something to eat. Although it was the middle of the night, the place was bustling. Ross studied the army's morale, welfare and recreation posters advertising sightseeing tours, golf excursions and spa services, which sounded as exotic as a glass of French brandy. Before he'd enlisted, everyday luxuries had been commonplace in his life, thanks to his grandfather. Ross was returning hardened by the things he'd seen and done. But at least he was keeping the promise he'd made to his grandfather.

Please be okay, Granddad, he thought. Please be like a wounded soldier who gets patched up and sent back out into battle. At the next layover in Baku, Azerbaijan, he had the urge to bolt and travel like a civilian, but he quelled the impulse and bided his time, waiting for the flight to Shannon Airport, in Ireland. He couldn't allow himself to veer off track, not now.

Because now, it seemed his grandfather was acting crazy, giving up on treatment and haring off after a brother he hadn't bothered to mention before.

During his deployment, Ross had learned a lot about saving lives—but from shrapnel wounds and traumatic amputations, not brain tumors. There was an image stuck in his head, from that last sortie. He kept thinking about the boy and the wounded old man, trapped in that house, clinging to each other. Everything had been stripped away from those two, yet they'd radiated calm. He'd never found out what became of the two villagers; follow-ups were rare.

He wished he'd checked on them, though.

Three

"Well, now," said George, buckling his seat belt. "That was exciting."

Claire pulled back onto the road, trying to compose herself. "I can do without that kind of excitement." She drove slowly, with extra caution, as though a thousand eyes were watching her.

George seemed unperturbed by the encounter with the cop. He had politely pointed out that it was a free country, and just because certain family members were worried didn't mean any laws had been broken.

Officer Tolley had asked a number of questions, but to Claire's relief, most of them were directed at George. The old man's no-nonsense replies had won the day. "Young man," he'd said. "Much as I would enjoy being held captive by an attractive woman, it's not the case."

Claire had produced her state license and nursing certificate, trying to appear bland and pleasant, an ordinary woman. She'd had plenty of practice.

The effort must have succeeded because ultimately,

the cop could find no reason to detain them. He sent them on their way with a "Have a nice day, folks."

"Still all right?" she asked George, spying a service station up ahead. "Want to stop here?"

"No, thank you," he said. "We're nearly there, eh?"

She indicated the gizmo on the console between them. "According to the GPS, another eleven-point-seven miles."

"When I was a boy," said George, "we would take the train from Grand Central to Avalon. From there, we'd board an old rattletrap bus waiting at the station to take us up to Camp Kioga." He paused. "Sorry about that."

"About what?"

"Starting a story with 'when I was a boy.' I'm afraid you're going to be hearing that from me a lot."

"Don't apologize," she said. "Everybody's story starts somewhere."

"Good point. But to the world at large, my own story is not that interesting."

"Everyone's life is interesting," she pointed out, "in its own way."

"Kind of you to say," he agreed. "I'm sure you are no exception. I'm looking forward to getting to know you."

Claire said nothing. She kept her eyes on the road— a meandering, little-traveled country road leading to the small lakeside hamlet of Avalon.

Which Claire would she show him, this kindly, doomed old man? The star nursing student? The single woman who kept no possessions, who lived her life from job to job? She wondered if he would see through her, recognizing the rootless individual hiding behind the thin veneer of a made-up life. Occasionally one of her patients discerned something just a bit "off" with her.

Which was one reason she worked only with the terminally ill. A grim rationale, but at least she didn't fool herself about it.

"Trust me," she said to George, "I'm not that interesting."

"You most certainly are," he said. "Your career, for example. I find it a fascinating choice for a young woman. How did you get into this line of work, anyway?"

She had a ready answer. "I've always liked taking care of people."

"But the dying, Claire? That's got to get you down sometimes, eh?"

"Maybe that's why my clients are rich old bastards," she said, keeping her expression deadpan.

"Ha. I deserved that. Still, I'm curious. You're a lovely, bright young woman. Makes me wonder…"

She didn't want him to wonder about her. She was a very private person, not as a matter of choice, but as a matter of life and death. She lived a life made up of lies that had no substance, and secrets she could never share. The things that were true about her were the shallow details, cocktail party fare, not that she got invited to cocktail parties. The person she was deep inside stayed hidden, and that was probably for the best. Who would want to know about the endless nights, when her loneliness was so deep and sharp she felt as though she'd been hollowed out? Who would want to know she was so starved for a human touch that sometimes her skin felt as if it were on fire? Who could understand the way she wished to crawl out of her skin and walk away?

Back when she'd gone underground, she had saved her own life. But it wasn't until much later that she'd realized the cost. It had been simple and exorbitant; she'd given up everything, even her identity.

"Tell you what," she said, "let's keep the focus on you."

"I've never been able to resist a woman of mystery," he declared. "I'll find out if it kills me. It might just kill me." His amusement wasn't necessarily a bad thing. Humor had its uses, even in this situation.

"You have better things to do with your time than pry into my life, George. I'd rather hear about you, anyway. This summer is all about you."

"And you don't find that depressing? Hanging around an old man, waiting for him to die?"

"All kidding aside," she said, "things will go a lot better if you decide to make this summer about your life, not about your death."

"My family thinks you're not right for me."

"I guessed that when they called the police on us. Maybe I'm not right. We'll see."

"So far, we're getting along famously." He paused. "Aren't we?"

"You just hired me. We've only been together for three days."

"Yes, but it's been an intense three days," he pointed out. "Including this long drive from the city. You can tell a lot about a person on a car trip. You and I are getting along fine." Another pause. "You're silent. You don't agree?"

Claire had a policy of trying to be truthful whenever possible. There were so many lies in other areas of her life, this need not be one of them. "Well," she said almost apologetically, "there was the singing, back in Poughkeepsie."

"Everybody sings on car trips," he said. "It's the American way."

"All right. Forget I said anything."

"Was I really that bad?"

"You were pretty bad, George."

"Damn." He flipped through a few pages of his notebook.

"Just keeping it real," she said.

"Oh, I don't mind that you hated my singing," he said. "But you're making me rethink something on my list. Ah, here it is. I wanted to perform a song for my family."

"You could still do that."

"What, so they won't be sad to see me go?"

"You just need a little backup music for accompaniment, and you'll be fine."

"Are you up for it?" he asked.

"No way. I can't sing. I'll find someone to help you."

"I'm going to hold you to that."

Simple, she thought. All she needed to do was find a karaoke place. And get his family to show up. Okay, maybe not so simple.

"Judging by our encounter with Officer Friendly, your relatives are pretty unhappy with me," she said. She didn't much care. As her client, George was her sole concern. Still, it always went better if the family was supportive of the arrangement, because families had a way of complicating things. Sometimes she told herself that the lack of a family was a blessing in disguise. Certainly it was a complication she never had to deal with.

She often imagined about what it was like to have a family, the way a severe diabetic might think about eating a cake with burnt-sugar icing. It was never going to happen, but a girl could fantasize. Sometimes she covertly attended family gatherings—graduation ceremonies, outdoor weddings, even the occasional funeral—just to see what it was like to have a family. She had a fascination with the obituary page of the paper, her attention always drawn to lengthy lists of family members left behind. Which, when she thought about it, was kind of pathetic, but it seemed harmless enough.

"They're too quick to judge," he said. "They haven't even met you yet."

"Well, you did make all these arrangements rather quickly."

"If I hadn't, they would have tried to stop me. They'd say we're incompatible, that you and I are far too different," he pointed out.

"Nonsense," said Claire. "You're a blueblood, and I'm blue collar—it's just a color."

"Exactly," he said.

"We're all in the same race," she added.

"I'm closer to the finish line."

"I thought we were going to try to keep a positive attitude."

"Sorry."

"This is going to go well," she promised him.

"It's going to end badly for one of us."

"Then let's not focus on the ending."

There were known psychological and clinical end-of-life stages people went through when facing a devastating diagnosis—shock, rage, denial and so forth. Everyone in her field of work had memorized them. In practice, patients expressed their stages in ways that were as different and individual as people themselves.

Some held despair at bay with denial, or by displaying a smart-alecky attitude about death. George seemed quite happy to be in that phase. His wry sense of humor appealed to her. Of course, he was using humor and sarcasm to keep the darker things at bay—dread and uncertainty, abject fear, regret, despair. In time, those might or might not materialize. It was her job to be there through everything.

All her previous patients had been in the city, where it was possible to be an anonymous face in the crowd. This was the first time she had ventured somewhere like this—small and old-fashioned, more like an illustration in a storybook than a real place. It was like coming to a theme park, overrun by trees and beautiful wilderness areas and dotted with picturesque farms and painted houses.

"Avalon," she said as they passed another welcome sign, this one marked with a contrived-looking heraldic shield. "I wonder if it's named after a place from Arthurian legend." She'd gone through a teenage obsession with the topic, using books as a refuge from a frightening and uncertain life. One of her foster mothers, an English professor, had taught her how to live deeply in a story, drawing inspiration from its lessons.

"I imagine that's what the founders had in mind. Avalon is where Arthur went to die," George said.

"Not exactly. It's the island where Excalibur was forged, and where Arthur was taken to recover from his wounds after his last battle."

"Ah, but did he ever recover?"

She glanced over at him. "Not yet."

The first thing she did when arriving at a new place was reconnoiter the area. It had become second nature to plan her escape route. The world had been a dangerous place for her since she was a teenager. Avalon was no exception. To most people, a town like this represented an American ideal, with its scrubbed facades and tranquil natural setting. Tree-lined avenues led to the charming center of town, where people strolled along the swept sidewalks, browsing in shop windows.

To Claire, the pretty village looked as forbidding as the edge of a cliff. One false step could be her last. She was already sensing that it was going to be harder to hide here, especially now that she'd been welcomed by the law.

She took note of the train station and main square filled with inviting shops and restaurants, their windows shaded by striped and scalloped awnings. There was a handsome stone building in the middle of a large park— the Avalon Free Library. In the distance was the lake itself, as calm and pristine as a picture on a postcard.

It was late afternoon and the slant of the sun's rays lengthened the shadows, lending the scene a deep, golden tinge of nostalgia. Old brick buildings, some of them with facades of figured stonework, bore the dates of their founding—1890, 1909, 1913. A community bulletin board announced the opening game of a baseball team called the Hornets, to be celebrated with a pregame barbecue.

"Are you a baseball fan?" she asked.

"Devotedly. Some of my fondest memories involve going to the Yankee stadium with my father and brother. Saw the Yankees win the World Series over the Phillies there in 1950. Yogi Berra hit an unforgettable homer in that game." His eyes were glazed by wistful sentiment. "We saw Harry Truman throw out the first pitch of the season one year. He did one with each hand, as I recall.

I've often fantasized about throwing out the game ball. Never had the chance, though."

"Put it on your list, George," she suggested. "You never know."

They passed a bank and the Church of Christ. There were a couple of clothing boutiques, a sporting goods store and a bookstore called Camelot Books. There was a shop called Zuzu's Petals, and a grand opening banner hung across the entrance of a new-looking establishment—Yolanda's Bridal Shoppe. Some of the upper floors of the buildings housed offices—a pediatrician, a dentist, a lawyer, a funeral director.

One-stop shopping, she thought. A person could live and die here without ever leaving.

The idea of spending one's entire life in a single place was almost completely unfathomable to Claire.

She stopped at a pedestrian crossing and watched a dark-haired boy cross while tossing a baseball from hand to hand. On the corner, a blonde pregnant woman came out of a doctor's office. The residents of the town resembled people everywhere—young, old, alone, together, all shapes and sizes. It reminded her that folks tended to be the same no matter where she went. They lived their lives, loved each other, fought and laughed and cried, the years adding up to a life. The residents of Avalon were no different. They just did it all in a prettier place.

"Well, George?" she asked. "What do you think? How does it look to you?"

"The town has changed remarkably little since I was last here," George said. "I wasn't sure I'd recognize anything." His hands tightened around the notebook he held in his lap. "I think I want to die in Avalon. Yes, I believe this is where I want it to happen."

"When was the last time you visited?" she asked, deliberately ignoring his statement for the time being.

"It was August twenty-fourth, 1955," he said without hesitation. "I left on the 4:40 train. I never dreamed another fifty-five years would pass."

That long, thought Claire. What would bring him back to a place after so much time?

"Would you mind pulling in here?" George asked. "I need to make a stop at this bakery. It was here when I last visited."

She berthed the van in a big parking spot marked with a disabled symbol. On good days, George could walk fairly well, and today seemed to be a good day. However, they were in a new place and she didn't want to push their luck.

The Sky River Bakery and Café had a hand-painted sign proclaiming its establishment in 1952. It was a beautiful spring day, and tables with umbrellas sprouted along the sidewalk in front of the place, shading groups of customers as they enjoyed icy drinks and decadent-looking sweets.

She went around to the passenger side of the van to help him. The key to helping a patient, she'd learned from experience, was to take her cues from him. *Respect* and *dignity* were her watchwords.

Though she had a wheelchair available, he opted for his cane, an unpretentious one with a rubber-tipped end. She helped him down and they stood together for a moment, looking around. His somewhat cocky persona slipped a little to reveal a face gone soft with uncertainty.

"George?" she asked.

"Do I look…all right?"

She didn't smile, but her heart melted a little. Everyone had their insecurities. "I was just thinking you look exceptionally good. In fact, it's kind of nice to tell you the truth instead of having to pretend."

"You'd do that? You'd pretend I looked well, even if I didn't?"

"It's all a matter of perspective. I've told people they look like a million bucks when in fact they look like death on a cracker."

"And they don't see through that?"

"People see what they want to see. In your case, there's no need to lie. You're quite handsome. The driving cap is a nice touch. Where did you learn to dress like this?"

"My father, Parkhurst Bellamy. He was always quite clear on the way a gentleman should dress, for any occasion—even a bakery visit. He took my brother and me all the way to London for our first bespoke suits at Henry Poole, on Savile Row. I still get my clothing there."

"Bespoke?"

"Made-to-measure and hand tailored." He glanced at himself in a shop window. "Do me a favor. If I ever get to the stage where I look like death on a cracker, go ahead and lie to me."

"It's a deal." She hesitated. "So do you expect to see someone you know in the bakery?"

He offered a rueful smile. "After all this time? Not likely. On the other hand, it never hurts to be prepared for the unlikely." He squared his shoulders and gripped the head of the cane. "Shall we?" He gallantly held the shop door for her.

The bakery smelled so good she practically swooned from the aroma of fresh baked bread, buttery pastries, cookies and fruit pies, and a specialty of the house known as the *kolache,* which appeared to be a rich, pillowy roll embedded with fruit jam or sweet cheese.

A song by the Indigo Girls drifted from two small speakers. The shop had a funky eclectic decor, with black-and-white checkerboard floors and walls painted a sunny yellow. There was a cat clock with rolling eyes and a pendulum tail, and a hand-lettered menu board. Behind the counter on the wall was a framed dollar bill and various permits and licenses. A side wall featured a number of matted art photographs and articles, including a yellowed newspaper clipping about the bakery's grand opening nearly sixty years ago.

George seemed like a different person here: gentle and pensive, shedding the impatience he'd shown occasionally on the drive from the city. A small line of patrons were clustered at the main counter. George waited his turn, then ordered indulgently—a cappuccino, a *kolache* and an iced maple bar. He also ordered a box of bialys and a strawberry pie to go.

She ordered a glass of iced tea sweetened with Stevia.

They took a seat at a side table decorated with a large travel poster depicting a scene at the lake. A guy in a flour-dusted apron and a name tag identifying him as Zach brought their order. He was an unusual-looking young man, his hair so blond it appeared white—naturally, not bleached. Claire had changed her own hair color enough times to know the difference.

"Enjoy," he said, serving them.

"You didn't order anything." George aimed a pointed

look at her glass of tea. "How can you come to a place like this and not want to sample at least one thing?"

"Believe me, I want to sample *everything*," she admitted. "I can't, though. I, um, used to have a pretty bad weight problem. I really have to watch every single thing I put in my mouth."

"You're showing remarkable self-denial."

So much of her life boiled down to that, to self-denial. What she couldn't tell him was that her diet was not a matter of vanity alone. It was a matter of survival. As a teenager, she had used food as a comfort and a crutch, turning herself into the dateless fat girl. She was the nightmare everyone remembered from high school—overweight, reviled and given over to foster care.

When everything fell apart, her survival had depended on altering the way she looked as much as possible. In addition to changing the cut and color of her hair, the way she dressed, acted and talked, losing weight had been a key element of disguising her former self. Thanks to her young age at the time, and the stress of being on the run, the pounds had come off swiftly. Keeping the weight off was a daily battle. It was dangerously easy to pack on the pounds. It started with a simple, innocent-looking pastry like the one George was holding out to her.

But she had the ultimate motivation—staying alive. "Thanks, you go ahead and enjoy that."

"And what the devil are *you* going to enjoy?"

"Watching you eat a *kolache*," she said.

He shrugged. "My funeral. Whoops, I'm not supposed to be saying things like that, am I?"

"You can say anything you want, George. You can

do anything you want. That's what this summer is going to be about."

"I like the way you think. Should've lived my whole life that way." He took an indulgent bite of his pastry and chewed slowly, his face turning soft with quiet ecstasy. He opened his eyes and saw her watching him. "Well," he said, "there's good news and there's bad news. The bad news is, I'm not going to heaven. The good news is, I'm already there."

"According to the GPS, the resort is only ten miles from here, so I'll make sure you get a steady supply of those pastries," said Claire.

"Honestly, it's that good. Are you certain you can't be tempted with one?"

"I'm certain. And it's nice to know there are *kolaches* on the menu every day in heaven. Do me a favor and take a bite for me." Sipping her tea, she checked out the other patrons. Another paranoid habit of hers was checking to see if she was attracting attention, and scoping out escape options—the swinging door behind the counter, and the main entrance to the street. Seeing no telltale signs of trouble, she studied the framed art poster on the wall. "That's a beautiful shot of Willow Lake."

"It is," George agreed.

The image captured the placid mood and quality of light that pervaded the forest-fringed lake. She noticed a scrawled signature where the photographer had signed and numbered the print. "'Daisy Bellamy,'" she read. "George? Any relation to you?"

"Possibly." A tiny smile tightened his mouth, and she could see him forcibly shifting gears. "It's a singular sensation," he said, alternating bites of the pastry with sips of his full-cream cappuccino. "After decades of having to watch my cholesterol, I'm not going to die of a heart ailment after all." He sampled the maple bar. "I wish I'd known."

She decided against pointing out his circular logic. One reason he'd enjoyed good health as long as he had was probably because he watched his diet.

"I could even take up smoking," he said, blotting his mouth with a napkin. "Cigars and cigarettes won't kill me. I could pursue it, guilt-free."

"Whatever makes you happy."

"I'm working on it," he said.

"On what?"

"On making myself happy. All my life, I told myself I'd be happy someday."

"And now that day has arrived," she said.

"It's hard," he said quietly.

"To be happy? Tell me about it." She took his arm and moved toward the door before he could question her. "Come on, George. Let's go buy you some cigars."

They left town and headed northward along the lake-shore road. In the last part of the afternoon, the golden light deepened to amber, orange and fiery pink. Claire was silent, undone by the splendor of it. She wasn't accustomed to being surrounded by so much riotous beauty, and it pierced her deeply, causing an unexpected welling of emotion.

Here I am, she thought. Here I am.

"This forest has grown so lush," George remarked. "The area used to be all logged out. It's good they replanted it. This is as it should be."

She could feel his excitement spiraling upward as they

approached Camp Kioga. It was their ultimate destination—the camp where he'd spent the summers of his
boyhood. He eagerly pointed out landmarks as they passed
them—mountains and rock formations and lookout points,
a waterfall with a bridge suspended high above it.

The final approach took them deeper into the forest,
where the foliage was so dense that for the first time
Claire relaxed into a feeling of safety, false though it
might have been. The resort came into view, its lodge and
outbuildings nestled in the splendid wilderness at the
northern end of the lake.

According to her hastily read brochure, the resort had
recently been renovated and was run by a young couple,
Olivia and Connor Davis. Yet the place retained its
historic character in its timber and stone buildings,
handmade signs, wild gardens, wooden docks where
catboats and canoes bobbed at their moorage. The
resort's Web site, which she'd browsed the night before,
explained that Camp Kioga had reached its pinnacle
during the era of the Great Camps in the mid-twentieth
century, when families from the city would take refuge
from the summer heat.

The deep history and beauty of the place made her
yearn for things she couldn't have, like people who knew
who she really was. What a gift it would be if she could
stop running.

Gravel crunched under the tires of the van as they
trolled along the circular driveway leading to the main
lodge. Three flags flew over the landscaped garden in the
center of the driveway—the U.S. flag and the flag of New
York, and lower down, another one she didn't recognize.

"It's the Camp Kioga flag," said George. "Nice to see

they didn't change it." It depicted a kitschy-looking teepee by the lake, against a background of blue hills.

She pulled up next to the timbered entryway and went to help George. There was no one around. It was early in the season and a weekday afternoon, and the place was virtually deserted.

After a few minutes, a young teenager in coveralls, who had been working in the garden, came over, peeling off his canvas work gloves.

"Welcome to Camp Kioga," he said as she opened George's door. "My name's Max. Can I give you a hand?"

"Thank you, young man," George said. "Perhaps after we check in you can help with the bags."

"Will do," said Max. He appeared to do a double take, studying George for a moment. Then he held the door open for them.

Claire could feel tension in George as they stepped into a magnificent Adirondack-style lodge, constructed of tree-trunk timbers and river rock. It smelled faintly of wood smoke, thanks to a fireplace that was large enough to walk into.

The reception area, which was decorated with rustic furniture and primitive art, felt like another place in time, a place Claire had never been except in her imagination. The decor was subtle, with muted colors and light filtered through mica-shaded windowpanes and colored lampshades. A side room housed what appeared to be a well-stocked library, and there were stairs leading down to a game room.

Beyond the reception area lay an elegant dining room and a darkened bar. The dining room was being readied for dinner service, with white linen tablecloths and napkins. One wall was completely filled with wine bottles. French doors lined the far side of the room, offering access to a vast deck overlooking the lake.

She saw George's fist tighten on the head of his cane. "Are you all right?"

"Very much so."

A pleasantly efficient woman named Renée checked them in and gave them a quick orientation to the hundred-acre resort. Each accommodation on the property had its own character and name—the Winter Lodge, the Spring-house, Saratoga Bunk, the Longhouse, and so forth. Claire and George would be sharing a well-appointed two-bedroom cottage named the Summer Hideaway, according to the illustrated property map. When she'd made the booking, Claire had requested a wheelchair-accessible accommodation, and this one turned out to be the most elaborate on the property. It had its own private dock and boathouse, and, according to the literature, was "the perfect place to escape and dream."

The daily rate took Claire's breath away, but George didn't blink as he handed over his bank card.

Renée ran the card, then paused before handing it back. "Bellamy," she said. "The resort's owners are the Bellamys. Any relation?"

"Possibly," said George, though he offered no further explanation.

"You might qualify for the friends and family discount, then," she said.

"That won't be necessary. Excuse me." George made his way across the empty dining room and out to the deck.

Claire joined him there a few minutes later. She didn't say anything. He stood there, bathed in the last of the sunlight, his hands braced on the railing as he gazed out at the lake. The water was placid, showing only the faintest of ripples in the wake of a pair of water birds paddling along. The light struck a bright ribbon of color across the water. In the distance lay a small island with a dock and gazebo, inked in black against the darkening sky.

As she watched George, she realized he wasn't seeing the incredible scenery. He was looking out, but she sensed he was gazing inward, toward a lifetime of memories.

After a while, he let out a sigh. "Am I a foolish old man to come here, in search of my lost youth?" he asked.

"Probably." She offered her arm. "But don't let that stop you from enjoying it. George, it's so beautiful. It's a privilege to be here." She had never seen a place like this before. She'd read about this sort of thing in books, maybe seen a glimpse in the movies. "This place is a dream," she added.

"I suppose if I get to choose where I say goodbye to it all, I might as well choose this."

She frowned. "Don't you go all *On Golden Pond* on me. Come on, let's go settle in."

The boy named Max escorted them with their bags to the Summer Hideaway, driving a gas-powered golf cart with obvious enjoyment. As they passed the various areas of the camp, George turned animated again, pointing out familiar sights. "There used to be an archery range here. And see that waterfall? We'd sit around the campfire, telling ghost stories about a couple who committed suicide off the hanging bridge above it. Never figured out whether or not there was any truth to the story. Oh, and there…I learned to play tennis right there on those courts," he declared. "And I'm proud to say, I could hold my own against everyone. My first year here, anyway. When my brother and I teamed up for boys' doubles, we were virtually unbeatable."

Max parked in front of the lakeside residence and helped them with their luggage. George thanked him with a tip big enough to make the boy protest.

"Sir, it's not necessary."

"A tip never is," George said. "We appreciate your help."

Claire caught the boy's eye and offered a shrug.

The cottage was a dream, far larger than most houses Claire had lived in. The furnishings were deceptively simple but supremely comfortable. The place had a rustic elegance that didn't seem manufactured or contrived. It was bright and airy, and George's room featured a picture window with a window seat.

"Do you need to rest?" Claire asked.

"I do far too much of that," he said.

"How about you have a seat and I'll help you unpack," Claire suggested. She herself hadn't brought much along. She was prepared to disappear at a moment's notice. She always had an escape plan—a bag packed with a few basics—hair coloring and scissors, a wallet with ID, cash and credit cards, a new background and personal history. If something happened, she simply had to retrieve the bag from its hiding place and she would be gone.

At the moment, the bag was hidden under an electrical box near the parking lot of the resort. She hoped she would never have to use it, because she already knew she was going to love it here. She checked her phone and saw a missed call from "number unavailable," another name for Mel Reno. She made a mental note to phone him later.

George had packed with neat efficiency, things from pricey clothiers like Brooks Brothers, Ted Lapidus, Henry Poole, Paul & Shark. There was a briefcase filled with papers and documents, and a box of books and photographs.

"Family pictures and old journals, that sort of thing," George explained. "We can go through them later. I'll want to enjoy my mementos in the living room, I imagine."

Claire resisted an urge to ask him if he preferred pictures of his family over the real thing—or if they hadn't given him a choice. She reminded herself to reserve judgment.

"When we checked in," she said, "the woman asked you if you were any relation to the Bellamys. Is there anything more you want to tell me about that?"

He lowered himself to an overstuffed chair that was angled to take advantage of the view. "I have plenty to say about that. In due time."

"It's up to you." She went to the desk and picked up a leather-bound volume embossed with the words *Resort Guide*. "It says here there are no phones in the unit."

"I have a mobile phone," he pointed out. "I'm not fond of using it, but it'll do in a pinch."

Claire steered clear of cell phones herself. Of necessity, she had one, a no-contract phone for which she'd paid cash. She bought the minutes card with cash, too. She had schooled herself to leave as light a footprint as possible wherever she went.

"No Internet, either," she told George, "except in the main lodge."

"I rarely use the confounded thing," he said.

Claire used the Internet for its conveniences, when necessary. "Same here," she said. "There are better ways to spend time than looking at things on the Internet. Like taking in a view like this." She gestured at the sunset out the window. "Would you like to go sit on the porch for a bit?"

"A lovely idea."

The cottage featured a railed porch furnished with white wicker chairs, a swing and an intriguing cot suspended from chains. She helped him to the swing, and he leaned back, surveying the calm water. Then he took out the cigars they'd bought and lit one up. Almost instantly, he erupted with a coughing fit, waving his hand in front of his face.

"George!" She took the burning cigar from him and stubbed it out. "Are you all right?"

"I am now. There's one regret I don't have." He shook his head, sipped some water. "Smoking used to be so fashionable, back when."

"I'm glad you weren't a slave to fashion."

George picked up his journal and paged through it. "My list is long. Is that unrealistic?" he asked.

"There aren't any rules."

He nodded. "We've accomplished one already."

"You have?"

He drew a firm line through item number seventeen and handed it to her with a flourish.

She studied the entry for a few moments. "Visit the place where I first fell in love," it read. She handed back the journal. "You did this?"

"Today."

"The resort lodge, you mean?"

He looked a bit bashful. "Before that."

She mentally retraced their journey. "I don't under— Wait. George, do you mean…?"

He nodded again. "The Sky River Bakery." He sighed, stared down at the item for a few more moments with a distant light in his eyes.

"Are you hungry, George? Would you like to go to dinner at the lodge?"

"I'm a bit tired, actually. I'm happy just resting here awhile."

"Of course. I'll get your meds." Steroids and other palliative meds were keeping the symptoms at bay, but the effects were only temporary. The upside was, he stood a chance of enjoying a decent quality of life as opposed to endless days of chasing painful, time-consuming treatments that ultimately would fail.

When she came across the Viagra, she tried not to react, but something must've shown on her face. George didn't seem sheepish at all, just matter-of-fact. "In case I get lucky. Is that a foolish hope?"

"As soon as you stop hoping to get lucky, it's all over," she said with a grin.

He gifted her with a burst of laughter. "Something tells me we're going to get along just fine."

She brought him a Hudson's Bay blanket of brightly dyed wool, and a few pillows. Propped against the pillows, he scowled at a page in his journal. Across the top, he'd written *Charles.*

"Your brother, right?" said Claire.

George nodded. "He's the main reason I've come here."

"I bet he's going to be incredibly happy to see you, George."

"Of that, I'm not so certain."

"What do you mean, not certain?"

"Charles and I haven't spoken in fifty-five years."

Four

Claire woke up to silence. She wondered if she'd ever get used to the absence of honking horns and gnashing air brakes, the shouts and whistles of vendors and workmen. The void was filled with birdsong, the hum of insects and breezes ruffling the leaves and rippling across the water. The smells drifting in through the screened window—flowers and grass and the fresh scent of the lake—were utterly intoxicating.

She went to the window of her small loft bedroom and felt the irresistible pull of the outside. She had an urge to be a part of it—and it was the perfect time for a morning run. Hastily dressed in nylon shorts and an athletic bra and T-shirt, ankle socks and her favorite runners, she tiptoed downstairs. She tucked her monitor receiver into a pocket and drank a big glass of water. Then she stepped outside and headed for the trail, choosing the five-mile route marked Lakeside Loop.

In the city, she would be plugged into an iPod to cover up the babble of urban life. Here in the wilderness, she welcomed the sounds of nature and the feel of the fresh air on her skin, and she started her morning jog with a smile on her face. And of course, she had the requisite shot of pepper spray clipped to her waistband, but that was more out of habit than any real fear she'd encounter trouble on the lakeside trail.

The beauty of her surroundings seemed almost unreal, as though she had stepped into a dream.

This morning, she tried to clear her mind. It was exhausting, always trying to think ahead, plan the next move, anticipate disaster. She pushed aside the constant tension and sank into her enjoyment of the woodland trails of the resort. One couple jogged past, nodding at her, and there was a single person in a kayak out on the lake, out for a morning paddle.

Birds flickered in the trees, and she spotted the occasional deer or rabbit. Sunlight glimmered on the lake, and the willow trees at the shore gracefully dipped their fronds in the water. Such a beautiful world. Too beautiful, she thought with a familiar twinge of yearning. She wished she had someone to share this moment with. Yet the fact was, she had no one to bear witness to her life. Sometimes that realization was overwhelming.

Over time, she had taught herself to tolerate the self-isolation. There really wasn't any other choice.

The rhythm of her feet on the pavement alternated with the cadence of her breathing. She tried to imagine absorbing the beauty of the day through her pores, somehow keeping it with her. Maybe that was the magic of this place—that even after you left, you could take it with you. Maybe that was why George still thought about it even after half a century had passed.

We haven't spoken in fifty-five years.

A lifetime, she thought. George and his brother had let a lifetime slip by. Last night, she'd suggested they call Charles Bellamy—he was listed in the local phone book. George had balked and looked tired. "When Ross comes," he'd said.

Ross. The favored grandson. She hoped like hell the guy was on his way. For that matter, where was the rest of George's family? According to George, his sons and daughters-in-law expected him to return to the city in a matter of days.

This morning, George had been out of sorts. He'd stayed close to the house, only venturing to the porch or dock to catch the sun's early rays. There was no further talk of Charles Bellamy, and Claire didn't bring it up. For the time being, George was in no shape to face the emotional turmoil of a reunion with his long-lost brother.

Her plan for the day was to let each hour unfold at a pace that seemed to suit her patient. In the resort's eclectic library, she had read up on Camp Kioga, trying to fill in the blanks for herself. There was a multivolume scrapbook filled with photos of people and events connected to the resort. It had started out as a big agricultural parcel at the north end of the lake, deeded to the Gordon family to settle a debt. The camp itself had been founded by Angus Gordon in the 1920s. *Kioga* was, as far as anyone knew, a fake Mohawk word which Angus claimed meant *tranquility*.

The campground was later run by Angus's son and then inherited by his granddaughter and her husband. The current owners' names had leaped off the page at her: Jane and Charles Bellamy.

Exploring the woodland trails that wound through

the area, Claire imagined the past here, and wondered if she would ever learn the reason for the brothers' estrangement. A brother shared a person's history and background the way no one else ever could. Yet something had torn George and Charles apart. Something had made George walk away and stay away for fifty-five years.

She was so lost in thought that she didn't notice someone approaching from an oblique angle behind her. At the last second, she spied a shadow—large male, baseball cap, arm outstretched—and reacted instantly, with all the force and decisiveness she'd learned in her self-defense training. In a fluid movement she turned, right leg kicking out at groin level, the heel of her left hand crunching upward into the assailant's face. In less than a second, he was down, doubled over, and she was running for her life, her every nerve lit by adrenaline, the pepper spray in hand.

Claire gauged that she was about five minutes from the spot where her bag was hidden, going at top speed. As for George Bellamy, he would have no idea what became of her.

She felt bad about that. She hoped he'd find his brother, and she hoped the Bellamy family wouldn't drag the old guy back to the city and force him to submit to brutal treatment.

The concern wasn't enough to stop her.

A shout from her assailant, however, definitely was. "Tancredi," he said, his voice a rasp of pain.

The single word—a name almost never uttered—froze her. It brought back everything she had left behind, including the person she'd been before she'd disappeared.

She allowed herself a quick look back.

Her assailant was on all fours, struggling to rise. Good. On all fours, he wouldn't be drawing a weapon.

The baseball cap had fallen off him, revealing a mane of salt-and-pepper hair.

Oh, God. *Mel.* It was Melvin Reno, the only person Claire trusted with her secrets.

She instantly switched direction and ran to him, dropping to her knees by his side. "Are you insane?" she asked. "You huge idiot, you shouldn't have sneaked up on me. I could have done you permanent damage."

"Maybe you did." He glowered at her through tears of pain.

"Sit," she said, noting the shocky gray cast to his face. "Pull up your knees at a forty-five-degree angle and put your head between them."

With a groan, he complied.

"Breathe in through your nose," she instructed. "Out through your mouth."

"I think you broke my face."

"Is your breathing okay?"

"Just peachy."

"Then it's probably not broken."

"I guess that's the advantage of being a nurse," he said, his voice muffled. "You can kick a guy's ass and then put it back together again."

"I was doing exactly what I was trained to do. By you, I might add. Fight, run, ask questions later but don't believe the answers, isn't that what you always say?"

He nodded without raising his head.

"How bad is the pain?" she asked. "Subsiding any?"

"Depends," he muttered. "What if I say no?"

"Then you might need to be checked out. An ultra-

sound can determine whether or not there's a testicu-
lar fracture."

"A fracture? A *fracture?*"

"If there is, you'll need surgery. Mel, I'm so sorry."

"In that case, the pain's going away."

She winced, watching him try to catch his breath. He
was the one person who could connect the dots between
the quiet, studious Clarissa Tancredi of the past and the
present-day Claire Turner.

And she had just kicked him in the balls.

"Sorry about kicking you in the balls," she said again.

"I'm not looking for sympathy," he said. "If the target
had been anyone but me, I would say I'm proud of you
for knowing the moves." He lifted his head and she
studied his face—blunt features, kind eyes, a rough-
hewn handsomeness that had probably been more refined
in his youth. It was a good face, approachable and trust-
worthy. There were few blessings in the life Claire had
been given. But Mel Reno was one of them.

He slowly climbed to his feet and limped to the side of
the trail at the water's edge, taking a seat on the ground.
"So anyway," he said, "thanks for the warm welcome."

"What were you thinking?" she said, annoyed. "What
are you doing here? Is everything all right?"

"Give me a minute." He looped his arms around his
drawn-up knees.

She studied him, relieved to note his coloring and res-
piration already seemed to be easing back to normal.

He took a deep breath and relaxed a little. "I called
you yesterday. Why didn't you call me back?"

"I got busy, Mel. I'm sorry."

He frowned. "That's not like you."

"Well, you didn't have to come tearing upstate after me." She always kept him informed as to her whereabouts. Otherwise, he worried.

"I kind of wanted to see this place. Damn, it's nice here."

"I woke up this morning thinking I landed in the middle of a…" She paused. He'd think she'd lost it if she mentioned the enchanted world. "Special place." Far in the distance, a floatplane landed, skimming like a dragonfly across the surface of the lake.

"Coming from where I do," he said, "I tend to forget there are places like this in the world."

A retired federal marshal with a troubled past, he lived alone in a tattered but quiet neighborhood of Newark. He was on disability and had dedicated his life to looking after people like Claire—witnesses who were hiding or running from something too big to cope with on their own. He had been an expert in identity reassignment and redocumentation, and when she'd gone to him in desperation, he'd given her a comprehensive security suite. This included a name borrowed from a deceased person, a new personal history and legitimate documentation. All new paper on her was official—birth certificate, driver's license, social security card. Thanks to Mel, she had been reborn and given a chance at a new life.

Although she'd known him for years, she didn't really *know* him. He was absolutely committed to helping people caught in the shadow world of anonymity. It was probably what made him tick. She had once asked him why he bothered with people like her. He said he'd been in charge of protecting a family of witnesses, and they'd all been killed.

Claire had stopped asking after that. She didn't want to know more. If she got too close to him, he'd be in danger from the same monster who had sent her into hiding.

"Are you staying at the resort?" she asked.

"Right. Do you know what this place charges per night?" He shook his head. "I got a day use pass."

"So where are you staying?"

"There's a conservation department campground not far from here. It's called Woodland Valley."

She frowned. "You're camping?"

"I'm camping."

"Like, in a tent, with a sleeping bag?"

"Yeah, like that."

She tried to picture him in the tent staked out in the wilderness. "So, um, how is that working out for you?"

"I didn't come all this way to get laughed at."

She caught a note of apprehension in his tone. "What?"

"I got a bit of news. You're not going to like it."

She braced herself. "Just tell me."

"The Jordans applied to be foster parents once again."

Despite the heat of the day, she felt a curdled chill that took her breath away. Her throat went dry; she had to swallow several times before she could bring herself to speak. "For God's sake, two murders and a third kid missing, all of which happened on their watch—that doesn't stand in their way?" she demanded. "No way will Social Services approve them."

Mel was quiet. Too quiet, for too long.

"Right?" she demanded.

He stared out at the water. "I talked to about a half-dozen people at Social Services."

"And?"

"Apparently they dismissed me as a crackpot."

"That was risky," she said, "you pointing the finger at Vance Jordan. I'm the one who needs to blow the whistle on him, not you." As soon as the words were out of her mouth, she realized the decision was already made. It had been percolating for a long time, the need to end her self-exile. Coming to a place like this had only firmed her resolve. "It's time, Mel. Past time. I can't do this anymore. I'm done waiting."

"Claire—Clarissa. He's got too many friends all along the chain of command, and the ones who aren't his friends are scared of him. Exposing yourself now won't accomplish anything."

There was a good chance he was right, but the thought of Jordan with another foster child made her stomach churn. "I'll figure out something," she said. "On my own."

"You want to talk about risk—"

"That's why I want you to stay out of it. Look, I'm doing this for myself, okay? I have to stop running." There might have been a time when she'd accepted her life underground, but that time was over. She simply couldn't keep it up. Instead of getting easier, being in hiding was getting harder. She was dying inside, unraveling with need. Her mother had been alone in the world, and sometimes Claire was convinced that was what had made her live so recklessly and die so young.

Claire sometimes heard of protected witnesses who came out of hiding and got themselves killed. People thought they were foolish, but she understood why they couldn't stay anonymous forever.

"I won't let you," he snapped. "Just wait, okay?" he said. "I'll figure out the next step."

She merely nodded, pretending to agree with him. Then they parted ways in secret, like illicit lovers. That was the way all their meetings went. It was best not to be spotted together. She knew he was furious with her for insisting on risking herself in the Jordan case, but he must have known she wouldn't sit still and watch Vance Jordan become someone's foster father again. There was a ninety-day period before approval was granted or revoked. Ninety days to figure out how to come forward with what she knew—and to make someone believe her.

The prospect excited Claire as much as it frightened her. Mel had always insisted the chances of success were slim and the risk of exposure too great. But she kept thinking about how her life could change if Vance Jordan were arrested.

In her job helping people at the end of their lives, she had learned much about the importance of the way a person spent her time on earth. Running and hiding was not a life; it was just getting through the day.

George Bellamy was adrift. These spells came upon him in the gauzy numbness between waking and sleeping, courtesy of his disease. He was sometimes treated to an unprompted magic carpet ride through time and space, and at the end, he was amazed to find himself in the here and now. Here—in this paradise of a place, so beautiful it almost hurt to look at it. And now—at the last part of his life, which had not always been beautiful. It had never been boring, though.

Once he was gone, he imagined people would say he'd fought a brave battle with cancer or some such nonsense. In fact, he was not brave in the least; he was scared shitless. Who the devil wouldn't be? No one knew for certain what awaited him in the vast infinite, no matter what one's teachings were.

But still. Death was one of the Great Inevitables. George was working hard on accepting his fate, but a few things were holding him back, like the last uncut anchor ropes that kept a hot air balloon from soaring. If he wanted to fly free with boundless energy, he was going to have to find a way to untether himself.

Hence the visit to Avalon, to excavate a past that had always haunted him. Yet now that he was here, he felt himself balking. When Ross comes, he'd told Claire. Then he'd pay a visit to his brother.

George was grateful for Claire. He'd gone to a great deal of trouble to find precisely the right person—not just for him, but for Ross. Because Ross was one of those uncut tether ropes.

George wondered what Claire thought of this place, and of the glimpse into the past he'd given her. She was easy to talk to, this quiet young woman. Perhaps it was her gift, or perhaps it was something people in her profession were trained to do. Once she learned the rest of the story, she wouldn't judge him or show disapproval. And honestly, in the place where he was in his life—what was left of it—he didn't much care.

How much was the truth worth to a dying man? He'd been wondering about that lately. Perhaps he would discuss it with Claire. She was easy to talk to, this quiet young woman.... He frowned, frustrated to find his thoughts looping back on themselves.

Claire Turner. *Turner.* George wondered what made her so guarded, so hard to know. He hoped she would open up for Ross. The two of them... George had a good feeling. They could really be something together, if they'd allow themselves that possibility.

He worried about Ross, of course, coming back from the war. George had no doubt his grandson had seen horrors beyond imagining. Ross would need to learn again that the world was a good place to be. Maybe Claire would be a part of that process. George certainly hoped so.

By the time he got himself up, he was feeling rather better. He shaved and dressed himself in chinos and a fresh golf shirt, and put on his favorite hat, the sporty one that covered his too-short hair. Then he went outside to see what the day was like. Moving slowly, with cane in hand, he went down a path that ran along the lakeshore. The air was so sweet it nearly took his breath away, and a searing grief streamed through him. How was it possible to leave all this?

"Hello," someone said behind him.

Startled, he turned to see a woman seated on a bench by the path. She had white hair and wore a violet dress and sneakers with no socks. Just the sight of her made him smile. "I'm sorry," he said. "I didn't see you there. Too busy admiring the lake."

"I don't blame you. Would you like to have a seat?"

"Thanks. Nice morning," he said. "Are you here on vacation?"

"My married grand-niece and her husband persuaded me to come. I happened to mention I'd spent summers at Camp Kioga as a girl and young woman, so they insisted that I should visit once again. It turns out the resort, in its new incarnation, offers a fifty percent discount to anyone who used to attend Camp Kioga." She offered a charming smile. "I love discounts. It's my favorite thing about being a senior citizen."

George chuckled, liking her more by the minute. "You don't say. We have something in common, then. I used to come here, too. It was a long time ago." Now he was thoroughly curious about this woman, who had nice brown eyes and a somewhat impish expression. He checked her hand. No wedding band.

He must not have been very discreet, because she smiled straight at him. "I've never been married. I suppose that makes me a professional spinster."

"I'm a widower," he said. "And I've never much cared for the term spinster. There's something lonely and unattractive about it, and you hardly appear to be either."

"Thank you. And for the record, I have never spun a single thing in my life, so the label is inaccurate, as well."

"I'd best find out your name, then."

"It's Millie. Millicent Darrow," she said.

Recognition—remembrance—nudged at George. "Millie Darrow. I should have recognized you from our college days. You and your sister Beatrice went to Vassar."

"Why, yes. I graduated in 1956." She leaned forward and peered at him, hard. "George? George Bellamy."

"It's good to see you, Millie."

She took off her sun hat and fanned herself. "This is extraordinary. What a surprise. What an incredible gift."

She had no idea. She was the first person he'd seen in months who didn't know George was sick. He liked that. He was glad for the hat covering his peach-fuzz hair. "You look wonderful, Millie," he said.

"So do you. How is your brother Charles?"

It was too complicated to explain the situation, so George said simply, "He's fine. Thank you for asking."

"I always thought you were the handsome one."

"Liar," he said, laughing.

She replaced her hat. "It's the truth, George Bellamy."

"And I thought you were the sweet one," he said.

"How long are you staying here?" she asked.

"As long as I can," he said with an unbidden lurch of his heart. "As long as I possibly can."

Five

Because Ross Bellamy's discharge had been expedited by request, he was supposedly moved faster than normal through outprocessing and demobing. Still, the journey home seemed to take forever. After debriefing at Fort Shelby, Alabama, he was finally sent on his way. He felt out of place on the commercial airliner to Newark, unfamiliar with the culture after so many months in the service. There were a number of soldiers aboard, and they chattered madly the whole way, revved up by nerves and excitement as they prepared to reenter civilian life.

Ross found himself seated in an exit row between two other soldiers—a woman who had not yet turned twenty-one, and a guy in his thirties who drank and talked the whole way, preoccupied with the taste of beer and a girlfriend named Rhonda.

"I don't know why I'm so excited," he confessed. "We did a lot of Skype and e-mail, so it's not like we've been totally incommunicado. I guess it's just the seeing-in-person thing, huh? There's no substitute for it."

"Makes me glad," said the female soldier. "You

don't want technology to take the place of everything, right?"

Ross paged through an old copy of the New Jersey *Star-Ledger.* Gang murders, sports reports, community news. A headline about the state prosecutor's office caught his eye; he scanned a story about corrupt state troopers. One of the prosecutors mentioned was Tyrone Kennedy. Father of Florence, the last friend Ross had made in Afghanistan.

"How about you, Chief?" the other soldier asked Ross. "You got a family waiting for you at home? Wife and kids?"

He shook his head, offered a slight smile. "Not at the moment."

"Interesting answer," said the female soldier. "Is this something you're putting on your agenda?"

Ross chuckled. "Never thought of it in that way, but yeah. Maybe I am. Being in country so long makes you realize…having a family gives a guy something to hold on to."

"Sometimes the only thing," said the woman. "Sometimes it's the thing that saves you."

Ross knew she was right. The bond of family was a powerful, invisible force, feeding the will to survive. He'd seen wounded soldiers keeping themselves alive by sheer determination alone. Sometimes there was more healing power in the sight of a loved one's face than in a team of surgeons.

"Yeah, one good thing about deployment is it makes you appreciate the life you have," said the beer-drinking soldier. "Because nobody's life sucks as bad as bunking in the desert in winter."

"Hey, don't be so sure," said another soldier, turning around in his seat. "You haven't met my wife."

"Okay, now you're scaring me," said Ross. He knew he was joking as much as the soldier. In his life so far, he had done everything he was supposed to do as a Bellamy. He'd acquired a fine education and learned a useful profession. He'd served in the military. He just assumed the rest would come to him, that he wouldn't have to go looking for it.

He liked women. He dated a lot. But he'd never found someone he wanted to wake up next to for the rest of his life, someone he wanted to have kids with, build a life. He hated the way his last relationship had ended just before he enlisted. It had faded away—not with an explosion of emotion but something possibly more devastating—disappointment. He'd been faced with the sinking realization that he'd made a huge mistake, convincing himself he was in love when he really wasn't.

"It's been my experience that love happens when you least expect it," Granddad had said. "Sometimes it's not convenient. So what you do is you simply stay open to the possibility, all the time."

Ross tried to do that. Before going overseas, he'd dated a lot. He had good times. Great sex, sometimes so great he felt a flash of emotion and mistook it for love. But nothing ever lasted. He always ended up with a hole in the middle of his life. Without someone to share everything with, the future was just an endless string of days.

He wanted more than that. He needed more. The realization had been so clear to him on that final evac mission. He had vowed then to find a life that meant something, rather than waiting around for life to find him.

They landed in Newark. Civilians whipped out mobile phones and soldiers jumped up, grabbing their gear for the final push to the jetway. Families were gathered just past the TSA security point. There were women with kids clinging to them, spouses holding hand-lettered signs, parents and siblings, faces beaming through bouquets of flowers and balloons. A couple of contraband pets had been smuggled in.

Returning soldiers were enveloped by their loving families, many of them literally surrounded and swallowed up. Tears flowed and laughter erupted. Camera flashes strobed the area. Spontaneous applause erupted from onlookers.

Ross skirted the excited crowd, his duffel bag balanced on one shoulder and held in place with an upraised arm. Just seeing the rush of love that greeted everyone filled him with satisfaction. These soldiers had earned it. They'd fought and bled and wept and despaired, and they had earned the right to be home with their loved ones at last.

He was not naive enough to believe every single one of them was headed for some life of unrelenting familial bliss. Indeed, they would face hardships and disappointment and setbacks, just like anyone else. But not now. Not today.

He left the homecoming lovefest behind and scanned the throng for his mother. He tried not to seem too eager or desperate. But hell, he'd been gone a long time, long enough to start thinking of her fondly and remembering the good times.

There was a group at the back of the crowd, gathered under a sign labeled Any Soldier. It appeared to be some grassroots organization meant to provide a warm welcome home to any service person, particularly those who, for whatever reason, didn't have anyone to meet them on the ground.

Did they really think some soldier would avail himself of their greeting? They might as well be holding up signs labeled Losers Register Here.

To his surprise, a big-shouldered guy with sergeant stripes approached the group. At first he was tentative, his bashfulness at odds with his massive size. Someone in the group noticed him, and he was immediately enclosed by the friendly mass. After that, a few more soldiers approached, some looking almost furtive, but then pleased to have a hand to shake, a friendly word to exchange.

Ross walked on past the strangers. Any port in a storm, he supposed. Family meant different things to different people.

To others, he thought, spying his own name on a hand-lettered sign, it meant not a whole hell of a lot.

The sign read R. Bellamy, and it was held by a white-gloved, uniformed stranger in a banded hat. He wore a badge that said Royal Limo Service.

Great, thought Ross. His mother had sent a car service to pick him up from the airport. His stomach sank, and he mentally kicked himself for expecting anything else.

"That's me," he said to the limo driver, offering a brief handshake. "Ross Bellamy."

"Welcome to New Jersey, sir," the driver said with a vague accent. "My name is Pinto. Can I take your bag?"

"Thanks." Ross handed over the duffel.

"Baggage claim is this way," said Pinto. "Did you have a pleasant flight?"

"It was fine."

"Where you coming from, then?"

"Afghanistan, the eastern part of the country, by way of Mobile, Alabama."

Pinto gave a low whistle. "You mean you was on deployment." He set down the duffel and shook Ross's hand. "Glad you're back, man."

"Yeah." The handshake felt ridiculously good.

The limo was actually a Town Car, which was a relief to Ross. A big stretch limo ran the risk of seeming ostentatious. The plush leather of the car's upholstery sighed under his weight as he slid in and fastened his seat belt. His mother had clearly ordered the VIP package. There was an array of amenities—ice and drinks, cocktail snacks, mints, a phone for customers' use.

He picked it up and dialed his mother's number. "Mrs. Talmadge's residence," said her assistant.

"It's Ross," he said. "Is my mother available?"

"Hold a moment, please."

"Ross, darling." Winifred Talmadge's voice trilled with delight. "Where are you?"

"On my way from the airport."

"Is the car all right? I told the service to send their best car."

"Oh, yeah, it's great."

"I can't tell you what an utter relief it is to know you're back. I nearly lost my mind worrying."

It was natural, even normal for a mother to worry. When your son was in a battle zone, it was to be expected. "Thanks," he said.

"I mean, what can he possibly be thinking?" she rushed on. "I haven't slept a wink since he announced his intention to go off to the Catskills in search of his long-lost brother."

"Oh," said Ross. "Granddad. That's what you're worried about."

"Well, aren't you?"

"Of course. Listen, traffic doesn't look bad at all. I should be there soon. Can we talk about it then?"

"Certainly. I'll have all your favorites for dinner."

"Great, thanks."

She paused. "Ross."

"Yes?"

"Just refresh my memory," she said. "What *are* your favorites?"

He burst out laughing then. There was nothing to do but laugh. Here he'd been thinking she might be having a moment. Might be genuinely sentimental about him.

"Hey, anything that's not served in a metal compartmentalized tray is fine with me," he said.

He rode the rest of the way into Manhattan in blissful silence, leaning back against the headrest. In a way, he was grateful for the mother he had. Seriously, he was. He learned as much from her bad example as other people did from having good mothers.

Winifred Lamprey Bellamy Talmadge was a creature of her own invention. Lacking what she regarded as the right background, she had invented a whole new persona for herself.

Few people knew she had grown up in a seedy section of Flatbush, in a thin-walled apartment above her parents' pawn shop. Early in life, she'd learned to be ashamed of her humble roots, and had made it her life's mission—as she'd put it when Ross questioned her—to rise above it. She'd made a study of the upper classes. She practiced speaking in an ultrarefined, boarding school accent, slightly nasal and beautifully articulated. She studied the way the wealthy dressed and ate and comported themselves. She totally hid who she was.

She buried her past, insisted on being called Winifred instead of Wanda. She feasted on novels of the mannered elite. As a high school girl, she set a goal to attend Vassar College—not so much for the education, but for its traditional social affiliation with Yale. She wanted to marry a Yale man, and attending Vassar was the way to do it. With the focus and dedication of a nationally ranked scholar, she applied herself in high school. She knew she had to work twice as hard as the privileged girls of private schools. And she did, even winning lucrative scholarships. Such dedication, her teachers had said. Such discipline. She'll probably do something extraordinary with her life.

It could be argued that she had, in a way. He had to give her props for that. It was no small feat to pull oneself up by one's bootstraps, in a single generation going from Flatbush to Fifth Avenue simply by sheer force of will.

Ross knew all this about his mother because his grandfather had told him. Not to gossip or be mean but to try to give a hurting, grieving boy some perspective with regard to his mother, who had all but turned her back on him after the death of his father. Ross would never understand a person who ran from her past and hated who she really was. But he learned to put up with her paranoia and self-absorption, and his grandfather had, in time, made it cease to matter.

Ross gazed out the car window at the landscape passing

by en route to the city—first the tenements and creaky wooden row houses of the outskirts, the industrial mid-urban zone of boxy brick and metal buildings, and finally the tunnel leading to Manhattan, vibrant and congested, smelly and full of energy. His mother's neighborhood, on the upper west side, was a calm oasis of residences with wrought-iron gates leading to fussy gardens.

Though Winifred had her widow's benefits from her late husband, she still managed to live beyond her means. Her former father-in-law, George Bellamy, assured her that he was keeping her in the will. Granddad had vowed that as the widow of his first son and the mother of his first grandson, she had earned the privilege.

After being widowed by her first husband and divorced by her second, Winifred didn't know what else to do, having never made a career for herself. All the promise her teachers had seen in her, all the promise that had won her scholarships and a coveted spot at Vassar, had served one purpose and one purpose only—to marry well.

And indeed she had. The Bellamy family was wealthy and influential with roots that could be traced, not to the mongrel rebels who had arrived on the *Mayflower,* but to the genteel nobles who stayed in England and conquered the world. To Winifred, marrying Pierce Bellamy had been like grabbing the brass ring on the merry-go-round.

There was a catch, though. Something no one ever told Winifred. Or Pierce, for that matter. And the catch was that certain things couldn't be gleaned from a book. The finest education in the world could not instruct someone how to marry for the right reasons, or even to know what those reasons were. The best schools in the country could not teach a person to be happy and stay that way, let alone keep someone else happy.

For now, Ross would let himself be glad he was home. He would be grateful for every day that didn't involve surface-to-air missiles, sucking chest wounds, evacuation under fire or war-shattered lives. And he would do everything in his power to convince his grandfather to fight his illness rather than give up.

He dialed his grandfather's number, predictably getting a prerecorded voice mail message. His grandfather had a cell phone, too, and Ross tried that, as well. It went straight to voice mail, meaning the thing was probably turned off or had a dead battery. Granddad had never quite warmed up to having a cell phone.

Tonight, Granddad, Ross thought. *I'll find you tonight.* Never mind that his mother was going to serve all his unremembered favorites. He would borrow the roadster and drive up to the wilderness camp where his sick and dying grandfather had gone, in the company of a stranger.

Ross picked up the phone again. He only had a few friends in the city. Educated abroad, then serving in the army, he hadn't really settled down anywhere. He was ready now, though. More than ready.

He tried calling Natalie Sweet, whom he'd known since ninth grade and who lived here. Thank God for Natalie. Other than his grandfather, she was probably the person closest to Ross. He got her voice mail and left a message. Then he did the same for his cousin Ivy, and was secretly relieved when she didn't pick up, since she wept each time they spoke of their grandfather.

The car pulled up at a handsome brown brick building.

It was nominally the place Ross called home. In actuality, he had been moved around so much after his father was killed that he never quite knew where home was. Had it been the Bellamy family retreat on Long Island? His uncle Trevor's place in Southern California? His grandfather's apartment in Paris? He had no emotional ties to this particular patch of upper Manhattan, no true anchor, except wherever his grandfather happened to be.

The doorman, Cappy, greeted him warmly. So did Ross's mother, to be fair, the moment he walked through the door and Salomé told him Madame was in the living room.

Winifred hugged him close, and her arms felt taut and strong around him. When she pulled back, tears shone brightly in her eyes. "I've missed you, son."

Tall and slender, she maintained her looks with regular visits to salons and spas. Her hair looked polished, her makeup perfect, despite the tears. In her own needy way, she did love him.

"I'm so relieved to have you back, safe and sound," she added.

"Thanks," he said, taking a seat by a window that overlooked a manicured park, crisscrossed by pathways. "A little something I brought you," he said, handing her a flat jar with a colorful label. It was caviar from the Caspian Fish Company Azerbaijan. "Slim pickings in the souvenir department."

"Thank you, Ross. You know I love caviar."

"Sure. I want to hear all about Granddad. What's going on?"

She reiterated the words that had brought him racing across the globe: *glioblastoma multiforme.* Grade four—

which meant rapid progression. Refusing treatment. "He said he wants to make the most of the time he has left," she explained, her voice tinged with indignation. "And then what does he do? Hires some woman who is obviously after his money, and goes looking for some lost branch of the family. I think it's complete and utter nonsense."

Ross wasn't sure what she was referring to as complete and utter nonsense. George's diagnosis or his reaction to it? His quest to reconnect with his brother or the fact that there were other Bellamys in the world?

"Did you know anything about Granddad's brother?" asked Ross. "Did Dad?"

She waved a hand in dismissal. "Pierce knew about the brother. It was no secret. It was simply a fact. George had a brother and the two never saw each other or spoke."

"And you didn't think there was anything wrong with that?"

"It's not my place to judge. Nor is it yours. I always assumed they had gone down separate paths. Your grandfather was an expatriate until he retired a few years ago, and his sons are… Why, I scarcely know where anyone is these days. It's easy to lose track."

"Uncle Gerard's in Cape Town, Uncle Louis in Tokyo and Uncle Trevor's in L.A. It's not rocket science, keeping up with family members. Something else must have happened."

"He's being a foolish old man," Winifred pronounced. "That's what happened. I don't know if his lack of judgment is caused by the cancer, or if he's simply old and foolish. I hope he'll listen to you, Ross. You're the only one who can reason with him. He's acting out of panic, going with a strange woman to a strange town when he should be here, with us," his mother said, her voice taut with insistence.

Ross felt a surge of pity. Yes, she was self-centered. But she and Granddad shared a common bond. Ross and his grandfather were perhaps the only ones in the family who understood that Winifred was terrified of another loss, and it wasn't all about the money.

Once a year, on the anniversary of Pierce's death, Winifred would go to the war veterans' cemetery in Farmingdale on Long Island. There, she would weep as she lay a wreath at the unadorned headstone that was indistinguishable from all the others there, in the endless rows, except for the name chiseled in it. Each year she was joined in this ritual by her father-in-law, who would visit from Paris or wherever he happened to be working.

"He's a selfish, foolish old man to do this to his family," she repeated.

"Oh, that'll bring him rushing back," Ross pointed out.

"I would never tell him that."

"Sometimes you can sense someone's opinion without having it expressed directly." He paused. Then something made him ask, "Did you ever really know Granddad, Mom? Did you love him, or did you love the way he took care of us after Dad was killed?"

"Don't be silly. The two are inseparable." Then she burst into tears. "Of course I loved him. What on earth do you take me for?"

Ross touched her shoulder, knowing this was a rare glimpse at his mother's closely guarded heart. She patted his hand and moved away from him. The two of them had never been at ease in one another's company. Ross felt too restless to sit still. "I'm going to drive up and find

Granddad. If I leave now, I can beat the rush-hour traffic out of the city."

"You just got here," said Winifred.

"Come with me," he suggested.

"I couldn't," she said. "I have too much on my schedule."

Ross didn't let himself comment about that. "I can stay for dinner," he conceded. "Then I need to borrow the car."

"Thank God I caught you," said Natalie Sweet, exiting the taxicab. "Your mother told me I could catch you if I hurry."

In the remote parking facility where the car was stored, Ross set aside the car keys and opened his arms. She launched herself at him. They clung together for long moments and he inhaled the bubblegum-sweet scent of her hair. She was his best friend, and one of his oldest. He and Natalie had met at boarding school in Lugano, Switzerland. They had both been scared, skinny kids with mad skills at skiing and families that were far, far away.

Leaning back a little, he lifted her off the ground. "I'm glad you caught me."

"Welcome home, soldier," she said, and her voice in his ear was as welcome as an old favorite song on the radio.

"Thanks." He set her down. "You look fantastic, Nat. The writing life agrees with you."

She laughed. "Making a living agrees with me. See how fat and sassy I am?" She perched her hands on her hips.

"You look great."

She had always been pretty—to Ross, anyway. Not a classic beauty; she had typical girl-next-door good looks, with the wholesome appeal of a loaf of freshly baked bread.

"So things are working out at the paper?" he asked.

"I'll tell you all about it in the car." She grinned at his expression. "That's right, soldier. I'm coming with you."

"I don't remember inviting you."

She indicated a slouchy-looking weekender bag on the pavement. "You didn't. But you're going to need me and we both know it. We've got the Vulcan mind link up and running, right?"

In secondary school, they'd both been closet fans of *Star Trek: The Next Generation*, a crazy dubbed version that aired on the Italian national station. To this day, he still remembered how to say "Live long and prosper" in Italian.

"Look, it's really good of you," he said. "But I'm driving upstate by myself. It's not a pleasure trip."

"Haven't you figured it out by now?" she asked, giving him a slug in the arm. "I'd rather have a rotten time with you than a great time with anyone else. So we'd better get going, or we'll get stuck in traffic."

"You're not coming."

"Why would you waste valuable time in an argument you're going to lose?" she asked.

"Damn. You are one huge pain in the ass."

A few minutes later they were in a thick but moving line of traffic leaving the city behind, block by tattered block.

"Thanks for letting me tag along," Natalie said. "This car kicks ass."

He'd never argue about his mother's taste in cars. The Aston Martin roadster drove like a carnival ride. He could barely remember the last time he'd driven anything that didn't involve both hands and both feet simultaneously.

"You didn't give me a choice," he reminded Natalie.

"I love George. You know I always have, and I want to do what's best for him under the circumstances."

"That's why I need to see him," Ross said. "To figure out the circumstances. I can't go by what my mother reported to me. According to her, he's suffering from dementia. His judgment is impaired. He might be a victim of some predatory nurse."

She reached across the console, touched his arm. "I'm so glad you're back, Ross. I want to hear what it was like over there," she said. "When you're ready to talk about it."

"Yeah, I'm not really there yet," he said, knowing the trauma of his deployment was still too fresh to discuss with anybody—including himself. Eventually he would need to talk about his time overseas, describe the things he'd seen and done.

Just not now. Everything was all too fresh. It was very, *very* strange to consider that only hours ago, he'd still been in the military. Only days ago, he'd been embroiled in a life-or-death firefight, and still bore the healing scratches of that final battle. He felt as though he'd been plucked from one world and set down in another. Not that he wasn't grateful, but he hadn't quite adjusted.

During the long, intermittently scenic drive upstate, he thought about the more immediate issue. His was a messy, screwed-up family—more than he knew, apparently. No wonder Granddad had taken off. Maybe he'd gone in search of a less screwed-up branch of the Bellamy family.

"Well, when you're ready, so am I," said Natalie.

"I'd rather hear about you, Nat. So you say work is good?"

"Work is great. The world of sports journalism is my oyster. I had a big break last year—a piece on an up-and-coming baseball pitcher in the *New York Times Magazine*. My blog has a big following and I'm working on a book. Oh, and here's something I bet you didn't know. It's our twentieth anniversary." She touched his arm again, giving him a squeeze. It felt…unfamiliar. People in his unit didn't touch.

"No shit." He draped his wrist over the arch of the steering wheel. "I've never kept count. You mean we met twenty years ago?"

"Yep. And it was hate at first sight, remember? You totally made fun of my braces."

"You made fun of my haircut."

"It's a miracle we lasted five minutes together, let alone twenty years."

They had been forced to work together on a school project. The two of them came from completely different backgrounds, although that hadn't been the cause of their mutual dislike. Ross was an adolescent train wreck, grieving the loss of his father. He came from a family that *had* money—had rather than *made*. There was a difference.

Natalie, on the other hand, had been a scholarship student. Her parents were missionaries working in an East African principality that tended to erupt with military coups every few months.

The two of them had teased and fought their way into a genuine friendship. Their bond came from their shared pain; they were both kids who had been set aside—Ross by his mother, who could not abide the thought of having to raise him alone, and Natalie by her parents, whose humanitarian ideals left no room for their daughter.

Reverend and Mrs. Sweet believed they were meant for a higher purpose than merely being parents to a gifted but awkward girl.

"That officially makes you my oldest friend," she declared.

"Same here. So we're both old. When are you going to marry me?"

"How about never?" she asked. "Does never work for you?"

It was a running joke with them. They had struggled through dating woes in high school and commiserated at Columbia, where they'd both gone to college, she to study journalism, and he, aeronautics. On a single, ill-conceived night, fueled by too many boilermakers, they had lost their virginity to each other. They'd figured out then that they could never be together as lovers. The delicate alchemy of their friendship didn't transform itself into passion, no matter how hard they tried.

"That's not enough for me," she'd said. "Or for you, either. We're forcing this, and we shouldn't need to. When it's right, we won't have to force it."

He'd teased her about having a secret wish to be a psychoanalyst. He hadn't disagreed with her, though.

As for Natalie, she always claimed her boyfriends didn't work out because Ross had filled her head full of unrealistic expectations. She'd been serious about one guy awhile back; some musician. Like all the others, it hadn't worked out.

Every time she broke up with a guy, Ross would accuse her of holding out for him.

"You're killing me here," he said to her. "How many rejections can one guy take?"

"From me? The sky's the limit, dude. What's your hurry, anyway? Most guys I know run the other way when it comes to marriage talk. You sound like you're in some kind of race to settle down."

"It's not *like* that," he said. "It *is* that." Especially after what he'd seen over there. "I'm tired of being alone, Nat," he said. "I want to be someone's husband. Someone's dad, eventually."

"Because you lost your own dad at such a young age," she said softly.

"You're probably right, Dr. Sweet. The happiest time of my life was when I was little, with my dad."

"And now you want to recapture that by becoming a dad yourself." She fiddled with the radio, stopping on a mellow Ingrid Michaelson song. "Hate to tell you this, but it probably doesn't work that way. I wish it did, because you deserve it, Ross. You deserve some woman who will light you up for the next fifty years, and a bunch of kids to worry about."

"Don't forget the house with a white picket fence," he said, chuckling. "And the dog. I've never had a dog."

"Okay, now you're getting greedy." She fiddled with the radio dial again, this time opting for some rock song he didn't recognize, with shouted lyrics. "It's about damn time."

"What's that supposed to mean?" he asked, turning down the volume.

"You're always looking out for somebody else. It's about time you wanted something just for you."

"What I want," he said, "is to help my grandfather. To

figure out what's really going on with him." He told her
what he knew of his grandfather's condition.

She cried a little, yanking Kleenex out of her purse.
"Damn it. That sucks. I can't even tell you how much it
sucks. I'm so sorry, Ross."

"Thanks."

"And you say he's with some kind of private nurse?"

"Apparently."

"Sounds kinky."

"For his sake, I kind of hope it is."

"You're such a guy. And what about the rest of your
family? Why are you the one who gets to go chasing after
the old dude?"

*Because he's Granddad. Because I can't stand to lose
him.* "Everyone assumes I'm the only one who can make
him see reason. I think they're expecting him to return
to the city as soon as I talk some sense into him."

"And if he doesn't?"

"Then I think the Bellamy population in this little town
is likely to swell. I can't believe Granddad never mentioned
his brother, Charles, to me." As Ross had hastily packed
for the drive upstate, his mother had disclosed what little
she knew of the situation. Charles Bellamy was younger
than Granddad by about four years. They both went to Yale.
And then, the year Granddad graduated from college, they
parted ways and fell out of touch.

"How did Charles end up in Avalon?"

"My mother said he married a local girl and they ran
some kind of camp or resort—her family's business—on a
seasonal basis. In the city, Charles had a career in law. Now
they're retired and live in Avalon. That's about all I know."

He grew quiet with anxiety as they crossed into Ulster

County, heading west toward the Catskills Wilderness. The truth was, he was afraid for his grandfather. If the two brothers hadn't spoken in such a long time, there had to be a huge reason for it. If that reason still existed, his grandfather could be in for a world of hurt.

Six

Getting started with a new client was, for Claire, a little like dating, only more one-sided. And maybe there wasn't such a great payoff. But like someone embarking on a date, she found herself preoccupied with George, uncovering who he was, trying to figure out the nuances of his heart. In a weird way, she had a crush on him—not a romantic crush but an emotional one. The liking deepened into familiarity. She started to recognize his signals. She could tell when he was getting restless or uncomfortable, or when he was feeling content.

He'd had a quiet day, resting and eating little, but he'd asked her to go to dinner with him at the main lodge. A little after seven, she went to check on him, and he appeared to be asleep. It was tempting to leave him be, but he'd been insistent about the plan for the evening. He claimed he didn't want to miss dinner service. Tonight, he was determined to dine in style.

"George," she said, gently touching his shoulder. "George, wake up. Time to get ready for dinner."

His face was soft and mild as if he was in the midst

of a beautiful dream. He sighed and blinked slowly; she could see him orienting himself. There was the picture window, framing the lake. The bedside table with meds lined up. The buzzer that would summon her at the push of a button.

"Still interested in dinner? If not, I can bring you a tray again—"

"No. I'm done acting like an invalid. All this fresh air and sunshine is making me feel better."

She nodded. "It's seven-fifteen. We have an eight o'clock table."

"I'll be ready."

In the tooled-leather binder in Claire's room, there was a request that guests dress appropriately for evening dinner service in the main lodge. Casual dining was offered elsewhere on the property, but the Starlight Dining Room was meant for dinner and dancing.

She wasn't entirely sure what would be deemed appropriate. More than any other of her past job assignments, this elegant resort scene was a whole new world. Since finishing nursing school and specialty training, she had served a number of clients, but never one remotely like George Bellamy.

For dinner, she dressed in a beige matte jersey sheath and midheeled shoes, just a touch of makeup, her hair swept to the side and fastened with a celluloid tortoise-shell comb. It was not glamorous. It was...nondescript, and that was the goal. While some people strove all their lives to be above average, she aimed for average. People noticed and remembered the extremes. She wanted to be the woman everyone forgot—the one in the insurance agency who helped you file a claim. The taxi driver. The math teacher, not the art teacher. The line cook, not the chef. Studying herself in the mirror on the back of the bathroom door, she knew a moment of wistful fantasy. As a small girl being shuffled between her erratic mother and a variety of foster homes, she'd had a favorite story— Cinderella. There was something in every girl that longed for a dramatic transformation. It was a metaphor, of course, a reward. The power of Cinderella's goodness transcended all the bad luck that beset her. And the trans- formation had to be huge. A girl wanted to go from rags to riches. Not rags to middle-of-the-road average.

Maybe just once, Claire yearned to put on something that would stop everyone in their tracks, cause them to stare, maybe whisper behind their hands—*Who's that girl?*

She could only dream of such a moment. Her job was to blend in, not stand out. She considered herself a master of this art. Regarding the girl in the looking glass, she saw the ultimate average person, neither tall nor short, fat nor thin, beautiful nor ugly. She was simply… average. If she was to walk across a crowded room and people were later asked to describe her, no one would remember her.

George Bellamy had no limitations on making himself look good. When he came into the sitting room to meet her for dinner, she couldn't stifle a gasp.

"Wow, look at you. You look like a million bucks."

He turned in a slow circle, palms out, a smile on his face. "I feel like a million bucks." He paused. "Maybe not quite a million."

"An even million," she contradicted him. "Let's put it this way. If Richard Gere gets very, *very* lucky, he might end up looking like you one day."

"Well, now. A movie star? That's quite a compliment."

"The suit looks amazing on you. Is it from the tailor shop you told me about—Henry Poole?"

"Indeed it is. You have a good eye."

"It's perfect on you." And it was, down to the precise break in the hem of the trousers. His shoes were a lustrous black leather, polished to a gleam in the last light of the day. Every fold of his shirt bore a crisp crease, as though attended by an invisible valet. There was precisely three quarters of an inch of cuff showing, studded by silver cuff links with a stylized fish design. "A gift from my father," George said when he saw her looking at the cuff links. "He gave matching pairs to me and my brother. I shall have to think about what to do with these," he added. "I have six grandsons."

"That many?"

"We Bellamys are a prolific lot."

She led the way down to the golf cart, which they'd rented for getting around the resort. "Your chariot awaits. Would you like to drive?"

"Certainly." He elected to leave his cane behind, for he was feeling spry.

They arrived at the main pavilion at precisely eight o'clock. George offered his arm and they went in together. The dining room looked beautiful in the evening light. The setting sun, reflecting off the glassy surface of the lake, bathed everything in a wash of pinkish gold. The tables were aglow with candlelight and set with gleaming signature china, polished silver, stemmed crystal glasses. A slender young woman effortlessly played piano, a gleaming Steinway. She was accompanied by a guy on muted trumpet and another on percussion; the number was an old-fashioned one Claire didn't recognize.

The crowd was made up of couples, mostly, or small groups. There were a few families with fidgety kids or sullen teenagers. But overall, the impression was of couples on a romantic getaway. Not that Claire had ever been on a romantic getaway. But she read a lot of books.

Although she shunned attention, the same could not be said of George. She was not the only one to admire his bespoke suit, his snowy-white hair and studied, upright posture. Heads turned as he passed; voices dropped to murmurs.

And inevitably, attention then went to Claire. She felt several dozen pairs of eyes on her. People were undoubtedly speculating about her and this exceedingly handsome older gentleman. Was she his daughter or his trophy wife? Perhaps he was her sugar daddy.

She tried to dismiss the looks and speculation. She waved away the resort photographer who circulated among the tables, offering to take people's pictures.

Claire had not willingly had her picture taken since her junior year of high school. It was in an annual somewhere, "Clarissa Tancredi" squeezed between ChiChi Tambliss and Ginny Thompkins. The girl in the photo had been round-cheeked, with railroad-track braces and long brown hair, and a look in her eyes that was full of hope, despite all she'd been through. Within weeks of School Picture Day, that girl had ceased to exist. The long hair had been cropped and dyed black. The braces were removed with a pair of needle-nose pliers, in a ladies' room on the Jersey Turnpike. And that expression of hope would never, ever return.

The maître d' seated them at a table by the French doors near the deck—prime real estate in a prime restaurant, she noted.

"I do believe this is the best table in the place," she said. "How did we rate the royal treatment?"

"Must be your overwhelming beauty," said George, then winked when he saw she wasn't buying it. "Either that, or the fact that I gave the maître d' a tip the size of Chicago."

She raised her water goblet in his direction. "To you, Mr. George Bellamy, international man of mystery. Thank you for bringing me along on this journey."

"Don't thank me yet. Summer in a rustic cottage is not everyone's cup of tea. I hope you don't go batty with boredom."

"Highly doubtful, George." She noticed him glancing around the dining room. "Looking for someone?"

"I ran into an old friend from college," he said. "I thought she might be here tonight."

"That's nice for you," she said. "Is it a coincidence, or—"

"Total coincidence. I'd forgotten all about Millie until just this morning."

"I hope I get to meet her." His pleasure in the meeting was completely endearing, she thought with deepening affection. Wanting to connect with people was so very human. Even impending death didn't stave off the impulse. No wonder self-imposed isolation was so hard.

She studied the menu in bewilderment and delight. "I don't know what half this stuff is. And I can't actually pronounce it."

"Shall I order for us both?"

"Yes, please. Just remember, I'm watching my weight."

"I remember. How could I forget? You're the first person in history to turn down a pastry from the Sky River Bakery."

When the waiter came, George did the ordering—a salad that included something called frisée, garnished with fresh flowers. There was an entrée of local trout with sautéed wild ramps and chanterelles. He ordered wine, too, a white Burgundy from France.

Claire wished she could have more than a sip or two of the wine, but she couldn't allow that, any more than she could gorge on the menu items. She had to retain full control of her faculties at all times, and getting buzzed on wine was a risk she could not take.

Despite the restrictions, though, she was enchanted by the beautiful restaurant with its lakeside setting. Being here with George, for however long they stayed, gave her a chance to live a different life, even for a short while. This was how some people actually spent their time, in quiet conversation, smiling across a beautifully set table at a spouse or lover. What a concept. She tried not to want it too much.

George sat back, studying the surroundings with a bemused expression.

"Is it what you were hoping for?" she asked.

"For the most part, yes. I was hoping it hadn't changed beyond recognition, and it hasn't. There was always this view of the lake. I think the stage was in the opposite corner."

"Was there live music?" she asked.

"Every night," he assured her. "There were live acts, too. Not just crooners but all kinds of entertainers. Magic acts, stunts, comics, you name it. A lot of them were quite good. Being so close to the city gave the resorts in this area access to all kinds of talent."

"Did you have a favorite?"

"Sure. There was a magician named Marvel who sawed off his assistant's head twice a night. I remember being completely flummoxed when I saw her under the dock later, smoking a cigarette. I saw Henny Youngman right there on the stage one night," he said. "Ever heard of Henny Youngman?"

"Sorry, no."

"He was a comedian, a big deal in his day. The Everly Brothers played here. And the Andrews Sisters—they were regulars on the circuit."

With his stories of a rarefied, forgotten era, he took her to another place and time. There had been a whole subculture of monied families in the city who retreated to the lakes upstate each summer, and the Bellamys were part of that tradition.

Claire could scarcely imagine it. She had never done anything as a matter of tradition. Her childhood had been a series of ever-changing acts of survival and in the end, she had performed the ultimate act of her own, and disappeared.

A few couples danced to the gentle piano music. Watching them, Claire felt something in a soft and secret place inside her—a sadness, a sense of futility. She'd never allowed herself to see falling in love as an option. She couldn't. It was too dangerous. She could never have any kind of lasting relationship. Anyone she got close to would face the same dangers she faced. Or worse, they would be used as leverage against her.

Oh, but she dreamed. When she saw people together

like the couples on the dance floor, their love a palpable thing, she dreamed of what it might be like, and could not stop her heart from yearning. Then she would remember what it was like to be forced to run for her life and disappear. She wouldn't wish that on anyone. Convincing Social Services to bar Vance Jordan from being a foster parent was going to expose her to an insane level of risk. The last thing she needed was for someone else to get tangled up in her mess.

Providing skilled, compassionate care to terminal patients was a vocation few people understood, yet it was perfectly suited to Claire. She loved her patients while they were in her care, and her heart broke when she lost them. But she had come to discover that the heart was a sound and sturdy organ, capable of mending itself.

She could already tell she was going to love George very much. He was so dapper in his dress suit, proud and yet uncertain in the wake of a terrible prognosis, like a nervous bridegroom. She hoped he would find peace and clarity and eventually, acceptance.

They ordered dessert—he had crème brûlée with raspberries; she had just the raspberries. He ordered small glasses of ice wine from a vineyard in western New York and she allowed herself one sip. It was an intense, sweet wine made from grapes gathered after the frost. The flavor was deep and complicated, like nothing she'd ever tasted before. "This is nectar," she said, shutting her eyes briefly. When she opened them, she saw George watching her with an indulgent smile.

"What?" she asked.

"You're really quite a lovely young woman," he told her. "Ross is going to like you enormously."

Ross again. The grandson. "I'm here for you, George. You know that." She rested her chin in her hand and watched the couples on the dance floor.

He finished his glass of ice wine. "You're bored with me already. I can tell."

"Nonsense. I'm just getting to know you," she said.

"It's on my list, you know," he said.

"What's that?"

"Dancing. I never learned to dance."

"I'm surprised," she admitted, turning to look at him. "You seem like the kind of guy who would know how to dance. I figured it was a social skill, like knowing how to order wine or tie a bow tie."

"You're right, and in general, it is exactly that. In fact, dancing lessons were given right here at Camp Kioga, but I avoided them. Because, you understand…"

"Cooties," she suggested.

He chuckled. "Yes, there was that, early on. But now I'm sorry I never learned to dance, because I'd like to know what it feels like to be out on the dance floor in a beautiful place like this."

"Now that," she said, "is definitely something I can help you with. I'm actually an okay dancer." She went occasionally to dance clubs, which gave her the illusion of having close friends or even a boyfriend. It was one of the quirky things she did to preserve her own sanity. Over time, she'd learned a good number of dances, and some of the retro numbers were her favorites.

"Excellent," he said. "When shall we start?"

She set down her napkin. "There's no time like the present."

He looked momentarily disconcerted. Then resolute.

"Your point is well taken." He got up and moved to her side of the table, offering his right hand with a flourish. "May I have this dance?"

"I'd be thrilled," she said, taking his hand. "And I'm having a hard time believing you've never done this. You look like a pro, standing there."

"*Standing* is the key word. I've watched a lot of Fred Astaire movies in my day. I couldn't ever get past the asking, though."

"We're about to change that," she said.

The small ensemble was playing "Stardust Memories," which lent itself to a simple box step.

"The nice thing about dancing," she said, "is that you really only need to know two things—how to hold a frame, and how to engage with your partner. Don't worry about feet and legs. Those will come after."

"I certainly hope so," he said.

"Trust me. You have to trust me."

"Fine. Tell me what to do. I'm all ears."

"First, forget about everyone else in the room. Pretend it's just the two of us. I swear, we're not that interesting."

"Done."

"Now, hold up your hand, just like that, yes." She slipped her own into his. "Your other hand needs to rest at my waist. Yes. You're very good."

"I haven't done anything."

"You feel polished and confident," she said, "the way a true gentleman should. You smell good, too."

"Nice of you to say."

"I'm being honest, George. You smell wonderful. Now, about the dance frame. It's not very technical. It's based on common sense and consideration for your partner."

He had a natural flair for the hold. Next, she showed him the basic footwork. He caught on quickly enough, and seemed to have a strong sense of rhythm. The look of concentration on his face morphed into delight, and he laughed aloud, the sound eliciting smiles from the other dancers.

"Hey, you're a natural," she said, though the attention made her feel self-conscious. They danced some more, and George laughed some more as she coached him through a couple of moves.

"I don't think we'll win any trophies," he said, "but I'm having fun. Makes me wish I'd taken this up before my sons' weddings."

She decided to voice the question that had been nagging at her since their arrival. "Where are they, George? Where is your family now?"

"That's not the real question," he said. "The real question is, why aren't they here?"

"I suppose that is the question. And you needn't answer it unless you want to."

"They think I'm on a fool's errand, coming to Camp Kioga."

"And they've stayed away because…"

"Because they're convinced I'll be back in the city before they can even get their bags packed."

This was exactly as she'd suspected. Most loved ones tried to cling to denial as long as possible. "Just don't make this a battle of wills, George. Nobody wins that kind of fight."

"Not to worry. I have thought about this journey long and hard, to make sure it's something I'm pursuing for the right reasons, not just to be stubborn."

The inner workings of a family held endless fascination for Claire. Perhaps this stemmed from her lack of one. She was intrigued by the way people loved each other, and fought and turned their backs on each other, and then came together again. She was intrigued by all the ways people learned to forgive and grow and strengthen their bond. There was such richness in their efforts, and such grace, whether those efforts led to success or failure.

George was so studied in the way he dressed, so fearful and sweet at the same time. She thought about how he had carefully ordered the food and wine and how much he'd savored her enjoyment.

If you were my grandfather, she thought, *wild horses couldn't keep me from you.*

It was dark by the time Ross and Natalie arrived in Avalon, a cluster of glowing windows and gaslit streets nestled beside Willow Lake. He was only vaguely familiar with the many little lakeside towns and villages of upstate New York, but Natalie claimed she'd been to Avalon before.

"Several times, as a matter of fact," she remarked, folding away the road map.

"Here? I never knew that."

"My folks settled in Albany after they came back from overseas. This was one of my favorite train stops on the way upstate." She indicated a place called the Apple Tree Inn, a converted mansion with a lighted front porch and a sign advertising fine dining. "A guy asked me to marry him right there, about ten years ago."

"Yeah, right."

"I'm serious. It was Christmas Eve. I was mortified."

"What, mortified it wasn't me?"

"Very funny."

"You never told me that," said Ross.

"I don't tell you everything. And honestly, it wasn't…my finest moment. He was adorable, but we were too young. I wonder whatever became of Eddie."

"Nothing," Ross said. "His life was over the second you turned him down."

She laughed. "I'm so glad you're back. I don't know what I did without you."

"Sent me jokes in e-mail," he reminded her. "Several a day."

"Well, it's nice having you back where I can make fun of you in person."

They stopped at a service station for directions to Camp Kioga. "It's a good thing I came along with you today," Natalie said, squinting at the unlit wilderness that surrounded them after they left the town behind. "A really good thing. It's pitch-dark out here. And deserted, too. I feel like we're in one of those teen scream movies."

"Except we're not teenagers and there's nothing to scream about."

"Speak for yourself." She shuddered. "How about you pull over and put up the top."

"It's still warm outside. Let's leave it down."

"There are probably slimy nocturnal creatures everywhere."

"I'll try not to run over any of them. And let's hope nothing drops on your head."

"Ross, I swear—"

"Quit being a baby."

The lakeshore road took them northward. They passed a few farms and residences, and then…nothing. Finally, in the middle of nowhere, they spotted the sign: Historic Camp Kioga. 2 Miles Ahead. The pavement turned to gravel, and Ross slowed the roadster. The headlamps lit the surrounding dense forest, creating a tunnel of green. The shadow of an owl swooped over them, and occasional watching eyes flashed in the underbrush.

"Okay, this is seriously creepy," said Natalie, turning up the volume on the radio. A bouncy song about love gone wrong was playing, which seemed to lighten the atmosphere a little.

"Scaredy-cat," said Ross. "Finally, here we are."

The old-fashioned entranceway was constructed of two large timbers connected by an arch. *Camp Kioga* was spelled out in wrought-iron twig lettering. "Jeez, even the sign looks creepy," Natalie remarked.

The remainder of the driveway was illuminated by path lights leading to a big lodge at the lakeside. "Now, this is more like it," she declared, regarding the glowing windows with obvious relief. "It's even prettier than the brochures promised." Inside, they could see candlelit tables, waiters in black coats, dancing couples. It was the picture of vintage rustic elegance, the kind of place that invited nostalgia. Or, thought Ross, old men in search of old memories.

He and Natalie went inside to a big lobby area and stood for a moment, looking around.

Peeled timber ceiling beams soared above the lounge area and registration desk. The room had a timeless atmosphere; it felt like the sort of place people imagined other, more functional families than their own visited together, a couple of generations back. Maybe in Granddad's day.

At the registration desk, an earnest-looking woman waited expectantly. Adjacent to the lobby was a dining room, complete with live music and dancing couples.

"He might be there," Ross said.

Natalie touched his arm. "Go ahead," she said, following the direction of his gaze. "I'll get us a place to sleep for the night."

Leaving her at the desk, Ross went into the dining room. It was getting late and the crowd was thin. Ross surveyed the room, scanning the light dinner crowd, mostly couples. A small ensemble, on a raised dais in the corner, was playing the old tune "Stardust Memories," and several couples danced to the languid melody. His gaze skipped past them; it was well-known in the family that Granddad didn't dance. Then Ross heard a sound he hadn't heard in far too long—the ringing tones of his grandfather's laughter.

His gaze made another sweep through the dancers, this time focusing on a tall man dancing with a slender, dark-haired woman.

Ross froze, his chest constricted with emotion.

George Bellamy was dancing. He wore a tailored dress suit with a crisp white shirt and narrow tie. His close-cropped, snow-white hair caught flickers of light from the rustic chandelier. He looked lost in pleasurable concentration, with a small, crooked smile on his face.

A thousand thoughts crowded into Ross's head. He was unprepared for the sucker punch delivered by the sight of his grandfather. Striding toward the couple on the dance floor, Ross had an urge to physically remove the strange woman from his grandfather's arms. Maybe Ross's mother and aunt were right. Maybe the stranger was shameless, worming her way into Granddad's life.

"Granddad," he said, keeping his voice low and his temper reined in, for now.

George Bellamy stopped dancing, stepped away from his partner and turned. Just for a moment, he appeared confused, disoriented in a way that made Ross's pulse speed up in panic. Then George's face lit with a blissful smile. In the dim, kindly light, he looked youthful, perfectly healthy and utterly delighted. "My boy," he said, reaching out with his arms. "My boy. I knew you'd come."

The woman moved aside. George hugged Ross close, right there on the dance floor. Ross could feel dozens of eyes on him, but he didn't care. He was back. His grandfather's relief was palpable, and Ross knew George was thinking of the son who had gone to war and never came home.

A soldier's homecoming was meant to be a joyous occasion. Yet the joy in this moment was muted by a sense of sadness. In his grandfather's embrace, he was that young boy again, grieving and afraid. It was astonishing how quickly those feelings came rushing back, as though they had been hovering just below the surface, never really gone, waiting to reemerge.

"My boy," Granddad said again. "My dear, sweet boy. Welcome home."

"Thank you," Ross said, wanting to hold this man close and never let him go. "Can we go have a seat?"

"Of course. I'm so pleased you came, son. I didn't know when you'd arrive."

"I got here as fast as I could. My mother says you hired some phony tart who's going to fleece you bare."

Granddad stepped aside. Ross had no idea the hired

woman was still standing nearby, overhearing this. "Son, I'd like you to meet Claire Turner," said Granddad.

"The phony tart," she added helpfully.

"Great," said Ross.

"Miss Turner, this is my grandson, Ross Bellamy."

"Delighted," she said.

Ross knew there was ice in his gaze as he offered her a greeting of curt politeness. He would soon be having what he expected to be a short, dismissive conversation with her. Yet there was something unsettling about her. No, there was something about *him,* regarding her. *This woman is going to be trouble,* warned a quiet inner voice. At first glance, she didn't look like a gold digger. She wore no jewelry, little or no makeup that he could see. Her thick, dark hair was pulled back, revealing an undeniably pretty face. She wore a plain dress that did not have to loudly advertise the obvious—she had a knockout figure.

"Pardon me," Ross said. "I'm going to have a word with my grandfather."

"Of course," she said. "Why don't you go to the bar where it's quiet. I'll settle things here."

I'll just bet you will, thought Ross, watching her go. She was mesmerizing to look at, with a soothing voice and manner that had probably won George over from the start. Ross felt nothing but contempt for her, yet against his will, that contempt was tinged by curiosity.

Natalie came to greet George. As she gave him a hug, she immediately burst into tears.

"This is not helping," said Ross.

"I just don't know what to say. I'm sorry you're sick, Mr. Bellamy, and I feel so helpless."

"You've helped enormously by coming here with Ross," said George.

"I'm sorry," she murmured again, and handed Ross a key. "The cabin number's on the tag," she said. "I'm heading over there now."

"Charming creature, I've always thought," said Granddad as she withdrew. "There was a time when I wondered if the two of you might marry." He smiled at Ross's expression. "It's one of the few perks of being terminally ill. I get to speak my mind without getting in trouble for it."

"Nat and I…we're not like that."

"I know. You have a wonderful future ahead of you, my boy. Just not with her."

The bar was quiet, and furnished with comfortable wing chairs and low tables. George ordered two glasses of brandy, looking pleased to see that it was Rémy Martin, properly served in crystal globe snifters.

The two of them sat together, facing a glowing fire in the river-rock fireplace. On the table between them was a chess set, the pieces already lined up for battle. George settled back and lifted his glass. "To my grandson, the war hero."

"And to my grandfather, the exaggerator. I'm no hero."

"You came home alive and well. In my eyes, that makes you a hero."

Ross was quiet. He had accomplished what George's son could not. He had come home in one piece. "Whenever I got in trouble over there," he said, "I thought of you. And when I did that, the only option was to make it home."

"And for that, I am profoundly grateful. I hope you're planning to stick around, because…well, you know." He took a sip of brandy, closing his eyes as he swallowed. "How are you?"

"I'm completely freaked," Ross admitted.

"That was my initial reaction, as well. It's one thing to grow old as I have, knowing I shan't live forever. It's another to discover my actual expiration date."

Ross had always understood how hard it would be to lose his grandfather. But it had always seemed a distant eventuality, something that would happen someday in the nebulous, undefined future, taking him by surprise, like a sniper attack.

Instead the loss was predicted to happen this summer.

Ross hated that. With every fiber of his being, he hated the heartless prognosis.

Leaning forward, George nudged a pawn on the chess-board in his favorite opening move, the French defense.

"So, about this illness…" Ross kept his voice low, but even he could hear its intensity. Almost independently, he answered the opening move with one of his own. He and Granddad had always played chess, almost compulsively.

"We can go over all the technicalities in the morning. I promise not to die tonight." George advanced another pawn and regarded him with shining eyes. "Dear God, how I've missed you. I worried about you every moment."

"I'm sorry for that. The work was hazardous but I'm glad I served. I know you were opposed to my going, but it was just something I had to do."

"And I couldn't be prouder. And now you're back, and it means the world to me."

The center of the chessboard was fairly crowded now, with flanks of pawns. The queen's black bishop was hemmed in and useless.

Ross didn't give a shit about his future at the moment. "Look, Granddad, I don't care how sick you are. I want to know what the hell is going on. Where's everyone else? Uncle Louis and Gerard and Trevor? Why aren't they here with you?"

"Well, as you know, the elder two are overseas, but they'll be in New York soon. Trevor and Alice flew in from L.A. when I ended my treatment at the Mayo Clinic. They're staying at the apartment," he said, referring to his residence in Manhattan. "I invited them to Camp Kioga with me, but they declined. They all think I'm on a fool's errand, and they're hoping you'll be the one to make me see reason and escort me back to the city."

"Yeah? So how am I doing?"

"Not so well, because I intend to stay here." His face turned mild, reflective. "Ross, I had to make a choice. I've lived a full life. I've had my share of blessings and losses. I came here to face my greatest regret, and that is the long estrangement with my brother, Charles. Full-on treatment would 'give me' maybe a few more months, but every day would be eaten up by appointments, painful and invasive procedures and tests. So I chose to come here, and invite my family up and have a day like I did today. I sat in a porch swing, did the *New York Times* crossword and prayed you'd be here soon." He offered a smile that made Ross want to cry. "Now you're here. I'm sure the others will join us soon."

"But why here? And what's this about a brother?"

"Now that I'm out of time there are some things I see clearly, and the need to reconnect with my brother is one of them. Things that happened in the past…I can't let them matter now. All my priorities have shifted. My bank balance? Doesn't matter what it is, either. It doesn't matter if I missed the latest episode of *Grey's Anatomy* or if my damned socks match. What matters is making sure I come to terms with things in my past, and share my heart with my loved ones."

Ross wasn't quite sure what his grandfather needed to come to terms with. What could be powerful enough to divide brothers for a lifetime? Whatever it was, he hoped they could make this quick. Suffer through an awkward meeting with the brother, then head back to the city and find a doctor—a team of them—who could find a way to beat this disease.

He nodded his head toward the dining room. "And why *her?*"

George frowned at the game board. "She's exactly what we need."

Ross ignored the *we*. "But, Craigslist, Granddad? Seriously?"

"I was told one could find anything on the Internet. Apparently this is so. I simply listed the attributes I needed, and Godfrey put it all on the line." George took one of Ross's pawns with his bishop.

"On the line?"

"You know, the Internet."

Ross's mouth twitched. "Online, you mean."

"Yes. Within hours, there were applicants queuing up to meet me. Godfrey prescreened them. It was disheartening, I tell you. Nothing like those match-up services they're always advertising. I wish you could've seen some of the candidates." He chuckled. "Did you know there's a variety of tattoo known as the 'tramp stamp'?"

"Granddad—"

"Don't worry, Claire doesn't have any tattoos. None that I know of. At any rate, I nearly gave up the search, and then I met Claire. Almost from the first moment, I knew she was the one. I had a feeling about her."

"Yeah, about these attributes—did you check her references? Her qualifications?"

"Of course. I had to make certain she was exactly what I was looking for. I'm sure you'll come to like her, too. At first glance, she seems a bit plain, but you'll soon realize that's not the case at all. She has a quiet sort of beauty. Doesn't seem to want to play up her looks the way most women do."

"To be honest, I don't give a shit about her except where you're concerned. Level with me, Granddad. How did you happen to decide on this girl?"

He took out a small notebook. "Well now, let's see. I started with a list of qualifications—age twenty-five to thirty-five. Female, of course. Someone with a positive attitude and a sense of adventure. Heterosexual. Must love children of all ages. Must be open to relocation. No emotional baggage. Nursing skills a plus."

"I don't get what you were thinking. This doesn't sound even remotely like a notice for a nursing position."

"How so?"

"I think when you specify age, gender and marital status, it's more like a personals ad."

"I had certain requirements. And those were some of them. You know I have nothing against homosexuals. But for this position it had to be a woman."

Ross grabbed the list. "Nursing skills a plus?" he read. "A plus? Like it's optional or something?"

"It's secondary to the other attributes," Granddad said.

"Not to get too graphic on you, but as this business progresses, my needs are not going to be terribly complicated."

"You can't know that."

"She's available, you know," George pointed out.

Ross stared at him, incredulous. "Did I hear you right?"

"Indeed you did."

"What the hell do I have to do with any of this?"

"A great deal. Now, you're not going to like hearing this, but it has to be said. I'm all you have, son, and I'm not enough family for you." He raised his hand to stave off the objections he clearly anticipated. "I know you, Ross. Your heart is big, the way your father's was. You were made for the kind of life filled with family. And it's not a weakness. It's a gift. And introducing you to Claire—that's a gift. Perhaps my final one to you."

"I don't need— Granddad, she's the last woman I'd want to date."

"Why? She's lovely. Intelligent, soft-spoken—"

"Whoa. I'm here for you, okay? Can you just please remember that?"

"As you wish. I do want you and Claire to get along, though. She's not going anywhere, so you'd best plan to make an effort."

Ross took a moment to absorb what Granddad was saying. He needed a moment. It wasn't every day he encountered someone who saw him so clearly. George had always possessed that ability, Ross reminded himself. He could see into Ross's heart. It was one of the reasons they'd always been so close and why he trusted his grandfather so much. But this…

"Let me get this straight. You hired Claire based on the fact that you thought I'd be attracted to her."

"Yes," George admitted.

"Are you out of your mind?"

"That's quite possible. I might be, yes. This disease is notoriously unpredictable." He studied the board. "I'm still giving you a schooling at chess, though."

"You'd better send her packing, because it's not going to work."

"On the contrary. I saw the way you looked at her. You're intrigued."

"And this comes as a surprise? Christ, you've seen her. Of course I'm intrigued."

"Excellent. And the good news is, she's going to be entirely smitten with you."

"Did she say that?"

"Of course she didn't say that. You just met."

"Then how do you know?"

"Good question. She hides it well. She's a complicated creature. Your favorite kind. You are wearing that confounded expression again, Ross."

He let out a sigh, steepled his fingers together. "We have a lot to talk about."

"I agree. I hope we'll have time for plenty of talk this summer."

"I've got all the time in the world," Ross told him. "It's crazy, going from having every minute of the day spoken for by my Dustoff unit to having nothing to do."

"Nothing but trying to figure out the whims of a dotty old man suffering from a diseased brain."

"Not funny," Ross pointed out.

"It wasn't meant to be." Granddad's smile was thoughtful. "You look wonderful, Ross. Soldiering agreed with you, just as it did your father. You look so much like him, I nearly forgot who I was talking to. Thank you again for coming."

"I'm here for you," said Ross. "I'm here for whatever you need from me."

"Now, that is music to my ears. Precisely what I was hoping to hear." He nudged a pawn into position, putting Ross's queen in dire straits. "Your move," he said.

Ross sacrificed his queen, as George must have known he would do. Then he hid behind the balloonlike brandy snifter to take a sip. He was lying through his teeth, of course. He was here to take his grandfather back to the city and persuade him to save his own life. He finished his brandy and set down the empty snifter.

George reached over to do the same. He missed the side table and the glass shattered in a shock of brilliant crystal shards.

"Occasional intermittent blindness," Claire explained to Ross Bellamy in a low voice. They had brought George back to the lake house and helped him to bed. Now she stood with Ross on the porch. She was trying to keep her professional facade in place, but it was hard. The guy looked like he'd stepped out of her best fantasy—tall and fit, a chiseled face, soulful eyes. *Dimples.* "That's likely why he dropped the glass. I'm afraid disorientation and lack of coordination are also common symptoms."

At the moment, standing in the moonlight and gazing out at Willow Lake, it was Claire herself who felt disoriented, and Ross Bellamy was the cause. The last thing she'd expected was…him. Sure, George had sort of prepared her by explaining that Ross had been in the service, that he was tall like George and shared the Bellamy blue eyes, but still, she hadn't been prepared. The guy was like some kind of action hero come to life, even in civilian clothes. When he'd approached her and George on the dance floor, she'd been caught off guard—and being caught off guard was a dangerous thing.

It wasn't just that she hadn't expected him—which she hadn't, not tonight. The thing that truly caught her off guard was her own reaction to him. The attraction had been as instantaneous and powerful as heat lightning. Sure, she'd been attracted to men before; just because she lived a borrowed life didn't mean she was immune to sexual chemistry. This was even more intense. It didn't matter that the man clearly resented and distrusted her. It didn't even matter that he'd come with his girlfriend. From the moment he'd drilled her with that "who-the-hell-are-you" glare, she'd been spellbound.

She focused on the issue at hand. "There's nothing to be done about it," she told Ross, "except to keep an eye on him and help him with his mobility."

In the glow of the porch light, she could see Ross's jaw tighten with anxiety. She stifled an urge to take his hand; she sensed he'd find no comfort in her touch. She felt for him, though. The broken glass was probably Ross's first concrete evidence that George's illness was no fiction, but something real and inevitable, an enemy he couldn't fight.

"Is that your medical opinion?" Ross asked. "Or personal?"

"Medical," she said. "I've spent hours familiarizing myself with his case."

"His case. Yeah, I guess he's just a case to you."

"He's a man who needs me. He needs you, too, and

all those who love him. George deserves to find a sense of peace and closure. As horrible as this is, there will be unexpected gifts, too. Not everybody gets a time like this—to spend or waste however he likes. For some people, everything is snatched away in an instant." She stopped, wondering if she'd revealed too much of herself in that statement.

Ross stared at her. "What he *needs* is a damn team of doctors. I put my faith in surgeons and scalpels. That's the way lives are saved."

"On the battlefield, that's true," she said.

"He told you about me?"

"He told me you were a medevac pilot in the army." Claire could feel the tension rolling off Ross, and she sensed he was suppressing a lot. It was not uncommon, but it wasn't good for her patient. He couldn't be fully present for his grandfather if he was bottling up real feelings. There were things that needed to be let out. "I can't imagine what it was like for you."

"You don't want to imagine it. Nobody does."

"You saved lives," she said. "And every life you saved was connected to countless others. Your grandfather is extremely proud of that, rightfully so. I hope knowing what a difference you've made brings you peace."

He shrugged. "Guys like me, we don't keep score. We don't know how many people we've saved or how many we lost. None of the crew ever knew—or wanted to know—what happened to patients after they were airlifted."

"You never had a follow-up? Never wondered about someone?"

"There've been a few guys who figured out how to get

in touch with me," he admitted. "A couple of e-mails to say thanks." He pushed the tips of his fingers together, and his eyes looked lost in memories. "I'm one of the lucky ones, you know? I went to war for two years and never had to kill anyone. Going out flying and bringing guys back—it was a hell of a job."

The less he said, the more her mind filled in the details. She tried to create a mental image of Ross at the controls, piloting a helicopter through the firestorm of battle, but it resembled a scene out of a movie. Maybe it was his movie-star looks, which shone through his grief and anger.

"As for wondering about someone—hell, yeah," he admitted. "I wonder about every single one of them. And then I leave it at that. Trying to follow up on everything makes you crazy."

"Your grandfather calls you a hero."

"Maybe I was just an adrenaline addict."

"Did you always want to be a pilot?" she asked.

He shook his head. "Never quite knew what I wanted to be, so for a long time, I was an asshole."

She kind of wanted it to be true, so she could stop feeling so drawn to him. "Your grandfather didn't tell me that part."

"Yeah, he wouldn't. I partied my way through college and a couple of jobs I didn't much like. Enlisted almost on a whim, and it turned out to be the right thing for me." He rubbed his jaw, looking weary. "Deployment wore me down, though, two years of it. I thought I'd come back to the States and work as a civilian in medevac. Everything's on hold now."

"I know it must be hard, coming home to this."

He paced the length of the porch, stopping a few feet

from her. "Listen, the last thing I need is for some hired New Age nurse to be doling out platitudes to me. I'll tell you what's hard. Coming home from a war to the news that my grandfather's dying—that's hard. Finding out he's given up on getting better—that, too. Oh, and realizing this is all going to go down in a strange place, surrounded by strangers—that's pretty damn hard."

She watched the way his hands gripped the porch rail in a fury of tension. Though she couldn't tell him the truth, she was painfully familiar with the aftermath of trauma. One day, she'd been a high school girl; the next she was a fugitive. Though it wasn't quite the same as surviving a war, she could recognize the lingering stress in Ross.

He subjected her to a penetrating stare, and a part of her almost wished he recognized that lonely girl, hiding inside her.

She wished his contempt was more of a turnoff. But it wasn't because she recognized his rage for what it was—a shield against the terror of losing someone he loved. "I'm sorry," she said. "I should have said that right off the bat. I'm so very sorry. George is too nice a person for this to be happening to him."

"I guess we agree on one thing." He turned away to stare out at the lake, a mirror of ink in the darkness, where the reflection of the moon created a shimmering silver disc. "Damn, it's quiet here. Kind of like night ops, only we're not being shot at."

She tried to picture him in uniform. She had issues with guys in uniform, but for some reason, she felt okay around Ross Bellamy. "Night ops?"

"Mandatory exercises," he said. "You have to learn to

do everything in the dark. That's when the worst part of war happens."

"And there's a best part of war?"

"It's known as boredom. In my line of work, there were two modes of operation—boredom or full-on adrenaline. Not much in between."

She wondered about the memories he carried inside him. "This is a big adjustment for you. If you need to talk to someone about it—"

"What, you're a shrink, too? Jeez, lady, you're one-stop shopping."

"I was going to say there's a vet center in Middletown."

"Shit, sorry. I know you're trying to be helpful. I'm okay for now. During demobilization, they gave us info about PTSD. Last thing I want to do is have a meltdown when I'm supposed to be taking care of my grandfather."

"Then we agree on two things," she pointed out.

"No, we don't. I'm here to help him get better, and you seem fine with letting him get sicker, out here in the middle of nowhere."

"I'm not 'letting' him do anything," she said. "He's here by choice, and the things that are happening to him can't be helped or stopped."

"You claim you're some kind of nurse," Ross said. "Isn't it your job to help people?"

"I *am* a nurse, and yes, that *is* my job."

"So where does the dancing come in? Is that part of my grandfather's treatment, dancing in restaurants? What the hell was that about, Nurse Turner?"

"It was about taking care of my patient. He said he always wanted to dance."

His shoulders sagged just the slightest bit. "I guess

you've noticed—my grandfather is everything to me. He's the best man I know. And what's happening to him…" His voice broke off on a rough note. "We need to stop it, Claire. Please."

It was the first time he'd addressed her by her first name, and it signaled a slight shift. She wanted to weep for him; she probably would later, in private. "There's no stopping it," she whispered. "The best way to help your grandfather is to give him as many good days as you can, for as long as you can."

Ross shook his head. "It's like he's giving up on himself. What's worse, he came here to see some guy who hasn't given him the time of day in what, fifty, sixty years. He's going to get his heart broken, and he doesn't deserve that, either."

Even through the gloom, she could see the brightness of tears in his eyes. "Please listen. There's no easy way to say this, but try to understand. This is his life and he gets to choose. Now, you can either support him and wish him well, or you can begrudge him this time and criticize the choices he's making."

"So if he wishes to jump in the lake wearing cement boots we should let him because he wishes it?" Ross demanded.

"Now you're being ridiculous."

"For wanting my grandfather to seek treatment for an illness so he can get better? Come on, Claire. Help me out here."

"Help *you* out?"

"I have to persuade him to come back to the city. I'm sure there are more doctors he can see, more courses of treatment to explore."

Claire's heart ached for him. She wished things were different, that she could agree with Ross. Instead she said, "Don't you think he'd treat this if there was a possibility of a decent outcome? There's not. I hate to be so blunt, but there's not."

He winced. "Look, all I'm asking is for him to keep an open mind. Or for God's sake, to listen to reason. To actually seek treatment for his condition instead of giving up and retreating to some obscure hideaway like a wounded animal holing up to die."

Claire placed one hand in the other, quelling the urge to touch his arm, or the back of his hand. "He's here with his doctor's blessing, did he tell you that?"

"Then he needs to find a new doctor."

"He's been working with a whole team. Any one of them will be glad to go over the case with you. And what they'll say, with the deepest of regret, is that surgical resection is not an option. Chemo and radiation are strictly palliative measures, and the side effects are so severe, they'd strip away any quality of life he might have. Your grandfather's doctors will tell you there's no further surgical or medical intervention for this. Not a single one will say that any life is better than death. I'm employed by your grandfather, and he's made his choice. This can't be about you, Ross. It has to be about George. Can you allow that? Please?"

He said nothing, but it was an angry silence.

"You don't have to like me," she said, struggling to keep the barriers in place. "I don't need for you to like me. But the sooner you figure out a way to be okay with your grandfather's wishes, the better it'll be for him."

"Right," said Ross. "Got it." He fell silent again and

stayed that way awhile longer. She waited, listening to the rustle of night creatures in the underbrush, the lapping of the lake on the shore. Finally he said, "Has he contacted the brother yet?"

The brother. She sensed Ross wasn't too happy about that development and wondered how much of the background he knew. "Not yet," she said. "I think, actually, he's been waiting for you."

In the lake, a fish jumped, and something slipped into the water from the shore. Ross continued to survey the scene for a moment. Then he said, "I'm going to turn in. If he needs anything at all, you come and get me."

"Of course."

He turned and walked away, striding across the compound to an A-frame cabin.

Claire stood on the porch in the moonlight, peering into the darkness, feeling a crazy jumble of emotions. The guy's moods changed like the swing of a pendulum, which was not uncommon in ex-soldiers. He was the last guy she expected to feel attracted to. It made absolutely no sense. He was freshly back from war, he was her client's grandson and he had shown up with a woman named Natalie—a girlfriend?

Claire knew she wouldn't do anything about the heart-lurch of yearning she felt. And as for Ross, he was going to be preoccupied by family business that promised to be complicated.

Families were so messy, she reflected, hearing the door to his cabin open and shut. People hurt each other so much. Even when they tried to do the right thing, when they acted out of love, they hurt each other. Family members worked so hard to be together, and for what?

So they could fight and cry and butt heads. Being a member of a family was a recipe for pain and strife.

So why did she want it so much?

Seven

Ross awakened to birdsong and sunshine streaming in through his window. For a few minutes, he lay perfectly still, reorienting himself as he savored the miracle of a perfect morning. He'd grown used to being awakened by the sound of explosions, alarms, chugging generators and radio calls, the descending whistle of a Soviet-made bomb or the champagne-cork pop of rifle fire.

Last night, Claire Turner had mentioned a nearby vet center. For now, he didn't need that. He just needed the gentle, quiet morning by the lake. He kept his mind in the moment, something he had learned to do to keep his sanity while in country.

The bed in his rented lakeside cabin was seriously comfortable, with crisp white sheets and an eiderdown that was thick but weightless. The foot of the bed faced a window with sheer, pale curtains rippling in the breeze, framing a view he'd only glimpsed by moonlight when they'd arrived.

Willow Lake more than lived up to its name on the welcome sign—the jewel of the Catskills. The water's surface resembled hammered gold, reflecting the rising sun. It was fringed by every sort of tree, predominantly willows. In his mind, Ross heard the iconic strains of Grieg's "Morning," though a much more prosaic reality penetrated the fantasy. Elsewhere in the cabin, a radio was playing Jay-Z rapping out "Big Pimpin'." Natalie was up.

He forgave his friend her choice of music because she'd already made coffee. Its aroma permeated the place. He pulled on a faded pair of jeans, which fit him like old friends from his civilian days, and headed into the cabin's tiny kitchen.

Natalie was dressed in running shorts and a T-shirt. She was sipping coffee and gazing out the window. She turned to him, her gaze lingering on his bare chest. "Why, Chief Bellamy. The military life agrees with you."

"You mean I graduated from the scrawny kid you used to make fun of?"

"Definitely."

It had been boredom more than vanity that had driven him to spend hours in the workout tent. Between the adrenaline-rush moments of rescue ops, there wasn't much else to do. He also had to admit he'd succumbed to an element of competitiveness among the men. It was part of the rarefied culture of the remote outposts where he'd spent the past couple of years.

He helped himself to coffee—strong, dark coffee with real cream. It tasted so good he thought he was dreaming.

"You guys stayed up late last night," Natalie observed. "Your granddad okay? For now, I mean."

Dream over, thought Ross, setting aside his coffee. "Apparently he sometimes has trouble with vision and maybe coordination. He still managed to school me at chess, though."

"For what it's worth, I couldn't tell he was ill," she said. "And the nurse? Is she… How's that working out? For what it's worth, she doesn't look like a grandpa-kidnapper."

"My grandfather seems to like her. We'll see." *Claire Turner.* He was still trying to figure out how he felt about her, so he didn't say any more. "Thanks for renting the cabin, Nat," he added. "In my rush to get here, it never even occurred to me to make a reservation."

"No problem. It's early enough in the season so there was plenty of room."

The cabin they'd been given was an A-frame, which stood shoulder to shoulder in a row with the others, facing the lake. A framed printout on the wall offered a brief history of the unit. The original structures had housed seasonal farm workers back when the area was agricultural, in the dust bowl days. Later, when Camp Kioga was in operation, the A-frames had housed camp workers or visiting entertainers.

Natalie had declared it perfectly appointed, with its Hudson's Bay blankets of colorful striped wool, vintage prints on the walls and retro furniture. The main floor had a raised bed facing the view, and there was a cozy loft in the peak of the A, accessed by a sturdy ladder. Ross and Natalie had flipped a coin for the loft, and she'd won it.

"I'm off for a run," she said. "After that, I'll need a lift into town. I need to be on the noon train."

"You're leaving already?"

"I have a grown-up job, remember?"

"You're going to miss all of the fun," he said. "In addition to my own family, there's apparently a mystery brother."

"No offense, but I have my own screwed-up family. I don't need to borrow yours."

He walked outside with her. The cool air felt fresh on his skin. He inhaled deeply, put his arm around Natalie. "Thanks for driving up here with me."

"That's what friends are for." She drew closer with surprising ferocity and lifted herself up on tiptoe to whisper in his ear, "I wish this wasn't happening."

He squeezed her tight in a bear hug, lifting her slightly off the ground. She felt both sturdy and feminine in his arms, but as always, his feelings toward her were platonic; she was like a sister to him. An extremely loyal sister. "You're awesome, Ms. Sweet," he said.

"Aren't I, though? I'll come back for a visit." She pulled out of the hug, and he saw that she was crying. "These tears are not for you," she quickly pointed out.

"I know," he said, taking a deep, unsteady breath. "I know who they're for."

When they separated, he noticed Claire Turner standing on the deck of his grandfather's cabin, observing them. She offered a brief wave of greeting, then went back inside. Ross wondered what was on her mind. He wondered a lot of things about her.

"She thinks we're a thing," he said to Natalie.

Natalie gave his arm a slug. "Dream on, Chief."

"Do me a favor."

"Anything."

"When you get back to the city, see what you can find out about Nurse Claire Turner."

"You think she's scamming him?"

"I don't know what to make of her." Based on his conversation with her the night before, Ross knew he was a long way from figuring the woman out. But he also knew that when he looked into her eyes, he felt something that was both strange and real, as though the two of them shared something.

"I'll put on my investigative reporter hat and see what I can dig up," Natalie said, and took off for her morning run.

Ross had a quick shower before heading over to see his grandfather. The air had a watery smell and a light breeze ran its fingers through his damp hair, a welcome contrast to the grit and fleas that had plagued him not so long ago. After deployment, there were certain things he would never again take for granted, such as consistent hot water and a temperate climate.

Granddad's summer rental was much more than a cabin. It was a whole house, with a dock and furnished porch, complete with accessibility ramps. The porch was hung with baskets of fresh flowers and a couple of hummingbird feeders. Ross knocked at the screen door. "Granddad," he called, "you up?"

"Good morning," his grandfather said. "Splendid day, isn't it?" He was dressed and seated in a sun-drenched breakfast nook with the *New York Times* open in front of him.

Ross felt an unbidden beat of emotion. It was an ordinary, familiar sight, his grandfather with the morning paper, but now everything seemed fraught with importance. Don't die, Granddad, Ross thought. I want you to live forever.

His grandfather regarded him placidly. For a disconcerting moment, Ross felt as though his thoughts had been heard.

"Join me," Granddad said. "I was just finishing the paper. And look—my old fly-tying kit. Remember this?"

How could he forget? The kit was a treasure trove of string and bobbins, wing burners, tiny pliers and scissors, grips and holders and every sort of material, from deer hair to speckled pheasant feathers. Just the sight of it unleashed memories of the distant past—Granddad's big fingers, guiding Ross's small ones as they smoothed back the fibers and wrapped a thread around the hook, fastening the end with a whip finish. Tying flies was a curiously intricate and intimate activity, one that seemed to lend itself to talk.

Granddad used to talk to him about everything. Maybe not everything, Ross realized now. There was the small matter of the brother he'd never mentioned.

He was about to broach the topic when Claire Turner came into the room. "Good morning," she said, speaking in a neutral, well-modulated voice. The voice of a professional nurse—matter-of-fact yet determinedly pleasant. He couldn't tell what she was thinking, or if she had any thoughts at all about seeing his and Natalie's embrace earlier. Not that it was any of her business, or any of his concern what her opinion was, but he was just curious.

Okay, more than curious. She was an enigma to him, in her Bermuda shorts and plain white collared shirt, dark hair pulled back, no jewelry other than a watch. She reminded him somewhat of a female soldier, trying to downplay her femininity, hiding her thoughts and feelings behind a mask of neutrality. Ironically the harder she tried to conceal her looks, the more attractive she appeared. But Claire wasn't in a war, which made him wonder why she was so guarded. What battle was she fighting?

"More coffee?" she offered.

He shook his head. "Thanks, I had some earlier. Just came by to see my grandfather and figure out what the plan is for the day." He tried to sound polite but dismissive.

She clearly got it. "I'll leave the two of you alone, then." She handed George a small paper cup of pills, which he washed down with orange juice. "Can I get you anything else, George?"

"Not at the moment, thanks."

"I'll be outside, then. Just give me a buzz if you need me." She slipped out, swallowed up by sunshine as she crossed the porch and walked out onto the dock.

Granddad indicated a small box. "Electronic apron strings, I call it," he explained. "I push this button, and Claire comes running. Or vice versa—she can summon me from her end. Wish I'd had something like this back in my youth. It would have made dating easier. Push a button and presto, a beautiful woman appears."

"Very handy," said Ross, watching the way the morning sun outlined her. Was she beautiful? Damn, after the past two years, every woman looked beautiful to him. He sidestepped the thought. "Listen, I need to give Natalie a ride to the station in a little bit. When I get back, let's talk. Okay, Granddad?"

"Of course. I'd like nothing better."

"She's not his girlfriend," George said to Claire.

"I beg your pardon?" She realized he'd caught her staring out the window at Ross as he loaded Natalie's things into the trunk of his sports car.

"Natalie Sweet," said George. "She's not his girlfriend."

"Not whose girlfriend?"

"You know very well who."

She watched them drive off together, then turned back to George. "And I need to know this because…"

"Why do you think, Miss Turner?"

"George. You are not trying to fix us up."

"I certainly am."

"You're wasting your time."

"Give the man a chance."

"Trust me, the man does not want a chance with me." She tried to suppress a small twinge. The loneliness of her situation was unbearable sometimes, particularly in the wake of meeting someone like Ross Bellamy. He was everything she secretly wished for—kind and caring, undeniably good-looking, the sort of guy she could picture surrounded by friends and family—but everything she couldn't have.

"Humor me," George said. "The prospect of a blooming romance gives me something to dwell on besides my grim fate. I want my grandson to meet someone wonderful—"

"I'm sure he will one day," she said hastily.

"Perhaps he already has. He's the finest young man I know, Claire, and my wish for him is to have the life he deserves."

"You can't make someone's life happen, George."

"But I can introduce him to someone like you."

She decided to change the subject. "I've been rereading an old favorite. *The Great Gatsby.*"

"That's a favorite of yours?"

"Sure. I like the romanticism of it, the tragedy. The impossibility."

George nodded. "I'd always meant to read Fitzgerald's other works but never got around to it. I wish I'd been a faster reader. For that matter, I wish some of my favorite writers were faster. To my eternal dismay, I probably won't ever read the new Ken Follett." Bracing his hands on the arms of his chair, he got up. "Help me with this box. I want to put some family pictures around the place, since I'm planning to stay awhile."

For his sake, she wished his family would get over itself and quit expecting George to head straight back to the city. Maybe now that Ross was here, he'd persuade the others to come.

The box turned out to be a time capsule of George's life. He showed her a black-and-white shot of his family from the 1940s. "This was taken right here at Camp Kioga," he said.

Even in the monochromatic photo, the place seemed like something out of a dream. The four of them were posed on a dock, and in the water was a sleek wooden Chris-Craft boat.

"I was about thirteen in this picture, and Charles was ten," George continued.

"What a beautiful family," said Claire. "I hope you were as happy as you look in this photo."

"I suppose we were, a lot of the time."

The mother was flawlessly groomed, in a wasp-waisted dress and high-heeled sandals, which, oddly enough, did not look out of place on the dock. The father stood slightly behind her, his posture very correct.

"He lost his right arm in the first all-American air attack on Germany," George said. "1942—he was a senior officer in the army air force. He was supposed to be at a command post far from the action. But there was a shortage of personnel, and he went up with a bomber group." George regarded the photo quietly. "That was not supposed to happen."

"No one's ever supposed to lose a limb," Claire pointed out.

"He was awarded a Purple Heart and later a medal of honor."

"You must have been proud of him," said Claire.

"I never really knew him," George said.

She heard regret in his voice. "Didn't you tell me he took you and your brother to Yankees games? I bet you knew plenty about him."

"In some ways, yes, I could tell you plenty. I could tell you how he traced his ancestry back to the Norman Conquest and that the first Bellamys came to the New World on King James's business. I could tell you he was educated at Yale and expected both his sons to do the same. I could tell you he married an heiress who had even more money than he did. But I never really knew his heart."

"So now you know what your children and grandchildren need from you," she pointed out.

He sat back, took off his glasses and polished them. "Suppose I show them who I really am, and they don't like me?"

"Aw, George. It's not your job to make them like you. It's your job to be who you are."

"Even if what I am is a cranky old bastard?"

"Even if," she agreed. "However, you're neither cranky nor a bastard."

"Just old." He chuckled as he took out two small

boxes. One of them contained a few tarnished coins and an old-fashioned silver earring in the shape of a daisy. He gazed at the earring for a few seconds, then put it away. The other box was made of the unmistakable signature blue of Tiffany's. He opened it, showing her a diamond ring.

Claire went nuts for it. "That's the prettiest ring I've ever seen. Was it your wife's?"

"No. I never had a chance to give it to the one it was bought for. That was back in 1956." He handed over a leather-bound certificate. The ring was signed and numbered, certified as to color and clarity.

"Wow," Claire said, "I hope it's insured."

He studied the ring, on its pristine cream-colored pillow. Maybe he'd tell her one day. "It's never been worn," he said, then put it with the other box.

She was dying to know more, but didn't want to badger him. She picked up another framed picture and removed the tissue paper. "So who are these people?"

"That was taken at my youngest son's wedding," said George. "I brought it along because we were all so happy that day."

It was a joyful photograph, with everyone dressed to the nines and smiling, some even laughing. She focused on a young, skinny Ross, whose broad grin was framed by those irresistible dimples, and found herself wishing she'd known that boy.

"That's the French Riviera in the background," George said. "Louis and Lola were married in Cap d'Antibes. Ah, what a day that was."

"You'll have to give me a who's who," she said. "Your wife is so pretty in this shot. When did she pass away?"

"It's been ten years." He paused. "There was…an accident."

Claire hadn't been expecting that. "I'm sorry."

He gazed at the tall, elegant woman in the picture. "There was a treacherous road involved, and a large motorcycle. And an Italian lover—did I mention that?"

"Um, no."

"She and her Italian lover, a man in his forties, went off the road on his motorcycle."

Ouch, thought Claire. "I'm really sorry."

"We were actually in talks about a divorce, but I ended up being widowed instead. I can't say I was happy about that, but it would be a lie not to admit she saved me a great deal of trouble, she and Fabio."

"Fabio. His name was Fabio?"

He nodded glumly. "Try explaining that to your family. And may I just say, Miss Turner, how much I'm enjoying the expression on your face right now?"

"Sorry. It's just…this is quite a story."

"I have many more of them, of every sort—happy, tragic, funny, or simply inane. Life is long, Claire. There's room for everything to happen to you, if you let it. I can't quite bring myself to regret my marriage. Jacqueline was the mother of my children and I would never speak ill of her."

"As for your children—you have three sons," she said, switching gears.

"I had four boys," he said. "One died."

Claire touched his hand, brushing her fingers over the cool, dry skin. "You don't have to talk about it if you don't want to."

"I'm never really far from Pierce," he said. "Yet losing a child is one of those horrors from which the heart will not mend. Ever. It's actually the one thing that brings me a perverse sense of peace about reaching the end. To not have to face every single day with a sense of grief and loss is a comfort to me."

"I'd like to hear about him one day," she said.

"I would be pleased to tell you. Better yet, Ross could tell you."

Her heart skipped a beat. "Pierce was Ross's father."

He took out the last framed photo and sat it next to the others. "He was killed while serving in the military, during operation Desert Storm."

She had only the vaguest recollection of the conflict. She had been in grade school when it was going on, and the conflict had been as remote as a space shuttle launch. Seeing the man in the picture, with his hauntingly familiar smile, suddenly made it real to her. "I'm terribly sorry."

"Pierce was the best of them," George said. "I know it's wrong to compare one's children, but it's true. He was the best. And Ross is like him in many ways."

Claire's throat heated with tears. "He was lucky to have you, then."

"I hope he thinks so." George took out the last framed photo, this one showing a large group. "I have a dozen grandchildren in all. Ross is the eldest, and Micah, who's twelve now, is the youngest. And somehow, I fear this will be the hardest on the two of them, for different reasons. I suspect you'll find out more about that as you get to know Ross better."

You are my client, not Ross, she thought, but didn't say. "Now that he's here, you can see about contacting your brother."

George looked away. "Suppose he refuses to see me."

"Then at least you'll know you tried. And honestly, that seems unlikely." She gestured at the oldest photo of George and his brother with their parents. "There's a foundation of love. That's how it looks to me."

"Oh, there was love, for certain." George's eyes were glazed with memories as he turned toward the lake. "But that didn't stop us from fighting like cats and dogs."

Eight

New York en route to Camp Kioga,
Avalon, Ulster County
Summer 1944

"Mama, George won't share with me!" Ten-year-old Charles Bellamy's voice piped from his window seat on the hot, creaky train. "He's hogging *Superman* all to himself."

"Am not." George peevishly hugged the comic book to his chest.

"Are so."

"Am not."

"Give it here," whined Charles, his voice climbing to a crescendo.

"You don't even like Superman," George grumbled.

"Do so."

"Do not."

"Do—"

"George Parkhurst Bellamy. Let your brother read the comic book."

"But—"

"*George.*" When Mother took that tone, she meant business.

With a decided lack of grace, he slapped the book against his brother's chest. "Here, baby. And don't ask me to read any of the big words for you."

Charles stuck out his tongue, reeling it back in when their mother leaned over the seat to check on them. She was always exhorting them to be on their best behavior on account of their father was Overseas, where the fighting was.

George didn't understand how his best behavior was going to help Father, though. Gone was gone, and acting like a perfect angel even when Charles was being a pest was not going to bring him back. Not this summer.

Maybe not ever.

Mother said he was in the diplomatic corps, working for the Office of Strategic Services, which was not as dangerous as being a soldier. Father had been a soldier at the very start of the war, and he'd lost an arm in battle. He could have returned to his family after that, but Parkhurst Bellamy claimed he had a duty to serve his country, and if that meant being a diplomat, then that was what he would do. You didn't need two arms to be a diplomat. You needed to speak several languages and know which wine to pick and which gifts to give.

Yet even being in the diplomatic corps was risky. Most kids didn't watch the newsreels before a Saturday matinee, but George paid close attention. There had been a very bad Nazi bombing in Tunis, in North Africa. George knew for a fact that his father had worked in Tunisia, and it was just pure dumb luck he hadn't been there in the explosion that had blasted several people to smithereens.

Usually Mother wasn't told where Father was, as a security measure. Father was always doing Top Secret things. And anyway, grown-ups tended to think "Overseas" was enough of an explanation for kids. Now that he was thirteen, George considered himself in between a kid and an adult and he wished they would tell him more. He was like Clark Kent. He wanted the real story.

Most kids, including his little brother, Charles, professed their devotion to Superman. George had even caught Charles paging ahead in the latest comic book, skipping whole chunks of the story.

"Looking for the exciting parts," Charles had explained with a goofball grin.

Here was the thing about George. When every other kid idolized Superman, paging through the comics to find the caped crusader in action, George tended to linger over the parts that appealed to him much more—pages that featured Clark Kent in the newsroom of the *Daily Planet,* or Clark Kent in pursuit of a story. In George's opinion, Clark Kent was lots more interesting than Superman. You always knew what would happen when Superman came into the picture. With Clark, things were more uncertain.

Now, there was excitement, George would think. A regular fellow, rooting out the truth. To George, that was more intriguing than some guy from outer space, swooping around in a cape. That storyline was out of the realm of possibility. But Clark Kent on a hot news tip? Now, there was something that might really happen.

George was a boy who liked writing things down. He took notes about everything from the big stuff like D-Day, which had taken place two weeks earlier, to small details about his life, like the vendor at Grand Central Station who had just sold him a batch of homemade saltwater taffy. Ever since having his tonsils out last spring, he'd craved things like taffy or horehound candies to soothe his throat. The vendor had been gaunt and clad in rags, around the same age as Charles. The sight of a boy with nothing made George feel guilty.

"Mother!" shouted Charles. "He's got candy! I want some!"

"George Bellamy, you give me that." She grabbed the candy by its torn wax-paper wrapping.

"Hey," George protested. "I bought that fair and square, with my own money. There was a kid at Grand Central—"

"You bought candy from a street beggar?" His mother rushed to throw the taffy out the window, then spritzed her hands with rosewater from her carpetbag. "Honestly, what were you thinking? You could get a disease."

"Aw, he was just trying to make some spare change," protested George.

"Never you mind that. You know better than to take food from strangers." His mother shuddered, then turned her attention to the rotogravure she'd been reading.

Charles fidgeted, slamming the heels of his Buster Browns against the footrest as he pretended to read the comic book. Sometimes George got sick of having a little brother tagging after him. Especially a kid like Charles who assumed he was George's equal. He was nearly four years younger than George, yet he insisted on doing everything his big brother did.

Scowling with ill humor, George decided to write in his journal. He was pretty sure Clark would have kept a journal when he was George's age. You didn't get to be a crack reporter overnight. You had to practice for years, so George was giving himself a head start.

It was challenging, writing on the train, using the small table mounted under the window. His penmanship wobbled with the motion of the railcar, but he kept doggedly at it.

"En route to Camp Kioga, in Avalon, Ulster County, New York, United States of America, Planet Earth," he wrote. He felt very grown-up because his mother had allowed him to use his good pen, the one he had been given as a prize for winning the school spelling bee.

He had a vial of Skrip Spillproof Ink in the best color, which was peacock-blue. He reckoned Clark Kent used peacock-blue ink.

George focused on his task with total absorption. He wrote a very good article about street vendors in New York City, making sure all his punctuation was perfect. The story was so good he could imagine it being published in the *New York Times*. Everybody knew the *New York Times* published all the news that was fit to print. It said so right on the masthead.

George decided to make his own masthead. He needed a slogan. He wrote,

"All the News That's Fit to Print."

Maybe he should think up something of his own:

"The Printed News, All the Time."

No, that wasn't right. Maybe:

"If It Fits, Print It."

"What're you doing?" asked Charles.

"None of your beeswax," said George.

"Let me see." Charles reached for the notebook. His hand bumped the unspillable ink bottle, and the vial toppled over. Unfortunately, unspillable did not mean unbreakable. The neck of the bottle snapped off and ink spilled across George's story, obliterating two pages of painstaking work.

"Uh-oh," said Charles.

"You little pest," said George. "I ought to knock your block off."

"Go ahead and try it," Charles said. "See what it gets you. It was a...an accident, you big bully." His face reddened, and his chin trembled.

George was completely disdainful of his brother's show of emotion. "Go on with you," he said. "Go away, baby."

"Sure I'll go away," Charles declared. "I don't care if I never see you again. Ever ever ever."

Charles's threat proved to be impossible to carry out, since the lakeside bungalow that would be theirs for the summer required them to share a room with a bunk bed. They fought over who would sleep on the top or bottom. They fought over having the lamp on or off at bedtime. They fought over everything, bickering until their mother threatened to send them to Reform School.

Neither boy knew precisely what Reform School actually was. But it sounded like nothing good, and the threat of it stopped them from fighting for whole minutes at a time.

Eventually, however, the magic of Camp Kioga took over. The mothers would play bridge and smoke cigarettes and paint fake stocking seams on each other's legs as they talked about the war. The kids would go on expeditions deep in the forest. They would climb mountains to find the source of a spring, or take turns jumping off the high dive into the cold, clear lake. In the evenings there would be shows, sometimes an act from the city, or a sing-along led by Mrs. Gordon herself, the wife of the camp's owner.

The kids would stay awake late into the night, huddled around a campfire, telling ghost stories. George's favorites were the ones that were so scary they made his younger brother cry.

Meals were served family-style in a big dining room in the timber main lodge, which also had a loggia and deck overlooking the lake, a library and music room, and a billiard room. The food was delicious, because in this part of the world, food rationing didn't matter so much. Right on camp premises there was a victory garden, and a dairy and chicken farm. It was considered patriotic to grow one's own food. Every day, the tables were laden with big bowls of mashed potatoes with butter and cream, and cobblers made with stone fruit gathered from trees on the property.

Outward signs of war were subtle here, for the most part. Both George and Charles came to some understanding that they were meant to be America's elite. Princes of society, they were called by a reporter from the *Washington Post,* who was at Camp Kioga doing a piece on the War at Home.

Maybe he was just doing the assignment so he could rusticate at a glamorous resort, but George didn't care. He was more interested in the reporter—Mr. McClatchy—than he was in the topic. Mr. McClatchy took notes and asked questions. He was old and kind of fat, and wore thick glasses. He was no Clark Kent but he clearly had a passion for what he did.

Journalism, he declared, shone a light in the darkest places of the world.

"But what's the story here?" asked George. "Princes of society? Who cares?"

"People who buy advertisements in the paper, that's who. They want to read about folks who aren't like them, folks who live a different way."

"How does that shine a light?"

"You never know. Sometimes it doesn't. And sometimes you're John Steinbeck."

George had read *The Grapes of Wrath* on the sly, because it was considered shocking and scandalous. He had devoured page after page, with a sense of complete fascination. And he wasn't scandalized by the ending, which had caused the book to be banned all over the place on account of some lady kept a guy from starving by feeding him her mother's milk. He thought it was heroic and beautiful in a weird way, like the rest of the book. It wasn't the kind of thing George aspired to write, though.

"Mr. Steinbeck writes fiction," he pointed out.

"He's a war correspondent now, for the *New York Herald Tribune*."

"I keep a journal," George offered.

"It's a good habit to get into," Mr. McClatchy said. "Organizes your thoughts. Just make sure it never falls into the wrong hands."

"Yes, sir."

George behaved like the prince he'd been dubbed. He

was the best in sports, winning all the races, leading expeditions, basking in the admiration of the other kids. It all came naturally to him, and always had. Even in winter, the Bellamys spent several weeks in Killington, Vermont, at a ski resort. It was there that George had decided to join the elite Tenth Mountain Division of the U.S. Army. He'd be a ranger on skis, like some kind of superhero—except he would be for real.

Figuring out what his superpower would be this summer was a challenge. The ability to see long distances, maybe, he thought one day as they were returning from a woodcraft expedition to the summit of Watch Hill. He shaded his eyes and surveyed the area, fancying he could see beyond the vast lake and ridge of mountains, clear across the Atlantic Ocean to the secret place where his father was.

"Who are those people?" asked Charles, pausing to point at a group in a clearing much closer at hand. It appeared to be a family in the yard of a boxy clapboard house. Some kind of celebration was taking place.

"Let's go see," said George. "Say, Warren, are you coming?"

They'd made friends with a boy from Larchmont named Warren Byrne, who thought he was important because he had attended camp every summer from the beginning of time, to hear him tell it.

"We're behind enemy lines," George said, signaling Charles and Warren to drop low and fall into one of their favorite fantasies. They were getting pretty good at not making a sound while skulking through the forest.

As they drew closer, the thin, scratchy sound of a Victrola could be heard, along with laughter and conversation. There was a banner strung up over the front porch that read Farewell, Stuart. We Love You.

"This is where the Gordons live," explained Warren Byrne. The Gordons owned and ran the camp.

George had never thought of them as a family, just as workers who kept the dining room going and made sure the sheets were changed and the garbage taken out, the cabins cleaned and swept, the lawns mowed. And here, tucked away on a forgotten acre of the camp's premises, they had a whole separate life.

Stuart, it appeared, was a soldier.

"He's a marine," George told the others. "You can tell by his sage-green uniform. And he's wearing an overseas cover, so I betcha he's shipping out. Marines call that kind of cap a pisscutter," he added, eliciting snickers from the younger boys.

"Stuart's my big brother," said a voice behind them.

George's stomach dropped. They'd been caught, behind enemy lines. Should they make a run for it? Fight their way free? Surrender immediately?

Warren Byrne scampered off, like a coward.

"Jeez, it's only some girl," Charles said, grabbing George's sleeve and pointing out the intruder.

"I ain't some girl," she said. "I got a name. It's Jane. Jane Gordon. And Stuart's my big brother and what are you doing spying on us?"

"We were just exploring," George said peevishly. He didn't know why he was peeved. Maybe because she'd caught them, or maybe because she was just a dumb girl. She was about Charles's size, maybe a little bigger, with frizzy reddish hair and big teeth and one skinny arm threaded through a wire basket. She wore overalls of faded blue denim, the cuffs rolled up above scabby knees. The shins were bruised and the feet were bare.

"Stuart's going to the Specific Ocean," she announced with lofty authority.

"You mean the Pacific Ocean."

"I mean what I mean." She sniffed. "He's gonna be fighting in New Guinea. You know, like a guinea hen. And I have to go. Just because there is a celebration going on doesn't mean I can put off my chores."

"What kind of chores?" asked Charles.

"Come on," said Jane. "I'll show you." Without looking to see if they followed, she marched along a beaten path, her dirty feet kicking up puffs of dust.

George hesitated, but Charles gamely followed along. Then curiosity got the better of George, and he brought up the rear. They came to a clearing with a big garden, its rows divided by long wooden planks. Nearby was a chicken coop, surrounded on all sides and the top by wire.

"I have to gather the eggs," said Jane. "Twice a day no matter what. It's my job."

"Sounds like fun," Charles said.

"It's not." She stood in front of a latched gate. "Shows what you know."

"What's not fun about it?"

"Him, mainly. That bad rooster." She pointed out a colorful bird with gleaming beads for eyes and colorful plumes arching from its tail. "He's mean. He's so mean."

"What's a rooster doing in there anyway?" George demanded. "He's sure not laying any eggs."

"Jiminy Cricket, don't you know anything?" Jane said with a sniff. "Keeping a rooster around the chicken coop protects the chickens from predators. Plus, you need a rooster in order to keep the flock going. There can't be any baby chicks without roosters. Anyways, the rooster pecks because he thinks humans are out to harm the flock." Jane rolled her eyes.

"That's stupid," said George.

"They're chickens," she said. "They're supposed to be stupid."

"The rooster doesn't look all that dangerous. It's just a bird," George pointed out.

"With a sharp beak," she said. She put her hand on the latch, visibly screwing up her courage. In that instant, George started to like her.

"You want some help?"

"No, I'll catch fire and brimstone if one of you gets hurt." She slipped through the gate and headed for the nesting boxes. "Shoo!" she said to the rooster, flapping her hand in his face. "Go on with you."

The rooster lowered its head and rushed forward with amazing speed, sharp beak brandished like a knife. She swung out with her basket. "Get away, you bad rooster!"

George stood outside the gate, torn by indecision.

Charles sprang into action, ignoring protests from both his brother and from Jane. He chased the rooster away, waving his arms and making crazy noises. Jane moved quickly, plunging her hand into each nest and snatching the eggs. Within a couple of minutes, they were safely outside the pen, the wire basket full.

Charles's face was flushed with excitement. "Hey, that was something," he said, running along the side of the pen, keeping pace with the rooster. "That was really something."

Jane batted her eyes like a matinee princess. "That's the first time I didn't get pecked in a long time."

"It's a cinch with two people," said Charles. "I'll come and help you every day."

"That's real nice," she said, grinning at him.

George felt oddly out of sorts about the whole exchange. "You can't just drop everything and come here to do farm work," he said to his brother.

"Sure I can," Charles said, predictably. "Maybe I like farm work."

George scowled at the basket. "The eggs are no good," he said. "They're filthy."

"Nonsense. These are farm fresh eggs. None fresher."

"They've got straw stuck to them, and…and…" He struggled to think of a polite way to say it.

"Manure," she said matter-of-factly. "That just means the eggs are fresh as can be."

Charles giggled.

"It's disgusting." George regarded the eggs with revulsion.

"What did you eat for breakfast this morning?" Jane demanded.

"A cheese omelette."

"Ha. It was made from eggs gathered yesterday, just like this. I bet it was delicious." She headed down the path. "Come on, you can help me wash them in the creek." She called it a *crick* but George saw that she meant creek.

She waded right in and crouched down, dipping the wire basket into the deep, fast-flowing water.

"I'll help," Charles said with his typical eagerness. He leaped for a river rock.

"It's all right, I can—"

She didn't get a chance to finish. Charles missed the rock and plunged into the stream. He sputtered and flailed, fighting the current.

George was trying to figure out what to do. Should he jump in and rescue his brother, or—

"I gotcha." Jane grabbed the back of Charles's collar and tugged him toward her. He slipped and fell again, and down she went with a great splash, careful to keep her basket upright and above the water. They came up laughing, and sloshed over to the bank, their clothes plastered to their skin and their hair in straggles.

"We broke two eggs," she said.

"I'm sorry."

"It's okay, you didn't know." They were both dripping wet and grinning like fools.

"I have to get back," she said, wringing out her hair. "It's my brother's last day."

They walked her as far as the property edge. The afternoon sun beat down and Jane declared it lucky, as it was drying out her hair and clothes. "I'll see you around," she said.

Charles and George stood watching her for a few minutes. She entered the yard through a gate and set her basket on the ground. Then she ran to Stuart, a tall, lanky young man with a huge smile and military haircut.

He picked her up and swung her around, and she tilted back her head, laughing uproariously as she clasped him around the waist with her legs. The rest of the family gathered around, watching with fond smiles.

"Hey, you," Stuart said, "you're all wet. You smell like the crick. And like sunshine! I'm sure going to miss you, Sunshine."

This was the kind of thing Mr. McClatchy ought to be covering for his paper, thought George. A family like this, one that didn't have a fancy house and expensive things. They had each other, and were bound by a love even a stranger could see.

McClatchy would probably say a story about an ordinary family wouldn't sell papers. Even though stuff like this made John Steinbeck famous.

"I miss Father," Charles said as they hiked back to camp.

George slung his arm around his brother's skinny shoulders.

When they returned to their cottage, Charles bubbled over with stories of their adventure. As George knew would be the case, their mother was not amused. She scolded him about getting his shoes wet and said, "You are here to make friends with the other guests. Not with the workers' children."

"Does it matter?" asked Charles.

"Of course it matters."

"Why?"

"Because the other guests are like you. They're the sort of people you'll be surrounded with all your life."

"What if I don't want to be with people like me?" Charles demanded.

George snickered. "Now you know how *I* feel, having to be around you."

"Nuts to you," Charles said.

Nine

Deep in the wilderness, the children made their own rules. They played out stories from myth, legend, fairy tales…or whatever George happened to scribble in his notebook the night before.

Jane, who was a little older than Charles and a little younger than George, turned out to be a good match for both brothers. She declared herself a royal princess and claimed dominion over all she surveyed. Charles indulged his usual obsession with Superman. George told them the story of the Three Musketeers—Athos, Porthos, Aramis— and the way they always fought as an inseparable unit, protecting each other from all harm. He taught them to say "one for all and all for one" in French. The Three Musketeers became their favorite game.

Despite the disapproval of George's mother, the three became fast friends. The Gordons didn't approve of the threesome any more than the Bellamys did. They, too, believed the hosts and guests should never mingle socially, but Mrs. Gordon was usually too busy running things to enforce many rules.

Their favorite expedition was the hike to the summit of Watch Hill. From the very top, all of Willow Lake could be seen, even the town, ten miles away on the opposite end of the lake. They could see the curvy lake-shore road that hugged the perimeter of the vast lake. From this perspective, Camp Kioga resembled a miniature model fort from colonial times. Spruce Island, the wooded atoll in the middle of the lake, rose up like a mystical green enchanted isle.

George had been getting headaches for a few weeks running, but he didn't tell his mother, because he didn't want to be confined to his cabin. Today the pain was stabbing like a knife. Ignoring it, he crept out on a rocky outcropping and sat with his knees drawn up to his chest, watching the progress of a shiny black car on the road, far in the distance. You didn't see too many cars in these parts, what with gas rationing in force, just the occasional farm vehicle or bus, and quite often, a horse and buggy. Even wealthy people left their cars at home as a sign of patriotism.

"What are you looking at?" inquired Jane, sitting beside him.

He gestured. "That car."

The approaching car gleamed with importance. It was as black as a hearse, and left a trail of dust behind it.

They watched for a few minutes. The sun was just starting to slant toward afternoon, and its heat was so intense it seemed to pulse. Crickets sang in the tall grass, and the green smell of summertime rode the breeze. Bees browsed in the wildflowers that covered the hillside. Beside him, Jane was very still. She had a smell, too— her mother's homemade soap, scented with evergreen.

For a few seconds, it was so quiet he could detect the cadence of her breathing. It was even and slow.

And then she gasped, startling him so that he nearly fell off the outcropping. "That car is turning up the camp road!"

She jumped up and George gave a curt command to Charles—*Let's go*—and for once his little brother didn't argue or demand an explanation.

The three of them ran hell-for-leather down the hill. George told himself not to think or speculate. A reporter didn't judge or prognosticate until he had all the facts. George didn't let himself imagine what he would do if the car brought news of his father.

But the car kept rolling past the camp.

And that was when George knew. He knew Jane understood, too, because he could hear her gasping with sobs.

When they got to the Gordon house, the polished official vehicle was already there. They were too far away to hear what was being said. But in the end, it didn't matter. They could see it playing out before them—an officer in fancy dress uniform, cap removed and tucked ceremonially under his elbow. His posture straight, arm snapping in a smart salute.

Jane's mother, coming out into the yard with her apron still on.

There was a brief exchange. Mrs. Gordon sank to the ground as though her bones suddenly melted, her own strength not enough to hold her up. The officer scrambled awkwardly to help her.

Jane turned to Charles and George, her eyes already haunted with unbearable knowing. "I have to go," she said. She spoke with a curious dignity that made her seem older.

Wiser. As if the girl who had gone up the hill was a different person from the one who had come down it.

"I have to go," she said again. "My mother needs me."

The news made its way slowly through Camp Kioga—Stuart Gordon was dead. He'd gone to the Pacific to fight in the war, and at the age of eighteen he'd been killed in action "in the performance of duty and service of his country," according to the hand-delivered telegram.

George kept seeing Stuart in his mind's eye, twirling a laughing Jane around and calling her Sunshine. He imagined similar scenarios unfolding all around the country. Families were interrupted in the middle of dinner, the middle of the night, the middle of their lives, to be told somebody young and strong and beloved was dead.

Charles started having nightmares. He would thrash and whimper in his bunk and wake up crying for his father.

Someone said Mrs. Gordon was suffering from a terrible heartache and would be going to New Haven to stay with relatives for a change of scenery. Losing her son was simply too tragic for Mrs. Gordon to contemplate the future without him.

Jane tried to explain. "Everything here reminds her of him. I heard my aunt Tilly say it's causing a nervous disorder." She scuffed her bare heel into the dusty ground. "That's a code word for crazy."

George paid closer attention to accounts of the war in the newspaper. That was when he realized what he ought to do with his life. He ought to write for newspapers and magazines like Mr. McClatchy did. Somebody had to tell the world what was going on. Somebody had to tell the story behind the casualty numbers. If more people understood the true price being paid for the war, they might find a way to end it.

Jane was going away with her mother. Her father would stay and run Camp Kioga, but her mother couldn't bear to be here, where memories of her lost son lurked around every corner. Jane came to tell the Bellamy boys goodbye and said there was time for one more expedition through the forest, to their special place high on Watch Hill.

George felt cranky and out of sorts. He had that same headache, the one that pounded hard no matter whether or not his mother gave him a headache powder. He felt sleepy, too, but it was a beautiful day and he was not about to stay inside.

He didn't exactly know how to act around Jane. He felt like he should treat her differently because she *was* different. She seemed more serious to him, maybe a little quieter, a noticeable change since she was usually so animated and bubbly.

The hike to the top of Watch Hill made him especially tired. He felt more hot and sweaty than he'd ever been in his life. He and Charles and Jane stood at the summit, surveying the view below like gods of myth and legend.

There was something wrong with George's vision. The entire landscape blurred together like a watercolor—the lake in the woods. The sky and the long squiggle of the road. Everything spun like a pinwheel. The voices of the others sounded hollow, like echoes shouted down a tube.

"My mother doesn't want to help run the camp anymore," Jane was telling them. "She told my father it makes her too sad. Pa and I love Camp Kioga, though. It was started by my grandfather, and I want it to be mine one day, and I aim to make that happen."

She sounded adamant, like she was in one of the melo-dramas they put on at camp.

George thought he should commend her for her loyalty and lofty commitment. The words swirled around in his head. He must have made some kind of noise, because the others turned to stare at him. Their faces expanded and contracted as though viewed in a fun house mirror. Their voices sounded funny, too, like the Victrola when it needed a turn of the crank.

And even though George meant to tell Jane she was brave and strong and that he admired her, something else came out. He fell to his knees while vomit erupted with undeniable force.

He had just barely enough consciousness left to feel humiliated.

He lost track of time and forgot where he was. Jane yelled something and Charles sped off down the hill. Then Jane crouched beside him and tried to give him water from her round, flat canteen. George couldn't swallow the rusty-tasting liquid. Could barely even open his mouth. Could see only pinholes of light. He felt the water dribbling away, could hear Jane crying, and he wanted to tell her it was all right but that would be a lie. It was not all right. Something was terribly wrong and he was just as scared as she.

An eternity passed. A lifetime. Maybe he slept. Maybe he died. No, sleep, because he became aware of a shadow falling over Jane, an eclipse plunging her into darkness, swallowing her whole.

Help. He couldn't say it, but he thought it. He needed Superman, not Clark Kent.

The hulking forms of strangers surrounded George.

Somebody scooped him up. Maybe he was being swooped to safety by Superman.

But he wasn't safe. Things melted together and things fell apart. He had only blurred impressions, couldn't tell what was real and what was in his head. He sensed Jane Gordon being snatched away, reeled in, kept at a distance, growing smaller and smaller…disappearing. His own brother Charles was pulled away, too, disappearing, separated from him, forbidden to go near him.

Vague impressions floated past George, and he struggled to separate the real images from the nightmares. He thought he saw men in special vulcanized coats arriving and shutting down everything—the dining hall, the cabins, the sporting facilities, the pool, everything.

Official signs from the health department were posted everywhere: *Quarantined by the Ulster County Board of Health.*

George was shrouded in blankets, piles and piles of them, even though his head was on fire.

He was plunged into a zinc tub filled with icy water.

He saw white lights. Naked bulbs staring down at him like monster eyes. His skinny, bloodless body no longer belonged to him.

Too weak to cry out. But his soul cried out. His heart cried out. Nobody heard him. There were noises in his head, sounds and voices. He didn't know what was real and what was in the comic book.

All around him, white light. White sheets in the hospital room, white blinds on the window, a long white passageway with no end.

His father. Concerned frown, lower half of his face wearing a surgeon's mask, sleeve tied up at his left shoulder where his arm used to be. Why? Why? What was Father here for?

Voices in the stark echoing hallway. *Highly contagious… Commonly transmitted via contaminated food…* They spoke as if he could not hear. Maybe he couldn't. Or maybe this was just something else from the comic book in his head. The voices, though. He knew them. Mother, crying—long, desperate sobs. Father, coughing. No, not coughing. He was sobbing, too. George had never heard his father weep before.

And the doctor had not yet spoken the dreaded word—the true diagnosis. It was as if Mother and Father already knew. A scream came from his mother like a howl of pain from a wounded animal.

George told the ringing bells in his ears to be still so he could hear. He concentrated very hard on what the doctor was saying. A good reporter did that. He listened. He concentrated. He did not miss anything.

"I'm afraid…" The doctor—Bancroft was his name— Dr. Bancroft cleared his throat and started again. "Mr. and Mrs. Bellamy, I'm so sorry. I'm afraid it's the worst possible news," he said. There was a pause, filled with the sounds of George's parents, still weeping.

"It's polio."

Ten

"George has a list," Claire said to Ross. "Did you know that?" They were on the porch, waiting for George to wake up from his nap. She had just collected the mail from the main lodge. George had friends all over the globe, and had already received a couple of cards and letters. It was a day of soft breezes and sunshine coaxing new blooms from the lilac bushes and inviting the wildflowers to open up. George had slept most of the day, and Ross had been on the phone with—she assumed—various family members.

Claire was seated on the cushioned swing, listening to the *clack* of the chains as she moved. Ross sat nearby in a wicker armchair. Despite the relaxing setting, he seemed tense and restive.

"What kind of list?" asked Ross.

"It's a kind of…I guess you'd call it a list of things he'd like to accomplish in the time he has left." She watched Ross's shoulders stiffen, and it hurt her to look at him. He was still so far from accepting the situation. She wished she could comfort him with a gentle touch or soothing word, but she sensed he didn't want that from her. Not yet. Maybe not ever.

"Like finding his long-lost brother," said Ross.

"That's on the list."

"Today?"

"Let's see how he feels when he wakes up."

When he'd told her about his boyhood summers at Camp Kioga, giving her a glimpse of the vanished past, she could picture the two brothers exploring together, never knowing one day they'd be enemies, looking back on the long-ago time of their youth. She could picture him and his little brother, Charles, and the girl named Jane Gordon playing at Three Musketeers, deep in their fantasy world.

She'd wanted to tell him he was an idiot. A man who didn't contact his brother for five decades needed to have his head examined. But…no. She couldn't allow herself to project her own issues on her patient.

And so she'd listened. That was a huge part of her job. Exploring the events of the past and reconnecting with family tended to bring a sense of peace. She hoped this would be the case for George.

Like a dark fairy tale, the golden summer had turned shadowy with the Gordons' tragic loss of their son and George's diagnosis of polio.

Claire had only a passing knowledge of the disease from a unit in an advanced practice course in nursing school. Like every other doctor and nurse she knew, she'd never seen an acute case. There were a few known late effects, and now she saw them in George's muscle and joint fatigue. The atrophied muscle at the base of his right thumb was a classic presentation, yet she hadn't connected the dots until he told her.

"Did your grandfather tell you he's a polio survivor?" she asked Ross.

He spun around to face her. Sunlight slashed across his face. "Granddad had polio?"

"You didn't know." She swallowed, feeling guilty. "My apologies, then. I thought he might have told you."

"Jesus," Ross said. "*Polio.* Okay, I had no idea."

"I've been reading up on something called post-polio syndrome—PPS. Later in life, it can be the cause of joint and muscle pain."

"He's in pain?" Ross asked. "How much pain?"

"I ask him that every day, and he says it's manageable."

"Polio," Ross said again. "He never told me."

"You should ask him about it. He came down with the disease right here at Camp Kioga in 1944. He's a wonderful storyteller, as I'm sure you know, and these days, stories of polio are incredibly rare."

"If he can live through polio, then why won't he fight now?" Ross demanded. "He was saved by medical science, sixty-something years ago—"

"He was saved by a damned miracle," she said. "There was no cure for polio. There still isn't, just a vaccine."

"Oh, so we should just sit around in the wilderness, waiting for a miracle? Is that what we should do?"

"What we should do is what George wishes." Claire's heart ached for Ross, because his eyes were full of everything he would not say. Being here in this beautiful place was lovely, but she knew every moment Ross and George spent together was bittersweet, tinged by the shadow of George's illness.

In her profession, grieving relatives came with the territory. She had seen a whole range of reactions, from open hysteria to stoic acceptance, and everything in between, including those who tried everything to stave off death. People wrung hands and offered prayers, reminisced and baked and wept and comforted each other. They also fought, showing her everything from bickering to rage. Her least favorite were the ones who pretended to care when in reality, they were desperate to claim their piece of the inheritance pie.

Ross was still processing the raw shock of reality, she could tell, even from the way he held his hands, flexing and unflexing them.

"Shit," he said, watching a hummingbird dart in and out of the hanging plants.

"That's not on the list," she said.

"What the hell good is a list?" he demanded. "Was this your idea? What are you, some kind of bad fairy, feeding an old man's fantasies?"

She didn't let herself get mad. This was not about her. "We all have goals," she pointed out, "whether or not they're written down. Some part of us wants to keep track, you know?"

"Bullshit."

She could already read his moods. Maybe, she thought, that was one of the reasons she felt drawn to him. He was—or seemed to be—entirely honest and let his feelings hover close to the surface. She understood that he didn't trust her, and had decided not to fight it. She could never be fully honest with anyone. Sometimes the urge to explain everything was unbearable, building with painful intensity in her chest. She was desperate for someone to know her, not just her circumstances the way Mel Reno did, but *her*. She yearned for someone to affirm that she mattered.

Clearing her throat, she asked, "So are you willing to help your grandfather reconnect with his brother?"

"Suppose I said I'm not," said Ross.

"Then you're not the person he told me about, with such pride. But I think you are," she said simply. She held out a slip of paper. "This is Charles Bellamy's contact information."

He grabbed the note from her and stuffed it in his pocket.

"He's going to be so grateful, Ross."

Ross ran his hand back and forth over his cropped hair. She wondered what it would look like when the military crew cut grew in. She would probably never know. And how pathetic was that, having relationships that were shorter than an army haircut?

"His freaking brother," Ross muttered. "They haven't talked in an entire lifetime. Now suddenly there has to be some phony reunion thing."

Claire thought about what George had told her about that long-ago summer. "I don't think it'll be phony."

"Okay, but doesn't he get it? The time to act like brothers is when they're living, not dying. When being together and knowing each other and being close could do him some good, instead of just depressing him."

"There's no reason to assume he'll be depressed. It's what he wants," Claire said. "When you get to the place he is, you quit worrying about what's needed and you do what you want."

Ross was quiet for a time. Then he asked, "So what else is on the list?"

"Everything from serious talks with family members— not just his brother—to small gestures, like reading a special novel or playing a round of golf, to big thrills."

He turned to her, cracked a smile. "What kind of big thrills?"

"Actually the biggest one of all is something you might be able to help him with, in your capacity as a pilot."

"What, he wants to fly a chopper? I guess I could arrange it."

"Not fly it," she said. "Jump out of it. Out of a plane, actually. You know, skydiving."

"Skydiving," Ross said, glaring at her. "Are you kidding me?"

"You know me," said George, stepping out on the porch to join them. "I wouldn't kid about something like this."

"George," Claire said, stopping the swing with her foot. "I didn't hear you get up." She did a quick visual assessment. He looked somewhat refreshed by his nap, and he was moving well, his eyes alert behind the glasses.

"I'm pleased to find you discussing my list," he said.

"Among other things," said Ross. "I never knew you were a polio survivor. Why didn't you ever tell me?"

"It happened so long ago," George said. "It hardly matters. Did you know the greatest strides in rehabilitating polio patients came from a nurse?"

"Sister Elizabeth Kenny," said Claire. "She demonstrated that polio patients who underwent physical therapy had a better chance of recovery than those kept immobilized. Is that how you recovered?"

George nodded. "Eventually. I was in an iron lung at first."

Her heart lurched as she recalled seeing all the old black-and-white photos of encased children, rows and rows of them in special hospital wards. How trapped they must have felt, how helpless.

"My brother, Charles, used to read to me," George said quietly. "Patients with acute signs of the disease aren't contagious, so he was allowed to visit. And the majority of people can be exposed and never come down with polio. Charles was probably one of those. They would let him come to the ward, and he would read books to me." His eyes turned distant with memories. "When you're confined to an iron lung, you live for the moments that take you away. Books did that for me. And Charles in particular. Although he was quite young, he was a remarkably good reader. He would entertain the entire ward. I recall him reading *The Jungle Book, Peter Pan,* Hardy Boys mysteries."

She glanced at Ross and could tell he was warming up to the idea of approaching Charles Bellamy.

"Books were marvelous companions for me," George said. "But it was hard to count one's blessings from inside an iron lung."

Her heart lurched, and she met Ross's gaze. He looked amazed to learn this whole new part of his grandfather's history. In college, Claire had studied the history of epidemiology. It was one thing to read about the polio epidemic, to study the statistics and patterns of contagion, the progression of the disease and the race to develop a vaccine. But until George, she'd never met someone who had the disease.

"I should have been more appreciative," George added. "In many cases, too many cases, a diagnosis of polio was a death sentence."

"I'm glad you didn't die, George."

With a wink at Ross, he said, "I'm certain my grandson would say the same. In later years, I was always self-conscious about having a lame leg. I spent too much time brooding about what the disease took from me. But I was young, and couldn't help feeling robbed. I gave up on any sort of sport or physical activity."

"I didn't realize the leg still troubled you," Claire said. "It's much less apparent than you think."

"At this point in my life, I'm past worrying about other people's opinions. It's remarkable how easy things are becoming now that I've stopped worrying about what people think. Should have done it a long time ago. I'm sure I'll say the same of skydiving—"

"Yeah, about that," said Ross. "I'm not so sure you need to be jumping out of an airplane."

"That's why I waited so long to try it," said George.

"Come on, Granddad. Seriously?"

"Serious as a heart attack," George assured him. "It's not very original, I admit. Everyone mentions skydiving as something they'd like to do before they die. I think it's a universal yearning to fly. We all want that freedom."

"Trust me," Ross said, "it's overrated."

"You're lying," said George.

"Okay, it's a kick in the ass," Ross admitted with a hint of a smile. "But only if you've had major training and preparation."

"I don't have time for that," said George, matter-of-factly.

"How about I take you flying. Do a couple of stunts—"

"Skydiving," Granddad insisted. "Nothing else will do. I want the freedom. The long fall. What are you afraid of, Ross? That I'll get hurt? That I'll die?" He leaned back, folded his hands behind his head. "Look at it this way. If the skydiving kills me, you won't need to worry about helping me with anything else on my list."

"The list is bullshit. It was your idea," Ross accused Claire.

"I was hoping to find the two of you getting along better," George said. "You've only just met, and you're bickering like newlyweds."

Claire flushed. "Ross is very concerned about you. He wants you to go back to the city. He wants you to keep pursuing treatment."

Ross looked startled; clearly he'd been regarding her as the enemy. "It's true, Granddad," he said. "I want you to fight this thing."

"Of course you do, my boy. You're a fighter. Always have been."

"You do have that option," said Claire.

"You know what I think of that option."

She nodded. Folded her arms in front of her. "You can change your mind anytime you want. There will be no questions asked. This isn't a competition or test of any sort. You get instant compliance with what you want."

"I won't change my mind." He took a seat next to Ross. "Don't you think if there was a chance—*any* chance—to stay with you, I would?" he asked softly.

Claire had to look away from the expression in Ross's eyes.

George, bless him, managed to summon a smile. "Take me skydiving, Ross. I've always wondered what it was like."

"But—"

"I know it's dangerous, son. I don't care. If I die in the attempt, I've only done myself out of a few weeks, right? Months, at the most. Sorry to be so blunt, but that's my thinking on the matter."

"And I'm supposed to help you with this?" Ross said, incredulous.

"We were thinking you could make the arrangements," said Claire.

"You're certified in tandem jumping," George said. "We could do it together."

"Sorry, give me a minute with this visual. You want to jump out of a plane, strapped to me?"

"That's correct," said George. "I would consider it a complete privilege."

Ross clenched his jaw and glared at Claire. "I'll think about it. Maybe make a few calls."

She knew then that he would do it. He had a reluctant-but-willing look on his face. "Speaking of your list," she said, "this came in today's mail." She handed George an express mail packet.

He turned the packet over in his hands, checking the return address. "Penguin Group publishing," he said, and his eyes lit with delight. "Young lady, is this what I think it is?"

"Why don't you open it and see?"

His hand trembled a little as he opened the parcel. Out slipped a book, bound in plain card stock, labeled Advance Reading Copy—Not For Sale. There was a worldwide publication date of September 28.

"*Fall of Giants* by Ken Follett," said George. "This is top secret stuff, Claire. The most hotly anticipated novel since that vampire craze. How on earth did you get a copy?"

"I have my ways," she said. She almost never stayed

in touch with families of former patients, but in this case, she'd made an exception. She'd looked after the mother of a production intern at a publisher, and he was so grateful for her help that he'd offered her any book on the company's list, at any stage of production. For George's sake, she'd called in the favor.

"I shall enjoy this immensely. Thank you, Claire." George turned to Ross. "She's extremely thoughtful."

"Uh-huh." Ross clearly didn't want to hear about her thoughtfulness. "So, let's talk a little more about the list, Granddad."

He tapped his breast pocket. "The main reason I'm here is to try to make amends with my brother, if that's possible. I need to see if there is anything left after fifty-five years of silence."

"With all due respect," said Ross, "why haven't you called him yet?"

George smiled. "I confess, I'm hesitant to disrupt other people's lives. My own—well, that was thoroughly disrupted by this confounded diagnosis. Still, that doesn't give me the right to barge in on unsuspecting people."

Claire watched them both closely, noting the strong family resemblance. In Ross, she could see the young man George might have been at one time. And in George, she could see the mature man Ross might become one day.

Sometimes she wondered about her own background, though she tried not to dwell on unanswered questions. She'd never met any of her grandparents. She knew of exactly four photographs of her mother, but was in possession of none of them. Even now, it was too dangerous to carry any connection to the past. The photos—one Polaroid and three snapshots—were being safeguarded by Mel, but Claire had memorized each one. Yet when she looked in the mirror, she didn't know if she could see her face in her mother's face, or if there had ever been a time when her mother had looked at her and seen something familiar.

There was a slight tremor in George's hand as he took the small leather-bound volume from his pocket containing his list. "When I first heard my diagnosis, and my prognosis, I did pick up the phone. Many times. Such a simple thing, picking up the phone and placing a call. But between the time I held the phone in my hand and looked at the number I had tracked down for Charles, I could see the passing of a lifetime. I'll just say it—I turned cowardly. This is too important for a simple telephone conversation. I didn't want to ruin my one chance. I want to get it right, so I need to come up with the best way to go about this."

"Well, for one thing, you might want to do it before you jump out of a plane," Claire suggested, and caught a glare from Ross. "I'm just saying."

George let loose with his big laugh, the one that crescendoed and tapered in a way that was impossible to resist. "But seriously," he said, "jumping out of an airplane might prove to be easier than having a reunion with my brother." His laughter subsided, and his voice grew quiet. "It's time," he said.

She felt a chill creep over her skin. She didn't look at Ross, not wanting him to see her concern. Many patients had a very keen sense of the progress of their illness, and their urgency sometimes came from a place of deep knowing, a place no doctor's test could reveal.

* * *

"What do you mean, she's not coming to dinner with us?" George asked Ross as they made their way to the main pavilion that evening. "Was it something I said?"

"No, of course not."

"Was it something *you* said?"

Probably, thought Ross. He'd been borderline rude to Claire all day. He was torn between feeling grateful for her compassion toward his grandfather, and resentful of her insistence on letting Granddad choose to forego treatment for his illness.

"She wanted to give us time alone together," Ross explained, because that was simpler. "That's what she said, anyway."

"Pull over," Granddad said. "Right here, pull over."

Ross stopped the golf cart at the side of the trail. "We're not going back for her."

His grandfather waved a hand in impatience and got out of the cart. There was a colorful flower garden nearby, with a bed of lilies surrounding a small stone marker. Ross saw that it was engraved with Stuart Gordon's name and life span, 1926–1944.

Now that he knew a little more Bellamy family history, Ross was beginning to understand his grandfather's emotional ties to this place. The marker read, "We will never forget the love you gave to us. God alone can tell how much you are missed."

The same words could be said of Ross's father, and every other soldier who'd served his country. Granddad stooped down and plucked a couple of white flowers. It made a strangely beautiful picture, an old man picking flowers in the golden light. The sun's rays shone through his almost translucent hair, giving him a peculiar glow. Just for a moment, Ross had a vision of his grandfather in another time, younger and more hearty, at the Tuileries gardens in Paris, grinning as he reached past the *pas de prendre les fleurs* sign and helped himself to a carnation.

"A gentleman is never fully dressed without a boutonniere," George declared as he climbed back in the golf cart. "You never know who you're going to meet, so it's best to be prepared."

Ross pulled the flower stem through a buttonhole of Granddad's lapel. He held a smile in place even though he wanted to break down and cry. *Holy crap,* he thought. *Holy crap, Granddad, don't leave me.*

Hiding his grief and fear, he said, "You've been giving me that same advice for years. So far, nothing's panned out."

"No reason to stop trying." George reached out to affix Ross's flower, the way he used to when Ross was a geeky kid. His hand shook, and Ross had to guide it to the buttonhole.

"Are you all right?"

"Aside from this brain tumor, I'm fine." His voice was bright with irony. "One of my meds causes the tremors. Don't worry about it."

Right, thought Ross. *I won't worry.*

George settled back on the seat. "Claire likes picking flowers," he said. "This morning, she put a few in a juice glass on the breakfast table. Something tells me the two of you are going to get on very nicely."

Ross's gaze flicked to the ever-present buzzer. "Granddad—"

"No, hear me out. I don't want to be overly dramatic, but if something needs saying, I'm damn well going to say it."

"How is that different from the way you've always talked to me?" asked Ross.

"I'm simply going to level with you. You're not meant to be alone, Ross. You're meant to find someone special."

"Then don't shove some stranger at me."

"She won't stay a stranger for long, if you keep an open mind and open heart. You might even fall in love. You've never done so, and I think you'd enjoy it."

Ross threw back his head and laughed. It felt good to laugh. It felt almost normal. "Sure, Granddad. I'll get right on that."

"I'm not joking."

"Well, I appreciate the sentiment, but—"

"It's one of the things on my list," said George.

Ross paused. "I'm starting to get an attitude about this list."

"It's essential. I want to make sure I don't leave anything undone, if I can help it."

"Fine, but it's your list. I've got no business being on it," Ross said.

"I'd like to see you settled into the life you deserve. It would bring me a great sense of peace."

Granddad could be a manipulative old dude when he wanted to. "I'll work on it," said Ross. "Just bear in mind, if and when I find someone, it's not likely to be a nurse you hired through a personals ad."

Ross parked near the lodge and headed inside with his grandfather. He didn't really care about his own future. What mattered to him was getting his grandfather to listen to reason. In that regard, maybe the meeting with the brother could serve a purpose. The sooner the two old men decided to bury the hatchet, the sooner Ross could work on getting George back to the city and checked in to the hospital to fight for his life. Maybe, he thought, the brother would help convince George to keep trying.

He caught a glimpse of the two of them in the glass doors of the dining room, and was struck by the sight of himself in civilian clothes. He still wasn't used to that. "You were right about the flowers," he said, giving his grandfather a thumbs-up sign. "We look good."

They were seated at a table with a view. Nearby sat an older lady with a younger couple. The moment she saw George, she patted her hair and sat up a little straighter. Granddad brought Ross over and introduced them. "Miss Millicent Darrow," he said with a flourish. "Millie, this is my grandson, Ross."

Granddad had already made a friend here. Was it something in the water?

The white-haired, well-dressed lady beamed at them. "He's as handsome as you, George," she said.

Granddad seemed to glow with pride. And there was no denying he seemed to hold himself a little straighter, his shoulders squared, under her regard. As they took their seats again, Ross leaned forward and murmured, "She's sweet on you."

"I believe the feeling's mutual. She and I might be living proof that romance knows no age barriers. And I might try the filet for dinner tonight," George said. "Stayed away from red meat for years, and now I find I enjoy living dangerously."

At the next table, Miss Darrow tilted her wineglass in his direction. "I'll drink to that."

* * *

Claire was startled to see Ross approaching the cottage, alone and on foot later that evening. She hurried outside and was even more surprised to see that he'd changed out of his dinner clothes and was draped in fly-fishing gear. He looked impossibly cute in khaki utility shorts, a T-shirt under a vest with dozens of pockets, and a hat that should have looked funny but somehow looked sexy instead.

"Where's George?" she asked, an edge to her voice.

"Dancing with some woman. He said to tell you thanks for showing him some dance moves."

"You're kidding."

"Nope." He seemed to read her mind. "And don't worry, she's staying at the resort, and she has my number and yours."

The idea of George with a lady pleased Claire utterly. "So is this someone he just met?"

"He knew her years ago," Ross said. "Her name's Millicent Darrow. Apparently they both vacationed here with their families in the fifties. Since this place reopened as a resort, a lot of the old families have come back."

"Millicent Darrow," Claire said. "That's a classy-sounding name. She and your grandfather must have a lot of catching up to do."

"So it seems." Ross ducked his head, but she caught the flash of a rare grin. He had an amazing smile. "All I know is, he told me to make myself scarce and he'd call one of us if he needed anything."

"Well, I guess…I'll wait up for him," she said, feeling suddenly awkward.

Ross studied her for a moment, making her feel even more awkward. "You want to join me? I was going to try a little fly-fishing."

She glanced at the sky, deepening with sunset. "Um, now?"

"Twilight until dark is the best time for it," he said. "Come on, I've got all the gear we need."

"Really?" The prospect of fly-fishing sounded ridiculously appealing to Claire.

"Sure."

He must have had the happy plate special at dinner tonight, she thought.

They hiked a short distance along the lakeshore. It was another gorgeous evening, the scenery lovely enough to cause a sweet ache in her chest. She'd never known this quality of peace and quiet, so complete and all-pervasive. The lake was flat and glassy in the twilight, the water disturbed only by the occasional flicker of an insect or water bird.

They came to a waterfall pouring down a narrow gorge to a stream that emptied into the lake. "Over here," said Ross, moving to the reeds at the bank of the stream. "Ever been fishing?"

"Never." She could feel a light spray from the waterfall on her face. "It's so beautiful here," she said. "It's the most beautiful place I've ever seen."

"I'm starting to see why my grandfather wanted to come to this place. It's like going to heaven." He paused. "And that might be a damned poor choice of words."

She smiled. "I bet he'd disagree. He and Millicent Darrow might even be there now."

"Okay, not that I needed that picture in my head—"

"I was referring to the dancing," she said.

"I wasn't," he said. "Come on, let's see if I remember how this is done."

She followed him to the edge of the stream. The equipment was minimal—a rod and reel, lead and line—and the concept deceptively simple. She watched him for a bit, intrigued by the motion of the pole and the graceful dance of the translucent line upon the water as he aimed for the still, shadowy places behind the jutting rocks, where a fish might hide.

"I've never seen someone fly-fishing before," she said, entranced by the featherlight sweep of the lure on the end of the line. "Not in person, anyway. But in pictures and movies."

"Let me guess," said Ross. *"A River Runs Through It."*

She nodded. "I love that movie." She'd always been drawn to films and books about families. It was the source of much of what she knew about family life. Her favorite had been *The Cosby Show* reruns. In her dreams, she got to be part of a family like that.

"The scenery was nice," he said, casting into the shadows again, "except I'm not a big fan of death and dying in movies." He kept up the graceful rhythm of casting, the rod and line singing in the air and creating a black slash of motion in the deepening twilight.

"I'm not having much luck. You want to give it a try?" He indicated the fly rod.

His sudden accommodating manner startled her. "I thought you didn't like me."

"I thought so, too," he agreed, softening the statement with a grin. "Are you wearing waterproof sandals?"

She looked down at her KEENs. "Yes, but—"

"Let's move over there." He indicated a stony high spot on the other side of the rapids. "Grab my hand."

She did so without thinking, because the rocky bottom was slippery and uneven. His arm was completely steady, though, and hard with muscle. The water felt delicious, cool and swift as it eddied around her ankles. She was going to like fishing, Claire decided. She was going to like fishing more than life itself.

It wasn't as simple as it looked. He demonstrated the fluid motion of the rod and line, but her attempt was clumsy, and the beautiful little hand-tied fly was soon lost in the reeds on the opposite bank. "I'll try to find it," she said.

"Don't worry," he said. "I have more."

"Are you sure?"

"In the grand scheme of things, losing a lure isn't the end of the world. Granddad and I made some flies earlier today. It was like old times. He still ties the best knot I've ever seen. That's the whole point of fishing—to leave worry behind."

"I thought the point was to catch a fish."

"Secondary," he said, tying on another fly and demonstrating a graceful cast. "Fishing is all about connecting with nature, practicing an age-old art. Plus it's a kick in the ass."

"Give me that. I refuse to be defeated by a hook wearing a feather." She tried again, this time plopping the fly down practically at their feet. "What am I doing wrong?"

"Here, you need to pull back…I'll show you." He positioned himself behind her, his arm slipping easily around her waist. His hand covered hers. "Draw back like this. Don't try to kill it. Let the rod do the work."

With his coaching, she managed to improve. Before long she sensed a live tug on the end of the line; it felt different from the clumsy snags she'd felt earlier. "Oh, no," she said, "look, I'm getting a bite."

"Easy now." He spoke quietly, though his voice was taut with excitement. With unexpected delicacy, he cupped his hand around hers and helped her play the line. "You want to tease it along and then…there. It's on the hook."

"Really? Oh!" The fish fought, leaping in a fury of panic.

Ross showed her how to reel the thing in, then scooped it into a net. "It's a beauty," he declared, holding up the net.

She'd caught a rainbow trout, fat and shiny, curved into a gleaming U-shape in the net. Ross gently lifted it in one hand and eased the hook from its lip. "Barbless," he said. "This kind of hook doesn't do any harm. Want to say hello to your fish?"

She took it from him, trying not to flinch at the chill, slick feel of it. "Hello, fish."

Ross took a picture with his cell phone. She winced at the flash, never happy about having her picture taken. "Now what?"

"Now we let it go."

"I'm glad you said that. I wouldn't want to eat it, after meeting it face-to-face."

He bent down and lowered the trout into the clear water. "See you around," he said, straightening up and turning to Claire.

"So that's fishing."

"That's fishing. Catch and release." He was still smiling, but the flicker of sadness in his eyes was unmistakable.

"Tell me about fishing with George," she said.

"It was our thing, you know? Even before my father was killed, Granddad and I were close." He tied on another fly. "So what's your expert opinion, Nurse Turner? Is that going to make this easier or harder?"

She wasn't sure how to answer that. Ross was decompressing after two years of war, he'd lost his own father and now he had to deal with losing his grandfather. And in the midst of all this, George had some crazy idea that she and Ross… No.

"Give it another try," he said.

"What?"

He held out the rod to her.

"Oh," she said. "Sure." She was glad to have something to occupy her hands. "Every family is different, as you can imagine. People who are close don't have to struggle through unfinished business, because they've nurtured their bond over a lifetime. So in that sense, it's easier. You focus on each other instead of dwelling on past regrets."

"And in another sense?"

She found a rhythm and cast the line. This time it landed on the water, but nowhere near where she'd aimed it. "In another sense, losing someone you love with all your heart is the worst thing in the world."

"It is," he agreed. Two words, yet his voice reverberated with sadness.

"Your grandfather told me what happened to your father," she said. "I'm sorry. You must miss him so much."

"With all my heart," he said. "That's how I tend to be, I guess."

The way he said it gave her chills. She hoped her fascination with him didn't show. Fathers and sons, she thought. *Family.*

Turning away, she said, "My aim is terrible. Tell me how to control my cast better."

"Well," he said, stepping up behind her again, "it all starts with your posture. Stay relaxed." He slipped his arms around her again. With incredible patience, and an intimacy she hadn't expected, he guided her through the movements. The pretext was wearing thin, and they both knew it.

She didn't care. The cast was nothing. The only thing she could focus on was the sensation of being embraced from behind, even on the pretext of showing her how to throw the line. She reveled in the feel of his body pressed to hers, the warmth of his breath on her neck, the murmur of his voice in her ear. He felt so good. He smelled so good. It was all she could do to keep from turning around and kissing him on the mouth. The urge to do so was almost overwhelming. She wondered if he'd put her in this position by accident, or if this was a calculated maneuver.

"This was a mistake." His voice was quiet, but resolute.

She tried to focus on the motion of the fly. "Look, I'm doing the best I can."

"I'm not talking about the fishing." He lowered his head, speaking softly into her ear. "It was a mistake to touch you like this."

"Then we agree on something." Story of my life, she thought. She would never be anything but some-one's mistake.

"What I mean is…damn. This feels so damn good. I haven't held a woman in so long, Claire. You feel like a dream to me."

The fishing pole dropped onto the stones. Either she turned, or he turned her in his arms; she couldn't be certain. The next thing she knew, she was kissing him.

Just like that. Kissing a guy she barely knew, the grandson of her client. And she couldn't stop. And somehow, he seemed to sense that she was starved for closeness. She didn't have much experience with kissing, but she knew this was a good one. Better than good. World class. He was like that missing piece of a puzzle, now fitting perfectly in place, and his mouth was warm and soft, his arms a safe and gentle haven. She sensed real emotion from him; it seemed to radiate from his arms and even his breath as he gently explored her mouth with his. Maybe, freshly back from war, a soldier latched on to any human connection. Or maybe it was her. She wished she could ask him. She wished for so much.

Just that quickly, in a matter of seconds, he made her forget the world. This was the kind of thing she dreamed of, lying awake through so many sleepless nights when she felt so alone, she nearly came out of her skin.

It was the sweetest torture, this kiss. But it was torture, because in this single magical moment, she could taste everything she wanted but could never have.

Somehow she found the will to step back and extricate herself from his embrace. "Um, all right, then. Let's stick with the fishing," she suggested, trying for a light tone as she stooped to pick up the rod.

"Yeah, I kind of forgot about fishing for a minute there. I won't apologize, though. I liked that way too much to apologize."

She found herself wondering—was it better to have tasted something she could never have, or should she have avoided it altogether, never knowing what she was missing? Too late now. She knew what it was like, and she knew that one kiss would haunt her. "We can't...shouldn't be doing this."

"Funny, I was just thinking it was the best thing that's happened to me since my discharge. Felt better than a three-day furlough. Kissing you...just for a few seconds, it made me feel normal."

"Ross—"

"So do you have a boyfriend or something?" he asked.

"I wouldn't have kissed you if I had a boyfriend."

"Good."

"Why is it good?"

"Because...is the position open?"

"No," she said firmly.

"Why not?"

"It's...it's complicated."

"Fine, dumb it down for me."

"I didn't mean— Ross, I can't talk about it."

"Now I'm *really* hooked."

Quick, she told herself. Think up a lie. She should have said she had a boyfriend. But there was something about Ross Bellamy. She didn't want to hurt him, couldn't bring herself to lie to him. Yet she couldn't tell him the truth, either.

Why, oh why had she let this happen? Nothing but heartache could come of it. He was like a treat from the Sky River Bakery. Why tempt herself with something that was bad for her?

"I've got another fish on the line," she said, giving it a tug.

"Don't yank on it so hard," Ross said, "or you'll—"

"Oh. It jumped off. I pulled too hard."

"It happens."

"I think the lure is gone, too." She reeled in the line. "It's getting too dark to see, anyway."

They picked up the gear and waded back to shore. He held her hand to steady her, and didn't let go even as they walked along the pathway back to the cottage. The resort was illuminated by path lights and, like a fantasy, flickered with glimmering fireflies darting over the meadows and gardens. On the shore by the main lodge, the nightly campfire burned, and they could hear the muted sounds of other guests. Voices had a distant quality, adding to the sense of intimacy.

"So are things going to be awkward between us now?" Ross asked.

The man didn't mince words. She wouldn't, either. "Probably."

After the dancing, George offered to drive Millicent Darrow back to her cabin in the electric cart.

"I'd rather go to your place," she said.

He gave a burst of surprised laughter. "Your wish is my command."

Ross and Claire were nowhere to be found. George hoped they were off somewhere together, getting to know one another.

"Thank you for putting up with me on the dance floor, Millie," he said.

"You are not a terrible dancer. And you have the best cottage of the resort," said Millicent Darrow. "The largest and most private."

"Back in the fifties when we were here, this was the

boathouse. It's been beautifully refurbished. Come on in, and I'll show you."

"Perhaps in a while." She lifted her hair up off her neck. "It's so warm tonight. Do you mind if I dangle my feet in the water?"

"My dear, you can dangle anything you want in the water." The wine they'd sipped after dinner made him feel silly. It took so little these days.

"Fine, then I shall." She stepped out of her sandals and slowly lowered herself at the end of the dock. "Ah, that feels delightful."

He joined her, rolling up his trousers and sitting next to her. "Just like old times."

"Better than old times. I was never one of the fast crowd. You know, the kids who stole beer and went skinny-dipping."

"I can't say the idea of stealing beer appeals," he said. "But the skinny-dipping…"

"George Bellamy!"

"Don't act so shocked." Boldly he reached over and tugged at the sash of her dress. It was one of those light, flowy things anchored only by the sash, but he hesitated, to make sure this was what she wanted.

"I'm not shocked. At my age, I don't shock easily." She laughed, a bright unfettered sound that carried across the water. Then she stood up, leaving the dress pooled on the dock. George's joints creaked as he levered himself up, but he was quick to shed his clothes. Then, hand in hand, they jumped in. The cool water felt like silk as it flowed over him.

They paddled around for a minute, and he loved the feeling of buoyancy and the sound of her breathing, in soft gasps of delight. And he liked the idea that she didn't know he was sick.

"Are you all right?" he asked.

"I'm *wonderful*."

In the dark, he found her hand, pulled her closer and leaned in for a kiss. "Yes, you are."

"I still remember you from all those years ago," she said. "Goodness, I had such a crush on you. I desperately wanted you for my first husband."

He chuckled. "You were always the blunt one."

"Then I'll be blunt again. I desperately want you…not for a husband, either."

He almost couldn't believe what he was hearing. Sometimes he had hallucinations, thanks to his condition. Was she a hallucination? No, she was right here, soft and cool against him. He could hear her soft gasps of breath, could feel the press of her mouth against his.

Like errant teenagers, they got out of the water and snatched up their clothes. In the cottage, he found a pair of thick terry-cloth bathrobes. He paused to hang a Do Not Disturb sign on the door and swallow a pill—just in case. The master bedroom was equipped with gas logs, and he lit a fire with one press of the remote.

"That's lovely, George," she said. "Everything's lovely."

He didn't let himself think of failure, or the future, or anything but the moment. No, they weren't young and strong and beautiful. They were both quite elderly and out of practice, but so willing and eager it made up for everything else. There was surprise and delight and a glow of pleasure that made him feel, just for a moment, as though he were flying.

Eleven

Ross decided to approach the brother in person, rather than calling first. He figured it would be harder for the guy—Charles—to turn him down to his face. Besides, and Ross couldn't deny this, he was curious. He'd just found out about a whole unknown branch of the family; of course he was curious. And hopeful, too. Maybe the brother would give Granddad a reason to keep fighting for his life.

He checked the address again and drove through the tree-lined streets of Avalon. His mind wandered, as it seemed to every couple of minutes, to Claire Turner. Kissing her at the water's edge had been filled with unexpected magic. He might tell himself she could be anyone; the first woman he kissed after reentering civilian life was bound to seem special. But he was drawn to her in a powerful way he couldn't yet explain to himself.

He wasn't supposed to like her. He'd vowed to Granddad he would never like her. But just as Granddad had predicted, she intrigued him. And yeah, she turned him on. Right or wrong, he was far from done with her.

With an effort of will, he forced himself to focus. Today's task was about his grandfather.

Last night, after the fly-fishing, Ross and Claire had checked out the well-stocked library at Camp Kioga. Poring over scrapbooks and photo albums, they had learned quite a bit about Charles. In 1956, he'd married the daughter of the camp owner. The couple had divided their time between New York City and Avalon, raising four children—two boys and two girls. Charles and Jane had recently settled in Avalon full-time, having bought a home in town the year before.

The neighborhood was old and established, with nice but not-quite-ostentatious homes. There were front porches hung with potted flowers and sidewalks swept clean; the street was marked with Children at Play signs. From the outside, the house appeared to be a fine and comfortable abode, one that bore a plaque from the historical society, designating it a landmark. A small brass plate under the house number identified the name of the residents: Bellamy.

The name was not that unique, but it was a little disconcerting to consider that the strangers living here were his relatives. He squared his shoulders, cleared his throat and rang the bell.

Waited. Wished he could be anywhere but here, bracing himself for an awkward meeting. Wished the situation could be anything but what it was.

What the hell was he going to say? How did you phrase something like this? What did—

The door swung open. "Yeah? Can I help you?"

It was a kid, about high school age, with light hair and eyes, a Yankees T-shirt.

Ross hesitated. Maybe he had the wrong house. Except there was something weirdly, obliquely familiar about the boy. In the room beyond the foyer, a few others were playing Wii Golf on a flat-screen TV. Ross was familiar with video games of all sorts, having passed many an hour playing them overseas, racking up car thefts and bonus points between sorties and rescues.

"Hello," said Ross. "I'm looking for Mr. Charles Bellamy. Is he in?"

"I'll go see if I can find him," said the boy.

At the same moment, a female voice called, "Max? Who is at the door?"

"Some guy for Granddad," Max said over his shoulder. *Granddad.* Just like George's grandchildren called him.

Behind the boy Ross could see a hall tree hung with hats and jackets, an umbrella stand and a table. The wall was lined with framed photographs of smiling subjects posing by the lake, or on a ski slope, or in some undefined setting that probably meant the world to them. These could be Ross's aunts and uncles, his cousins.

An orange cat lay on the carpeted stairs, its front paws tucked under its chest, fluffy tail gently swishing back and forth. A white-haired woman came into the foyer, wiping her hands on a tea towel. She studied Ross curiously. "Yes?"

"I'll go find Granddad." Max headed down the hallway.

Ross caught himself maintaining a military bearing, there on the front porch. "Mrs. Bellamy?" he asked.

"Yes?" She tilted her head to one side, the light glinting off her eyeglasses. He wondered if she saw something in him. Did he look like Granddad? Some said he did.

"I'm sorry to disturb you, ma'am. My name is Ross Bellamy. I'm George Bellamy's grandson."

The tea towel dropped from her hand. For a moment, her face went slack with surprise. Neither of them moved to pick up the towel. She touched the edge of the hall table as if to steady herself. Ross hadn't really thought about what reaction to expect, but it probably wouldn't have been this pained vulnerability. And something else. Fear? But the woman had nothing to fear.

"I didn't mean to startle you," he said quickly. "May I come in?"

"Oh," she said. "Oh, certainly. I'm Jane, by the way," she said, though Ross had already guessed as much. She stepped aside. "Jane Bellamy. And yes, please, come in."

Granddad had wondered aloud if Charles's marriage had lasted. Apparently it had. Ross had often wished his grandfather's marriage had worked out better. He and Jacqueline—Granny Jack, as Ross and his cousins called her—had lived an eventful, glamorous life. But losing their son had wounded them in hidden ways and sent them spiraling off in different directions, each trying to cope with a devastating grief.

Even though he'd been a kid himself at the time, and shell-shocked by his own grief, Ross had realized his grandparents' marriage was deteriorating under the strain. They never got around to divorcing each other, but in the end, the two of them had led separate lives. The way she'd died with her lover had been a shock to everyone—except maybe Granddad.

"Let's, er, let's go in here where we can sit down." Jane Bellamy gestured down a short hallway.

"Thank you." Ross stooped to pick up the towel and handed it to her.

She led the way to a sunroom overlooking a broad,

well-kept backyard, away from the noise of the grandson's Wii game. "So is George…has something happened?" She held herself very still as though bracing for bad news.

"Granddad's in Avalon. He's got a place up at the Camp Kioga resort."

"My goodness. I should have guessed it. The assistant manager, Renée, mentioned a Mr. Bellamy had checked in. But I thought it was a coincidence. I never imagined George would come back. Never in a million years."

"He'd like to see his brother, Charles," said Ross.

"I just never imagined," Jane said again.

Just then Ross's grandfather stepped into the room. For a few disoriented seconds, Ross thought it actually was Granddad, tall and slender and gentlemanly, with thick white hair and blue eyes. "Imagine what?" he asked his wife. The voice was Granddad's, too.

"This young man is Ross Bellamy," Jane said. "He's…George's grandson." Her voice changed as she spoke Granddad's name.

Charles did not exhibit any of the fear or vulnerability his wife had shown, just a benign neutrality. "How do you do?" He offered Ross his hand.

"George would like to see you," Jane added.

"When?" he asked bluntly.

"At your convenience, of course," said Ross. "But soon, if possible."

Charles's mouth quirked momentarily into a smile. "All right, then. A visit from my brother George. He couldn't have come here in person?"

"He didn't want to disturb you, or put you on the spot." Ross was wary of Jane's silence and the guarded neutrality he observed in Charles. This was precisely why his grandfather's plan for the summer was such a bad idea. These people had the power to hurt Granddad. "He wanted you to have the opportunity to think it over."

Jane and Charles regarded each other briefly. Jane looked away first, smoothing her hands down her apron. Although Granddad had characterized this as a dispute between brothers, Jane appeared to be the most agitated of all.

Charles either kept a poker face or he genuinely didn't care. "What brought this about?" he asked. "Why now? And why would he come here?"

Granddad had admonished Ross not to beg. "But what the hell," he'd said with a touch of dry humor, "go ahead and tell them I'm dying. No sense in holding back on the truth, and I'm not too proud to play the sympathy card."

"My grandfather's not well," said Ross. And then, to his complete surprise and horror, a thick heat formed in his throat, a gathering of tears. From the moment he'd first received word of grandfather's illness, Ross had not wept. And now, with a few short words uttered to a pair of strangers, he was about to lose it.

"Sorry," he said, staring down at the floor and pushing his fists together hard. He forced himself to look at them. Get a grip. *Get a grip.*

Jane started to say something. Charles caught her eye and gave an almost imperceptible shake of the head. Charles looked so much like Granddad, Ross wanted to scream. It wasn't fair that this younger brother got to be so vital and healthy, while Granddad suffered with a fatal disease.

Ross cleared his throat. "The prognosis isn't good,"

he stated in a rush. "That's the reason for the timing of this…request."

The big orange cat came in, padding delicately around Ross's ankles.

"Let me get you something to drink. I've got some lemonade in the fridge." Jane seemed eager to do something.

"Thank you," said Ross. "That sounds good." He hoped he'd be able to keep it down; he felt sick to his stomach with unexpressed grief. It had been swelling inside him like a silent, invisible storm, and for some reason, it had chosen this moment to break the surface.

"We're very sorry," Charles said. "I can see this is a sad time for you. So George is…he's not in the hospital, then."

Ross shook his head. "For the moment, he's doing all right. But…that's temporary. He stopped treatment but I'm trying to persuade him to start again. So for that reason, I'm hoping you'll agree to see him as soon as possible."

Jane placed her open hand against her chest, like someone having a heart attack. Ross could see her struggling for composure. "I'll just get those drinks," she murmured, and hurried into the kitchen.

"If I could ask," Charles said, "what did George tell you about me?"

"Frankly, sir, he never mentioned you until recently. Most people in the family weren't aware he had a brother." Ross pressed the tips of his fingers together. "To be honest, I'm not sure why he's so adamant about seeing you. But there's nothing I won't do for my grandfather. I'm probably closer to him than I am to anyone else in my life. He's just…he's everything," he repeated.

"I understand. There was a time when I felt the same way about George."

Ross was surprised to hear something so honest and personal from Charles, who had been circumspect until now. "I'm sure my grandfather would like to talk to you about that."

"And I feel likewise."

Their gazes caught and held. Ross felt a terrible kind of relief in finding something in common with this stranger.

Jane returned with a tray of lemonade and cookies. "Feel likewise about what?" she asked.

"About my brother. I was just telling Ross here that I'd like to talk to George about times past. We went from being the closest of brothers to being strangers on different sides of the Atlantic," said Charles. "This could be our one chance to figure out what went wrong, and perhaps even try to make it right."

As Jane was leaning to set down her tray, one of the glasses toppled over. It landed with a bang on the antique cocktail table, ice cubes and pale liquid fanning across the surface, the glass shattering.

Both Ross and Charles stood up.

"Stay right there," Jane said urgently. "It's my mess, and I'll clean it up. I need to blot that up before everything is ruined."

Twelve

Avalon, Ulster County, New York
Summer 1945

There was always a special excitement in the air on arrival day at Camp Kioga. Jane Gordon had done a countdown on her wall calendar, marking off each day with an X as summer approached. Of course this year, things were different in several ways, none of them particularly good.

Stuart was nearly a year gone. He would never again be around to help out, to tease everybody and make chores seem like fun. No one would ever hear his off-key whistling as he mowed the grounds, made fresh lines of white lime on the tennis courts, strung up the volleyball nets, repaired the bunks.

Their mother wasn't present, either. After the double shocks last year of Stuart's death, followed by the hasty closing and quarantine of the camp when George Bellamy came down with polio, something had happened to Mama. Something had caused her to change until she didn't seem like Jane's mother at all.

Before the news about Stuart, she used to sing as she gazed out the kitchen window over the sink, enjoying its view of the lush lawn and dirt road leading to the house.

Ever since that road had been traveled by the shiny government car, bringing the news about Stuart, Mama had not been the same. She behaved in strange ways, still gazing out the window but no longer singing. Sometimes she would just wash the same juice glass or salad plate over and over again, until Jane or her father noticed and took her by the hand and led her away to the sofa or porch swing.

No one said much, just that Mama was so sad and quiet, but as time went on, things got even worse. Jane had awakened one night to a rhythmic sound—*shush, shush, shush*—and had gone downstairs to find Mama in her kerchief, methodically sweeping the porch. It was pitch-dark.

It had frightened Jane to see her mother behaving so strangely. "Mama?" she'd said softly, "It's the middle of the night."

"Yes, yes," Mama had said. She wasn't looking at Jane at all, not one bit. She hadn't really looked at Jane since the day of Stuart's memorial.

"Mama, you should come inside," Jane said.

Mama stared straight through Jane, and said, "Oh!"

A puddle appeared on the porch floor at her feet.

"Mama! You, um, gosh, Mama. I think you wet yourself," Jane had said in mortification.

A few days afterward, Jane's father took her aside and said her mother had suffered something called a Nervous Breakdown. She had to go away for a while, to a place called a sanitarium. There, she'd be with doctors and nurses who would help her get better.

As the weeks and months passed, Mama gradually did get better. Every Sunday afternoon, Jane and her father went to visit her at the clinic in Poughkeepsie. She was nothing like her old singing, piano-playing self, but she could carry on a conversation, dress herself and do her hair.

She tried coming home to Avalon a few times but it was too much for her. Eventually it was decided that she would stay with her sister in New Haven.

Jane tried never to feel sorry for herself but sometimes she couldn't help it. When she started feeling the blues, she would slip into a canoe and paddle on the lake for hours, exploring the deep and secret places of the forest-bound water.

Despite the troubles with her mother, there was something irrepressible in Jane that made her look forward to the coming summer. Some days, she even forgot about Mama, which made her feel guilty. When she confessed this to her father, he held her close and said, "It's all right to live your life, Janie. It's the only thing to do sometimes, just live your life. Come on now, you can help me hoist the camp flag for opening day."

As camp hosts, they were never supposed to play favorites, but Jane couldn't help herself. Last year her most favorite guests of all had been the Bellamy brothers, George and Charles, and when she learned they would be back again this year, she was beside herself. She had loved their adventures together, the Three Musketeers exploring the world, watching out for each other. She was thrilled to know they'd be together again this summer.

"I was so worried, Pa, you know. About George."

Her father nodded. "Everyone was. If the polio had killed him, I think we would have heard."

She threw her energy into the pulley to raise the flag. "I can't wait to see him! I'm so glad he's all right."

"Janie, he might not be—"

The tolling of the camp bell interrupted him, and they both hurried to offer a Kioga welcome to the guests. People arrived in big buses. Because of gas rationing, almost no one took a private car, not even the wealthiest of them.

Feeling grown-up at age twelve, Jane wore a new sailor dress and her best Mary Janes. She had her hair in ringlets, and Mrs. Romano, the head cook, said she looked just like Shirley Temple. She'd worked very hard all day to stay clean.

With her father and the rest of the staff, she greeted guests old and new. When someone asked about her mother, Jane gave the reply she'd rehearsed again and again, until she could say it without crying: "She's spending the summer with her sister in Connecticut."

Jane even managed to smile at Violetta Winslow, who was a terrible snob with nothing good to say about anyone. Mrs. Winslow declared that the new paint job on the cabins looked nice, but that she hoped the interiors had been refurbished, as well. "I'm sure you'll find everything to your liking," Jane said.

It was almost unbearable, waiting for Charles and George to exit the bus. Jiminy Cricket, she thought. Were they going to be the last ones off? It wasn't fair to make her wait. It just wasn't.

She had big plans for them this summer. She wanted to find the source of Meerskill Falls, the cataract that tumbled down from the soaring heights above Willow Lake. She wanted to swim to the very bottom of the deepest part of the lake. She wanted to ride the river rapids and climb the rocks of the gorge.

A slender woman in an elegant sundress emerged from the bus. She wore a red scarf and dark glasses, which made her look like Lana Turner. Could it be…?

Yes. It was definitely Mrs. Bellamy. At last, Jane's favorite guests had arrived. Charles came bounding out of the bus. He had grown much taller, Jane saw, weaving her way through the milling guests. He looked wonderful. Oh, they would have so much to talk about, they—

Mr. Bellamy got off the bus next, his empty shirtsleeve pinned up out of the way. He turned and spoke to someone behind him, and a large, burly workman appeared, holding George in his arms.

Jane stopped, the contents of her stomach curdling with dreadful apprehension. Why was George being carried off the bus?

She knew why, though. She didn't want to understand, but she did. She stood frozen in place as a camp worker brought out a folding chair and set it up. No, it wasn't a folding chair but…a wheelchair.

Jane had never seen one up close before. She watched in fascination as the workman stooped and lowered George into the chair.

George did not look wonderful. Thin and pale, he stared straight ahead, unsmiling, as his father went down on one knee in front of him to adjust the footrest on the chair. The expression on George's face was completely blank, yet even from a distance, Jane could see his eyes were haunted.

A small but extremely shameful and terrified part of her wanted to run away. She simply did not know how to act in this situation.

It was too late to hide, so she continued forward, and approached the Bellamy family. "Welcome back," she exclaimed, and was rewarded by a delighted grin from Charles. She caught George's eye, too, but saw no pleasure in his thunderous expression.

"I didn't realize you were…"

"Go ahead and say it," George taunted. "A cripple. I'm a cripple."

"I was going to say, I didn't realize you were coming until Pa told me yesterday. I'm glad you didn't die of polio," Jane stated baldly.

"Well, that makes two of us."

And just like that, a flash of inspiration told her how to act in this situation. Not as if everything were normal and the trouble did not exist. That would be a mistake.

After Stuart's death, some people said stuff like, "He's with the Lord now," and "He died while serving a higher purpose," but Jane never felt comforted by the well-meaning words. And some people simply didn't acknowledge that there was anything strange going on with Jane's mother. They acted like it was completely normal for a woman to freeze solid for two days straight, or to stare at nothing for hours. They pretended it was normal for her to go to a special hospital and then tell her husband and daughter she could not live with them anymore.

And somehow, pretending nothing was wrong hurt more than taking the trouble head-on.

What Jane needed was for someone to notice the pain and confusion she felt every day. She wanted someone to tell her how awful it was. Maybe that would mean she'd have to admit there was no end in sight. But maybe then she could come to believe life was still worth living no matter what.

She was not going to pretend with George. What had happened was terrible. The least she could do was be honest with him.

"Welcome back to Camp Kioga," she said to the Bellamys. "We've made quite a few changes around here. I can't wait to show you. Come on, let's go."

Charles fell in step with her. No one else moved. Jane stopped walking. "George, are you coming?"

Fury burned in his eyes, as though he suspected her of mocking him. "Show my brother around. I have to be wheeled everywhere I want to go, in case you didn't notice. I'll just go to our cabin."

There was a tense, quiet moment of challenge. Jane saw through his anger. One thing she had learned in the time after Stuart's death—people got mad to cover up for feeling sad. And they always wanted someone to rip away the mask.

"Come on," she said. "There's nothing to do at the cabins except read books and listen to the radio while the grown-ups talk their faces off."

"That's all I can do, anyway."

"You got eyes to see, don't you?" she asked.

"Yes, but—"

"Come on, then. There's a new swimming dock. Can I push you in your chair?"

"No."

"*I* can," Charles said, and took hold of the handles.

Thirteen

Jane embraced her mission. She was relentless when it came to George Bellamy. Coaxing him out of his shell of anger and despair became her personal quest. Of course, she had her chores around the camp, which were many now that she was older and her mother was away. But the rest of the time was devoted to George.

She could usually find him on the porch of the Bellamys' lakefront cottage. Pa had installed a ramp so George could be wheeled up and down. Each day, she thought up a reason to coax him out. "There's a nest of robins that just hatched" was today's suggestion.

"No, thanks." He clung to glum hopelessness.

"Mr. Jacoby said we could come and see his worm farm. Ever seen a worm farm?"

"No, and I don't want to."

"What's wrong with you?" Charles asked, coming out on the porch. "Who doesn't want to see a worm farm?" He stomped away in disgust.

Jane felt torn between the two brothers. She really did want to show them her neighbor's worm farm. On the other hand, she wanted to stick with George and see if there was anything she could do to make him feel better.

"How about this?" she asked. "How about you tell me what you want to do, and we'll do it."

"I don't want to do anything."

"Even doing nothing is doing *something*. Just sitting here is something, but it's not very interesting. You have to pick."

"Who says?"

"I say."

"Who are you to boss me around?" He jutted up his chin, glaring straight ahead.

"I'm the daughter of the owner of this camp, that's who," she said. "Now, pick something, or I'll do the picking."

He turned his furious eyes on her. Finally, with utmost reluctance, he said, "I'm supposed to learn how to maneuver this thing by myself."

"Then why don't you?"

"Because it's impossible."

"No, *you're* impossible. I think moving the chair is just hard. That's different from impossible."

"Easy to say when you're not the one doing it."

"You're not doing it, either."

"Because I can't."

"Because you won't. And won't is different from can't."

"You're just a dumb girl."

"You're just a lazy boy. I'll make you a wager. I wager if you can get yourself down the ramp to the path, I'll make it worth your while."

"In what way?"

"You'll see, after you get down the ramp. I promise it will be worth it."

"It'll be the bee's knees," said Charles, coming back to join them.

"What do you know?" George asked.

"I know when something is worth seeing."

In the end, his curiosity won out. He puffed and strained and grew red in the face with the effort, but he made it down the ramp without tumbling over. Jane didn't congratulate him; she sensed that making a big production of his progress might only make him shut down again.

"This way," she said. "It's not far." She led the way to the barn. It was near her house, through a boundary marked Employees Only. Going into a restricted area was irresistible to the boys, she could tell.

"All right," George said, his temples running with sweat. "I'm here. What were you going to show me?"

She motioned them into the barn, warm and fragrant with the scent of molasses-coated feed and dry hay. Making a *shushing* gesture with a finger to her lips, she bent down and moved aside a pile of straw in an old manger box. There, in a bar of sunlight streaming through the rafters, was a black-and-white mama cat, her body curved around a litter of powder-puff kittens.

The boys' faces lit up.

"Can we hold them?" asked Charles.

"Not yet. They're too little. Salem's really tame, though. She'll let you, when the time comes."

The three of them took to visiting the barn every day. Charles usually grew restless and amused himself by climbing to the hayloft or playing on the tractor. George showed enormous patience with the kittens, talking softly to them, making friends with Salem. Within days, the kittens were venturing forth from their nest, exploring the world around them.

George's parents had given him a Kodak Brownie camera, and he took pictures of everything. "They each have their own personality already," he pointed out. "That one is really bashful—the black one. The one next to him is always finding something to play with. And the one that looks like Salem is curious about everything. I call him Doctor. I brought him a toy today." He took out a string with a button tied on the end, and played it along the floor.

It quickly caught the kittens' attention. Following the lead of the ginger-colored kitten, they all eventually went to inspect the irresistible toy. At first, one would bat it and then slink back to see what it would do. Then, as they gained confidence, they would seize the button, engaging in a tug-of-war for possession. George brought the button closer and closer to his feet, then his knees, then his lap. Eventually the kittens climbed his legs and settled into his lap. Soon, he was able to cuddle and pet them.

"All it takes is a little patience," he said, offering rare, sweet laughter as one of the kittens batted its paws at his shirt buttons.

"They're wonderful, aren't they?" said Jane. She loved the sight of the kittens, crawling all over him. "Here, I'll take a picture."

"No." George spoke sharply, startling a couple of the kittens.

"Fine, I won't." She didn't push, knowing he probably didn't want a photo of himself in a wheelchair.

"What's going to happen to them?"

"My father will let us keep one," she said. "And I'm

going to ask him if I can take one to my mother in New Haven."

"Your mother's in New Haven?"

"She lives there now."

"Forever?"

Jane nodded, swallowed a knot in her throat. "Ever since my brother was killed, she hasn't wanted to live here."

George grew quiet. "Because she misses him too much?"

"We all miss him too much. Being here at the farm and Camp Kioga made her sad all the time. She can't do everyday things anymore." Jane had no idea how she managed to push out the rest of the words. "In a way, it's better that she's there, staying with my aunt. See, when she's having a bad spell about Stuart, I, um, um…I get kind of scared of her."

Jane was surprised to discover it was possible to talk to George there in the dim barn, with shadows plentiful enough to duck into. In a way, she felt screened from him, the way she did in the confessional at church. The sense of privacy made it easier to speak honestly.

"I'm sorry," George said.

She'd heard the phrase so many times in the past year, she wanted to scream. Everybody was sorry. Sorry Stuart had been on a boat that got hit by a Japanese shell blast. Sorry he'd been blown to kingdom come. Sorry there wasn't even enough left of him to send home in a box. Sorry her shattered mother couldn't be pieced together again any more than Stuart could.

Everybody was sorry but no one could fix anything.

"I bet you hate hearing that," George said as though

reading her mind. "I bet you hate hearing people say how sorry they are."

She shuffled her bare foot through the straw on the floor and nodded her head. How had he known?

"I hear it a lot, too," he added. "Lots of people were sorry I got sick. They were so sorry all the time that I started being sorry, too, and feeling sorry for myself. So the reason I said just now I was sorry is that I want you to know, I'm going to quit feeling sorry for myself. Right now. Right this minute."

Jane paused, not sure she had heard correctly. But she had; there in the barn, quiet but for the mewling of the kittens in his lap, there could be no mistaking what he'd said. Very slowly she raised her head. Her face lit with a smile that nearly lifted her off her feet. "Was it the kittens that convinced you?"

He shook his head. "Nope. Not the kittens."

She waited for him to say more, but he just stayed quiet, his expression a little mysterious.

After that day, the three of them—Charles, George and Jane—took to going on long hikes with Jane leading the way, sometimes having to pry big rocks out of the path or use her father's pruning shears to clear away branches. Day by day, George grew stronger, his arms quicker and more sure as they pumped the large wheels of his chair. When they came to the steep parts, Charles would push the chair from behind, never daunted by an uphill slope, even one that made his face red with exertion.

Charles turned sinewy and suntanned from his daily efforts. Jane's skin was perpetually scratched from insect bites and forays in the underbrush. And slowly, gradually, George changed, too. He went from being a passive participant in their adventures to taking part in his own way. They still played games of Three Musketeers or Pirate King or Superman, but not the way they had in the past with the three of them racing and jumping and climbing. Perhaps George could no longer run through the forest like a Mohawk on the hunt, but he could narrate stories of danger and adventure, while Jane and Charles listened, enraptured, or acted them out. Sometimes George's stories made them do things that were risky or silly, but they always ended with laughter.

At first, Mrs. Bellamy would fret and wring her hands every time Jane conceived of another adventure. But Mr. Bellamy would always give them permission, and off they went, out into the summer forest. Jane was even allowed to take them to the camp's rifle range, and under supervision, the boys were given shooting lessons by the resident marksman, a war veteran who had lost a leg. George seemed inspired by the idea that a man with one leg had mastered a sport. He practiced hard at his lessons and was soon the best shot at the camp.

Jane loved seeing George come out of his shell. She loved being one of the Three Musketeers again. He taught her and Charles to play chess and backgammon. They worked crossword puzzles together and held spelling bees with the other campers.

One night, Jane organized a game of hide-and-seek. She grew frightened when everyone but George had been found. She and the others called and called, and her heart beat faster every second, like a panicked bird.

"Over here," Charles called. "He's been calling for us, but our yelling drowned him out."

George sat on the ground at the edge of the woods. There were burrs and bits of grass in his hair and clinging to his shirt, but he didn't seem injured.

"He's fine," one of the other kids yelled. "Not even bleeding or nothing." This caused the others to lose interest, and they all dispersed.

Her knees wobbly with relief, Jane sank down beside George. "What happened?" she asked. "We were so worried."

"I took a spill," he said, swiping angrily at his cheeks.

"I'll go find your chair." Charles went thrashing off into the dark.

Jane stayed with George, trying to make her pulse slow down. "Are you all right?" she asked him. "George, you're shaking."

"I got lost and my chair tipped over, and I had to crawl out of the woods. Do you know what that's like, crawling through the woods in the dark?"

"No, I don't. Maybe now you'll realize you'd better figure out how to walk," said Jane. She knew better than to baby him, particularly when he was being a baby.

"I can't, you ninny. Don't you think if I could walk, I would?"

"I think you're scared to try, same as you were scared of pushing your own chair when you first got here. But you managed to get around all by yourself. All it took was a lot of hard work."

He stared down at his left leg with an expression of extreme concentration. "Do you know what tracers are?" he asked in a small voice that was almost a whisper. "In polio victims, I mean."

She shook her head. "Never heard of 'em."

"Tracers are tiny threads of live muscle tissue in the damaged area. If you have tracers, supposedly those live muscles can be developed and will eventually replace the tissue that atrophied. Do you know what *atrophied* means?"

"Damaged, I guess."

He nodded. "Pretty much. In the hospital, I used to sit for hours studying my leg, looking for tracers."

"And did you find them?"

He shrugged. "I don't have a trained eye."

She wanted to touch him, maybe give him a hug or smooth her hand over his hair the way her father did when he told her good-night. Instead she challenged him. "Maybe you have to find those muscles by trying to use them. Like trying to walk."

"You don't get it," he snapped. "Walking's different."

"Why, because it's hard? Jiminy Cricket, you're not scared of hard work, are you?"

"No, but what if I do all the work, and it does no good?"

She thought about that for a moment. "What's the worst thing that can happen? You'll fail? Believe me, some things are worse than failing."

Fourteen

❧❦❧

Family Dance Night at Camp Kioga was a silly affair. That was what Jane had always thought, anyway. The dance instructors came from the city, and they always acted as though dancing was the most fun anyone could have. Jane secretly did think dancing was fun, though she'd never admit that to the other kids, especially Charles and George. They would surely make fun of her.

"I'm not going," George said, balking at the entrance to the dining pavilion. There was a five-piece ensemble and couples of all shapes and sizes on the dance floor. The men had pressed slacks and shiny shoes, and the women looked like flowers in their full skirts, underlaid with crinolines that belled out when they twirled.

"Sure you are. There's peach melba for dessert tonight," Charles pointed out.

"Fine, I'll eat the peach melba but forget about the dancing."

"Everybody dances," Jane said in her bossiest voice. "No exceptions."

"That's baloney."

"Huh. Shows how much you know."

"I can't dance. I can't even walk."

"Then dance however you can," she stated. "Come on."

She didn't look to see if the brothers followed. Usually if she just forged ahead, they went along with her. A famous ensemble was playing that night—the Klinger Kabaret from downtown Manhattan. They were so good that, along with the peach melba, they brought a smile to George's face. The dance instructors had Jane dancing with every boy in the place, and some girls, too, since there were always more girls than boys.

Charles was pretty good, for a boy. He was especially good at the bumps-a-daisy and the jitterbug, which was all the rage. Jane picked him for the last dance of the night, and they jumped and jived like a pair of professionals. As they swooped around the dance floor, she spied George and did a double take.

"Charles," she said, practically yelling above the brassy blare of the band, "look at George. Am I seeing things?"

"You're not seeing things."

They nearly tripped over each other's feet as they stared at George. He was in his chair off to the side, drinking a root beer soda. And he was tapping his feet to the music.

Jane and Charles descended on him. "You're moving your feet, George!" she exclaimed. "Good for you! You're moving your feet."

"Yeah," he said. "So?" He couldn't keep the grin from his face.

"So nothing," she said. "Dance with me."

"Dance with you? You're crazy, you—"

"Charles will help," she declared, and plopped herself right into George's lap. At the same time, Charles zoomed the wheelchair out onto the dance floor. The other dancers barely took note, they were so caught up in the wildness of the number.

George laughed aloud, and it sounded wonderful to her. She knew a moment of fleeting happiness then. It was a flash of perfection, a sense that everything was all right. She was in George's lap with her head thrown back in laughter. Charles pushed the chair in crazy circles as the three of them spun in time with the music, their spirits enmeshed, three broken pieces momentarily bound together.

After the dancing, Jane insisted there was nothing George could not do, and she set out every day to prove it.

"Come swimming with us," she said one afternoon after escaping Mrs. Romano's constant demands in the kitchen. She was wearing a hand-me-down romper swim-suit from one of her cousins, and she hated it, but the day was burning hot and she was dying for a plunge in the lake.

"Nope," said George.

"Come on." Charles nudged George's shoulder as he grabbed a couple of towels. "It's hotter than hades today."

"You go ahead," George said.

Jane turned on her heel. "Let's go, then. He's not interested."

"Have fun stewing in your own juices, George," said Charles, following her.

Jane knew George wouldn't last long on his own. He didn't anymore. He always found a way to join in, even if it just meant sitting in the shade and watching her and Charles play. True to form, he ended up going with them to the swimming dock. They found a nice shady spot near the locker that housed the towels and life vests, and George parked himself there.

Charles gave an Indian war whoop and pounded down the dock, doing a cannonball off the end, creating a huge splash. Jane felt torn, not wanting to abandon George but yearning to join in with the other kids.

"Go on," he urged her. "I brought my camera. I'll take some pictures."

With a squeal of delight, she ran to the dock and launched herself. The cold water felt like silk on her skin.

"Over here," said Charles. "We're playing water tag. I'm it!"

Jane swam madly, determined not to be tagged. More and more swimmers joined in until there were at least a dozen kids involved. It was the most glorious summer day imaginable. The only thing that could have made it more glorious would be—

Jane stopped swimming to tread water. She looked around for George, but he'd moved from his spot. Then she spied him. He was pumping his wheelchair as fast as he could down the dock. He'd strapped a life ring to the chair, but not to himself. The chair gathered speed as he spun the wheels faster. Jane tried to call out, but her voice was gone, stolen by shock.

The rolling chair ran out of dock and kept going. George was ejected and hit the water with a big splash. For a stunned second, everyone was frozen by dread. Then the chair bobbed to the surface, buoyed by the life ring.

The chair was empty.

Jane screamed. Charles swam toward the dock, his arms and legs churning like eggbeaters.

After what seemed like an eternity, George broke the

surface, hauling in a huge breath of air. "I'm okay," he called. He looked around at the other kids. When they realized he was all right, they started hooting and clapping.

"You creep," Jane accused him, paddling over. "You scared us to death."

"Look at me now," he said. "I'm swimming."

Not very well, she noted, but he was. He was *swimming*. He paddled slowly and clumsily toward the dock. Charles and the others lost interest in the drama and went back to their game of tag. Jane followed George, and they both clung to the ladder attached to the dock. "I'm real proud of you," she said. "I am."

"When I first went off the end," he said, lowering his voice so no one else could hear, "I sank like a stone. And it crossed my mind that I might drown if I just quit fighting and let myself go. But all of a sudden, I knew I had to get stronger and save myself. And so I started swimming."

"George!" She put her arms around him and gave him a swift, wet smack on the cheek. Instantly realizing what she'd done, she shoved away from him and swam in the opposite direction. She couldn't resist looking back at him, to see if he was as embarrassed as she was.

He didn't look embarrassed. As long as Jane lived, she knew she would never forget the expression on his face.

"Hey, look up here!" yelled Charles. He was standing on the dock with the Brownie camera. "Smile!"

Treading water, George and Jane grinned up at the camera box.

"Hold on to Doctor, will you?" George said, handing the orange kitten to his brother. "Don't let her get away."

"Sure," Charles said, cuddling and nuzzling the little creature.

The kitty was Jane's parting gift to the Bellamy brothers. Summer was over, and the time had come for them to go back to the city. Jane's father had told her she could give one of the kittens to them, and of course they chose Doctor, who was as sweet as her mother, with the same coloring. Now it was time for all of them to head home.

Jane tried not to feel too despondent as she stood watching George, who had wheeled his chair to the edge of the chipped-gravel parking area, where everyone waited for the buses to the train station in town. He had that special fire in his eye, the one that flared when he was about to say "Checkmate" in chess, or when he'd thought up a really good story to tell her.

"What's going on?" she asked.

He didn't answer. Instead he set the brake of the wheelchair and braced his hands on the armrests. Through the summer, his hands and arms had turned so brown and strong, he reminded her of Stuart, who used to pick up and toss around hay bales as if they were nothing.

Frowning with concentration, George folded up the footrests of the wheelchair and planted his feet on the ground.

Jane held her breath. Every instinct urged her to step forward and help, but she resisted. The last thing he needed was for her to interfere, or to caution him not to take a risk. She glanced at Charles and saw him practically biting a hole in his lip.

George lurched forward, but fell back into the chair. He didn't look at either Charles or Jane. She crushed her teeth together to keep from telling him not to rush, not to feel as if he had to do this right now. He tried again. Failed, twice more.

Sweat beaded on his forehead. He wiped his hands on his trousers. Planted his hands and feet…and levered himself up out of the chair.

The kitten mewed in protest, and Jane glanced over to see Charles ease his grip on the little creature. George took a step forward. One, then another. Then he stopped. His face was damp and livid from the effort. Jane couldn't stand it anymore; she rushed forward and took his arm. He was trembling, but smiling.

"Good for you, George," she whispered. "I knew you could do it."

"I had to. My mother wants to put me to bed and treat me like an invalid for the rest of my life. My father thinks I should go back to the Children's Institute, and I don't want to do either. So I better figure out how to walk on my own." He wobbled, and she held on harder, helping him back to the chair.

"Three lousy steps," he said.

"It's a start," she replied. "You'll do more tomorrow, and more every day. Promise me you will."

"All right, but you have to promise me something."

"Anything, George. I swear."

"When I come back, you have to promise to dance with me."

Fifteen

"What are you doing this evening, Granddad?" asked Ross.

"I have no plans. Unfortunately my friend Millie has gone up to Albany to visit friends and won't be back until tomorrow."

"So you and Millie…" Ross was slightly freaked by this development. He wondered if the old lady had spent the night.

"We had a lovely time. And a gentleman will say no more."

Ross gave a nervous laugh. His hat was off to the old dude, but he was content to let the matter rest. "Anyway, about tonight…"

"What did you have in mind?" George took off his reading glasses and set them aside.

"Do you feel up to a visit with your brother?"

George sat forward, gripping the arms of his chair. "Absolutely."

"And his wife, Jane? Should she come, too?"

"She…" Granddad cleared his throat. "She most certainly is welcome." He leaned back in his chair, somehow managing to look both relieved and apprehensive. "Tonight. I can scarcely believe it. Claire, did you hear?"

"I did, and I'm really happy for you, George."

After some discussion, it was determined that a private dinner, catered by the resort's kitchen, would be served on the veranda of George's house on the lake. This would keep the reunion as intimate as possible. Things were bound to get emotional. He felt the building tension later that day, as he helped his grandfather get ready.

"Tell me again what he's like," Granddad said. "What was your first impression?"

Ross passed him a handheld mirror. "Take a look. The two of you might as well be twins."

Granddad beamed. "People used to say we shared a strong family resemblance. In our younger days, I was always the athletic one. Then, after I fell ill, I turned into the bookish one." He rubbed his thigh.

Now that Ross knew about the polio, he saw his grandfather in a different light. Granddad had endured a devastating disease. One that had changed him forever. Yet he had gone on to a good life. Ross hoped to persuade him to put up a new fight now. Maybe seeing his brother would motivate him.

"I can't thank you enough for arranging this, son. It means the world to me," said Granddad.

"More than happy to do it. You know that."

"Did you like him? And Jane?"

"They were surprised when they met me. But…cordial. I liked them well enough. For strangers, that is."

"Did they tell you anything about…the past?" Granddad sounded tense.

"No. It's between the two of you," Ross said. "You can tell me or not. It's up to you."

"Maybe my foolishness will be a reminder to others not to let something like this happen."

"Since I'm an only child, it's not likely," Ross said jokingly.

"You have your stepbrother and stepsister," Granddad pointed out.

"Good old Donnie and Denise. How could I forget?"

"Ross—"

"Don't worry, Granddad. I get along fine with them."

"I wish I'd been so sensible, back when all this happened."

"All what?" Ross held out a dress shirt.

George threaded his arms into the shirt. "It was a volatile time for both of us, our college days. We were rivals, competing over everything from grades to club memberships."

"That's what brothers do. But they don't usually quit communicating for fifty years because of it."

"I confess, the rivalry went deeper than that."

"Obviously. What was it? I don't get it," said Ross.

Granddad hesitated, then picked up a silver cuff link. "I didn't approve of the girl he married."

"Jane."

"That's correct. I made no secret of my disapproval. I know it sounds impossibly snobbish in this day and age, but…things were different back then. A person's background used to matter more. I like to think I didn't consider our family superior to Jane's, just different. The Gordons were farmers and the owners of Camp Kioga. They didn't get rich doing it, and Jane did domestic work. All those years ago, she worked as a housekeeper in New Haven. Charles and I were students at Yale. The contrast was quite pronounced. And then when Charles announced his intent to marry her, well, our parents were beside themselves. She was definitely not their idea of a proper daughter-in-law. It made for an extremely tense time. Extremely tense."

A tremor started in his hand, and Ross had to help him with the other cuff link. "You were a product of your time," he said, determined not to judge his grandfather.

"I'm not proud of the way I was back in those days. I held on to my righteous indignation, and Charles married Jane. After that, we just…stayed apart. Each of us went on with our lives. I moved to Paris, married your grandmother. We both had families, careers, busy lives. One year, when the children were little, our parents invited Jackie, me and the boys on a ski holiday in Gstaad, Switzerland. In a magnanimous moment, they invited Charles and Jane and their kids, as well. But by then, Charles was serving in Vietnam. And of course, Jane declined. Your grandmother and I didn't go, either. I couldn't get away from the paper and Jackie was drowning in little boys, as she liked to put it. My parents ended up going on their own. Then we received word at the *Trib* about a devastating accident on the aerial ropeway to Les Diablerets Glacier. A cable had snapped. The tram car, crammed with eighty passengers, plunged a hundred meters." He paused, shuddering a little.

Ross had heard the story, growing up, but the incident had always seemed distant and unreal. He wasn't sure why that was. Losing his own father in a single moment of violence had turned the world upside down. Granddad's loss had been just as hard. Perhaps harder, losing both mother and father in the same instant.

"It must've been a nightmare for you," he said.

Granddad nodded. "I should have reached out to Charles then. Under normal circumstances, we would have seen each other, but he wasn't able to attend the funeral."

"Because he was serving in Vietnam." Ross sensed there was more to the story, much more.

"Time passed," his grandfather went on. "It just slipped away. I let it, and I suppose Charles did, as well."

Ross studied his grandfather's face, weathered by the years, his eyes a pale and distant blue. He seemed drained and diminished by the memories as he took out two ties. "Which one, do you think?"

Ross grinned. His grandfather was like a kid getting ready for a dance. "The stripes, for sure."

"Excellent choice." Granddad turned to the mirror and looped the tie around his neck. "I taught Charles to tie a tie. Our father wasn't so good at it, with his one arm."

"You taught me, too," Ross reminded him.

Granddad crossed one end of the tie over the other. "The Windsor knot. The most basic of gentlemanly arts." He looped the other end through, and then stopped. A frown creased his brow.

"Granddad?"

"I just… I don't know…" He looked flustered, and his left hand trembled. "I've done this ten thousand times."

Ross tried not to let his worry show. "Let me," he said, taking his grandfather's hands. "Please." Ever so gently, his heart breaking, he tied the tie into a perfect Windsor knot. Then he took his grandfather by the shoulders and turned him toward the mirror. "I love you, Granddad," he said. "You look like a million bucks."

The cottage had been readied by the resort staff, with fresh flowers, dinner and wine. The table was set with three places; Ross and Claire thought it best to have dinner elsewhere. Jane and Charles Bellamy arrived at the appointed time. They looked nervous as they walked through the door. For a moment, all three of them froze. The two brothers stood facing each other, their hesitation painful to watch.

For no reason he could fathom, Ross took Claire's hand and held on hard. Jane put a hand on her heart. It rested there lightly, like a bird about to take flight. Charles and George simply stared for several moments.

Finally Granddad said Charles's name and they shook hands. The handshake quickly escalated into a hug. The moment they touched, the tension seemed to melt into some other emotion. Ross couldn't see their faces, but their body language said it all—relief and comfort, cautious joy. After a long moment, they stepped back.

"I'm glad you came," said George.

"Of course I came," said Charles. He stepped aside and gestured Jane forward.

Granddad gave her a hug, this one briefer, more stiff. She was clutching a wad of Kleenex. "I came prepared," she said.

"You've met my grandson," said George. "And this is Claire."

As she greeted them, Claire's face glowed. She seemed to take true pleasure in the reunion. Ross let go of her hand, having forgotten he was holding on. For the umpteenth time, he wondered if she was for real. Because right now, she seemed too good to be true. She had arranged the dinner perfectly, working with the catering staff to make sure everything was just right. Even the soft music playing in the background was right—a swing era hit from the forties or fifties. She was completely centered on his grandfather's needs, and had been as nervous as any of them about this reunion. "I'm so glad you could come on short notice," she said.

"As am I," said Granddad. "We've got a lot to talk about."

Jane was already perusing the family pictures he'd placed around the room. "Ah, George. I can't wait to hear. It's wonderful, the three of us, together again. The Three Musketeers. That's what we called ourselves as children," she explained.

"Un pour tous, tous pour un," said Granddad.

"I think a toast is in order," Charles added.

Claire took Ross's hand again. "We're out of here, then," she said.

Jane beamed at them. "You make a lovely couple, you two."

Claire snatched her hand away. "Oh! We're not... I'm here for George. In fact, he knows how to get in touch with me if he needs anything. I've posted my number by the phone, too."

"Thank you," said Charles. "I'm sure we'll be fine."

It was nearly sunset when Claire and Ross left the lake house. She sensed his tension as he walked beside her, then paused to look back at the glowing windows of the cottage.

"Looks like they're getting along fine," she said, knowing he'd been worried.

As they watched, George poured a glass of wine and turned to offer it to Jane. But Jane didn't seem to notice; she was turned toward her husband. George stood holding the glass, and even from a distance he looked diminished, somehow.

Then Charles took the glass from him and handed it to Jane, and they poured two others, raising them in a toast.

"He forgot how to tie a tie," Ross said.

Claire's heart softened at the sad resignation in his voice. This was one of the hardest things about an illness like George's. You watched a person fade away, bit by bit. At the end of it all, everything fell away. The only thing left was the love you had in your life.

She shuddered, realizing when her time came, there would be nothing. Not unless she found a way out of hiding.

"He's lucky you were there to help him," she said gently.

Ross was quiet for a moment. Then he said, "There's something my grandfather's not telling me about the situation between him and his brother."

Claire had sensed the same thing, but she'd trained herself to let her patients' stories unfold in their own time—if at all. "This was a big step."

"Let's go grab something to eat," he suggested.

"We could go to the lodge."

"I have a better idea," Ross said, and took out his car keys. "Don't worry, we won't go far."

His uncanny ability to read her made Claire a little nervous. She wasn't used to people being able to see inside her. For the most part, people she met didn't even try; she'd been that successful at making herself anonymous. Ross was different. He was not the sort of person you could hide things from, not for long. This made him uniquely risky to know, yet she was intrigued. Even more so when she saw his car. "A convertible! Can we have the top down?"

He grinned and tossed her a baseball cap. "That's the point. Hop in."

"Why are you being so nice to me?"

"I'm always nice," he assured her.

She thought about how they kept butting heads about George's treatment. And then she remembered the kiss. Yes, he knew how to be nice.

He pushed a button and the top retracted. He put the car in gear and rolled out of the parking area.

She didn't know much about cars, but she could feel the power of the roadster as they rolled out onto the main road.

Claire wasn't much of a driver. At sixteen, she'd been taught to drive by her foster father, Vance Jordan. The very man from whom she was hiding now. It was chilling to think about how completely she'd placed her trust in him. Two nights before watching him murder two innocent boys, she had gone for a practice drive with him, shining with pride as he quizzed her about road rules in preparation for her driver's test.

She never did take that test, but in time, she'd obtained a license—under her new name, long after the girl she'd been then had ceased to exist. It had taken her a long time to be able to sit in a car next to a man without breaking into a cold sweat.

Ross Bellamy inspired much different emotions in her—longing and frustration. Affection and yes, lust. None of which were a good idea for someone in her situation. She tucked her hair into the baseball cap and fiddled with the radio, finding a station she liked. It was a perfect night at the leading edge of summer, the air sweet with the cool scent of new growth. They explored the area at twilight, and found an old-fashioned drive-in restaurant, where they ordered root beer floats, burgers and fries to go. Then they headed up to a scenic overlook by the lake, above a wide stretch of water rimmed by sheer rock. Float planes landed here, and there was a long dock where they could tie up. At present there was a toy-size single engine plane moored to the dock.

Claire shuddered, reminded of Vance Jordan. When she'd gone to live with them, Vance and Teresa had flown her to Pier 8 on the Hudson to celebrate. Back then, he had seemed like the perfect father figure, dashing and confident as he worked the controls.

She shook off the memory and dipped a long-handled plastic spoon into her cup, scooping up soft ice cream. She hadn't had a root beer float or a French fry in years, and it felt completely decadent to indulge.

The moon came up, bathing everything in a bluish glow. "Look at that," said Ross, leaning back in his seat. "Beautiful. *Clair de lune*—is that what you're named after?"

"No," she said. She was named after someone who had been deceased for twenty-five years, having appropriated the identity when she went underground. But of course, she couldn't tell him that.

"What's your family like?" he asked. "You never say much about yourself. Where do your parents live? What does your father do?"

"Abandons his family," she said. "No, wait. That would mean he stuck around long enough to abandon me and my mom." She looked away, lowered her head, instantly regretting what she'd just blurted out. The question had caught her off guard. "I don't really have much in the way of family."

She didn't get asked about the topic. Didn't let anyone get close enough to ask. "My mother died when I was young. I had a series of foster parents, and have been on my own since…high school."

"Damn," he said softly. "That's rough, Claire. I had no idea."

"I'm all right," she said, wishing she could say more. She hoped he wouldn't dig deeper, yet at the same time, a part of her wanted him to. She wanted to tell him everything about herself. The trouble with being in her situation was the constant battle to stay silent about things that truly mattered. "Sorry, but I don't really like talking about it," she said. "I didn't grow up with many opportunities to do things like this. Summers on the lake, sailing and fishing…it's like a dream."

"So how did you spend your summers?" he asked.

"I watched a lot of TV. My entire understanding of summer camp came from teen slasher movies."

"No wonder you like this better."

He had no idea. Her mother had been an only child, and had virtually nothing to say about her parents. Claire remembered asking her mother about this once. She'd been in third grade, and had brought home a flyer from school about Grandparents' Day.

"Not going to happen, baby girl," her mother had said, tossing the flyer in the kitchen garbage. "Like I always tell you, your grandparents aren't around. It's just you and me against the world." It was the only explanation Claire would ever get.

"You don't talk about yourself much, either," she said to Ross, determined to deflect further questions.

"Sure I do."

"Liar."

"Ask me anything. I'm an open book."

"Okay, when you were a kid, what did you want to be when you grew up?"

He thought for a minute, going back to the kid he'd been. "Everything," he admitted. "A ski racer, a rock star, a fireman, a Formula One driver, a spy and a rocket scientist." He paused and added, "An uncle. I really liked my uncles and wanted a bunch of nieces and nephews. It's tricky, though, when you're an only child. I tended to be drawn to things that were hard or impossible. Wonder what that says about me."

"That you're a big dreamer," she said. "It's no crime."

"When I was sixteen years old, my mother sent me to H.E.L.—the Human Engineering Laboratory. I'm sure the irony of the initials completely escaped the folks who ran the facility."

She frowned. "Sounds scary."

"It was a program meant to help kids figure out their affinities and aptitudes. They subjected us to a battery of tests, the idea being that if we knew what we were good at, we'd be better prepared to face the Real World."

"Did it indicate you'd be a good helicopter pilot?"

"I honestly don't remember." He scooped a bit of ice cream out of his float.

They were quiet for a few minutes, listening to the chorus of chirping frogs and watching the stars come out. It was incredibly relaxing, sitting with Ross Bellamy, eating a decadent meal and escaping the world, just for a while. "This is a great spot," she said.

"Reminds me of the kind of place where people go to park and make out."

She nearly choked on a French fry. "Don't get any ideas."

"Too late. I've been having ideas about you all evening."

"Bad idea." She set aside her dinner, her appetite gone. Just once, she would love to explore the suggestion she read in his eyes, indulge the desire that seemed to warm every inch of her.

"On the contrary, it felt like the best idea I've had in a long time. Kissing you—"

"Shouldn't have happened. It was unprofessional of me. I'm here for your grandfather and nothing more."

"But if something more happens…?"

"Trust me, it won't."

"Why not?"

"Because we won't let it. People shouldn't get emotionally involved in a situation like this. It's… It just doesn't make sense."

"When does love ever make sense?"

"Who said anything about love?"

"I just did." Ross laughed. "You're looking at me like I've got frogs coming out of my mouth."

Claire was inept at flirting, and it never led anywhere good. "Frogs, I can deal with. Flirting, not so much."

"Did you know my grandfather picked you because he thought I'd like you?"

"Nonsense." Yet she couldn't help remembering how adamant George had been about Natalie Sweet not being Ross's girlfriend.

"Ask him. He'll tell you."

"Why would he do something like that?"

"He's worried about me. Wants me to settle down, have a family."

Now it was Claire's turn to laugh. "With me? In that case, I'm sure he knows he's barking up the wrong tree."

"And why is that?"

She countered with another question. "Why is this so important to him?"

"He doesn't want me to be alone."

"And what do you want?"

"I want to make out."

Of course he did. He was a *guy*. "Ross."

"Just being honest."

She shifted uncomfortably, pressing her back against the car door. "You were the first person your grandfather told me about after he hired me."

"I suspect because I've given him the most to worry about." He pinched the bridge of his nose; his voice was anguished as he said, "Christ, I wish I'd spent the past two years with him instead of in a war zone."

"He'd hate to hear you talking like that," she pointed out.

"That's why I'm telling you, not him."

"You can tell me anything you want, Ross." She had an urge to touch him, but instead tucked her hands between her knees.

Ross stared straight ahead, though she sensed he wasn't seeing the moonlit curves of the distant hills. "He's the true North in my life. Always has been, but particularly since I lost my dad. I figured he'd quit worrying about me now that I'm out of the army, but now he's decided to worry about my future."

"Because he cares about you so much," she stated.

He set his cup in the drink holder and grew thought-ful. "He's right about one thing. I don't want to be alone anymore. I'm so damned ready to start a new chapter now that I'm back. Have a family of my own, make a life somewhere quiet and safe. After what I saw over there, I…it's all that matters."

It felt achingly intimate, getting a glimpse of his dreams. She could listen to him all night. Yet at the same time, she wanted to ask him what would happen if he dis-covered he wasn't able to have those things. Would he curl up and die? Or keep moving, avoiding attachments?

Finally he relaxed and turned to her with a grin. "First things first—how about we work on getting a date. Does this count as a date?"

She laughed, pretending she found his question amusing. "Yeah, sure." Flustered, she checked her mobile phone and the monitor receiver, to make sure she hadn't missed a message from George.

"Everything okay?" asked Ross.

"No news is good news," she said.

"How did you end up picking this sort of nursing, anyway? Ushering people out of this life? Is it something you grew up dreaming of?"

"Very funny. Sure, every little girl dreams of growing up to help people die."

"Then what's the appeal?"

"*Appeal* isn't exactly the word. It's more like a…calling. That suits me. Work that matters, and work that needs to be done well, and with love. I can love my patients with all my heart," she said. "I love them for as long as they have. And then I let them go and move on."

"I don't know how you do it," he said. "How can you stand it?"

"I just do." She paused, realizing her voice had turned rough with emotion. She did have a passion for her work, but she wasn't used to discussing it with anyone. Ross was so dangerously easy to talk to. "This area is something I found when I was doing practical training. It was easy to be drawn to the really gratifying areas—taking care of babies, clinical work, the E.R.—patching people up and sending them back to their lives none the worse for the wear. I liked those specialties. They were easy to like. Then I looked deeper at the work and at myself, and I realized nursing is a very nuanced profession, with so many ways of helping people. I learned that helping doesn't always mean curing. Sometimes it means doing whatever will help the patient to find comfort and closure. We talked a lot in our classes and evals about what constitutes a good death. It made for interesting discussions, but nobody really knows the answer."

"Congratulations, Miss Turner," he said with a gleam in his eye. "You win the round for which one of us is the better bullshit artist."

She didn't react other than to tilt her head to one side and regard him with a quizzical expression. "I'm sure I have no idea what you're talking about."

"I'm going to make a prediction," he said. "One of these days, you'll show me who you truly are."

The way he said it gave her chills. No one had ever talked to her like this before, and she didn't quite know what to make of him. "Are you accusing me of hiding something?"

"It's not an accusation. Just an observation. Feel free to prove me wrong anytime you want."

When Claire and Ross got home, Charles and Jane were just getting ready to leave. Claire thought George's coloring was off, but maybe that was the wine. He was smiling and relaxed, so she said nothing.

"It was wonderful," Jane was saying to Ross. "Thank you for bringing us together."

Ross nodded. "Thanks for coming."

Claire felt an echo of the warm buzz of attraction that had swirled through her all evening. Ross Bellamy was like a heady, dangerous drug.

"We have some big plans," said Charles. "There's going to be a family reunion."

"A fabulous one, right here at Camp Kioga," Jane added, bubbling over with a sense of mission. "I'm going to arrange everything—George's family and ours, all of us together here."

Claire shot a glance at Ross. His smile looked a bit strained. "Are you up for something like that, Granddad?" he asked.

"Absolutely," said George. He seemed pleased but tired. "If anyone can put something together on short notice, Jane can."

"We left a family album here so you can look at it, Ross," said Jane.

"I'll do that, thank you."

"Good night, George," said Charles. "We'll see you tomorrow." He held the door for his wife, and they left, Jane chattering away, already planning.

"It was a fine evening—harder in the anticipation than

in the actual doing," George said, his voice a bit wistful. "Charles and I were rivals in so many ways. It all seems quite foolish now."

"You sure you're okay with a big family reunion?" Ross asked again. "You're not just agreeing to make them happy?"

"It's precisely what I want," George said. "A chance to meet their children and grandchildren. I always wondered about him. Them." He frowned, rubbed his temples. "Help me to bed, will you, son?"

Apprehension sharpened Ross's features as he glanced at Claire. She tried to look reassuring as she said, "Good idea. I'll get your meds, George." She took her time, hearing their murmured conversation. She hoped they weren't talking about her. Dear God, no.

When she rejoined them, George was propped up in bed, paging through the photo album his brother had left for him. It was overstuffed with pictures in black and white, fading Kodachrome snapshots, Polaroids that had gone rusty at the edges and a number of printouts from modern digital cameras.

George was focused on a shot of Charles in a military uniform, surrounded by his wife and four kids.

"Granddad?" Ross said softly.

George blew his nose. "I'm sorry I missed all these years of my brother's life." Then he waved a hand impatiently. "Enough regrets. I'm feeling tired. I'll be better in the morning. Dim the light, would you? It's too bright."

"Here you go." Claire handed him a small cup of pills and a glass of water.

He swallowed the pills, then made a shooing motion

with his hands. "No more hovering. It's early. Go back to your date."

"We weren't on a date," she said, not looking at Ross.

"Then you're idiots, both of you. Any fool can see you're attracted to one another. Even my brother noticed. Go away. Let an old man get some rest."

They left the room, and Claire went to the kitchen to get started on the dishes.

"Leave that," Ross said. "The catering staff will do it in the morning."

"Do you know how foreign that sounds—'catering staff'?" She'd never even stayed in a place with room service.

"It's a Mohawk word for 'get your sweet ass over here and hang out with me some more.'"

Heat flared in her belly. "I think you'd better go."

"Whatever you say." But instead of heading for the door, he crossed the room and gently trapped her against the counter.

She put her hands on his arms, but she didn't push him away. He felt so strong, so...safe. And then he kissed her, first with a tender touch of his lips and then pressing harder, tasting her with an intimacy that made her dizzy.

After a moment, she managed to pull back. "What are you doing?" she whispered.

"Kissing you good-night,"

"You can't kiss me good-night."

"I just did. I feel like doing it again."

"Stop it, Ross. I mean it. There are so many ways this is wrong—"

"Except that it feels exactly right." He cradled her

face between his hands. "Do you know how long it's been since I kissed a woman?"

"About twenty-four hours."

"But before that, it was more than two years. Damn, you feel good."

"You should go now." But she discovered that she couldn't move. She didn't want to. She wanted to stay here all night, in his arms.

"In a minute." He bent to kiss her again. She told herself to step back, not to be an idiot...but her heart didn't listen. Her need was overpowering—not just for the kisses and the intimacy, but for the connection. He'd said he wanted her to show him who she was, and for the first time in her life, she saw that as a possibility. It was only fair to warn him, however, what he was getting into.

"Ross," she whispered against his mouth, "there's something you need to know about me."

"I want to know everything," he said. "Your favorite song, your favorite color. What your breathing sounds like when you sleep, the color you painted your apartment, the books you like to read—"

"I don't mean things like that," she said. Oh, she wished it were that simple. She wished she could tell him anything but the truth. She tried to imagine the words she would use. *I saw a cop commit two murders, and he'd kill me if he ever found me.*

Way to ruin the mood, she thought.

He kissed her some more, his lips gently nipping at the curve of her neck. "How about," he said, "we do this for a while, and then you can tell me later."

"Good plan, but—"

A thud sounded in George's room.

Ross sprang back as if she'd scalded him. "Granddad!"

They jumped up and ran to George's bedroom. George's monitor was on the floor, presumably knocked there as he'd reached for it.

"He's having a seizure," Claire said, rushing over to the bed. She checked his airway and turned him on his side.

Ross snatched up the phone by the bed. "I'm calling 911."

"You can't," she said, the words rushing from her.

"What?"

She knew he was going to hate what she said next. He was probably going to hate her. But she had to level with him. "You can't call 911 because your grandfather has a DNR order. Do not resuscitate."

Sixteen

Ross called 911.

He didn't care what Claire was saying about some bullshit DNR order. His grandfather needed help. Maybe she had a piece of paper that said he wasn't to be resuscitated, but that didn't mean he couldn't be treated.

Granddad was strapped to a backboard, his neck encased in a cervical collar, precautions to keep him stable during transport. He regained consciousness and said something, but an O$_2$ mask muffled his voice. As his nurse, Claire rode in the ambulance. Ross followed in his car.

At Benedictine Hospital, Granddad was whisked into the emergency department. By the time Ross parked and raced to the ward, Claire was already conferring with a doctor and a pair of nurses. Granddad lay surrounded by machines, wheeled trays, tubing, hovering residents and nurses.

"This is Ross Bellamy," Claire said. "He's Mr. Bellamy's grandson."

"And my grandfather's not DNR," he stated, refusing

to look at Claire. "He's full code, and that's how he's to be treated. So get to work."

Dr. Randolph, a young resident with a half-grown beard and tousled hair, stepped forward, holding the manila folder from Claire, filled with Granddad's medical records. "Just so you know," said the doctor, "full code means all possible lifesaving and support measures will be taken. Your grandfather's having trouble breathing. There might be obstruction or collapse of the upper airway. That likely means intubation and placement on a ventilator. Other measures might include catheterization, defibrillation, transfusions, feeding by tube…"

The list of horrors seemed to go on and on. Ross reminded himself these were lifesaving measures. He'd seen it in battle. The procedures were never kind, but at least the patient lived.

A loud crash sounded, drawing everyone's attention to Ross's grandfather. Somehow, he'd worked a hand free of its Velcro strap and had knocked over a tray of instruments. Claire rushed to his side, waved away the tech who had been working the bag valve.

"He seems to be breathing a little better," said Dr. Randolph.

Granddad coughed, waving his hand weakly. "For the love of God, Ross," he said. "What part of 'do not resuscitate' do you not understand?"

Though Granddad refused to be admitted to the hospital, he was kept for a few hours' observation. The emergency department was bright with glaring lights, noisy and busy with crying kids, babbling drunks, people moaning with sickness or injury, staffers calling orders back and forth. Ross gritted his teeth through some gruesome flashbacks to the war, but he shoved them into a dark corner of his mind so he could focus on his grandfather. A knee-length blue curtain offered a thin illusion of privacy.

"When you were off fighting," Granddad told him, "I was in a war of my own, at the Mayo Clinic. You think I didn't want to fight this disease? You think I didn't want to beat it? I gave it all I had, Ross. They numbed my head, screwed a steel frame into my skull and zapped me with gamma rays. Pumped me full of chemo—"

"You never told me, Granddad."

"And you never told me everything you saw in your war, either. Ross, the tumor keeps recurring. It won't stop, not ever. I won't go through that again. I won't. Not even for you."

George drifted off to sleep. Ross left the curtain area in a hurry, feeling his emotions unspooling fast.

Grief came to life like a spring thaw after deep winter. He had spent the past two years staying numb, lost in a bubble that separated him from everything. Now the bubble had burst; feelings he hadn't experienced in years were flooding through him—the desperation and sadness of his grandfather's illness, the sense of futility.

Granddad. Memories suddenly flowed through him, powerful, a raft of feelings.

Although he didn't make a sound, Claire must have sensed the shift in him. She followed him to a quiet area by the water cooler. He was crying. When the hell had he started crying?

"I told myself I'd be ready when the time came," he said, his voice rough and unsteady. "I lost my dad and dealt with it," he said, swiping his sleeve across his face. "I'll deal with this, too."

"Of course you will. It's the only way to honor your grandfather."

"Hell, I know that. But I'm not doing so hot." He took a deep breath and it surprised him to realize he was still alive. Because he'd always thought something that hurt this much would kill him.

"Yes, you are," she said.

"No. He's seen his brother. I want to get him back to the city. Back to the doctor—"

"What about what *he* wants? That's what's important here. You can break down. You can be afraid, but you have to keep the focus on George."

Ross knew what he was afraid of—being without his grandfather. Yet after tonight, he also knew dragging him back to treatment would mean pointless suffering. "Yeah," he said after a while. "I know. But I don't know what the hell I *am* going to do."

"Take things a day at a time. Maybe even an hour at a time. The best thing you can do for George is to be present in the moment. Have your meltdowns with me. I can take it. But if your grandfather senses you're worried and stressed, he'll be worried and stressed, too. When you're with him, just let that go."

Let go. Ross pictured himself letting go. A soldier's hand in the midst of an emergency. A fish caught at the water's edge. Let go, he thought. *Let go.*

Her simple words wrapped around his mind, rescuing him as surely as someone borne away on a medevac flight. Her gentle presence lifted him up, carried him away. The best way to love his grandfather now was to let go.

* * *

Ross called his uncle Trevor and told him what had happened. Trevor insisted he bring Granddad to the city right away.

"I think you'd better come here," said Ross. "Everyone should come here, and soon."

They argued, because the rest of the family still clung to the hope that Granddad would get better. Ultimately Ross was in charge. Trevor agreed to come to Avalon. His brothers, Gerard and Louis, would not be far behind.

Ross and Claire returned to the curtain area. His grandfather was still dozing, but when he woke up, they were going to take him back to Camp Kioga.

"Can he hear us?" asked Ross.

"Maybe." She straightened a corner of the institutional-blue blanket that covered him.

On the waist-high bed, Granddad looked lost somewhere, lost in a world of dreams. Ross looked around the area, gathering up his things. There wasn't much to grab—Granddad's bedroom slippers, his old cardigan with the patched elbows, left in a heap like yesterday's laundry. When Ross picked it up, something drifted from the pocket—a photograph. An old black-and-white print with deckled edges. It showed a boy and a girl in the lake, treading water, laughing up at the camera.

On the back of the snapshot, someone had written, "George Bellamy & Jane Gordon, Camp Kioga 1945."

Seventeen

Avalon, Ulster County, New York
Summer 1955

Charles and George were fighting over possession of the car keys. They often argued over which brother got to drive the DeSoto, but George was usually the one to give in. As he secured the canvas covering after folding away the convertible top, he tossed Charles the keys. The Camp Kioga parking lot was hot and dry, and a ride into town with the top down would be a refreshing break.

"Mother wants us to pick up a pie to bring to the camp picnic," George said. "You drive, and I'll check out the scenery."

A pair of girls—ponytailed, barelegged, in tennis whites—strolled past on their way to the tennis courts, and George followed them with his eyes. "I don't mind a little sightseeing now and then."

Charles took the wheel, driving with his elbow propped on the window frame and a grin on his face. "You go right ahead and flirt all you want," he said good-naturedly. "Me, I'll wait until the real thing comes along."

"Life is too short to wait around for anything," George declared. The breeze felt good on his face, and the air was sweet with the smells of summer—freshly cut grass, blooming flowers, the dry scent of the sun's heat on the pavement. "Burn that Candle" by Bill Haley and His Comets was blaring from the radio as they passed beneath the main gate.

"Back at Camp Kioga at last," Charles declared. "I can't believe it's been ten whole years."

Time had flown by. It was the summer before George's final year at Yale, and their mother had been struck by a wave of nostalgia. She wanted the whole family to return to Camp Kioga, vacationing together once again. This might be their last chance to spend summer as a family, she reasoned, because next year George would be on his own, a college grad, and the family would never be the same.

George didn't take much convincing. He often thought about his boyhood summers here. So much drama packed into such a short time—a series of childish adventures had ended abruptly with the twin disasters of a young man's tragic death and George's affliction with polio. The summer after that, he'd finally come to grips with his illness and realized that the true limitation to healing was himself. Drawing on reserves of strength he didn't know he had, George had fought his way back from the wheelchair to standing on his own two feet, more determined than ever to build a successful life.

Ten whole years. So many summers, stolen from him—from all the Bellamys, really—by polio. George's rehabilitation took more time and energy than he ever could have imagined. When he'd demonstrated the will to walk again, his parents had left no stone unturned, seeking out the best clinics and programs for him. He'd gone to Warm Springs in Georgia, where FDR himself had spent some time. After V-E Day, they'd taken him to the famed Institut Fleurier, in the Neuchâtel canton of Switzerland.

The hard and painful work of restoring function to his legs consumed him. FDR had said that once you'd spent two years trying to wiggle one toe, everything is put in proportion. George could relate to that entirely. Now he could walk, if not run or dance or leap tall buildings in a single bound. He looked like any other fellow, so long as his trousers covered the mechanical brace on his bad leg. His nurses and therapists claimed it was as good an outcome as could be expected.

Instead of Camp Kioga, the Bellamys had devoted their summers to George's rehabilitation. He'd lost time in school, too, and ultimately found himself only a year ahead of his brother Charles at college. He told himself he didn't mind, though he knew people compared the two brothers. George didn't understand why that was. He and Charles were so very different. Charles was the athletic one, the playful one, the one who pulled pranks and danced with girls and didn't seem the least bit shy about making a fool of himself.

George, on the other hand, was more serious and reflective. He carried on his boyhood habit of keeping a journal, and dedicated himself to his writing classes. Thanks to his many months in the Romandy region of Switzerland, he was fluent in French, and dreamed of being an overseas correspondent for a major newspaper.

But this summer, all four Bellamys were going back in search of something they'd left behind, or something they never really had to begin with—innocence, acceptance, simplicity. Camp Kioga offered that elusive promise; it was a place where everything seemed uncomplicated, bathed in golden sunlight, like a fondly remembered dream.

George often wondered about Jane Gordon, the frizzy-haired, knock-kneed girl who had made every day an adventure. He hadn't run into her yet; they'd only been here a few days. He wondered if he'd even recognize her; she'd be all grown up by now.

He made a big production of checking the time, glancing at a Breitling watch that had been a gift from his Bellamy grandparents upon his high school graduation. When Grandfather had presented it to him, he'd looked George in the eye and said, "Make the family proud, son."

Which, when it came to the Bellamys, meant go to the right school, move in the right circles, marry the right girl and live in the right neighborhood. It was a simple enough formula. Do all the right things and you'll end up with a successful life.

According to Bellamy family tradition, both George and Charles were on track. They had attended Andover as boarding students, manfully leaving the nest and pretending not to be homesick. George in particular had stood out, managing to juggle his exercises with a rigorous course of study. Now the brothers were both at Yale, the alma mater of their father and grandfather.

Neither brother had yet found the girl he was meant to marry. Privately George found the girls he met at school mixers boring. Their flat personalities and studied mannerisms held no appeal for him. At the nightly dinner dances held at the main lodge of Camp Kioga, his mother would chide George. "I do wish you'd join in the dancing, really. I can see a half-dozen girls here who would love to cut a rug with you."

He was always ready with a smooth answer. "Mother, I'm not the dancing type. I'll let Charles do the honors."

The fact was, George had never learned to dance. The last time he'd been on a dance floor, it had been right here at Camp Kioga. He'd held Jane Gordon in his lap while Charles pushed the chair, the three of them whirling together to the strains of a Guy Lombardo tune. He wondered if either of them remembered that moment as vividly as he had.

Once he'd recovered the ability to walk, he'd been disinclined to attempt dancing for any reason, even though it was considered one of the key social skills of a gentleman. He probably could have muddled his way through a couple of numbers, but he chose not to. Because above all other things, George Bellamy cared about appearances. He would rather avoid dancing altogether than risk looking bad in front of people.

His mother didn't push too hard. She had suffered the fright of her life with George's illness, and he knew she was so grateful for his recovery that she would never ask another thing of him.

Charles did enough dancing for both brothers, and he did it well. The jitterbug, the Lindy hop, all the fast and fun dances, were a good fit for his natural exuberance.

Millicent and Beatrice Darrow, two sisters from Boston, happened to be staying in the cottage next to the

Bellamys, and George and Charles were expected to squire them around this summer. George thought they were a swell pair of girls, students at Yale's sister school, Vassar College. Both young women had the handsome and vaguely horsey good looks that tended to be associated with fine New England breeding, and they spoke multiple languages with a broad, flat accent. As far as the Bellamys were concerned, the girls were a perfect match for their sons. George wasn't so sure about that, but he had promised to bring them a cherry pie from the Sky River Bakery.

"Holy smokes, look at this stuff." Charles practically fell to his knees in front of the display case, which was stocked with glazed crullers and berry tarts, pies and cakes and cookies.

The town bakery was crowded with folks provisioning for their weekend parties and picnics. Recently founded by an immigrant couple named the Majeskys, the place was already famous, thanks to the variety and quality of the goods.

"Jiminy Cricket," someone said, the voice cutting through the others in the bakery, "I can never make up my mind about my favorite flavor."

Something about that voice—its timbre or inflection—resonated deep inside George. It made the hair on the back of his neck stand on end. Scanning the crowd, he spotted a girl in a camp shirt and shorts, surrounded by a group of children. She wore the uniform of a Camp Kioga counselor, including the signature bandanna around her neck. The kids were all in camp uniforms, clustering around her or clamoring for baked goods. There was something in her laugh, some note or special tone, that resonated inside George like the plucked string of an instrument. He felt the sound all through him, which was kind of crazy; from where he stood, he couldn't really see her face.

She stood in a glare of light streaming in through the shop window as though the sun itself had singled her out, yet other than that, there was nothing particularly extraordinary about her. She was of average height and build, maybe a little more curvy than average, curly dark red hair caught in a high ponytail. The shorts showed off a fine pair of legs.

He must have been staring hard enough for her to feel his curiosity. She paused in what she was doing, stood up straight and turned to face him directly.

He felt her regard like the beat of his own heart. The moment of recognition seemed to hit them both at the same time. *Jane Gordon.*

She'd changed in a hundred ways, but the things he remembered best about her were exactly the same— wide hazel eyes, a saddle of freckles across her nose and a broad, expressive mouth and ready smile. Everything about her was open with exuberance, just as it had been when they were kids.

In a matter of seconds, he understood what was missing from people like the Darrow girls and others his family deemed a good match for him. They lacked whatever it was Jane exuded, some kind of irrepressible spark that was instantly apparent to George.

And although he and Jane were strangers now, thanks to the passing of the years, they shared a moment, fraught with memories. He could see the recognition in her eyes.

He also sensed the spark of something new, something

that hadn't been there when they were young kids. Neither of them had spoken a word to each other across the crowded shop, yet George could have sworn the air crackled around them. Every instinct he possessed urged him to take action. Simple, direct action. He ought to walk over to Jane, to reacquaint himself with her…and ask her out.

He could tell she wanted him to. Despite the long absence, he sensed the invitation in her eyes, the openness of her smile.

The time wasn't right, though. She was clearly busy with her young charges from Camp Kioga. He was on an errand and the bakery was jammed with people.

Life did not offer many moments like this—moments in which a single word or gesture might change everything. To let the opportunity pass would be to allow something special to slip through his fingers.

He took a tentative step toward her. A joint in his leg brace made the faintest creaking sound, unnoticeable except to him. Yet even that was enough to plant a kernel of doubt. What the devil was he going to say? "Hello, what are you doing for the rest of your life?" "Excuse me, but I think I'm falling in love with you?" Anything he might say would surely sound ridiculous. Besides, what would a lively girl like this want with a gimp like George?

"Ho-lee smokes," said a voice behind George. "Save my place in line. There's someone I have to talk to."

With long, brash strides, Charles made his way through the crowd and went up to Jane. She looked momentarily nonplussed. And perhaps, just perhaps, she shot George a plea, as though she wanted him to be the one to approach her first, not Charles. That, of course, could always be in his imagination.

In truth, he would never know what she was thinking in those first moments. The only thing he knew for certain was that three lives were changed forever, right there in the crowded bakery.

"Who'da thunk it? I'm already half in love with Jane Gordon," Charles declared as they gathered in the Fireside Lounge for drinks before dinner that night. His eyes sparkled with eager sentiment as he regarded George and his parents. "Do you believe in love at first sight? Because I'm pretty sure that's what happened to me."

"Baloney." George felt a cold rock of resentment in his chest. Once again, Charles had beaten him to the punch. This time, the stakes were much higher than a set of car keys. All afternoon, George had played and replayed the scene in his head. If he hadn't second-guessed himself, if he'd ignored the encumbrance of the leg brace and acted a split second sooner, then he would be the one glowing with excitement, telling his parents he'd met a special girl.

"And to think she's been living in New Haven all this time, and we never even knew," Charles went on. George took a small, controlled sip of his highball.

"We don't know any Gordons, do we?" their mother asked. "Still, that name sounds familiar. Are they staying at the resort?"

Charles laughed, his abundant blond hair gleaming in the glow of the candles on the table. "Here's the crazy thing," he declared with a grin of pure exuberance. "They're not staying at the resort. They *run* the resort."

With his typical blithe disregard for convention, Charles had chatted up Jane Gordon right there in the bakery, and learned that she spent most of the year in New Haven with her mother. Even a decade after losing her son in the war, Mrs. Gordon was still unwilling to live in Avalon, and Mr. Gordon insisted on staying and running the family business.

How odd, thought George, that the girl spent most of her time right in New Haven, yet they'd never run into her there. In his mind, he'd preserved the image of Jane as a skinny, funny-looking little girl with big teeth and laughing eyes. Now the ugly duckling had become a swan.

"Oh, for heaven's sake, that's why the name is familiar," said their mother. "They're just a local family."

When he heard the pronouncement, George felt the knot in his chest unfurl. He no longer felt regret that he hadn't approached her in the bakery; he felt relief. A local girl. *Local* was code for *beneath us*. Local meant a girl from the working class. A girl who didn't fit in with the college set. Neither he nor Charles had any business getting romantic with her. He certainly wasn't going to battle his brother for possession of her heart.

A romance with Jane Gordon would be doomed from the start, anyway. They had nothing in common. Once the initial attraction wore off, there would be nothing to sustain them. Perhaps that attitude was snobby or elitist, but he hadn't made the rules.

Thanks to Charles, George had avoided a sticky situation. How awkward it would have been to flirt with her, perhaps make some overture, only to be rebuffed because he had a bad leg and didn't fit into her world.

Yet as Charles went on and on about her—Jane Bonnie

Gordon, a farmer's daughter raised right here in Avalon—it dawned on George that his brother didn't understand.

"Son," their father said to Charles, "we don't blame you for enjoying a little summer flirtation, but don't make it into anything more than that."

"Too late," Charles said breezily. "It already *is* more than that."

Their mother fanned herself. "Dear heaven, do you mean—"

"Of course not," Charles said quickly. "We only found each other today. She's swell, and you're going to love her."

"And where does she go to school?" Mrs. Bellamy asked pointedly.

"Jane's not in school. She says her father's barely getting by, trying to keep this place in the black. But I want you to understand, I'm going to ask her out, court her the way I would any other girl."

"She's not any other girl," their father said in a low warning tone. "She's not for a young man like you."

"Don't be a fuddy-duddy." Charles laughed. "This is not the nineteenth century. We're not in Bizet's *Carmen*."

The fact that he had brought up the opera—about a class struggle that had ensued when a cigarette-factory girl fell for a powerful aristocrat—proved he understood on some level. Jane was completely wrong for either brother. The sooner Charles came to accept that reality, the sooner they could both move on.

George was frustrated to discover, though, that his heart refused to obey his mind. In spite of all good sense, he found himself thinking endlessly about those moments in the bakery. Those few seconds had been like a key in a lock, finally clicking into place. Why hadn't he stepped forward? Why hadn't he spoken up when he had a chance?

Because he was afraid. He hid behind the rules of society to avoid looking like a fool. It was not George's favorite thing about himself.

"Oh, look who's here," said Mrs. Bellamy. "The Darrows will be joining us for dinner tonight." She glided over to greet them, and within minutes, they were all sharing a large table, two handsome families, dressed to the nines. Dinner was a convivial affair as they discussed topics that ranged from Churchill's resignation as prime minister to the introduction of the Salk vaccine for polio.

"What a blessing," declared Millicent Darrow, the younger of the sisters. "How fortunate that we won't have to worry about polio anymore."

George polished off a glass of wine and changed the topic to the imminent opening of an amusement park called Disneyland, which promised to be all the rage in California. Then, to his relief, the women launched into a discussion of the overheated bestseller that was all the rage, *Marjorie Morningstar.*

At the conclusion of dinner, the musical ensemble struck up "Dance With Me Henry," and the girls looked expectantly at the brothers. "My favorite," said Millicent.

"You'll have to forgive my brother," said Charles Bellamy to the sisters. "He refuses to dance."

The girls exchanged a glance. "Not even a tiny foxtrot? Georgie, say it isn't so." Beatrice tucked her lips into a pout.

George, who couldn't stand being called Georgie, offered his smoothest and most charming smile. "Think of it as a humanitarian gesture," he said. "I don't want to prey on some hapless girl and cause her irreparable physical harm."

The sisters laughed. "I assure you, we're made of sturdier stuff than that. Good Yankee stock."

"What about the psychological damage of being paired with the worst dancer ever to blight the floor?" he inquired, arching an eyebrow at them. "Believe me, no one can overcome that."

"True," Millicent agreed. "A reputation is more fragile than the physical body. A broken bone can heal. A ruined reputation stays ruined forever."

"Will you listen to yourself?" Charles looked incredulous. "You sound like an old biddy."

She glared at him. "Well!"

"But you look like a young biddy," he said soothingly.

"That's better." She batted her eyes at him, then turned to George. "Didn't you have to take dancing lessons at school? I thought it was considered one of the gentlemanly arts."

"You're right," he said. "It is. Perhaps that explains why I'm no gentleman."

They all laughed as if he'd made a great joke.

"How did you get out of dancing lessons? Where were you when everyone was learning to dance?"

In an iron lung, he thought. Fighting for my life.

He could feel his brother watching him. Charles had never understood George's reluctance to tell people about the polio. And George couldn't understand why it was so hard to grasp. Why the devil would anyone want to advertise such a weakness?

Unlike his older brother, Charles had led a charmed life. Everything came easily to him—grades and excellence at sports, ease in social situations, everything. He was the all-American golden boy, for sure. It was probably no wonder he couldn't relate to a polio victim with a game leg.

"We missed you at the bridge tournament this afternoon," Millicent said to Charles. "Where were you?"

"Around and about," Charles said.

George suspected Charles had managed to sneak off to spend time with Jane Gordon. Charles should know better. Then again, he'd always been one to follow his impulses, and damn the consequences.

"Who won the tournament?" asked Charles.

"George and Beatrice, of course," she said.

"My big brother always wins at everything," Charles said with a rueful smile.

"Don't be too impressed," George said, noticing Charles had managed to avoid actually saying where he'd been during the bridge game. "I tend to only try things I have a chance at winning."

"Ah, so that's your secret," said Millicent.

"I just disclosed it, so it's a secret no more."

"I shall have to think about this one," Charles said. "The key to success is to only do things you can succeed at."

"It works for me," said George. "Keeps frustration to a minimum, anyway."

The band struck up a lively version of "Moments to Remember," and a raft of couples glided onto the dance floor. "Are you sure you won't dance with me, Georgie?" Beatrice asked, making a new effort.

"Trust me when I say I value your health and mobility too much to inflict myself on you."

"Tell you what," Charles suggested, smooth as silk.

"Let's send George to grab another bottle of wine for the table. And I'll dance with both of you at the same time. We'll invent a new dance."

The girls were charmed by the prospect of two against one. As Charles stood up and offered each of them an arm, George shot his brother a look of relieved gratitude.

"Don't forget that wine," Charles said. "Make it a good one. Make it two."

"I'll be back in a jiff." George rose from the table, thinking about every step he took. For years, he had dedicated himself to hiding the ravages of the disease. A London tailor made all his clothes, from dress suits to casual wear. Every pair of slacks, even his golf chinos, had been designed to conceal the mechanical brace he wore on his left leg. As he crossed the big, busy dining room, he knew he moved with confidence because he had practiced it.

Since it was a Friday night at the lodge, the dining room was particularly busy. Friday was the day the men came up from the city to join their families at the summer retreat. Parkhurst Bellamy was no exception. Like the others, he had arrived at the cocktail hour and had been drinking steadily ever since. He and George's mother were deep in conversation with the elder Darrows. They made a good-looking and self-satisfied foursome, the personification of the American success story.

George discovered that if he blurred his eyes, everyone in the room looked the same. Pale and well-groomed, dressed in expensive clothing and smoking imported cigarettes dispensed from monogrammed cases.

At the edge of the crowd stood someone who didn't

fit in. Her hair was too frizzy, her features too vivid, her expression too unguarded.

Jane Gordon was working in the dining room that night. In a plain server's frock and apron, she stood at the dessert table, cutting slices of layer cake or adding dollops of whipped cream to the banana creme pie.

During a break in the action, he saw her slip out a side exit to the broad deck overlooking the lake. On impulse, he followed her. George rarely did things on impulse, but he couldn't stop thinking about his missed chance in the bakery. Besides, his dinner companions were all on the dance floor.

She didn't notice him at first, as she stood at the rail of the deck with her back to the dining room. A string of paper lanterns illuminated the deck, deserted now with everyone inside dancing. She faced the lake, which lay in placid splendor, bathed in moonlight. It was a soft summer night, the temperature just right, the breeze as gentle as a baby's breath.

George stood in the shadows, wondering what to say to her. Maybe his initial attraction to her had merely been a fleeting nostalgia, he thought. But no; judging by the way his heart sped up, the feeling was still there.

His stupid leg brace creaked. She turned quickly. "Oh!" she said. "I'm sorry, did you need something, sir?"

She spoke in a funny upstate accent. Back when they were kids, he hadn't really noticed that about her. "Hello, Jane," he said, stepping into the light.

She relaxed visibly at the sound of his voice. "George Bellamy. I saw you in the bakery earlier, but I didn't get a chance to say hi." A dazzling smile lit her face. "So…hi!"

"Hi yourself. I, um, should have said something in the bakery, but you seemed busy. I didn't want to distract you."

"I've been wondering about you all day, George."

Oh, boy, he thought. Maybe she'd felt the same magnetic attraction that had stricken him. "Jane—"

"Look at you! You're all better."

His heart sank as he realized what she was thinking. It had nothing to do with attraction. "Right," he said. "All better."

"It's kind of a miracle, huh? Last time we saw each other, you were in a wheelchair. Now you're standing there, ready to take on the world. And here *I* am, shirking again."

"Is that what this is?" he asked, all too eager to change the subject. "Shirking? It's very pleasant."

"Don't report me, okay? Old Mrs. Romano, in the kitchen, is a drill sergeant. I hate getting in trouble and letting people down."

"I can't imagine a girl like you doing that."

"Oh, believe me, I can be a lot of trouble." She fanned herself with her apron. "I just needed to get some air. Cigarette smoke bothers me."

It bothered him, too, so much so that he was unable to smoke like most men his age. Yet another legacy of the polio—the intolerance of smoking, thanks to his weakened lungs.

"Is your brother really dancing with two girls at once?" she asked, peering through the window.

"What can I say?" George inquired. "He's a man of many talents."

"How about you?" she asked. "Do you have talents of your own?"

"I keep them hidden," he said jokingly.

"Why?"

"Modesty. What about yourself?"

"I'm good at a lot of things," she said with a grin. "Like pie-cutting."

"That's admirable."

"Whipping cream," she added. "I excel at whipping cream."

"Not every girl can say that."

She giggled. Her gaze strayed to the window. Another dance was starting and the Darrow girls appeared to be exhorting Charles to stay with them.

"He's popular," Jane observed.

"You noticed. Does that bother you?"

"Not really," she said easily. "I'm not the jealous type. Besides, I have nothing to worry about. He's already half in love with me."

George was startled into laughter. "I beg your pardon."

"I'm not being vain, just truthful. Charles is half in love with me."

George was stunned by her frankness, and her confidence. And completely, unjustifiably envious. "And the other half?"

"Is waiting to see if the feeling is mutual." The moonlight made a beautiful bas relief of her face, accentuating its bone structure. Suddenly she didn't look like a local mongrel, but as refined as a princess.

"What are you waiting for?"

She touched her finger to her bottom lip. "Maybe I'm holding out for someone else."

He wondered if she was teasing—or if she was feeling the same electric attraction he was.

George gave himself a stern talking-to. Taking up with this girl would lead to nothing but disaster and heartache. She was a working-class girl with a troubled mother and a father who was just getting by. She had no education beyond high school. Nothing but blazing good looks and an innate personal charm that would one day make some man extremely happy. Just not a man like George Bellamy.

Besides that, Charles liked her, though the infatuation was bound to fade away by the time the leaves began to turn.

"You're wasting your time, holding out for someone else," George told her.

She moved close to him on the deck. "Are you sure? Are you absolutely, positively sure?"

Time stood still. Even the night breeze seemed to quiet as if the world was holding its breath. The chorus of crickets fell silent. George had the crazy sensation that his life had contracted to this one moment. He couldn't help imagining what it would feel like to put his arms around her. Would she feel sturdy and firm, or soft and willowy? He wondered what her hair would smell like, how her lips would taste. He was teetering at the edge of a cliff in the dark, about to take the plunge even though he had no idea what lay beyond.

And he didn't even care. For this moment, nothing else mattered but the girl standing before him. Passion and need swirled around him like a fog, obliterating everything that used to matter—common sense, status and background, education and family expectations.

George had never felt this way before. He'd *wanted* to feel this way about a girl. He'd certainly tried. Now he realized how different things were with Jane. This was no weak affinity contrived by his parents as they steered him toward an appropriate young lady. This was a raw and undeniable hunger he could not resist or combat in any way.

He took one more step closer. Exerting a huge effort of will, he moved with excruciating slowness. If he just grabbed her and kissed her with the full force of his passion, it might scare her. He didn't want to scare her. He didn't want to do anything but make her happy.

Now she stood just a heartbeat away. Her mouth was half-open, slack with anticipation. The air between them stirred as he whispered her name. He couldn't think straight. He couldn't think at all.

"Do you remember what you promised me, last time we saw each other?" Jane asked.

"It's been ten years."

"*I* remember. You promised you'd dance with me."

"As I recall, *you* promised I'd dance with you," he said.

"Aha. So you do remember."

He remembered everything. Every single second—the way she used to challenge and laugh at him. The kittens in the barn. Swimming in Willow Lake. Finding the tracers in his legs. Their first—their only—childish kiss. Everything.

"In that case," Jane continued, "you owe me a dance."

He was no good at it but a skillful performance wasn't the point. The moment he touched her, nothing else mattered. Nothing except his hand, snug against her trim waist. His other hand, holding hers. In that moment, he knew a happiness so complete, it made him laugh softly for no reason. Gazing down at Jane, he was lost in her, lost…

"There you are," Charles brayed from the doorway. "I've been looking all over for you. You out here stealing my girl?"

With a jolt of horror, George came to his senses and stepped back. "Uh-huh, stealing your girl. Good one, Chaz."

He hadn't met Jane's eyes. Later he would always wonder. If he'd looked, what would he have seen in her expression? Regret? Longing, confusion, or resentment? The fact was, he knew almost nothing about this girl and had no right to wish he did.

"I'd better get back to work," Jane murmured, and slipped inside.

Eighteen

⧽⧼⧽⧼⧽

A bittersweet nostalgia tinged the days of summer that year. All the Bellamys knew it would probably be the last time they would spend together as a family at Camp Kioga. By this time next year, George would be a Yale graduate. He would embark on his Grand Tour, the prize at the end of college. It was a tradition for young men of breeding to spend six weeks after graduation touring the great capital cities and countryside of Europe.

Privately George was glad to see the end of summer. It was painful seeing Jane Gordon every day, knowing she and Charles were secretly cultivating a love affair. He had to force himself to look the other way. Charles's ardor would fade with the season.

At last, summer's end arrived and the torment was coming to a close. Each year, the resort hosted a series of closing activities, including athletic contests, parties and sailing events, and a farewell songfest on the shore, with everyone gathered around a campfire.

The Bellamys went on a final sunset sail together. The wind was slow, but no one complained. Tonight, speed was not the point. The point was to absorb the splendor of the lake and surrounding wooded hills in order to keep a little piece of summer in their hearts to carry them through the winter.

"Sometimes I wonder what it would be like to live in a place like this, in an impossibly small town like Avalon," said Charles. "I think I should like it quite a lot."

"Nonsense," his father chided. "You'd be bored before the first frost."

"I don't know about that."

"I do. My sons are both going to be men of the world."

"Whatever you say, Father," George intoned, just to keep the peace. Honestly, he did want that. New York, Paris, Shanghai, even the ruined capital of Tokyo was said to have rebuilt itself after the war into the most modern city on the globe. He wanted to see the sights and meet people, write about the great issues of the day.

George's mother dabbed away a tear. "We've had such marvelous times here," she said.

"Yeah, like that time I got polio, just marvelous," said George.

"Not funny," said Charles. "People all over the place came down with polio."

Parkhurst Bellamy patted his wife's shoulder. "There, there, pet. We'll be back."

"I suppose we might, but never like this. Never the four of us as a family. My three precious boys with me."

"It'll be even better," her husband assured her. "Someday soon, the boys will be married. They'll have wives to bring and eventually, children of their own."

She sighed and leaned her head on his shoulder. "Do you hear that, my sons? You have a duty to your family."

They all laughed, though they knew she was only half joking.

Finally the day had arrived to say goodbye to Camp Kioga. As they cleared their belongings out of the bungalow and did a final walk-through, George felt a little queasy. He didn't know why, but he had a feeling he would not be back, despite what his mother said about future generations here.

Members of the camp staff were already swarming the cottages, getting them ready to close up for the season. He looked around for Jane, but didn't see her. Maybe she and Charles were sharing a private farewell. George pulled his mind away from the notion. He had no business speculating. Summer was *over.*

Their things were all loaded into the DeSoto, and Charles came loping up with his sloppy duffel bag, cramming it in the trunk. There was a suspicious ghost of lipstick on his cheek, in precisely the subtle coral shade favored by Jane Gordon. George had memorized the color, describing it in fine detail in his journal.

Hell's bells. He just remembered something. "I have to go back to the bungalow," he said. "I left my journal there."

"Oh, George," his mother said. "You'd forget your own head if it wasn't attached."

"I'll be right back." He walked quickly, trying not to favor his bad leg. He couldn't stand the idea of leaving behind his private notebook, in which he wrote his observations every night before bed. Some of the entries were merely prosaic, others profound; all of them were private. He'd left it in the drawer of the nightstand by his bed, along with his favorite pen.

Workers had already started on the bungalow, bringing out armloads of linens. In the bedroom, he found Jane Gordon, and froze. In her hands, she held the Moleskine notebook.

"I came back for that," he said, his gut twisting with anxiety. He couldn't tell whether or not she'd read any of it. Surely there hadn't been time. The idea of Jane reading his private thoughts—far too many of which were about her—made him furious. At the same time, he was fighting a fierce urge to kiss her, long and hard. He could barely look at her as he ungraciously snatched the journal from her. "Goodbye, Jane," he said tersely, and walked away.

Nineteen

George's son Trevor showed up the morning after the trip to the E.R. He brought his daughter, Ivy, who took one look at George and burst into tears as she collapsed into his arms. Then she spied Ross and squealed, leaping into a hug. "The family drama queen has arrived," said Ross, catching Claire's eye.

Ivy was adorable in every sense of the word—adorable to look at, a china doll with silky California-girl hair and a taste for bohemian chic; she had an adorable personality, too, with an air of complete sincerity and genuine sweetness. Though she greeted Claire with caution, she spoke kindly.

"Thank you for taking care of my granddad," she said.

"He's really wonderful," Claire said. "You're lucky to have a grandfather like George."

"I know." Ivy looked around the resort. "And it's incredible here. I'm glad we came, Granddad. The whole family will be here soon."

"In that case, I'm going to get some rest," said George, a gentle dismissal. "Later today, we can go into town together."

As they left the cottage, Claire said, "I have to go see the catering director. I'm organizing a special welcome dinner for the rest of your grandfather's family."

"That sounds nice," said Trevor. "Thank you."

"You're younger than I pictured you," said Ivy. "Have you been doing this kind of nursing for long?"

"Five years," Claire said. "I started right out of nursing school."

"It must be hard," said Ivy.

"Yes." Claire saw no reason to lie about it. "That's no reason not to do it, though. Every patient I've ever worked with has left me a gift." She smiled a little at Trevor's expression. "Not that kind of gift, despite what you might have been told. I mean, some part of their heart or wisdom, something to hold on to. My second private patient was a child, a nine-year-old named Joy. She's the one who convinced me to believe in miracles."

"She got better?"

Claire shook her head. "Not that kind of miracle. The miracle of what the human spirit can endure, and how much the heart can hold. I miss her. I miss them all, but this is not about me."

Ivy started to cry again. "She's fabulous," Ivy said to Ross, right in front of Claire. "No, I mean it, you are," she added, turning to Claire. "And Ross thinks so, too. I can tell."

"What I think," Ross said, "is we should keep the focus on Granddad."

"Yes. What happened last night? Why didn't he stay in the hospital? I thought you wanted him to get better," Ivy said.

"We all want that," said Ross. "We can't make it

happen, though. No one can. The doctor gave me a packet of information about this illness. It's grim stuff."

Trevor nodded. "I've been reading up on it, too. But are you sure this is right?"

"Hell, I'm not sure of anything. But at the hospital… We're not putting him through that. He just wants to be with us. In fact, there are some pretty specific things he wants. He made a list."

While Ross explained the list to his uncle and cousin, Claire headed to the main lodge. It was a relief, knowing Ross was an ally now.

George had an appointment in town, and he was dressed for a business meeting.

"You're seeing a lawyer, Granddad?" asked Ross. "Seriously?"

"Is there any other way to see a lawyer?" asked George.

"You have Mr. Matlock in the city," Ross pointed out. "He's been your lawyer for years."

"This is a small bit of work, an amendment to a document," George said. "Hardly worth bothering Sherman with."

"What kind of document?"

"Now that you're back, I'm giving you power of attorney, provided you don't use it to force me back to the hospital."

A look of apprehension shadowed Ross's face. "What about Trevor?" He gestured at his uncle.

Trevor raised his hands, palms out. "It's all yours."

"I want it to be you, Ross," said George. "For a number of reasons. There has always been a particular clarity between us, ever since you were a boy."

Ivy's eyes grew large. "Mom's going to have a cat."

"Ivy," her father said in a warning tone.

"Just saying." She turned to her grandfather. "We can all go into town together. Dad and I will explore the town and catch up with you later."

"That sounds like a splendid plan," said George.

The nameplate on the door indicated a partnership of three—Melinda Lee Parkington, Wendell Whitcomb and Sophie Shepherd. Ross held the door for Claire and his grandfather and they stepped into the reception area. The desk was occupied by a girl who resembled an escapee from an anime convention—pink hair, facial hardware, black lacquered nails. The Happy Bunny sign on her desk said Daphne McDaniel and the slogan, They Don't Pay Me Enough To Be Nice To You.

She looked up at the three of them, and focused on George, who held a thick legal-size envelope. "Can I help—"

"Make it happen, Wendell," said an angry male voice. A guy with flame-red hair strode out of one of the law offices. "It's what I'm paying you for. The mother of my kid took off with him and I have my rights." He paused at the reception desk. "I need to book a meeting next week," he stated.

"I'll get right on that," Daphne said coolly. "*After* I help these people. So have a seat, Logan."

"I'm kind of in a hurry."

She fixed him with a don't-screw-with-me stare. "Twizzler?" she asked, pushing a large glass candy jar in his direction.

He grabbed one and stepped aside.

"All righty then," she said to George. "I'm sure Sophie's eager to meet you. Right this way," she said, taking them to a conference room.

A moment later they were joined by the lawyer George had retained. Sophie Shepherd was blonde, chic and pregnant. Her hair was pulled back in a sleek chignon, and she wore pearls and a dove-gray suit with a pink silk blouse draped over her enormous belly. After greeting each of them with a handshake, she set a legal file on the table.

"I see congratulations are in order," said George.

"Thank you."

The sight of a pregnant woman never failed to give Claire a pang. Having a baby was out of her reach; it would be the height of foolishness to have a child when Claire had to be prepared to run at any moment. Still, she couldn't help envying women like Sophie.

"Your first?" asked George.

"My fifth, actually. I have two grown kids from my first marriage, and my husband Noah and I adopted two of our own. So this makes five for me. And speaking of kids, I need to let you know something in advance. I used to be married to Greg Bellamy."

"Charles's boy?" George smiled. "That's delightful."

"Granddad, he was her *first* husband," Ross pointed out.

"Oh, er, then…not so delightful," said George.

"I only bring this up in the interest of disclosure," Sophie explained. "My two oldest children, Max and Daisy, are Bellamys, so in that respect, there's a family connection. I've since remarried, but I wanted you to be aware of it. If you prefer to work with one of my associates, I'll understand."

"Not at all," George assured her.

Claire caught his eye. "George, if you don't need anything else, I'll wait outside." She didn't need or want to be privy to the details of any legal arrangements of her patients. She slipped out and made her way to the reception area.

The receptionist was just saying goodbye to the red-haired guy called Logan. Claire tried not to speculate about his dilemma, but she couldn't help herself. He was almost blindingly handsome in a youthful, intense way. She surmised from his angry remarks that some woman had taken his kid somewhere. Claire told herself this was a perfect example of the complications and pain she was avoiding by being entirely on her own with no ties to anyone.

Yet another of the many lies she told herself.

Daphne scribbled something on the back of a card and handed it over. He stuck it in his pocket and turned on his heel. The receptionist eyed him over her cat's-eye glasses as he yanked open the door and left. Noticing Claire's attention, she said, "Everybody needs a little eye candy." She opened the glass apothecary jar of Twizzlers. "Help yourself."

Claire smiled, but shook her head. "No, thanks." She paged through a copy of *Coastal Living,* her gaze lingering on photos of summer picnics and lakeside gazebos. Did people really live like this, surrounded by flowering shrubs and fancy patio furniture? She set the magazine aside and picked up the *New York Times,* giving herself a reality check by skimming a story about criminal proceedings against a mob boss.

The meeting with the lawyer didn't take long. By the

time they exited the conference room, George and Sophie seemed like old friends.

Sophie handed them a flyer. "My husband's band is performing at a benefit later today. It's a concert in the park, to raise funds for the local library."

"Your husband's a musician? How nice."

"Only as a hobby, but he loves it. Noah's the drummer—definitely not the star of the show. He's a veterinarian."

"Don't let her fool you," Daphne said. "Noah's a good drummer, and the band is *great*."

The invitation read, "Inner Child—One Performance Only. Sponsored by the Friends of the Avalon Free Library."

"What kind of music does the group play?" Claire asked. She pictured an elegant piano quintet...and drums.

"Mostly ska and old-school punk rock," said Sophie.

Daphne grinned. "Sophie, you need to work on your rocker-chick image."

They all went together to the library event. Claire was fairly confident George wouldn't want to stay long. He tired so very easily. Yet today, an afternoon nap and a dose of meds gave him a second wind.

The event was in full swing when they arrived. An outdoor stage had been set up in the park surrounding the library. It was a fine, breezy evening. Wind-borne seeds floated in the sunlit air, and delicious smells emanated from the booths and stands. Ross pushed his grandfather's wheelchair, passing booths for face painting, people dressed as characters from books, volunteers selling paving bricks with patrons' names, a stand offering *kolaches* from the Sky River Bakery. Claire watched families strolling around together, and she noticed Ross watching them, too.

"I love it here," Ivy exclaimed. "Ross, don't you love it here?"

His gaze tracked a pair of kids running around with balloons. "This is the kind of thing soldiers think about when they're overseas," he said.

He had a way of saying things with unvarnished frankness. She wondered what it would be like to simply speak her mind and not have to think about every word that came out of her mouth. Sometimes Ross seemed to sense she was holding back, but he'd never know how much. Every moment she was with him, it grew harder and harder to hide herself. More than anyone she'd ever met, he saw her heart, and the prospect frightened her.

A sharp blast of feedback screeched from the tall speakers. She saw Ross flinch, and suspected it was fallout from being at war. But he seemed to shake off the tension and turned toward the stage.

A guy with shaggy hair, wearing ripped, skinny jeans and a tight T-shirt stepped up to the mic. "I'm Eddie Haven," he announced, "and we're Inner Child." He introduced the band members—a girl named Brandi on bass, Noah Shepherd on drums, and on keyboard, Rayburn Tolley.

With a jolt of recognition, Claire studied the keyboard man. "That's the cop who pulled us over on the first day," she reminded George.

"Indeed it is. Ross and Ivy, your mothers set the law on us, did they tell you? That young man pulled us over."

"Good Lord." Ivy turned to Claire. "I'm mortified."

"He'd been told I was kidnapping George."

"At least he didn't give you a speeding ticket," George pointed out. "That was decent of him."

"I'd like to dedicate a song to your favorite librarian and mine, Maureen Davenport," Eddie Haven announced. He made a grand flourish on his electric guitar while the applause crescendoed. Looking pleased but hardly comfortable with all the attention, a young woman stepped on stage and issued a brief welcome.

"It's thanks to our community support that our library fund is growing," she said. "There's still a lot of work to be done. And don't forget, we're still looking for a sponsor who would like naming rights for our new genealogy annex. I know it's an ambitious request, but in working to save the library, I've learned to be audacious."

"That's what we love about her. She's bringing sexy back to the library," Eddie said, and was answered by wild hooting and applause.

The first number was an upbeat ballad that soon had a swarm of kids jumping around in front of the stage. Claire noticed George cringing a bit, and she gestured at Ross. They moved away from the speakers.

"Not to your taste, Granddad?" Ross asked.

"Apparently not, but I'm glad I came."

The music changed to a slow, emotional love song, and couples started dancing. Eddie Haven had a compelling voice, raspy with sentiment. "Go," said George, "the two of you. Dance."

"Granddad—"

"You heard the man," said Ivy.

Ross rolled his eyes, but clearly decided against further argument. "May I?" he asked Claire.

Despite the artificiality of the situation, she felt an

unbidden thrill. He held her decorously, but it still felt like a forbidden embrace. She loved the warmth of his hand in the curve of her waist, and the hardness of his shoulder as she leaned into him. Maybe it was his background as a soldier, or his profession as a medical rescue pilot; when she was with him, she felt irrationally—but gloriously—safe. It was embarrassingly romantic, under the circumstances. *Snap out of it,* she thought, but ignored her own inner voice. Nothing she told herself eased the crush she had on this man.

"Your hair smells like flowers," he whispered.

She tilted her head to look up at him. He seemed to hold her a little closer, and she enjoyed a few lost minutes, a brief fantasy of being with him, out in the open. When the song ended, they looked around and saw that George's chair was empty. After a momentary panic, they spied him with Trevor and Ivy, apparently chatting up the town librarian.

"What do you suppose they're talking about?" Claire asked.

"I bet he's propositioning her." Ross paused. "I think she likes it."

As they watched, the librarian hugged George, then stepped back, dabbing at her eyes. George was beaming as he returned to them. Ivy's eyes were shining with pride, and Trevor looked thoughtful.

"What's going on?" asked Ross.

"Well, now," George said, settling back into his chair. "That was a successful exchange indeed. I managed to help the library and cross off an item on my list."

"How so, Granddad?"

"I wanted to make an indelible impression," he said.

"What better way than to buy the naming rights to the library annex?"

"What," said Ross, "you're getting a building named after you?"

"Not exactly," said George, his expression softening. "After your father. The Pierce Bellamy Annex. Has a nice ring to it, don't you think?"

Claire watched Ross's throat work as he swallowed hard. "You're really something, Granddad," he said.

George nodded. Claire could tell by the way he was holding his head that he was done for the night. She caught Ross's eye, and a message passed between them.

"Let's call it a night," Ross said to the others, and they headed back to the lake.

Although George had rallied after the hospital visit, Ross sensed the progress of his disease in subtle ways. A misused word, a dropped utensil, or frozen moments in the middle of a conversation. Granddad slept a lot, but when he was awake, he seemed restless. The hospital incident had ripped away the last pretense of normalcy.

Ross couldn't believe it, didn't *want* to believe it, but he was moving into acceptance mode now. It broke him up to think of it, but what else could he do?

Trevor and Ivy went to town to meet with Jane Bellamy. They wanted to help her organize the family reunion, which was coming together fast. No one talked about the reason for the urgency, but it was on everyone's mind.

Ross's goal was to give his grandfather a good day. This morning, Granddad had said he wanted to go sailing on the lake.

"Give me a hand with the boat," Ross said to Claire. "We'll get everything ready, and then Granddad can join us." The catboat had a sleek hull and a good padded seat astern for his grandfather. It reminded him of the little boat they used to take out on Long Island Sound, back when he was a kid.

She followed him to the dock. "Just let me know what to do. I've never been boating before."

He caught himself staring at her legs and having completely inappropriate thoughts about her. "Watch that mooring rope, will you?" He indicated the rope loosely coiled around a cleat on the dock. "Grab the line. Do it *now*."

"What? What line?" Even as she spoke, the rope slithered into the water and the boat bobbed away. "Now what?" she asked, watching the boat in dismay.

"You were in charge of the rope, you go get the boat," he said.

"I'm not jumping in."

He shot her a look, then kicked off his shoes and peeled his shirt over his head. The water was cool and ribboned by sunlight, and within a few strokes, he'd grabbed hold of the mooring line and towed it back to the dock. "Thanks a lot," he said, levering himself up out of the water.

"No problem."

When he saw the way she was staring at his bare chest, he forgave her completely. And then he left his shirt off for a while. He hadn't taken his shirt off for a woman since getting a wound checked out after that last firefight. This felt totally different, even though she was a nurse. Her expression was anything but nurselike.

"Okay, you can help me seat the mast," he told her.

"You're going to have to tell me what to do."

"Try to keep your balance," he said. "I'll hold up the mast, and you guide it to that hole right there, in the bow. Watch your fingers."

She was nimble and cooperative, and he felt himself relaxing in spite of himself. In short order, they'd lowered the boom and raised the sail. Shading her eyes, she gazed up at it, her face lit with a sense of accomplishment. Ross regarded her for a long, quiet moment. He was crazy about her face, her eyes. He didn't want to be, even though it had been Granddad's plan all along. But sometimes, in unguarded moments, he could imagine her being everything to him. Damn.

As if she felt his gaze, she lowered her hand and looked at him. "What?"

"Nothing. Just checking you out and having a sex fantasy about you."

"Ross."

"I know, I'm a jerk. So sue me."

"You're talking nonsense." Her cheeks lit with a blush, which pleased him inordinately. She turned away. "How about you show me how to…I don't know. Batten the hatches. Rig up the lines."

Okay, so she didn't want to flirt with him. He showed her how to rig up the lines, then sent her to get his grandfather. Granddad looked remarkably the same as he had long ago, in his Top-Siders and V-neck cardigan and a frayed hat he'd owned for years. "Everything shipshape, Skipper?" he asked with a grin. Claire helped him with his life vest. Ross dropped the centerboard, cast off the lines and shoved away from the dock. A light breeze caught the sail, tugging the small boat gently toward the middle of the lake.

Manning the tiller, his grandfather gave the rudder a few good sculling pumps, with Claire providing the muscle to his direction until they found a good point of sail.

She looked completely thrilled. "Are we sailing yet?" she asked, her eyes dancing.

"We're sailing," said Granddad. "You'll want to sit up on the rail when it starts to heel."

"Any second now." Ross motioned her to his side. Almost on cue, the boat heeled. Bracing an arm behind her, he showed her how to counterbalance the motion. "Careful there. A boat like this wants to throw you in the water if you don't balance it out."

Her nearness felt good, her warm, bare shoulder pressed next to his. Her dark hair fluttered softly against his jaw, and its floral scent surrounded him. He let the simple pleasure of the moment fill him up. Instead of wishing he could get his grandfather back to more tests and treatments, he simply surrendered, just the way Granddad wanted him to. Sunshine on the water, a breeze in the sail, Claire beside him, Granddad's ringing laughter, the sweet trickle of water under the hull.

"Sailing is awesome," Claire said. "I had no idea. It's exhilarating and relaxing at the same time." She beamed at George. "This was a treat."

All in all, it was a golden day, filled with moments Ross hoped he'd never forget—his grandfather, in his funny Gilligan hat, his face lifted to the summer sky. And Claire, her eyes filled with wonder as she experienced sailing for the first time.

But when they moored the boat to the dock, Ross

could tell his grandfather was tired. "I'm going to lie down for a bit," George said.

"I'll help you," Ross offered.

A vase of freshly cut lilacs stood on a table, their scent wafting on the breeze. The lake was bright blue, reflecting its ring of willow trees at the edges. Granddad took off his deck shoes and settled back on the bed, letting out a sigh.

"You all right?" asked Ross. "Warm enough?"

"Just right," Granddad said. "Thank you for today."

"Are you kidding? I always liked sailing with you. I was six years old when you first took me out. We sailed until dark that day, remember?"

Granddad nodded, though his eyelids drooped with fatigue. "You asked me where heaven was. And my answer's still the same. Right here, my boy. Right here with you."

Claire watched Ross leave the house and walk to the end of the dock, lowering the boat's sail and zipping it away in the hull. She would have approached him and offered to help, but she could tell, even from a distance, that he was crying.

As a nurse, she often faced the balancing act of giving a family member what he needed, and allowing him the privacy to reflect, grieve, fall apart and then pull himself together. Grief had a pace of its own, as individual as each person and as deep as each loss. She would never be hardened to people's grief, but it was familiar to her. Expected. Anticipated, even.

Yet watching Ross—big shaking shoulders, big clenched fists—she felt a fresh twist of sympathy. She cared about him so much; it hurt to see him hurting. Until now, she'd been able to detach herself from other people's pain, yet Ross was different. Ross mattered far too much to her. The approach she'd used in the past wasn't working here. She was supposed to maintain that professional distance. Instead an intimate bond was forming with this man, almost against her will.

She very much feared she was falling in love.

Books and movies depicted the event as joyous, the start to a lifetime of happiness. In Claire's case, it marked a new roadblock. She needed to find a way around this situation.

Whoever had coined the term *falling* in love had been spot-on. There was that same sense of momentary weightlessness that came from a fall, and the same inevitability. A fall was something that couldn't be stopped or even reversed. And when you landed, pain was involved.

Twenty

Over the next several days, the rest of George's family arrived—his son Gerard from Cape Town and Louis from Tokyo, along with their attendant spouses and children.

They came to Camp Kioga like vassals summoned by a monarch, with George ensconced in a big armchair in the resort lobby to greet everyone. The reunions were tearful, for the most part, but tinged by occasional laughter and a constant stream of conversation. With each new arrival, George seemed to grow more comfortable, exuding contentment.

This, Claire knew, was the power of a family. The intimate ties of blood and history were woven together with an emotional bond, forming an invisible safety net. George wasn't going to find a cure for his illness, but another kind of healing was taking place. She could tell Ross saw it, too, as he watched his uncles and aunts and cousins dispensing hugs and tears and laughter. As awful as a terminal illness was, it did offer a chance for a family to come together. Claire was glad the Bellamys had decided to seize that opportunity.

Some of the relatives took rooms in town at the historic Inn at Willow Lake, which was owned by another Bellamy—Charles's son Greg and his wife, Nina. Most found accommodations at the resort. The lakeside cabins and bunkhouses were soon filled with people who had come to see George.

Trevor's wife and his other kids showed up. Louis and his wife were both amped up on coffee and jet lag. Gerard was twice divorced, with numerous children. A few of the relatives exuded an optimism that seemed either false or forced. And some, understandably, were just plain scared. The imminent death of a loved one had a world-shaking impact on people, and Claire knew for certain that the worst kind of terror was always borne of love.

Once all the relatives had arrived, everyone gathered at the main lodge for a welcome dinner. "Don't try to keep track of everyone," Ross advised her, surveying the busy lobby. "Eventually you'll figure out who's who."

"It's wonderful to have a big family."

"It can be a mixed blessing," he said.

"I've always wondered what people mean by that—*mixed* blessings."

"You're about to find out." He extended his arms to an attractive blonde woman who approached them, heels clicking on the slate floor. Claire guessed she was in her fifties, striving hard to look younger—but not too much younger. She had the taut, angular face and puffed lips of a woman who was no stranger to cosmetic surgery, and a smile that was studied and quite devoid of warmth.

"Claire," said Ross, "I'd like you to meet my mother, Winifred."

Hence the lack of warmth, thought Claire. "Nice to meet you," she said.

"And my aunt Alice," added Ross, presenting a woman who was slightly younger and plumper than Winifred, though equally fashionable and dour. "She's Ivy's mother."

"We're the ones who asked the local police to check on George," said Winifred.

At least she didn't pull any punches. "He's lucky to have a caring family."

"Yes, he is." Winifred subjected Claire to a thorough study. "Help me understand. Why on earth would a young woman simply take off with an elderly man?"

"I appreciate your candor," she said. And honestly, she did. It was so much worse to pretend. "The answer is, I'm a licensed private duty nurse, and George engaged my services."

Winifred and Alice exchanged a glance, heavy with doubt. "If you truly wish to help, you'll persuade him to return to the city," said Alice. "That's what he needs—people who want to do him some good." The two women turned resolutely and headed for the dining room.

"Speaking of which," Ross broke in, "I think that waiter is trying to find a taker for the last two cocktails." He motioned them toward a guy with a tray, and steered Claire in the opposite direction. "That would be the *mixed* in mixed blessing."

"I don't take their suspicions personally. They're worried about your grandfather."

"They're worried about his money."

"It's not so much about the money. It's more about holding on to what they have."

"You're a nicer person than most," he said.

"Thanks, but I can't agree. Just stating a fact."

"Christ, can you not take even the smallest compliment?" he said. "I just can't figure you out, Claire."

"Excuse me," she said, flustered. "I need to check on George. I think they're almost ready in the dining room. Do me a favor—bring him in when I signal."

She hoped George would like the welcome dinner. Everything had been arranged at the speed of light. In doing the planning for this, and for many of the other things on George's list, she'd had a strong dose of small-town life—and found it to her liking. She had to admit, things were easier when you forged relationships and connected with people. The notion made her a little sad, because a town like this could only be a temporary home for her. It took only a few phone calls to come up with a menu of George's favorites—including dessert from the Sky River Bakery, an extra microphone for the sound system and a karaoke setup.

Claire savored the expression on George's face when he entered the dining room. The other resort guests looked on with expressions of surprise and delight. Miss Millicent Darrow was present, but like Claire, she kept her distance, instinctively knowing this was family time.

"Thank you all for coming," George said from his place at the head of the table. "You honor me by being here. You make me remember everything good and beautiful life has to offer. I came here with a list of goals I hoped to accomplish. But honestly, if I don't fulfill a single one of them, my life will be complete anyway. Because of you I will always be here. Always. Because I have a family."

He lifted his glass, which was filled with a bright con-
coction of Midori, lime and vodka. "Special thanks to
whoever created the Bellamy Hammer. I've always
wanted a cocktail named after me."

"Hear, hear." Glasses were lifted in a salute.

"And now I must ask you to bear with me," said
George. "It's one of the world's small mercies that I will
be performing for one night only. This is something I've
always wanted to do—sing to my family."

"You've got to be kidding," said one of the teenage
grandsons.

"I'm afraid not, my boy. Now, help me to the stage."

The ensemble played a gentle riff as two of the boys
guided him up the three steps to the corner platform and
handed over a microphone. The glow of light from
behind limned his sparse, pale hair and outlined his silhouette, as he perched on a crooner's stool. The piece
started with a glissando on the piano and a shimmer of
percussion, followed by a series of familiar rhythmic
chords on the guitar. Then George launched into his ren-
dition of "L-O-V-E" by Nat King Cole. The first few
notes started with a waver of uncertainty. His voice was
thin, and after the first line, he hesitated.

"I'm sorry," he said, his shoulders hunching.
"I…wanted to be better for you."

"Granddad, you're fine," said Ivy, hurrying up to the
stage. "You're perfect." She signaled to the piano player,
and the song started again. This time, she sang along with
him, and turned the karaoke screen to face the audience,
urging everyone else to join in. Clearly bolstered by the
support, George sang in a smooth, surprisingly tuneful
baritone. By the end of the first chorus, everyone had

joined in, along with a blare of brass from the karaoke recording. Some were drunk with cocktails or wine, others with emotion. Egged on by everyone in the dining room, they ran through the song again. The second time around, George looked loose and comfortable, as though channeling Dean Martin.

Claire sang along softly, swaying a little to the classic melody. A few couples got up and danced. She glanced at Ross, and saw him kicked back in his chair, grinning as he sang, clearly enjoying his grandfather's moment. The set ended to appreciative applause, to laughter and, of course, tears.

You're all so lucky, Claire thought, surveying the family. Even the ones breaking down with sobs were lucky, because their lives had been enriched by George Bellamy, and as hard as the grief was, they would always have the love he was giving them now.

"I won't inflict any more of my singing on you," he said, seating the mic back in its stand. "I'll just claim my youngest granddaughter for a last dance, and then call it a night." He took the hand of his granddaughter Jessica, heavyset and self-conscious. The girl was red-faced from crying, but she went willingly enough to the dance floor, and they joined the other couples there.

A shadow fell over Claire, and there was Ross, holding out his hand.

She dabbed at her eyes with a napkin. "He's just so wonderful."

"Dance with me. He'll like that."

She had a moment of hesitation, then gave in for George's sake. Ross was a natural on the dance floor, exuding confidence. When it came to Ross's future,

George did not have a thing to worry about, Claire reflected, feeling dizzy with the closeness of him, his scent and the sturdy feel of his arms around her. Some woman was going to fall head over heels for his grandson one of these days.

Correction, she thought. Some woman already had. Unfortunately it was the wrong one.

The number was slow, and she rested her cheek lightly against his chest. She didn't even know she was doing it; the motion felt so natural and right. Maybe he felt the same way, because his hand at her waist pulled her just a little closer. She should have seen this coming—that one day she'd meet a man and lose her heart. She'd been so careful, though. How had this happened?

Reality intruded in the form of a vibrating pocket.

"Sorry." Ross pulled back and took his mobile phone from his breast pocket. The display was lit with a message she probably wasn't supposed to see, but he turned it in her direction. "OMG, U TOTALLY LUUURVE HER."

"From my cousin Ivy," he said easily.

Claire burned with embarrassment. "She's a big tease."

"Maybe. But sometimes she's right about things."

Now that the family had arrived, everything grew more complicated. They all but took over the resort. The girl cousins moved into a multibunk cabin called the Saratoga Bunk, and the boy cousins took its counterpart, the Ticonderoga Longhouse. Families settled into the A-frames along the waterfront. But the main gathering place, where everyone gravitated each day, was the Summer Hideaway, where Granddad could often be found relaxing, listening to music, challenging people to chess or Parcheesi, or reading a book. Conversations were often punctuated with his laughter, and sometimes when Ross closed his eyes, he could pretend everything was normal for whole seconds at a time.

The big reunion of both sides of the Bellamy family was still in the works, but there were plenty of other things to do in the meantime. Granddad proudly introduced his brother to all the guests. He wanted everyone to explore Camp Kioga, experiencing it as he had as a boy. The days were filled with boating and fishing, hiking and swimming, even archery and marksmanship. George couldn't always participate, but he seemed to take a special joy in seeing the others discover the timeless rhythm of summer. In one of the more bizarre developments, Uncle Charles organized a shooting party—not for skeet, but for targets, at the camp's rifle range. It was a big sport in these parts. It turned out Granddad was a keen shot with a bolt-action rifle.

With quiet competence, Claire orchestrated George's life from hour to hour. Granddad slept more and more, just as the doctor had predicted. Yet he didn't seem to be in pain, and his waking moments were happy ones. There was peculiar weightiness to each moment, and a melancholy sense that they were making memories, because all too soon, that was all they'd be left with. Ross knew he would never forget the sight of his grandfather on the porch, surrounded by his family, telling stories about his boyhood summers here. Granddad was a consummate storyteller. He'd made a career of it in newspapers, and now he brought his keen eye for detail and powers of recollection to summarizing the events of his life.

Everything was dictated by how he was feeling and

what he wanted. One evening, they all headed into town to the local ball field. Avalon had its own team—the Hornets—which was part of the Can-Am League of Independent Baseball. The team was expertly managed by Dino Carminucci, who had been part of the Yankees organization for years. And the club's biggest success story was that their star pitcher, Bo Crutcher, had gone on to a successful career with the Yankees.

Ross's friend, Natalie Sweet, came up from the city. A sports writer with a growing reputation, she was always up for a ball game. She didn't pull any punches when she saw Ross. "You look totally different," she said.

"Different how?" he asked.

"You seem… Okay, this is going to sound weird, under the circumstances. You seem comfortable here."

"Believe me, nothing about this is comfortable. But I have to keep reminding myself of what's important. My grandfather, and making sure every day is a good one."

"Wow. That's so…un-Ross-like. You've always been an action hero. Now you're Mr. Mellow."

"Claire's a good influence on me." The admission slipped out, surprising him as much as it did Natalie. "Hey, speaking of which. You were going to see what you could find out about her."

Natalie hesitated, then said, "Yeah, I've been busy. And look, buddy. We've got a baseball game to watch."

Surrounded by billboards for local businesses, the playing field was flooded with stadium lights. The bleachers were jammed and the concession stand busy selling hot dogs, beer and popcorn. Nasally organ music whined over the PA system, and excitement crackled in the air. The Hornets were playing a team called the Bremolos, and apparently it was a heated rivalry.

A local girl named Chelsea Nash sang the national anthem, followed by the traditional command—*Play ball!*

"Holy cow," said Ross's cousin Micah, shading his eyes, "that's Granddad down there."

"Ladies and gentlemen," said a mellow-voiced announcer, "we've got a VIP in the house to throw out the first pitch tonight."

"Cool," said Micah. "I betcha Granddad—"

"Just listen," hissed his sister, Hazel.

"He's back in Avalon for the first time since—wow—since 1955. Please welcome Mr. George Bellamy!" The announcer elongated the name, and applause erupted from the stands.

Arm raised in greeting, wearing an honorary Hornets jersey, Granddad walked out to the mound under his own steam. The sight of him in the glare of the stadium lights, with the organ playing the "Charge" theme, brought a lump to Ross's throat. He looked so frail, yet his smile was broad as he wound up and threw a pitch to the catcher.

"Okay, not totally humiliating," said Micah.

"Granddad's awesome," said Hazel, and started to cry.

Applause accompanied George's walk off the field.

Ross climbed down from the bleachers to find Claire. She had his cane at the ready, and the wheelchair parked nearby. "Thanks for that," he said, knowing she had organized it.

"It was my pleasure," she said, flushing a little.

They hadn't spent much time alone together since the dancing. Ivy had been teasing him endlessly about having a crush on Granddad's nurse, but Ross didn't mind. He *did* have a crush on her. In the midst of this family tragedy, he had an ill-timed but undeniable crush. Granddad had noticed, of course. He'd always been able to read Ross like a book. Ross tried to brush the issue aside, claiming he wanted all his focus to stay on Granddad.

"Nonsense, my boy," the old man had said. "There's never a bad time to fall in love. Look at me and Millie."

"You're in love?"

"You find that so unlikely?"

"I find it…quick."

"It's the only way to be when you don't have all the time in the world."

"You're going to break her heart."

"I explained my situation to her. It was pleasant, at first, to have someone who didn't know I was sick, but as we…as things progressed, I realized she deserved fair warning." He was quiet for a few moments as he took off his glasses, wiped his eyes, then cleaned the lenses with a corner of his baseball jersey. "She told me to go ahead and break her heart. Said she'd rather be with me for a summer than not at all. She's a remarkable woman, that Millie."

Ross saw Charles and Jane Bellamy in the bleachers, waving vigorously. George excused himself to go say hi. Jane held a drooling great-grandbaby in her lap. Ross had met a number of their family members—their younger son Greg and his wife, Nina, Charles's granddaughters, Jenny and Olivia, and their husbands and babies. Charles's grandson, Max, worked part-time at the resort. There was a granddaughter, Daisy, who had gone to live overseas for a time, and their eldest son named Philip, who was out of town on an extended trip with his wife.

At this point, they all seemed like relative strangers to Ross. They were nice enough, but strangers.

"What are you thinking?" asked Claire, watching him.

"All these new Bellamys—Granddad is just so eager for me to bond with them."

"Of course he is."

"A bond like that can't be forced or hurried," he said. "It's the kind of thing that grows over time together, shared experiences."

"He knows that," Claire assured him. "But it has to start somewhere."

True, thought Ross. But the feeling was bittersweet, because behind the sentiment was the knowledge of the void his grandfather would leave behind.

Granddad rejoined them a moment later, looking tired but happy. "It was a good pitch, wasn't it?"

"Outstanding," said Ross. "You always had a good arm."

"You're being too generous." He took his cane from Claire. "Another item accomplished."

"Way to go, George."

"Oh, I'm just warming up. There's lots more to do. You don't think I've forgotten about the skydiving, do you?"

A 150-mile-per-hour free fall with his grandfather strapped to him was well outside of Ross's comfort zone.

Granddad joked that if the fall killed him, he wouldn't have to worry about the rest of his list. Ross had found a company in nearby New Paltz with a flawless safety record and an array of the best equipment. Duke Elder, the owner-operator, was ex-army like Ross. He'd been a paratrooper during his term of service and later got his pilot's license, certified for a number of aircraft. In addition to the parachute jumping, he also ran an air transport service to Newark, Logan and LaGuardia.

They went to the airfield on a cloudless day. The family gathered around and watched a short instructional video. George looked as excited as a kid in his jumpsuit, goggles and helmet.

"A helmet, eh?" he'd observed wryly. "I'm not sure I get the point. If something goes wrong at ten thousand feet, I'm going to break more than my head."

Claire caught Ross's eye. "Then make sure nothing goes wrong."

"I see she doesn't hesitate to nag you," George observed. "I like that in a woman."

"You're joking, right?" Ross asked.

"It's a sign that she cares," George replied.

"It's a sign that she's a nag," Ross said.

"Or how about this?" Claire said in exasperation. "It's a sign she gets annoyed when you talk about her as though she isn't there." She stepped forward and clasped George in a hug. "Have fun," she said. "It's going to be amazing."

"I want to go." Ross's cousin Micah looked yearningly at the aircraft. Granddad took him over to check it out.

Winifred challenged Claire. "Did you put him up to this?"

"Why would I do that?"

"Well, I should think that's obvious," Winifred said.

"Mom." Ross sent her a low-voiced warning.

She ignored it. "The sooner George is gone, the sooner she gets her hands on his fortune."

"Excuse me," Claire said, and she walked away.

"There's something off about that girl," his mother said. "I can't put my finger on it. She's hiding something."

"Yeah, like the fact that you're out of your gourd." Ross lowered his goggles and went to board the plane with his grandfather. Everyone else stayed behind, in a small cluster of worry near the landing site.

The ascent was swift and loud. Granddad held himself very still, gazing out the hatch window. He caught Ross's eye, leaned over and handed him a tiny, folded bit of paper. On it, he'd written down a line from Plato's *Republic*. Ross stuck it deep in his pocket.

They reached thirteen thousand feet, and it was time to go. Just before stepping through the hatch, Ross checked in with his grandfather one final time. "You sure?" he mouthed.

Granddad nodded and gave a thumbs-up. He mouthed the words, "Your move." Behind the goggles, his eyes shone, and he was laughing, though the wind drowned out the sound. Ross was so damn grateful he was giving this to his grandfather. As he secured the tethers for the tandem jump, he just hoped like hell he wouldn't screw up the ending.

Ross had made hundreds of jumps; he'd felt the rush of exhilaration and the roar of air past his ears during training and drills. But sharing the 150-mile-per-hour fall with someone he loved—was a high he'd never felt before. The risk and trust involved in this filled him with tenderness and awe.

When his altimeter beeped, he gave a hand signal for "Go time." He extracted the pilot chute from its pouch and threw it into the surrounding airstream. The bridle of the pilot chute then pulled the deployment bag out, the lines releasing one stow at a time until fully stretched. With a dramatic gust of air and swift upsweep, the main parachute inflated.

Everything decelerated to a slow drift under the canopy. Ross steered with the control lines, giving his grandfather as smooth a ride as he could manage. He could feel Granddad's excitement like an electrical current. When he depressed both toggles, the wing slowed and the two of them swung forward, momentarily pitching the flight angle of the wing upward, like a brief ascent to heaven.

Twenty-One

The glow of success that emanated from George after the parachute jump was infectious. "I have a new rule for everyone," he declared at dinner that night. "Do not—I repeat, do *not* save your peak experiences for later. Have them now."

Claire found herself looking over at Ross, and quickly glanced away. George's words stuck with her, though, pointing out a painful truth. She wasn't just saving her peak experiences for later. She was saving *everything* for later.

She was sitting on the dock, in the moonlight, when Ross came to her. "What's up?" he asked.

"I have a slight…housing dilemma."

"What's that?"

"Miss Darrow."

"Millie?"

"Does that freak you out?"

"Are you kidding? It inspires me. In fact, this could work out well for us."

"I don't understand." Ah, but she did. She did.

"You're homeless," he said simply.

"I could try to sneak in…"

"And risk interrupting something? Forget it."

"I can bunk with your cousins. Ivy said there's plenty of room—"

"No way. I'm not going to pass up a chance to get you alone."

Her heart skipped a beat. "Why?"

"I'm done," he said simply.

"Done what?"

"Done pretending I don't think about you all the time. Done trying to keep my hands off you."

"Ross—"

"That's as honest as I know how to be, so it's up to you. Say the word, and I'll walk away and you won't hear me say this again. You have to tell me, Claire. The decision has to come from you." He paused, regarding her with an intensity that felt…physical. "I think you want to," he said. "I really think you want to."

She'd spent years trying to avoid exactly this situation. She'd succeeded, too, but not because she was so strong or smart or resourceful. It was because she hadn't met Ross Bellamy. Now that she had, she'd never be the same. Now that she'd felt his arms around her and his lips on hers, a door had been opened. She'd known she could never go back to her old in-between life, never forming more than a temporary or superficial connection with another soul.

"Well?" he prompted.

She shut off the part of her mind that was rational, stood on tiptoe and kissed him. There was a lifetime of yearning and need in the way she clung to him, which should probably warn him off. Instead he held her close, and she was filled with a feeling that was new and fresh and exhilarating.

If he walked away right now, she would never forgive herself.

His hands skimmed down her back and then pulled her closer, and the warm pressure of his touch stole her breath. She felt everything with a heightened awareness, not just his embrace but each tiny detail—the slight breeze on her skin. The fresh smell of the lake. The soft *churr* of a creature in the underbrush. The moon itself shone with a peculiar sharpness, as though she'd taken some drug. She hadn't, though; that was the extraordinary thing. Here was the world stripped bare for her, perhaps for the first time.

They walked hand in hand to his cabin, lost in a haze of desire. Even so, she took in the silver flow of moonlight on the lake, the flicker of a distant campfire, and the faint pulse of music from the main lodge across the water. She hadn't seen the inside of his place yet, and was not surprised to find it uncluttered and relaxing. He poured two glasses of ice wine, as if he'd somehow known it was her favorite. Out of long habit, she took her customary sip and prepared to set it aside. But the sweet, frost-cured wine was so delicious. One sip was not enough.

"Cheers," she said softly, and drank the entire glass.

"Now you're talking." He brought the bottle into the bedroom.

Into Ross Bellamy's bedroom. Oh, this was a huge step for her. He had no idea how huge. And he had no idea how much she wanted it. The lake breeze blew softly through the screened window, ruffling the pale curtains. In the dim light, she was drawn to the personal things in the room, like three different ties draped over a shirt on a hanger, as if he'd been trying to figure out which one matched. A stack of books on the bedside table—*The Complete Book of Fly Fishing,* a fat, dog-eared bestseller, and a slim volume with the unexpected title, *Meeting God in Quiet Places.* There was a shelf with things from his pockets—cell phone, scribbled notes, a knife.

And then there was the bed. The frame was made of vintage birch with a hand-painted rustic scene on the headboard. The linens were a pile of luxury, including a thick duvet and a folded Pendleton blanket. Her dress slipped away when he untied the sash. She heard him catch his breath, and it was a complete turn-on. She was so used to hiding herself, she hadn't been prepared for this sense of liberation. As for Ross, he was fresh out of the military and looked it.

They lay down together, and they shared everything—nervous laughter, sighs of delight, endless kisses, more wine, some good-humored but urgent fumbling with the condom. Claire was filled with an overwhelming urge to tell him everything, to shed her secrets like articles of clothing, stripped from her body, piece by piece. He was shaking as he sank down slowly, too slowly, and she lifted herself to meet him halfway and clasp him close, as close as she'd dreamed of. There was a moment of hesitation, a slight wince of pain, but she drew him closer still. He froze, holding himself with sinewed arms, his face in shadow but his voice a rasp of disbelief as he said, "No way."

"Way," she whispered. "I'm so glad I waited for you."

He kissed her and moved with exquisite slowness,

creating a deep rhythm of intimacy that made her feel as though she'd suddenly taken flight, and then burst into a thousand pieces. She cried out—his name, perhaps, or maybe it wasn't a word at all, and floated back to earth like a leaf on a breeze, settling safe in his arms. Neither of them spoke for the longest time. It wasn't necessary. He had discovered one of her deepest desires, and she surrendered it gladly. Gratefully, even.

Finally, here was someone with the uncanny ability to see who Claire really was, because he saw her heart. The secrets she gave up were the secrets of her heart— the loneliness and longing for someone who would love her. The sweetness of his embrace. Claire couldn't be honest with her words, but she could with her touch.

It was addictively pleasurable; it was a kind of searing pain, released from a hidden place deep inside her. This relinquishing of control was what she'd been protecting herself from. And no wonder. It was dangerous. It made her completely vulnerable. It made her feel as if she might die at any moment. It made her feel as if she might live forever.

Twenty-Two

Awakening slowly, filled with the pleasurable fatigue of intense lovemaking, Ross reached out to gather Claire closer to him.

His arms came up empty. Where the hell was Claire?

Granddad—some emergency with Granddad.

Ross yanked on a pair of jeans and sprinted barefoot across the compound. His grandfather was sleeping peacefully. Maybe she went to the lodge to get coffee.

He returned to his cabin to grab a sweatshirt and put on some sneakers. At the main pavilion, there was morning coffee. There were resort guests in tennis whites and golfers heading out for the day. But no Claire.

The morning desk clerk said she'd requested a ride to the train station. She'd left only a verbal message that there was a personal emergency, and she wouldn't be back. The early train had left more than an hour ago.

Thoroughly confused now, Ross wondered if he'd scared her off. It was possible. He'd had the shock of a lifetime when he'd discovered she was a virgin. *Was.* She was so *not* a virgin anymore, not after last night. He'd been her first, which totally blew his mind. Maybe it blew her mind, too. Maybe she'd freaked out and gone… where? He dug his phone out of his pocket and dialed her number. After a few rings, a generic voice-mail message greeted him. He hung up.

Then he called Natalie. When she'd come up for the baseball game, she said she hadn't had time to look into Claire's background. Maybe by now she had.

"I was wondering if you found out anything about Claire," he said.

"Oh my God, you slept with her."

Damn. How had she figured that out? "It gets worse. She took off. Pulled a classic disappearing act," he said.

"Ross, I'm really sorry, but I can't say I'm surprised. She's not… I'm pretty sure she's got a lot to hide. I was going to tell you at the baseball game, but…"

"Wait a minute. You knew at the game? Why didn't you say anything?"

"It didn't seem right. You seemed so happy with her, Ross."

"But she's a liar."

"I don't know what she is. Just…maybe her being gone is for the best, you know."

"I don't know, Nat. I don't know a damned thing."

He found his grandfather on the porch, drinking a cup of tea and staring at the compartmentalized pillbox with his medications.

"Claire usually helps me with this," he said, frowning in confusion.

"Claire's gone," said Ross. "She left word at the front

desk that she wouldn't be back, and took the early train to the city. No explanation, no goodbye. Nothing."

"That doesn't sound like her."

"Funny you should say that." Ross took the compartmentalized tray of pills and found the care notes on the chart. Every detail was documented with the time of day and Claire's initials, and her signature at the bottom of each page. *C. Turner.* Until this moment, he'd never even seen her signature. It seemed strange that he never had. Last night, as he'd held her and whispered in her ear, he'd had the sense that he knew every single thing about her. Right.

"Why is it funny?" asked Granddad.

"Because when it comes down to it, we don't really know what she's like." Ross gave his grandfather the same pills he'd had the day before and filled in the time on the chart. If Claire didn't return, they'd need to find a replacement.

Last night, everything had been vivid and clear. The attraction that had been growing between them all summer had turned into even more than he'd hoped that it could. He'd fallen asleep with the certainty of holding his destiny in his arms. Right again.

"I thought I had her figured out, Granddad," he said. "I was even starting to think I had *us* figured out."

"Son, once you have a woman figured out, the fun is over. There's nothing wrong with having more to discover."

"Yeah, I'm getting the feeling she doesn't want me or anybody to discover more about her. She gave me so damn little, now that I think about it. I should have asked for more."

"Perhaps," said Granddad. "Then again, perhaps she's already told you everything you need to know."

That she was quiet and thoughtful. Almost freakishly modest, devoted to her job, played a mean hand of pinochle and had a sly sense of humor. That she was vulnerable—yes. And cautious beyond all imagining. In a way, she reminded him of war refugees in Afghanistan, whose eyes were haunted by traumas they refused to talk about.

"What if she doesn't come back?" he asked his grandfather.

"Then you go to her," Granddad said simply.

"Like a stalker," said Ross. "I don't think so." He was already coming to terms with losing her. It wasn't right. They'd met under the most contrived of circumstances. Fresh out of the service and facing the loss of his grandfather, he'd been in no shape to take on an intense relationship.

"Baloney," Granddad burst out. "Son, I've given you plenty of advice through the years, but if you've heard nothing else, please hear this. Don't hesitate when you know something is right."

"But—"

"Let me finish." Granddad raised his hand, its tremor a grim reminder of his illness. "There are more opportunities lost to hesitation than I can say. Chances slip by while you're standing there weighing your options or rationalizing choices or putting together a damn decision matrix. If your heart tells you something, who are you to argue? There is more wisdom in one beat of the human heart than in an entire think tank filled with brain matter."

"Granddad, I appreciate what you're saying, but Claire and I aren't like that."

"I've been watching you together. The two of you are

exactly like that." He paused, gazing out at the scenery, aglow in the morning sun. "Powerful feelings tend to scare us," he added. "And when we're scared, we deny them. All I'm saying is, don't let all the extraneous nonsense in your head distract you from that which was true." He picked up his notebook, and a breeze wafted through the pages. "Believe me, I know whereof I speak."

Ross noticed the left side of his grandfather's face was pulled downward, and he was starting to slur his words. "Maybe you should lie down, take a nap."

"I'll sleep when I'm dead," he snapped. "And I'm not kidding about that. Look, I haven't lived a perfect life. Far from it. I'd like to claim I've gained wisdom through the years, and maybe I have, but there's really only one thing I can leave you with, and that's this. Live. Just live your life. Quit worrying about what people will think, and fling yourself into things. Make mistakes. It's amazing how much I missed because I was afraid to make a mistake. But if you realize you're going to make mistakes no matter how careful you are, then maybe you'll be less afraid."

Afraid? Ross wondered if he was afraid.

"Do the things that matter," Granddad continued. "I once spent a week of my life paving my driveway. The old one was a neighborhood eyesore, pitted and buckling from tree roots, and weeds were poking up through the cracks. So I spent an entire week supervising a crew of workers. I oversaw every aspect of the work, even dictating how the pavers were placed and the height of the shrubberies. Damn. I wish I had that week back," he concluded. "I'd spend the time so differently. That's all I'm saying. Don't trade your life for crap that doesn't matter."

"I won't forget," Ross assured him.

George scowled at a half-read novel Claire had left on a table. "You already are forgetting."

Ross reminded himself that no matter what his problem was with Claire, he had to stick by his grandfather. "You want to talk about what's really bugging you?"

Granddad was quiet for such a long time, he thought he might have nodded off. Then he said, "It was Jane. The rift between me and Charles."

"It was her fault?"

There was one beat of hesitation. Then he said firmly, "It was my fault. But Jane was…" He took a breath. "Charles and I were both in love with her. And of course, he was the brother who won her heart."

"Why do you say 'of course'?"

"Because he was always the decisive one. I tended to hesitate and analyze everything, asking myself how each hypothetical would play out. Charles, now, he was the reckless one, the plunger. He never questioned. He tended to feel something and then dive right in. Anyway, he fell for Jane and set about winning her heart. I fell for Jane and spun out the entire relationship in my head, concluding it would be a disaster. All I could think about was how different we were. I came from a background of privilege, and she was proudly working class. Our parents barely spoke the same language. None of this meant a thing to Charles, because he was an idealist. He believed that with enough love and commitment you can conquer the world."

"And how about you, Granddad?"

"I was the cynic. I believed the world made a mockery of love and sincerity. By the time Jane proved me wrong, it was too late to matter. She already belonged to

Charles. There was a moment when I thought I might have a chance, but…but I was wrong."

Again, a hesitation. A world of unexpressed thoughts lived inside that long silence.

"Granddad?"

"I simply don't know where to start."

"You've already started. You told me about coming here when you were a boy. And again when you were in college. I figured out from what you said that both you and your brother were sweet on Jane."

"It was all so long ago." His grandfather's eyes turned misty with memories.

There was something he wasn't saying. Ross couldn't put his finger on what that might be.

George's eyes were shut now. Ross got a blanket and gently laid it over his lap, to keep him warm when the shadows crowded in.

Twenty-Three

New Haven, Connecticut
Autumn 1955

In the journalism department at Yale, George was at the top of his class. He was known for his smarts. He'd made editor of the *Yale Daily News*, a campus paper that rivaled anything a college had ever produced. His colleagues on the paper called him Clark Kent because his investigative skills were legendary. His rivals called him "Clark Can't" because he seemed to have no luck with the ladies.

There was a reason for that, but no one would ever know it. George had given the girl he loved to his brother.

That was how he came to think of the situation. How he would always think of it. No one else was aware of his sacrifice, because he kept the truth in the deepest, most secret corner of his heart. Yet George's brother had no idea George had handed Charles his heart's desire.

There was no point in discussing it. George didn't want his sacrifice to be known. He wasn't a candidate for martyrdom. He was just seeking a way to escape into the future and stop dwelling on the past, stewing about things that might have been, if only he'd been more confident. More assertive. More willing to follow his heart.

Then again, he rationalized, a romance with Jane Gordon wouldn't have gone anywhere, anyway. They came from different worlds and would have been destined to break each other's hearts by summer's end. So it was Charles, not George, who would suffer that heartache.

Their parents would probably never know of the drama and rivalry surrounding Jane Gordon. Contrary to their mother's oft-expressed hopes, neither brother found himself tempted by the Darrow sisters. The Darrows and the Bellamys had harbored aspirations of a dynastic union between the families, but despite their best efforts, nothing materialized.

From time to time, someone would ask him why he was in such a lousy mood so much of the time, or why he didn't throw himself wholeheartedly into the fun and challenge of his senior year at Yale.

Many seniors were melancholy, already regretting the end of their time at Yale. Not George. He couldn't wait to be finished. To be gone. Because now, Jane Gordon was in the picture. It wasn't enough that the past summer had been filled with her. She was in New Haven, too, living with relatives and looking after her mother. Even worse, George had heard she had a job on campus. It was amazing to him that he'd never encountered her before.

George was determined to create an amazing future for himself. In order to do that, he had to quit thinking about Jane Gordon. He had to pretend he felt nothing for her, and he had to stop wondering if she felt the same way. They had never spoken of their feelings. He might be wrong. Might be making an assumption. Might be reading more into the situation than was actually there.

Except he wasn't. There was a small, barely acknowledged part of him that knew the truth—something unspoken but powerful had sprung up between him and Jane. He knew this as surely as he knew the principles of objective journalism.

And so did she, though she'd never said a word about it. Her attraction to him couldn't be seen or touched, but he felt it the way he felt the autumn rain on his shoulders as he crossed the campus between classes and seminars. Occasionally he wondered if he'd only imagined it. Then he'd remember the expression on her face, that night on the deck overlooking the lake, and he'd feel sure she was fighting an undeniable attraction as hard as he was.

George and Charles both belonged to different fraternities and different eating clubs at Yale. This was unorthodox within the same family, but the brothers instinctively felt the need to live separate lives. Their schedules rarely intersected, and Charles's obsession with athletics kept him busy at the boathouse for rowing practice, the tennis courts or golf course. George was a member of the shooting club and did no other sports. He saw very little of his younger brother. He dared to hope that Charles had come to his senses and realized it was better for everyone concerned to stop seeing Jane Gordon.

At a mixer with Vassar early that fall, George had the first inkling that she was still in the picture. He was waiting his turn at the bar when he heard one of the Darrow girls— he often forgot which was which—speaking sotto voce. Clearly she didn't realize George was nearby.

"Didn't you hear?" she said. "Charles Bellamy is seeing some local girl—a townie. They say she works as a chambermaid at the provost's residence."

"That can't be right," another girl said. "Charles Bellamy? He would never…"

George had heard enough. With a stone-cold feeling in his stomach, he approached his brother the next day.

He found Charles hard at work—at the campus squash courts, lobbing his way to a victory over his best friend, Samuel Lightsey. It was a golden Indian summer day, the temperature reaching toward eighty. Despite the heat, autumn was in full regalia, the quadrangle carpeted with leaves that scrambled before the breeze.

Watching his brother—strong and athletic, his every move shaped by the grace of self-confidence—George could not stave off a feeling of envy. The polio had taken much from him, but what he regretted the most was the loss of speed and grace. Although more than a dozen years had passed since he'd been stricken, he could still remember what it felt like to run like the wind, to master any sport he attempted.

All of that had gone by the wayside. George did his best to not let it matter. Ultimately, though, regrets washed through him every time he encountered a physical challenge. He pulled back from anything that might show the world his weakness. The swimming pool therapy and the exercises that had gotten him out of the wheelchair only went so far. He was grateful enough to have regained the ability to walk. He wished he could find a way to keep himself from yearning for more.

It didn't help to have a brother who was a natural and

effortless athlete, who dominated every sport he attempted. Charles never flaunted his prowess, but he didn't hide it, either. He loved sports and challenges too much to pretend he wasn't any good at them.

At the end of the match, Charles simply raised a fist in victory and then shook hands with his opponent. They noticed George watching from the sidelines, and Charles waved him over.

"Hiya, big brother. Just finished a match. You should have seen the way I schooled this fellow."

"I'll get you next time," Samuel vowed. "Gotta bounce. Meeting my fiancée for dinner. Gwen doesn't like me to be late."

George sensed Samuel's pride in his new status as a bridegroom-to-be. He had proposed to his sweetheart a couple of weeks before, and he'd been walking on air ever since.

Charles slung a towel around the back of his neck and found a seat in the shade. He took a long drink from a canteen and then offered it to George, who shook his head.

"Hey, Sam asked me to be his best man. How about that?" asked Charles.

"Terrific. Seems like guys are getting married left and right these days."

"Seems that way." Charles twirled his squash racket.

"I guess we Bellamy boys are late bloomers when it comes to girls," George suggested. "Unless there's something you're not telling me." He didn't want to have to repeat gossip, but he needed to figure out if there was any truth to the rumor.

"Well, now that you've brought it up," said Charles,

"there's something I've been meaning to tell you. I wanted you to be the first to know."

George already did know. In some part of his mind, the news had already embedded itself. Asking for an explanation had been a mere formality. He sat very stiffly, keeping his face from giving anything away. "Go on," he said.

"I got a girl," Charles said. "The most wonderful girl in the world, and I'm going to ask her to be my wife."

No, thought George. *Don't say it.*

"It's Jane Gordon." Charles blushed and grinned.

George's heart hit the pavement. His palms began to sweat, and his mouth went completely dry.

Charles didn't seem to notice. "Remember, I started falling for her last summer at Camp Kioga," he said. "She lives in New Haven, you know."

George did know. "I heard she does some kind of domestic work," he said dully.

"She keeps house for the school provost. I can't wait for you to get to know her again, now that we're all grown up. She's swell, like she's always been, ever since we were all kids. It's only natural we'd fall in love."

George shook his head. This sounded like a disaster in the making. "It won't work, Charles. I know she's…" An angel, he thought. A dream in the flesh. "…a nice girl. But it could never work."

There was one beat of hesitation, long enough for George to realize Charles wasn't completely naive about these things. But he held his ground. "We'll make it work."

"Mother and Father will never stand for it."

"They'll get used to the idea. Hell's bells, all they have to do is get to know her and they will love her as much as I do."

"You are delusional. This is our parents we're talking about. They'd disown you before they'd stand for you marrying a—a chambermaid." George tried to maintain a reasonable tone.

"Housekeeper. If they disown me for finding the girl I love," Charles said stubbornly, "then they're not the people I thought they were."

"Don't make them choose," George warned his brother. "They'll never forgive you."

"That's baloney." But a note of worry crept into his voice.

"And what about her family?" George persisted. "They're not going to approve, either. They wouldn't want to see their daughter trying to fit into a family where she doesn't belong."

"She belongs with me. Damn it, George, we're in love. Don't tell me there's anything wrong with two people being in love."

"It's not love," George snapped. "You're infatuated with each other. It'll fade away—"

"It'll last forever. I feel it in my bones. I thought you'd be happy for me."

"Happy to see you marching straight into disaster?" George demanded. "I just don't want you getting hurt." As he spoke, he wondered if there was another reason for his objection, buried deep inside.

"What hurts is being apart from Jane," Charles insisted. "Wait until you fall head over heels in love. Then you'll understand."

George crushed his hand into a fist, rubbed his bad leg hard. "Give it a rest, Charles. You are young. There's no hurry."

"That's why we're going to wait until next summer to get married."

Married. Charles and Jane, *married.* "It's not going to work."

"It's Jane, for God's sake. We've known her forever. We were the Three Musketeers, remember? One for all and all for one."

"We were kids, playing a game. This is life. Marriage isn't a game. It's playing for keeps. You'll end up miserable. She's a domestic, don't you get that? She comes from nothing. She has no education, no refinements. She'll drag you down—"

"Hell's bells." Charles glared at him. "At least I'm not a coward. You're a cripple, George, but not in the way you think. You're crippled by your own fears."

George couldn't believe what he'd just heard. "Go to hell," he said.

"Say, you just got me all riled up, George. I was going to ask you to be my best man—"

"Don't," George warned him.

"I won't," Charles said. "And I don't need your blessing. I'd like to have it, but I don't need it."

George was appalled by Charles's plan. It felt wrong in too many ways to count. But Charles was determined; he forged recklessly ahead, picking out a date the following August, planning an open-air ceremony at Camp Kioga. The guy had stars in his eyes.

Maybe, thought George, it was Jane who would see reason. Yes. He would talk to Jane, make her see what a mistake this was.

He waited one evening outside the provost's residence. It was a cool autumn twilight, the sky heavy with unshed rain. Visitors, faculty and administrators came and went. Then he saw a janitor come around the side of the building and realized the hired help would use a different entrance. He went to the mews behind the row of grand houses and leaned up against an old carriage house that had been converted into a garage. A row of dustbins and garbage cans leaned against the building.

He wasn't sure what he'd say to her; they hadn't seen each other since closing day at camp last summer. He halfway talked himself out of approaching her. Then, just as the lights came on in the windows of the big white house, a few people exited through the back. No one seemed to notice him as they headed to the street.

He picked out Jane immediately: a slender girl in a dark dress, with an apron and a heavy-looking satchel. Although he didn't want to feel it, his heart took a leap. She walked slowly, with a shuffling gait. He looked around, seeing students strolling between dining halls and libraries. In sharp contrast to Jane's somber dress, they looked lively and fashionable in argyles and sweater sets.

"Jane," he said, approaching her, trying not to limp.

"George!" Her face lit with a smile that made him catch his breath. "This is a surprise."

He glanced around. Then he felt ashamed for feeling furtive. "I didn't mean to startle you," he said. "I wanted to talk about, uh…" What an idiot. What a tongue-tied idiot.

She slowed her steps, tilted her head to one side. Something flickered in her face—recognition. Yearning. A tacit acknowledgment of the unspoken emotions that had flown between them last summer…before Charles had commandeered her attention.

George cleared his throat, battled his nervousness into submission.

"It's about Charles," he said.

Her eyes narrowed. The wind plucked at her apron. The expression on her face indicated that she understood just what the issue was. "Then shouldn't you be talking to Charles?"

"He won't listen."

She tossed her head and walked on, leaving the campus behind. George had no choice but to follow her. And a tiny part of him was willing to admit a twinge of curiosity about the way she lived, in a part of New Haven he'd never seen, despite his years as a student. The air smelled of rain, and the wind picked up, ripping dry leaves from the maples lining the streets. Within a few blocks, they came to a working-class neighborhood of nondescript buildings and row houses.

"Then why come to me?" she demanded.

"Because you will."

"What makes you think that?"

"Jane, you understand the way the world works. You know marrying Charles would tear both our families apart."

Her face paled. "He told you we were getting married?"

"Don't do it, Jane. It would destroy our parents—"

"Be honest, George. For once in your life, be honest. Tell me what your real objection is."

He regarded her, keeping his face devoid of expression, hiding everything. "You don't really want to know that."

The rain started in earnest, sheets of big drops. They took shelter in the doorway of a linen shop that had closed for the day. The breeze lifted her hair in whimsical tendrils, creating a crown of autumn-colored curls. Instead of flinching from his anger, she took a step toward him. There was a terrible unspoken plea in her eyes, a mixture of pain and passion and a longing that mirrored his own. She took another step, and he had the strangest fantasy. The shop window behind her displayed a draped ivory tablecloth, and for a second it resembled a bridal veil, spread out behind her. She stood so close he could practically taste her, the lips full and soft-looking as she said, "Yes, George. I do."

With her *yes* filling him completely, George forgot where he was. He swept his arm protectively around her, and that was his undoing. Her nearness and the feel of her next to him turned into a consuming fire, fed by all the moments of self-denial, finally burned to ashes by the simple, stark honesty of her touch. His will was not his own; desire became a force larger than himself. He could no sooner stop it than he could stop the wind. He grabbed her by the upper arms, hauled her against him and crushed his mouth down on hers. At last, he thought. At last.

A sound came from her—resistance? Surrender?— and there was a thud as her satchel hit the ground. Her fists dug into his shirt.

George tried to ease away. This was his brother's girl. Some small corner of his brain acknowledged that—his *brother's* girl.

But something kept him from letting go.

Jane. Jane held him there, clutching his shirt, kissing him with the same hunger he felt.

And then something shifted. A change in the wind, lashing like a ribbon of ice.

No, he thought. No no no.

With an effort that felt physically painful, he stepped back, holding her at arm's length.

She blinked against the driving wind, and tears streamed from her eyes. "George—"

"Damn it," he said, too afraid to hear her out. "We can't…." He fumbled for the right words. "I came to stop you from marrying my brother."

She stared up at him. She looked beautiful, shattered, her eyes begging him for something he didn't have in him to give. "George," she said softly. And then even softer, her voice all but drowned in the squeal of the wind. "You know what will stop me."

He did know. And it was the one thing he could not offer.

"Nothing but trouble can come from this," he said, his heart turning to stone even as he spoke. "Leave the Bellamy family alone, Jane. I'm asking you—"

"And that," she said, snapping the spell like a dreamer suddenly disturbed from sleep, "is why I refuse to do as you say."

"Jane—"

She picked up her satchel. "If you care about your brother, you will forget this ever happened."

"If *you* cared about him, you wouldn't have let me kiss you," he shouted above the wind.

"I didn't let you."

"No, you begged me for it."

Her face paled to a dull white. "If anyone is going to ruin anything, it's you, George. Unless you find a way to be the brother Charles needs you to be, then everything will be ruined. You have to understand that I want you—"

"No," he said. "Don't say any more—"

"I want you," she persisted, "to be happy for Charles

and me. To dance at our wedding as we celebrate our love."

"Your love?" he asked incredulously. "Your love?"

"Charles loves me," she said. "He's the one who dared to say it." With that, she tugged her shawl more tightly around her. Then, in a whirl of wind and icy sleet, she walked away with a curious dignity, her head held high, despite the lash of the rain in her face.

He called her name but the wind snatched it away. Her words echoed in his head. *He's the one who dared to say it.* Even louder was the roar of the words she didn't say— she had not said that she loved Charles.

Things were tense for the Bellamy brothers all that winter and into the following spring. George and Charles avoided each other, drifting further and further apart. George had made no secret of his disapproval of Jane. He had been a complete idiot about it, to be sure, but he couldn't unsay the words he had hurled at Charles. Nor could Charles unsay the things he'd leveled at George— coward. *Cripple.*

Ever since then, the brothers had dealt with one another on a perfunctory basis. Their manner toward each other was like an early frost—cold and brittle, though not very deep.

George's final year of schooling was challenging, and his plan to go to work abroad materialized. He was offered a chance to work at the *International Herald Tribune,* a prestigious paper headquartered in Paris.

Charles was more and more absent from the school social scene. He either didn't notice or didn't mind that people gossiped about him for having a "townie" girl-friend. George's parents found out about the situation and despaired over Charles, but he would not be swayed. The Bellamys clung to the hope that Charles was swept up in an infatuation that would wear off.

George wasn't so certain; Charles could be stubborn. George kept his own pain hidden behind a mask of disapproval. He steered clear of the provost's residence, not wanting to encounter Jane. He still believed Charles was making the mistake of his life with this girl, but he was done trying to interfere.

Until one windswept night in late March. Winter that year clung to the northeast with stubborn talons. Only the week before, there had been more snow. People worried aloud that springtime would never come. Freezing rain slung itself sideways against George's window, reminding him inevitably of another stormy night in the fall, and a kiss that still haunted him no matter how many months had passed.

As an upperclassman, he had the privilege of a single private room on the ground floor. His desk was situated below the single window. A narrow, Spartan bed was set against the opposite wall. He was up late as usual, working on a paper for a demanding professor. The rhythmic clack of his typewriter and the zip of the carriage return accompanied the din of the storm outside.

At first he didn't hear the knock at the door. Then the noise penetrated his consciousness, an urgent rapping. Mystified, he opened the door.

"Jane?"

"Please, I need to come in."

He stepped aside. "You're soaked to the skin."

She was crying, shivering from the cold. "George," she said through chattering teeth. "Oh, George."

"Over here," he said, grabbing her hand. Her skin was wet and icy cold. "You need to warm up, or you'll catch your death." He brought her over to the big iron radiator, which exuded a dry heat. "It's after midnight. What the hell is going on?"

She was trembling so much she had trouble speaking. "It's…it's Charles. And me. Both of us. We quarreled, and it's over between us, and the buses aren't running and I didn't know where else to go…" She shook with cold and with sobs that seemed to come from the deepest part of her.

George went to the door, looked one way and then the other. The hallway was completely empty. It was an infraction of the worst degree to have a female in one's room, though in practice it was quite a common occurrence.

Not for George Bellamy, though. For him, this was a first.

To his relief, no one seemed to be around at this hour. He shut the door quietly and turned back to Jane. Her face was pale as milk, her lips a vivid, alarming blue, and she convulsed with shivers.

He snatched his terry-cloth swimming robe from its hook on the back of the door. "Get out of those wet things," he said.

Her hands shook so much she couldn't unfasten her own buttons.

"Here," he said, "let me."

His hands were shaking, too. He forced himself to concentrate on the task at hand. She wore a shirt dress fastened in the front by nine buttons. He counted them as he worked his way from north to south.

The soaking wet fabric clung to her chilled skin. He

peeled it away, trying to maintain a clinical detachment, not really succeeding. He draped the wet dress over the radiator, and steam rose from it, creating an eerie light in the room.

Beneath the dress she wore a slip so sheer he could see everything beneath it. Without so much as a beat of hesitation, he peeled this off, as well. And even covered in goose bumps, even shivering and sobbing, she was unbelievably beautiful.

Swearing between his clenched teeth, he wrapped the big robe around her, held her close and rubbed her vigorously. Water from her dripping hair seeped into the shoulder of his sweatshirt. She felt like heaven in his arms.

She started to speak in broken phrases but was still too cold and upset for coherence. She had been drinking, too. He could smell the faint, yeasty essence of beer on her.

And all against his will, he was flooded with desire. He tried to focus on what she was saying. Over and over again she said, "We quarreled. It's over. He doesn't love me after all. I'm left with nobody to love me."

"Hush," George said, cradling her head against his chest. "Hush, it'll be all right." He knew he ought to ask her what happened with Charles, but the truth was, something else was happening here and he didn't want to say anything to stop it. He'd let an opportunity slip past before, and he wasn't about to do it again. Instead he let the soothing, whispered words come without thought. "Hush, Jane, it'll be all right. I'm here. *I* love you."

Her breath stopped, halting mid-sob. She gazed up at him, her eyes luminous in the glow from the desk lamp. "George?" She offered his name as a question, or maybe a supplication.

He couldn't think when she gazed at him like that. All

he knew was what his heart told him, with no regard for common sense. He was in love with her. He had been for a long time, but never allowed himself to express it until now. Simply saying the words unlocked a mystery that had hidden inside him all his life. Now he knew for certain what love felt like.

"Yes," he said, cradling her face between his hands, talking between kisses. "Yes, it's true, I love you. I never said anything because of Charles, but now I can tell you—I love you. I always have."

The robe parted, and he yanked off his sweatshirt one-handed over his head, filled with a wild need to feel his flesh next to hers. She was still chilled, but soon warmed in the press of his embrace, and within a few moments, a fire flared.

In the tiny, cramped dorm room, the only place to go was to the bed. He lay her down and kissed her with a long, searing kiss, half-drunk with wanting her. She was everything—the world, the universe, everything. He touched her everywhere and she was still crying, but softly now, and every few moments she would say the words "Please." And then "Don't." And then, "Stop."

Please don't stop.

George couldn't have stopped even if he had wanted to. The fire would not be put out. She was everything he'd ever wanted, every dream he'd ever had, and he was not going to stop. Ever.

The night went on and on. They were by turns urgent and then tender, impossibly slow and irresistibly quick. Emotion and fulfillment flowed like a river between them, and George finally knew the true meaning of ecstasy.

Did she know she was his first? He'd always been awkward with girls and self-conscious about his bad leg, and he'd never had a serious girlfriend. Now he was glad his heart had made him wait for Jane. He wasn't certain whether or not she realized that, and whether or not it mattered. At one point—he was sure he had not imagined it—she leaned down and touched his withered thigh, anointing his flesh with her tears.

George couldn't be sure he was doing everything right. He was too embarrassed to ask, so he focused on Jane and took his cues from her. If he touched her one way and her breathing changed, or if she made a tiny involuntary sound or clutched at him, he knew he was on the right track.

He felt drawn to her in so many ways. As kids, they'd clicked together like matching pieces of a puzzle. Even when he was recovering from polio that second summer, when he hated everything in the world including himself, she hadn't given up on him. She'd forced him to push to the edge of his limitations. To push beyond. When he saw her again last summer, so very different, yet fully recognizable, she'd taken his breath away. So much so that he'd been unable to speak.

That had been his fatal error. He'd missed his chance with her while Charles stepped boldly in. George regretted that moment so much, the hesitation that had cost him his heart. He would tell her he was sorry. He would spend the rest of his life making it up to her.

The rest of his life.

Suddenly the idea of making a life with Jane Gordon did not seem so insane. All his stupid prejudices fell by the wayside. The thought of stepping past artificial barriers erected by his parents struck him as incredibly liberating. No wonder Charles had been so convinced the world would embrace his romance with Jane.

Charles.

George wasn't ready to think about his jilted brother just now. Jane filled George's heart to overflowing. For the moment, everything he had to give was hers.

Though they scarcely spoke as the night pulsed away, moment by moment, they drew closer than mere words could ever bring them.

By the time they slept, replete, intoxicated with love, lying across each other in a state of dazed exhaustion, George was finally able to face the truth—his heart was lost entirely. The future he'd imagined for himself was gone now, like an unremembered dream.

Later in the morning, he awoke to an empty room. The swim robe was hung on the back of the door.

George sat up, squinted at the blinding flood of sunlight slipping into the room around the edges of the window shade. He went to the window, raised the sash and then the window itself to look out over the quadrangle. A host of songbirds greeted him. The storm was over, leaving a world washed clean. He could even smell the springtime—damp grass and budding flowers. Overnight, winter had gone away.

A sparkling layer of dew lightly blanketed the quadrangle. Few people were out and about at this hour. The cross-country team, in white shorts and V-neck undershirts, jogged past in a cluster. Ordinarily George would feel a pinch of envy at the sight of those well-honed bodies, graceful with the innate self-confidence that came from physical accomplishment.

Not this morning, though; not with the memory of the night before lingering so fresh in his mind. As she had that first summer after the polio, Jane had made him look past his limitations and celebrate the things he could do.

After last night, he had the feeling he could do anything.

"Hey, Bellamy, you putting on a show or what?" someone yelled, startling George from his thoughts.

He realized he'd been standing buck naked at the open window, lost in memories of his night with Jane.

"That's me," he yelled to his friend Jeffords, who was walking toward the dining hall. "A real showboater." He wondered how it could be that the world had changed overnight, and no one but him seemed to notice.

He turned back to the room, studied the slant of sunlight across the bed. The sheets and covers had been twisted every which way. Just looking at that bed brought back every touch, every kiss, every intimate detail of their night together. He could not believe how close they'd been.

At weddings people spoke of two becoming one. George had always considered that a lot of hot air. Each person was a separate entity, bound into his or her own skin.

Last night he'd learned otherwise, learned it was possible to break free of one's own self and cross some mystical divide to join with another. It wasn't just the sex, either. There was something even more powerful at work, something George hadn't been certain he believed in until last night—love.

Finally he came to understand why writers and artists through the ages created their work as a monument to the simple human notion of love. Men had waged war, crossed oceans, scaled mountain ranges, all for the sake of love. Epic poems, vast sculptures and even whole palaces had been created to celebrate it.

George Bellamy understood at last.

Whistling through his teeth, he grabbed his towel and robe to head across the hall for the showers. He paused and buried his face in the robe, hoping some of her essence lingered in the fabric. No such luck, though. It simply smelled like…his robe.

In fact, no trace of Jane remained in the room. She had left like a thief in the night, and somehow he'd let her slip away. In the future, he would have to keep her close.

No wonder Charles had been so adamant about marrying her.

The thought of Charles unsettled George. Last night he'd been blind and deaf to everything that wasn't Jane. And that included his brother.

This morning, by the stark light of a new day, he was forced to confront the notion that he'd made love to his brother's girl. His *former* girl, George insisted to himself. She had come to him, tearful and troubled. Until this moment, George hadn't let himself consider where his kid brother had been last night.

He'd undoubtedly been heartbroken. Perhaps he'd been full of rage, smashing things, tearing his hair out.

That, in fact, was quite unlikely, George conceded. Charles had always been a ladies' man.

Could be the reason for the rift was that Charles had strayed.

"Your loss, my gain," George muttered.

As he picked up his shower caddy, a gleam caught his eye. Bending down, he retrieved the object from the floor between the bed and nightstand. It was a silver earring in the shape of a daisy. Jane's earring.

George placed it carefully, almost reverently, in the top drawer of his bureau. He let out a burst of relief, and realized he had been holding his breath in, with a strange little insane worry.

The earring was evidence that the previous night had really happened. He'd actually taken Jane Gordon to bed.

It was a relief to have physical proof; otherwise there was a danger that he'd dreamed the whole thing.

Twenty-Four

George carried the earring like a talisman in his pants pocket, replacing his lucky rabbit's foot. He took it out while in French 505 as the professor was droning on about the nuances of the subjunctive case in the literature of French classicists.

"What've you got there?" asked Jeffords, holding up his textbook to whisper behind it.

"What's it look like?" George whispered back. In fact he'd never really studied a woman's earring up close before, never paid attention to how they worked. It was slightly shocking to see the way the earring was made. It resembled a tiny torture device, like a thumbscrew. Apparently it stayed in place by pinching the earlobe.

Ouch.

His friend lost interest in the earring and leaned over to whisper to the guy on his other side.

The morning dragged on interminably. He couldn't stop thinking about Jane. He couldn't wait to see her again, though he wasn't quite sure how to go about it. Swept away by last night's grand passion, he had neglected to extract the most basic information from her.

Such as where she lived.

And her telephone number.

And whether or not she even had a telephone. For although the twentieth century was more than half over, he knew some homes still lacked modern conveniences, such as a telephone.

The first hint that something was amiss came all too quickly, rolling in like stormclouds covering the sun. And that hint was carried in his pocket. Jane had not only slipped away while he slept, but she'd left nothing but the earring. Maybe it wasn't such a good luck talisman after all, he thought, turning the tiny screw one way, then the other. Why couldn't she have awakened him? Or at least left a note?

The only way he knew to find her was to wait by the provost's house for the end of her shift. He must have timed it wrong that first day, for he waited two hours and never saw her coming or going. Maybe it was her day off. The only one who might know how to contact her was the only person George would never ask—his brother, Charles.

On the second afternoon, he got there early and stayed late, until dusk painted the sky with smudges of charcoal.

Come on, Jane, he silently urged her.

He pictured her emerging from the ornate old house in her housekeeper's apron. She would spy him, and a smile would light her face. Then she'd fling herself into his arms. He'd catch her and hold her close and scold her for sneaking away without a word.

And she would laugh and say a Yale man ought to be smart enough to track down the girl he loves.

Mosquitoes came out as the light slipped away. George

slapped at the pests in annoyance. He was about to abandon his vigil when at last he noticed people at the servants' entrance. A small group of women emerged, all of them in domestic garb. They looked the same to him, like pilgrims in a play. He stood up, squinting in the light to try to pick out Jane.

The women were laughing together and chattering. There were six in all. Two of them hesitated and used a Zippo lighter to light up cigarettes. The group crossed the street to the bus stop to start their journey home.

At last he figured out which one Jane was, recognizing her slender silhouette and unruly hair escaping its combs. Unlike last time, she stayed with her coworkers, giving him no chance to speak with her alone.

Her name was on his lips, but he hesitated. If he called out, then what? Would he embarrass her in front of her friends? Worse, would they guess what had transpired that stormy night, in his dorm room? Would her reputation be ruined?

He didn't wish to be the cause of that.

While he deliberated and debated with himself, Jane looked over and seemed to spot him. She half raised her arm in greeting.

At that same moment, a group of fellows came out of the DeWitt House, where the unruly Gamma Delta society held their meetings. These men were at the top of the social echelon here at Yale. They were George's peers; he was one of them.

"Georgie Porgie, puddin' and pie," declared Greenhill, hooking an arm around his neck. A cloud of liquor breath fogged the air. They'd apparently started cocktail hour early today.

"Kissed the girls and made them cry," finished Sterling. "What the hell're you doing here all by your lonesome, Georgie Porgie?"

"Trolling for girls," brayed Akers. Then he spotted the domestics across the street, at the bus stop. "Oh, look. There they are now."

"The maid brigade," Greenhill shouted.

George had a bad feeling about this. "Guys—"

"Come give us a kiss, girls." Akers made a lewd gesture.

"I need to grab me one of those," declared Wilson. "The ideal woman. She lets you screw her any which way you like, and then she irons your shirt."

The others roared with laughter. George's stomach clenched.

The housekeeping staff huddled closer, turning their backs to the jeering men.

George didn't dare approach Jane now. Not with these jackasses around. He wished she could see his regret. He hoped she would understand he had abandoned her to avoid drawing attention to her. No point incurring the scorn of this lot.

"I heard the hired help can be hired to do a lot more than help," said Akers.

"Yeah, like when they say no, they mean yes. And don't means do. And stop means go."

"They can go all night. They never want to stop."

George couldn't escape the memories that drummed through his mind. *Please. Don't. Stop.*

Please. Was she begging him to leave her alone?

Don't. Was that what she'd meant? Don't touch me?

Stop. He'd heard her say it. But could he have missed her meaning?

Damn it. He had to talk to her.

"Maybe I'll just go grab me one of those right now," said Greenhill. "The redhead looks like a tasty morsel."

"Guys, I got a better idea." George grabbed the back of Greenhill's jacket and aimed him in the opposite direction. "Let's go see what they're serving at Kelly's Pub." He chattered away about nothing, knowing it would take some fast talking to distract them and make it believable.

They were mean, small minds, easily manipulated. Within a few moments he had convinced them to try their luck at Kelly's. He wanted to shout to the world that Jane was the woman he loved, but people like this would never understand.

He dared to look over his shoulder and saw her watching him, but she was too far away to read.

George tried again the next day, waiting for quitting time. For once in his life, he was going to be audacious instead of cautiously circling around, questioning himself and missing his chance. He'd gone all the way to Manhattan on the train, and he'd picked out a signed and numbered diamond ring in Tiffany's, cheerfully going into debt over the purchase. It had flawless color and clarity, and a leather-bound certificate declaring its perfection. He rehearsed his speech in his head. He planned to approach her directly, ask right in front of her coworkers if he could speak to her.

I'm in love with you, he would say. *It's a permanent condition.*

Come to Paris with me, he'd say. *Let's live together in Paris.*

It was the perfect solution. Paris—the city of lovers. A world away from his parents and from social snobs who didn't believe it was possible for a Bellamy to be with a working-class girl.

They would be thousands of miles away from prying eyes, and they'd have the world at their feet.

Yes. He felt the deep satisfaction of things coming together, a plan falling into place. He couldn't wait to tell her. He took a seat on the bench at the bus stop and tried to pass the time by reading the paper. There was a review of a new play, "Waiting for Godot," which had just opened at the John Golden. The author, Beckett, was an Irishman, but he lived in Paris, too. George took it as a sign that he was making the right decision.

The drama featured Bert Lahr, who had played the cowardly lion in *The Wizard of Oz.* George wondered if that might be a sign, too.

"Hey, stranger," said a voice behind him.

He glanced up from the paper, startled. "Charles."

George's brother was dressed in gray flannel slacks and a V-neck cashmere sweater vest. His hair was shiny with Brylcreem. In his hands he held a bouquet of flowers and a heart-shaped box of chocolates.

"What are you doing here?" he asked George. "Just enjoying the fresh air of springtime?"

George didn't know what to do, so he nodded his head while his mind raced. Spring truly had arrived, seemingly overnight. The lane was shaded by trees draped in pale green new leaves. Huge old lilacs bore lavish clusters of flowers. Every garden bed was crowded with tulips and daffodils.

"Right," said George. "How about yourself?"

"I'm meeting Jane," Charles said, gesturing. "She works just over there."

I know. George's mouth felt dry as dust. He had to figure out what was going on without disclosing anything that had happened. He cleared his throat, indicated the flowers and candy with a nod. "What's the occasion?"

Charles's ears turned red. "We had a little spat a couple of days ago."

A little spat. The kind that had sent Jane running out into a storm at midnight, convinced the affair was over. The kind of spat that had sent her into the arms of another man. Into his bed.

"We're good now," Charles said hastily. "I went to see her last night and she forgave me. I think her feelings are still a little tender, though. I've got a lot of making up to do." He lifted the bouquet to his nose. "Peonies are her favorites."

George stood up, feeling a twinge in his bad leg. He briefly considered sticking around, confronting the situation head-on. Yet if he did that, her reputation would be in shreds. Nothing good could come of exposing what they'd done. Not now, not like this. "I'd better get going. Got a journalism seminar tonight. Alfred Eisenstadt is speaking about his postwar photographs."

"Stick around for a few minutes," Charles suggested. "You can say hello to Jane. George, I'd really like it if the two of you would get to know each other. She's a really wonderful girl."

I know, George thought again. She was all he could think about—their night together, the whisper of his kisses across her skin, the desperation that had turned, by some magical emotional alchemy, into love.

"Charles, I'm sorry," he said, thrusting the newspaper into a nearby trash bin. "I just don't see that happening."

When it came to his personal life, George had never made much use of the skills and techniques he had learned as a journalist. He did now, though. Now he took advantage of everything he knew in order to discover where Jane lived. He found out her mother's maiden name was Swift and her aunt's married name was Scanlon, and that they lived on the east side of town. There was no individual telephone service in the neighborhood.

That evening, his search brought him to a clapboard-covered row house in a dilapidated section of Lower State Street. It was an area where workers lived between their back-breaking twelve-hour shifts at the wire plant or hosiery mill, where they yelled at their wives, raised their kids, played sandlot baseball, drank beer on their front porches and dragged themselves off to work the next day.

This was Jane's neighborhood, he thought, handing over cab fare to his driver. He'd never set foot in it before. Compared to the manicured greenswards of the Yale campus, this was like a different planet. How strange it must be for Jane to ride the bus each day between these two worlds.

"You want I should wait?" the driver asked.

"No…er, yes." He knew he wasn't likely to find another taxi in the area. "Can you give me ten minutes?"

"Sure. I got nothing but time."

George wasn't certain why he'd said ten minutes. Maybe he figured that was how long it took to find the woman you love, to lay your heart on the line for her. And when the ten minutes were up, you either moved on or moved in.

Simple.

A couple of doors down, a mongrel cur dog gave a husky bark. There was the sound of a door slamming. George squared his shoulders, crossed a weedy patch of grass that passed for a front yard. Through the window, he could see the family, an older couple who were probably Jane's aunt and uncle. The third woman must be Jane's mother, whom he had not seen since the summer of 1944. He scarcely recognized her, with her hair gone white, her expression blank, her hands frantically knitting, as though her life depended on it.

The four of them were gathered around a tall radio console, its dial glowing amber. The voice of Walter Winchell drifted from the speaker, clearly audible through the open window.

George was consumed by the urge to rescue Jane from all this, to sweep her away to a different life.

Paris was waiting for them, but there was just one obstacle. She'd said it was over with Charles. She'd never said she loved him.

He suddenly felt self-conscious about the Yale sweater he was wearing, the school colors blazing in the twilight. He pulled the sweater off and slung it around his shoulders. Then he made a fist and firmly knocked at the door. He prayed Jane would be the one to answer it, but no such luck. The uncle came, opening the door wide. The house exhaled a whiff of something oniony.

The uncle was a big man with a beer belly and an unshaven face, handsome in a rough fashion. He wore work trousers and an undershirt with a pack of Lucky Strikes twisted into the sleeve. "Yeah?"

"My name is George Bellamy," he said. "I'm here to see—"

"He's here to see me, Uncle Billy," said Jane, stepping through the door. "We'll be out on the front porch."

"Yeah, okay," said the uncle. He scowled at George. "I thought you was one of them religious boys that goes door to door, spreadin' the word."

"Uh, no, sir."

The man gave a nod, and headed back to the radio show.

It was all George could do to keep from grabbing Jane right then and there, and spiriting her away forever. Instead he said, "I'm here to plead my case."

"There's nothing to say, George." They sat together on the stoop, though it offered little in the way of privacy. The neighborhood was a busy place, people calling their kids in for the night, dogs barking, pots and pans clanking, couples fighting. Bikes lay abandoned in some of the yards.

"You came running to me," he said. "You spent the night in my room. You call that nothing?"

"I call it a mistake, made out of impulse and panic. I honestly thought I'd lost Charles forever. I had nowhere to turn, so I turned to you. All I wanted was someone to talk to."

"We did a whole lot more than talk." *Please. Don't. Stop.* He could hear her, plain as a radio broadcast.

"That was a…an accident. A mistake. I'd had too much to drink and I was confused. I didn't know…didn't expect—"

"Baloney," he burst out. "You came to me knowing how I felt about you, how I still—"

"No. I didn't know you felt anything but contempt. That's certainly all you ever showed me."

"Then why did you come to my room?"

"Because Charles respects you. I thought you might talk sense into him, convince him to change his mind."

"You knew better than that," he said. "Drunk or sober, you knew you had my heart, Jane. Don't deny it."

"Oh, George." Tears coursed down her cheeks.

"You felt it, too," he accused. "I know you did."

"But—"

"Hush, just listen. It's not too late for us. I have a job in Paris. I start next month, right after graduation. We can go to Paris together, live like natives there, in an old-fashioned apartment on the Rive Gauche. It'll be like a dream come true."

She smoothed her skirt over her knees and looked out at the beaten-down neighborhood. "Whose dream, George?"

"Ours, silly. It's Paris, for Pete's sake. Who doesn't dream of Paris?"

"You don't know anything about my dreams," she said brokenly. "I'm not going to Paris with you. I'm not going anywhere with you." She gestured at the weedy neighborhood. "This is my world. My life. I look after my mother. I help my father with the camp in the summer. How am I going to do that if I live in Paris?"

"We'll figure something out, find an arrangement—"

"We won't do anything of the kind," she said, swiping at her cheeks. "Don't you understand? I'm all my mother and father have. You can't 'arrange' for my parents to have another daughter, no matter how much money you have."

"Then I'll cancel my plans for Paris. I'll move right here to this house if you want," he blurted out. "I love you, Jane. I'll do anything to be with you." He plunged his hand into the pocket of his trousers, closing his fist around the small ring box.

"Stop it," she snapped. "You don't love me any more than I love you."

He let go of the box and touched his empty hand to her cheek, feeling the damp heat of her tears. "Then why are you crying? Answer me that."

"Because I'm frustrated. You won't listen. You need to understand, I'm with Charles now. We've reconciled."

"Three days ago you were with me," George reminded her, surprising even himself with the unblunted cruel edge to his voice. "You declared it was over with Charles and you came running straight into my arms. Into my *bed,* Jane."

"I should not have done that. I told you, I was upset, because all of a sudden, the future I thought I had was gone. It frightened me."

"I'll just bet it did. So you were scared of losing your rich boyfriend? Did you think to replace him with somebody equally wealthy, so—"

Her slap shut him up, a sting of heat he almost welcomed because it kept him from saying even more regrettable things. At the same time, the feeling was akin to the horror of being encased in the iron lung all those years ago. He felt trapped. He wasn't sure where his next breath was coming from.

The suddenness and violence of the blow seemed to startle her as much as him. "I shouldn't have done that," she said, wrapping her arms around her middle and leaning forward, as though her stomach ached.

"Does he know about us?" George demanded, determined to feel nothing.

"He can't ever know. It would hurt him too much. It would destroy him."

"What about us? We're destroying each other right now." That was how it felt to him. He was crushed. Devastated.

"For Charles's sake, we must put this behind us. As if it never happened."

"That's impossible."

"Anything is possible." She stood up, wiping her hands on her apron in a decisive fashion. "Don't contact me again, George. Go to Paris. Find your dreams there."

"I already found my dream," he said. "That night, in my room—"

Fresh tears gleamed on her face. "That wasn't a dream. It was an accident. A mistake."

"Don't do this."

"It's already done." She put her hand on the door latch. For the first time, he noticed the diamond ring, winking on her left ring finger.

The entire exchange had taken exactly ten minutes. George was glad he'd asked the cabbie to wait.

"Be happy for me, George." Charles sounded a little desperate as he dogged his brother's footsteps through the terminal of LaGuardia Airport. George was on his way to Paris, and Charles had come to see him off.

"I'm not going to pretend to be happy," said George, trying to stay focused on the bustling redcaps and liveried pilots hurrying to their flights.

"It's bad enough Mother and Father won't give us their blessing." Their parents had begged Charles not to marry Jane Gordon. They threatened to disinherit him, yet he refused to veer from his path. "I suppose I can understand Mother and Father disapproving. They're so old-fashioned. But you. Why can't you be happy for us?"

"Because I don't need a crystal ball to see what's going to happen. You're too different," George insisted. He kept up the argument about class differences because it was easier than telling the truth.

"Hey, variety's the spice of life," Charles reminded him.

"When it comes to *building* a life, you don't want it so spicy." George couldn't stand the thought of Charles and Jane together, having to smile through their wedding, through family holidays and gatherings, having to pretend he wasn't dying inside.

"I just don't get it," Charles said. "We've known Jane since we were kids."

"She'll break your heart," George blurted out. "She's trash."

Charles's chin snapped up as though he'd been punched. "Apologize."

"What, for wanting to spare you a lifetime of pain?" George asked. "Because that's what you're in for. I know you don't want to see that right now, but it's true."

"And *I* know you can get the hell out of my sight. Come back when you're ready to apologize."

"In that case, let's make it never."

Twenty-Five

Despite their bitter quarrel, George fully intended to man up and go to his brother's wedding that August. By then he was living in Paris, a Yale grad with a job doing exactly what he loved—writing. He covered stories and events that mattered to the world—armed conflicts in Egypt and the Suez, earthquakes and the Olympics.

He lived in a flat with a balcony overlooking the Place de la Concorde and kept company with literary friends. He visited the haunts of Hemingway, Gertrude Stein, Alice B. Toklas and J.P. Donleavy. He read banned books, drank absinthe and even seduced two women.

One of the women he seduced claimed she was falling in love with him, and he let her, because she was exciting. She was Jacqueline duPont, heiress to a champagne-exportation fortune. She was fiercely beautiful, sexually sophisticated and fashionable enough to have her photograph in *Women's Wear Daily*.

For about two seconds he considered inviting Jackie to attend his brother's wedding as his date. But George rejected the notion. It was out of the question. He could not imagine Jackie, in her Chanel suit with her heirloom pearls, witnessing Charles marry a chambermaid.

George buried himself in work and in a matter of weeks won the attention of a key editor at the paper—the *Trib* as it was called by insiders. He worked in a cramped and cluttered office alongside journalistic giants—the ascerbic Art Buchwald, the relentless Desmond Burke, and other revered veterans of journalism. From early on, George's career was guided by the same demanding editor who had overseen the Pulitzer prize-winning coverage of the Blitzkrieg.

Two days before George was due to fly to New York for the wedding, he was presented with a career-making opportunity. He would be given exclusive access to a high-level meeting of the North Atlantic Treaty Organization. General de Gaulle would be there.

George accepted without hesitation. This event was important to the world. He told himself he would do the job and catch a transatlantic flight in time to get there for the wedding. Sure, he was cutting it close, but that was the nature of modern journalism. You followed a story moment by moment, provided up-to-the-minute reportage. There was even a new term for it—breaking news.

He filed his story at the eleventh hour, sending it clacking over the Telex machine to be published not just in the *Trib*, but in the *New York Times*. Once this was accomplished, he discovered there was only one flight that would get him to the wedding on time.

Events conspired to delay him. That was what he knew he would tell himself later. The train out to Orly Airport ran behind. At the airport, he found himself crushed in a busy, jostling crowd. There was a line at the ticket counter. When he got to the desk, he discovered his pocket had been picked. He had no ticket, no passport, no cash. He talked the clerk into selling him a ticket with a promissory note, and hoped the border authorities would accept his story of the theft. The clerk told him he would have to run in order to catch the New York flight before it closed its hatch and taxied down the runway.

Running was not George's strong suit. He was in a leg brace, which he still had to wear on occasion, and the hinges and mechanisms simply did not allow him to move at a speed faster than a brisk walk.

He was a hundred meters or so from the departure doors when he saw the Pan American airplane pulling up its boarding stairs.

Did he shout loudly enough to be heard, or just loudly enough to say he tried?

In the end it didn't matter. A missed flight was a missed flight. He'd left himself one chance to make his brother's wedding and he'd missed it.

Thank God.

George plunged into work with a passion. He lived and breathed the news of the day. He produced story after story, covering topics as diverse as the opening of a new museum to state visits to violent uprisings.

He lobbied hard for the chance to interview Jonas Salk. He sat in the Prince de Galles hotel with the scientist and spoke with him about developing the live-virus polio vaccine.

He didn't tell Dr. Salk he'd had polio, for he wanted to keep the interview professional, not personal. But at the end of the conversation, as they shook hands and the staff photographer moved in to take a photo, Dr. Salk kept hold of George's hand, turning it palm up.

There was a telltale sign, so subtle no one ever noticed it—no one but experts. In an unaffected hand, the muscle at the base of the thumb was thick and healthy. In George's hand, the muscle was almost nonexistent.

Dr. Salk asked simply, "When?"

"The summer of '44," George said. He was surprised to feel a jolt of leftover emotion from that time—terror, rage and grief, knowing he'd contracted a disease from which he would never fully recover.

"I'm very sorry," said Dr. Salk.

George's mind flashed on Ward 8 at the polio clinic where he'd been sent in an attempt to save his life. Clear as yesterday he could hear the screams of other boys brought back from surgery, the wrenching sobs of parents being told their babies had died in the night. And always, like a nightmare, he couldn't escape, he heard the rhythmic suck and shush of the iron lung.

"I was one of the lucky ones," he said.

In December, George received a letter on his mother's personal letter-pressed stationery. Calls home via telephone were rare because the connection was usually quite poor, so he looked forward to his parents' letters. From Charles, he'd heard not a word; clearly his brother was sticking to his vow not to forgive George until he apologized.

For all that he was a prolific and tireless journalist, George was not much for writing letters. He didn't enjoy writing about himself. He'd sent Charles a telegraph the day of the wedding: "Missed flight. Nuptials must go on without me. Best wishes."

That had been their last communication.

George found it remarkably easy to avoid dealing with his brother and apparently it was the same for Charles. All George knew about Charles came via his mother's weekly letter. And Theodosia Bellamy had little enough to say about her younger son, only that he seemed to be doing well and intended to get his law degree.

Charles. A lawyer.

George wondered what kind of litigator he would be. He might sue his brother for breach of…what? Of brotherhood?

Then in December came unexpected news. Charles and his wife had a baby boy. His name was Philip Angus Bellamy, in honor of both his grandfathers.

At first George felt nothing but a small twinge of curiosity. No envy, of course; he was no fan of babies. They seemed to be noisy, puking, snotty things that disrupted people's sleep. No, thank you.

Later, sitting at an outdoor table at his favorite zinc bar in Montmartre, sipping cold, acrid pastis and reading *Le Monde,* a belated notion struck him. He drummed his four fingers on the enameled surface of the table.

Charles and Jane had been married in August.

They'd had a son in December.

His fingers tapped on the table: *tap tap tap tap…tap.*

August, September, October, November…December.

Five months was not the correct gestation time, was it? Not unless you were a Nubian goat.

AugustSeptemberOctoberNovemberDecember—

It was not uncommon for babies to be born prematurely. But not by four months. That was simply impossible. Especially since George's mother reported that Philip was a healthy eight-pound baby boy.

It was of course considered impolite to count, but George counted. He checked the date mentioned in his mother's letter. He opened his small leather-bound pocket calendar, the one he'd been given as a graduation gift. He took out a pencil.

Counted back nine months from the date the baby was born.

The point of his pencil broke as it landed on the day in late March. George tried every way he could think of to avoid seeing the truth. But there it was, staring him in the face.

That was the day—the night—he'd been with Jane. And nine months from that night, an ocean away, Jane had given birth to a baby.

George went a little crazy after that. He got roaring drunk and stormed the citadel that was Jacqueline duPont's flat on Avenue Marechal Foch, the one she shared with three other young women of privilege. He made love to her with a harsh insistence that surprised and delighted her, and she told him so.

"I'm glad you liked it," he said. "Let's get married."

She laughed and touched him in a way that was probably illegal in some parts of the world. "I thought you'd never ask," she said to him.

They eloped on New Year's Eve, taking a private jet to Monte Carlo, courtesy of the duPont family. Jackie was more adventurous than sentimental, and she regarded elopement as the ultimate adventure.

Amid the glittering lights of the French Riviera, they found a civil judge who was happy to take their money and officiate the union. There was no fanfare, just a hasty signing of documents and, at the Hotel Villa Mondial, a room service order that cost a fortune—champagne, oysters, caviar, chocolates decorated with gold leaf.

Although George's family was well off, Jackie's money made their lives worry free. It made them fun and exciting. George could have retired from the paper, but he insisted on staying and working harder than ever.

Jackie was prolific in her own way, giving him four sons in the first ten years of their marriage. He discovered that he loved babies after all, and lavished his adoration upon Pierce, Louis, Gerard and Trevor.

Their lives were a busy whirlwind. George rarely thought about home—the States, as the ex-pats in Paris referred to the U.S. It took no effort at all to maintain the silence with his brother.

It was through their parents that George learned Charles had volunteered to serve in Vietnam, and was now a JAG officer in some jungle outpost.

When their parents were killed in a cable car mishap in Switzerland, Charles was incommunicado, still serving overseas, and George took care of the arrangements. The estate was divided evenly down the middle. Within a matter of years, the brothers were living lives so separate they might as well have been strangers.

INVITATION

THE HONOR OF YOUR PRESENCE
IS REQUESTED
BY GEORGE AND CHARLES BELLAMY
ON THE OCCASION OF THE FIRST OFFICIAL
BELLAMY FAMILY REUNION.

SATURDAY THE 21ST OF AUGUST, 2010.
CAMP KIOGA, RR #47, AVALON,
ULSTER COUNTY, NEW YORK.

RUSTIC ACCOMMODATIONS PROVIDED.

Twenty-Six

Claire had been mere inches away from believing love could change everything. What she'd found with Ross was that powerful, a seismic shift. As she lay in his arms, feeling safe and protected and adored, she was able to forget the whole world. How had she lived so long without this? How could anyone?

Once found, her love for Ross felt as necessary and as natural as breathing.

She thought she'd mastered the art of detachment long ago. She'd taught herself to keep her distance from people, and had accepted that this was the way it had to be. It was working well for her—until Ross Bellamy came along. He had undone all her hard work, taking away the wall around her heart.

And like an idiot, she'd allowed it. One night with Ross had turned her into a different person, filled with emotions she'd never dared to feel before. The timing of the call back to reality had been cruel in the extreme. She'd been drowsing in Ross's arms, floating with happiness as she relived the night before.

The outside world had intruded in the form of a text message. She had glanced at her mobile phone where it lay on the floor by the bed, gleefully abandoned the night before. The message light was blinking insistently.

She had slipped from Ross's bed with painstaking care, praying there had not been some crisis with George in the night. There hadn't. This crisis was hers and hers alone. The message had come from Mel Reno many hours ago. She'd been so preoccupied with Ross that she hadn't noticed. It wasn't like her to be so careless.

Then again, she wasn't herself at all where Ross was concerned. He turned her into someone entirely new, re-invented out of whole cloth. With Ross, she became someone she barely recognized—a woman filled with love and joy and vulnerability, a woman whose future looked completely different from the bleak self-isolation she'd once envisioned for herself.

It was all a fantasy, as delicate and friable as spun sugar. She should have known better, of course. She *did* know better, but with Ross, she'd encountered something much more powerful than reason. But then, one glance at the message had driven home the insanity of what she'd just done. It hadn't felt crazy at the time, though. It had felt exactly right, and leaving him was like ripping a hole in herself.

She had gone quietly outside. The sun was just coming up, and a shimmery calm glazed the lake, reflecting the rich pink and amber light. The temptation to leave a note for George was almost overwhelming, but she had resisted. Though she'd come close to forgetting the rules last night, reality had slammed home with brutal force. The only way to stay safe and keep others from being harmed was to leave no trace, no footprint in other people's lives. She had tried calling Mel. Tried sending a text. There was no response. This was unheard of. He always responded, night or day, no matter what.

Though she purposely kept herself from knowing too much about him, she did have a number for his landlord. The guy was groggy, but the news galvanized her. Mel had been mugged. He was in the ICU at University Hospital. She called and frantically asked for a report.

"Are you family?" the receptionist had asked.

"I'm..." Not anything. She wasn't anything to anyone. "His daughter," she lied, scribbling the address and room number.

The report was bad. He'd apparently been left for dead and was in critical condition. There was not a doubt in her mind about why he'd been attacked. And not a doubt about what she had to do. She'd almost forgotten about the belongings she'd stashed by the resort exit. Almost, but not quite.

She retrieved the bag, caught an early train to the city and joined the anonymous stream of humanity, making her way on the subway from Grand Central to Penn Station and from there to Newark. She went straight to the hospital but outside the building, she balked. He'd almost been killed. By going to see him, she was exposing him to even greater risk. Still, she was a nurse. Perhaps she could fake her way in. She rummaged in her bag for her phone, but it was missing. She must have left it behind, or dropped it. Pacing back and forth near the round plaza in front of the hospital, she tried to remember what she'd done with it. Careless. She'd never been so careless. Falling in love with Ross had made her stupid on top of everything else. It was a given that she couldn't go back to Avalon. Ever. She'd never see Ross again, or any of the Bellamys. She wouldn't be with George at the end, wouldn't be there for Ross. *I'm sorry,* she thought, her throat aching. *I'm so sorry.*

She couldn't let herself dwell on what she'd lost. She had work to do, arrangements to make.

The plaza of the hospital campus was jammed with pedestrians sweltering in the summer heat. She didn't trust anyone in the department, but she couldn't put this off any longer. She needed to buy another phone and minutes card with cash, find an Internet café she knew of and—

"You are one hard girl to find," said a quiet male voice. "I suppose you know that."

She spun around, already in defensive mode. At the same time, recognition clicked in. *"Ross.* What are you doing here?" she asked, ignoring an urge to tumble into his arms. "How did you find me?"

He handed over her phone. "You left something behind."

He must have figured out where she was by the last number she'd called—the hospital. *Stupid.*

"And I flew, with Duke Elder," he added.

The parachute guy.

"You shouldn't have come," she said, but she already felt herself wavering.

"Sneaking out of a guy's bed isn't exactly unheard of," he said. "But I'm not stalking you. After last night, I thought… Claire, you can't just take off without any explanation."

She wavered some more. He looked wonderful to her. Tired and exasperated, but…wonderful. There was something undeniably thrilling about having a guy come for her, so fast and decisively, driven by passion. Before she could turn soft and weak with emotion, she started walking briskly away. "I don't think you're stalking me. This has nothing to do with you. It's a personal matter."

"Wrong," he said, falling in step with her. "It has everything to do with me. What's going on?"

He sounded angry, hurt. He had every right to be. And she had every reason to distance herself from him. "I can't explain, and I don't have to. The situation with your grandfather wasn't right for me."

"How about the situation with me?" he asked. "Was that right for you?"

It was the best thing that ever happened to me. She wished she could tell him. Falling in love had been a revelation, like seeing the ocean for the first time. In one incredible night, she'd seen a glimpse of a happiness so complete it brought tears to her eyes. "Last night was a mistake." The lies scratched her throat like sandpaper.

"I don't believe that for a minute, and neither do you."

"You don't know me," she lashed out in desperation. "You have no idea what I believe."

"Claire, I need answers to some basic questions. Like who the hell you are. I already know you appropriated the social security number of a child who died twenty-five years ago," he said.

"That's ridic—"

"And that's just the start. I can go deeper, and I will, if—"

"Please don't." She whispered the plea, and to her horror, felt her eyes burn with tears. "Please…"

"Then talk to me. I need to know what's going on."

His smile was gentle now, tinged with sadness. "You'd be surprised what I know about you. Natalie checked out your background—"

"Natalie should mind her own business."

"I asked her to. You've been on your own for a long time. You probably believe you'll go through life alone. And that's so insane, Claire, when all we both want is to be together."

"Speak for yourself," she said. "I'm not interested." *I can't be.* She felt a pounding sense of urgency. The longer he hung around here, arguing, the more danger he was exposed to. "Please go. I'm sorry for misleading you and giving you the wrong idea."

"You're apologizing?" He gave a bitter laugh of disbelief.

"Good point. I don't need your forgiveness," she said. "Goodbye, Ross. It's best just to part ways now." She felt the stares of passersby. Just what she needed—more attention. From the corner of her eye, she saw something. Police in uniform. They were looking around the crowded area, clearly in search of someone. One of them rested his hand on his holster.

Grabbing Ross by the shoulders, she drew herself into him, hiding against his tall, solid form. Forgive me, she thought, despite her earlier words. It was the quickest way she could think of to hide her face. As she held him close, she wished she could stay in his arms forever.

Instead she watched through slitted eyes. To her horror, the cops went inside the hospital.

She tore herself away. "I have to go." She hurried into the main entrance. One of her former patients had been here, and she knew the way to the neuro ICU. To her relief, the two cops were headed in the opposite direction, toward the emergency department.

Ross was right behind her. "Claire, you're acting crazy."

"I'm here to see a sick friend, if you must know," she said.

"You don't have any friends," he snapped. "Believe me, I checked."

"You had no right to check on me," she said, battling a fresh wave of tears.

"Excuse me?" He let out a laugh of disbelief. "Don't you get it? I love you, Claire. I want to know everything about you. And I'm not letting you go anywhere."

It was the *I love you* that broke her down. She swayed against him. "You have to," she said, even though she couldn't stop clinging to him. "You have to let me go." She knew he wouldn't. Not Ross. He embodied loyalty and caring; it was what she loved about him. Yes, loved. She wasn't going to kid herself anymore. She thought about how safe and cherished she'd felt in his arms. How smart he was, how much she trusted him.

The world seemed to blur into the background. She didn't see visitors and hospital staff walking by, didn't hear the elevator bells or pages over the PA system or the sound of aircraft in the distance. She only saw Ross, and the way he was looking at her—expectant, insistent. As if he cared about her more than life itself.

With slow deliberation, she pulled a tissue from her bag and dried her face. What if she told him who she really was, and he changed his mind about her? On the other hand, how could they ever have anything real between them if she constantly lied about her history? By the time her tears were gone, she knew she was going to let him in, come what may. You can never really escape who you are, she realized. You can change your name. Move to a new home. Make up a new story for yourself. But ultimately the person at the core couldn't change. She had needs and desires that would finally catch up and overtake her. She had a heart that couldn't help falling in love. The terrible reality was, she could not go on alone, not after meeting Ross.

"I do need to check on someone," she said softly, and found the charge nurse on duty. Though expected to recover, Mel was in an induced coma and on a ventilator. Standing next to Ross and watching through a wall of reinforced glass, she didn't recognize the draped figure surrounded by tubes and monitors. "He's the closest thing I have to a real friend," she said. "And this happened to him because of me."

"What?"

"There's a reason I don't have any friends," she whispered.

The charge nurse shooed them toward the exit. "You can call for a status check," she said.

Once outside, Ross studied her closely. "I'm not going anywhere."

"But your grandfather—"

"Already warned me not to come back without you, Claire. Listen, whatever happened…you can level with me."

"People who get close to me tend to get hurt," she said.

"I'll risk it."

All right, she thought. He'd made it through two years in a war zone. He was as stubborn and tenacious as his grandfather.

"Let's go in here," she said, heading for an Internet café near the hospital. "I need to show you something."

The atmosphere was dim and intimate, like a speakeasy. Although the webcam above the screen wasn't enabled, she stuck a Post-it note over the lens, for good measure. He bought them each a soda and Claire typed in an address and an old, scanned photo came up, showing row upon row of flat pavers with grass in between. "Fairacre Burial Ground," she said, and zoomed in on one of the pavers. The engraving was simple: "Mario and Joseph Balzano. D. 2001." The sight of their names brought back echoes of the old horror. They'd just been a couple of kids. Then a man they'd trusted and respected had attacked like a cornered wolverine. "I've never gone to see their grave in person," Claire told Ross. "I couldn't risk it."

"Who are they?"

She scrolled sideways to another paver marked "Clarissa Tancredi. D. 2001." It always freaked her out, seeing it etched into a gravestone.

"And who's that?" he asked.

"That," she said, starting to tremble. "Is me."

Twenty-Seven

The reason Claire had never slept with a guy had nothing to do with a set of moral standards or lofty ideals. The reason she'd never done it before was that she was afraid to make herself vulnerable. Yet with Ross, she'd wanted to do exactly that—to surrender, trusting him with the intimate landscape of her body…and her heart, as well.

She hadn't been prepared for how powerful it could be. In that long, magical night, she'd discovered that sex was not just sex. It was a way to show him who she was without saying a word. For someone who had been hiding her identity for so long, this was a gift beyond price.

Now she had to use her words. Now, in order to tell him who she was, she had to tell him her terrible secret. Maybe if he understood who she used to be, he'd understand who she was. This was a leap into the unknown for her. She had done it before, to save her own life. This time, she was saving herself from something else.

She led the way outside and scanned the area, then headed toward a shady parking lot. There were security cameras here and there, but she kept her back to them. She looked up at Ross, seeing nothing but love and acceptance in his face. Then she inhaled a long, slow breath, as though preparing to jump off a high dive. "There's something you have to know before I go on. If I tell you these things, you might be facing the same risk as I am."

"What kind of risk?"

"There's a guy who's out to kill me. I've been hiding from him since I was seventeen. I think he might be behind the attack on Mel."

"Whoa, hang on. Some guy wants to kill you?"

"Because of what I saw. Because of what Clarissa Tancredi saw."

"And what was that?"

"A double murder."

"You saw a double murder?"

Every night in my dreams, she thought. Even now.

She nodded, her heart speeding up as she realized what she was about to do. "The girl named Clarissa ceased to exist one sunny morning. I was reborn the next day in an alleyway behind a bar, when I walked away with nothing but a backpack and a large envelope filled with official documents. It was, um, the strangest, most radical thing you can imagine, dumping everything I'd been up until that point and becoming someone with a whole new story."

"You switched identities? Are you telling me you're in the witness protection program?"

"It's not like the ones you see on crime shows. Those programs are for people who've seen a federal crime. In the absence of a federal investigation, there's no program, regardless of what I saw. Murder is a crime against the state, so it's up to the state to protect any witnesses—or not."

He took her hand, carried it to his mouth and pressed a kiss there. "I want to hear this, Claire. And then we'll figure out what to do."

Her heart pounding even faster, she started from the beginning. The story came out in quiet whispers, like a slow leak of air from a balloon.

From the day she'd entered the foster care system until she was sixteen, the program had worked for Clarissa Tancredi. Thanks to the compassion and dedication of her case worker, Clarissa was cared for by families that enriched her life.

At sixteen, she'd been placed with a foster family deemed ideal by every standard of the state system. Her new family consisted of a work-at-home mom, Teresa Jordan, and her husband, Vance, a police detective. There were already two foster brothers in residence—Mario and Jo-Jo Balzano. The Jordans lived in Forest Hill, a venerable old neighborhood that defied everyone's preconceptions about Newark. Its historic mansions, tree-lined avenues and good schools made it a haven for prosperous families. The big house on Ridge Street was not the kind of place someone could live on a cop's salary, but it was said Vance's wife had money. She worked as a freelance theater set designer, more for the glamour than for the income. She was an aspiring playwright, though she'd never had anything produced. Her plays were intricately plotted, full of unexpected twists and turns. "I hate being predictable" was her motto.

When Claire was placed with the Jordans, she had every reason to expect the peace and security of a nurturing family life. That was what she'd been promised, anyway.

Vance and Teresa seemed like the perfect couple—affectionate and communicative, incredibly good-looking, interested in the kids. Perhaps their only fault was that they were a bit too indulgent, but they made no apology for this. Teresa had confessed that they were unable to conceive a baby. They decided to become foster parents, hoping in some small way to do their part for the community's less fortunate.

Being childless did have its benefits. While other parents were running themselves ragged, keeping up with all their kids' activities, Vance and Teresa put all their love into each other. A birthday or anniversary might be marked with an extravagant piece of jewelry. For his fortieth birthday, Teresa surprised Vance with flying lessons, and he ended up getting a pilot's license. After that, they took weekend float plane trips to Pier 8 in the city, or sometimes to remote lakes in the Poconos. It seemed like a dream life.

Yet in time, it became clear that all wasn't quite right. There seemed to be something almost obsessive, smothering, about the way Teresa loved her husband. Clarissa didn't know much about marriage, but she sensed Teresa's adoration of her husband was over the top. Then again, maybe it was a rare and lucky thing to be loved like that.

The only thing was, Vance was having an affair with his partner at work, a junior detective named Ava Snyder. The boys had told Clarissa shortly after she'd moved in.

They fancied themselves amateur detectives and tended to snoop around. They got away with everything because on the surface, they were just goofy kids who had been left behind when their mother, an undocumented worker, was deported. No one ever thought they had the smarts to solve a mystery or get away with spying on people, but that was exactly what they did. They'd seen Vance sneaking around with his partner, had hacked into his computer and tailed him like a couple of pros. Vance swore he would dump Teresa and marry Ava Snyder as soon as he could save up enough to break free of his wealthy wife.

If Teresa ever got wind of the affair, she'd freak out.

Or maybe not. She had a flair for drama, and a habit of saying, "I always have a plan B."

As things turned out, Clarissa was the one in need of a plan B. By seventeen, she'd had everything taken from her, including who she was—her name, her past, the few connections she had to people who cared about her, everything.

She didn't dare complain. At least she was alive.

Mario and Jo-Jo, her two foster brothers, had not been so lucky. They'd discovered Vance was stealing evidence and forfeited drug money. Apparently that was his plan for gaining freedom from his wife. Claire had been horrified, even though everyone knew police corruption was common and pervasive. It seemed like such a breach of the public trust. She and the boys approached Teresa about it, and Teresa was shocked, as well. "I can't rat out my own husband," she'd said, looking heartsore, "but you do what you have to do."

She'd given them the address of a substation in a

South Ward neighborhood, and told them to wait there for an internal affairs guy who would help them do the right thing. Clarissa had missed the bus; she'd called the boys to say she'd be arriving late to the meeting. By the time she arrived, it was nearly dark. Boarded-up houses, forbidding-looking brick buildings and steel garage doors topped with razor wire dominated the deserted streets. At first she thought she'd missed the meeting. Then she saw three guys halfway down the block. She'd nearly called out to them until she realized something wasn't right. Vance Jordan was herding the boys into an adjacent alley. He was yelling at them, and they were acting scared. She heard Vance demanding, "Where's Clarissa?"

"She don't know a thing," Mario had said. "Swear to God."

She froze and shrank into the shadows while the shouting continued. She found a rusty iron fire-escape ladder and hoisted herself to the first level, crouching on a grill overlooking the alley. She had no idea what her next move would be, so she made herself as small as possible and didn't make a sound. There was a flash and popping noise, and Jo-Jo dropped to the damp, grease-stained pavement.

The thing about killing two people was that you could only do one at a time. Mario fought back. He had a knife, maybe a utility knife. But it didn't matter. A second later, he was as still as his brother. She nearly passed out, trying to keep from making a sound. A thousand screams and sobs were trapped in her chest, clawing to get out. He'd shot the boys, one and then the other, with no more emotion than if he'd been swatting a fly. The boys had loved Vance. They'd idolized him, dreaming of one day being detectives themselves.

Vance Jordan scoured the area, removing traces of himself.

Don't look up, she prayed. *Don't look up.*

Jordan's hand was bleeding; maybe it had been cut with the knife in the struggle. He wrapped a cloth around his hand, but the cloth kept unraveling. With jerky movements, he nudged the boys onto their backs and emptied their pockets, maybe to make it look as though they'd been robbed. He used something to cut the pocket from Mario's jeans. Of course he would do that. A police detective would know exactly what evidence to look for at a murder scene, and exactly what he needed to remove.

Clarissa realized he was removing traces of his own blood. As he made his way to his car, something dropped from his bundle and fluttered to the curb, unnoticed. He jumped in the car and drove off. Clarissa let out a series of terrified sobs, still so shocked that she could barely think. She half jumped, half fell from the fire escape. At the edge of the alley where the bodies lay, she paced back and forth, hugging herself and shaking.

A car or two passed, one a low-riding clunker emitting loud music, another a sedan driven by a driver barely tall enough to see over the dashboard. She held her breath, nearly fainting as she waited for someone to notice her, or to see the bodies, or…

She spotted the object Vance had dropped in his haste. Every nerve of her body vibrated as she realized it was a pocket cut from the boy's jeans.

The fabric was stained with blood, most likely from Vance Jordan's cut hand. That's why he hadn't left it behind. She knew evidence shouldn't be handled too much. Holding it gingerly, she dropped it into a zipper pocket of her backpack. Her hand shook so much as she took out her phone that she couldn't dial. That was something they didn't show you on police shows—that in reality, your hands and fingers stopped working when you were scared. It took her several tries to dial 911. Her shaking thumb hovered over the send button. *Send.* Send what, exactly?

"Nine-one-one, what's your emergency?"

Another thing that stopped working—her voice. She felt as though she was being strangled.

"Hello? What's your emergency?"

She found her voice, formed words she never dreamed she'd be speaking: "I just saw a murder. Two boys— Mario and Jo-Jo Balzano. He…he killed them." She'd watched enough crime shows on TV to know this was an open-and-shut case. She knew the killer. She had a piece of physical evidence.

"Are you safe?"

"No…yes…I guess, for now. Please…"

"What's your name?"

Something kept her from saying it. "He… I saw who did it."

"Can you tell me his name?"

"It was Vance Jordan."

There was a pause, pulsing with disbelief. Then the dispatcher said, "Could you repeat that, please?"

Clarissa hit End. It should have been a simple matter to make a statement to the police. Instead it began a long nightmare that had no end.

A few minutes later, her phone vibrated—Caller

Unknown. Now what? NowwhatNowwhatNowwhat? The words bounced around in random panic. Her first instinct was to go home. But home was where the killer lived. She forced herself to think things through.

It occurred to her that the call from her mobile phone had been recorded. She knew this for certain when the next call came in from Vance Jordan. The dispatcher must have alerted him. "Clarissa, let's talk." His voice sounded the same as it always did. Calm. Fatherly. "It's not what you think."

"I'm not thinking anything. I know what happened."

"Kiddo, you've got it wrong. What happened is this— some lowlife dealer popped those boys. I'm sure the scumbag'll be arrested tonight, and it'll all be over tomorrow."

"That's a lie," she said. "I saw, and I can prove it."

"You can't prove shit, girlie. And the entire department's on my side. Hell, I play golf with the other general assignment detectives. I'm the fucking godfather of the primary investigator's firstborn, and the duty sergeants report to me."

She knew it was true. He was a golden boy in the department, surrounded by layers of allies. "I can prove it," she repeated stubbornly.

"Why, because you saw something? Do you know what a joke a single eyewitness is? Even the stupidest public defender would rip you to shreds. Nobody convicts based on a single witness, especially a girl like you. You'd probably end up doing time for perjury. So come on home, and we'll figure this out. Those boys were trouble—*they* would have hurt you if they hadn't been stopped. Come on, Clarissa. You know me. I'd never hurt you."

That was when she knew he'd kill her. There was something in his tone. She tried to sound normal when she said, "All right. I'll come home." She ended the call.

The phone vibrated again, its display window lighting like a beacon. *A beacon.* Some mobile phones were like tracking devices. Their whereabouts could be detected. She dropped it as though it were a live snake and turned to run. Then she changed her mind, ran to the next block and placed the phone under a seat on a transit bus. Maybe that would buy her a little time.

She spent the night in a gas station ladies' room, not sleeping, but shivering and crying and trying to figure out what to do. In the morning, she dragged herself out into the open. Jabbing coins into a pay phone, she called her case worker and babbled out her story. Sherri told her to calm down, and they arranged to meet. Sherri never made it to the meeting. She'd been taken to the hospital, the victim of a hit-and-run accident. She was not expected to live.

Claire had nearly gone crazy with grief…and guilt. She spent the day in the shadows, terrified Vance would find her next. She was afraid to call anyone else, afraid for anyone connected to her. When the bad guy was a cop, you couldn't call the cops.

Just as Vance had predicted, a lowlife gangbanger had been arrested for killing Mario and Jo-Jo. While in custody, he'd been stabbed to death with a prisoner's homemade knife. These things happened.

She racked her brain, trying to figure out where to turn for help. She remembered Mel Reno, a volunteer who coached the school chess team. A quiet, middle-aged guy, he was well-liked by the students, and brilliant when it came to chess. He had a past, though, which she'd found out from Vance himself. He had been talking to someone on the phone, probably Ava. Reno was a laughingstock, a disgrace, forced to resign from his job under a cloud. He'd been in charge of protecting a family of witnesses, and they'd all been killed. *Fucking bleeding heart,* Vance had said. *A couple of witnesses got popped, and he ran like a cat on fire. Fucking coward.*

Mel had believed every word she'd told him. She'd been jubilant, until he explained her fate. She was going to have to disappear.

And Vance Jordan was going to get away with murder. In the *Star-Ledger,* he was pictured with a grieving Teresa and quoted as saying, "They were always so troubled, those boys. We had no idea something like this could happen."

The way Mel explained it, the case was closed. With limited resources, the department was only too happy to go along with the explanation of the gangbanger who was stabbed to death right after his arrest. Even the existence of Mario's pocket stained with Vance's blood wouldn't be enough. If she produced the evidence and gave a statement, she'd be exposing herself to a terrible risk, possibly for no reason. Public prosecutors had difficulty protecting witnesses, particularly when the suspect was a cop. There was no staff or dedicated financing for witness protection. Sometimes a program could be cobbled together with a combination of petty cash, drug forfeiture money and general operating revenues. Sometimes relocation worked. But in a case like Claire's, she'd never make it long enough to testify. Mel felt sure of this.

The proof appeared in a footnote to the article about

the murders. The Jordans' foster daughter, Clarissa Tancredi, was assumed to be involved in drugs, just as the boys had been. Vance and Teresa were pleading for information as to her whereabouts. Her embarrassingly homely yearbook picture ran like a milk-carton ad.

Clarissa Tancredi had to disappear for good.

Sometimes, especially in the early days of her exile, she grew so exhausted trying to stay alive that she was on the verge of giving up and surrendering to her fate. She imagined walking into a police station and telling her story. She wouldn't let herself, though. She owed it to the boys who had been silenced to stay alive. She wondered if anyone—other case workers or Teresa Jordan or people at her school—wondered what had become of Clarissa Tancredi. Did they know why she'd disappeared without a trace?

Mel had set out the phony grave marker himself, a silent message that she was gone for good. The technique was common in witness security programs, but something had awakened Vance Jordan's suspicions.

Ross listened with his body held tense. She appreciated that he hadn't interrupted or questioned her. He'd just let her finish, as though sensing the need for the bottled-up story to come out.

"Mel recently found out Vance was going to be a foster father again," she explained. "Mel must have tried to alert the authorities." She stared at the ground. "It's my fault. I've known for years that Vance Jordan is a killer on the loose, and I was too afraid to do anything about it."

"Don't you dare do this," Ross said. "Don't you blame yourself."

"But—"

"There's something I need to know. Whatever happened to the evidence you picked up, the one with Vance Jordan's blood on it?"

"I've still got it. I thought I had the ultimate proof, because the report to the public never mentioned that Mario's pocket had been cut out. It's something that would only be known to someone who'd been there. Investigators often leave out key details as a way to test a witness's reliability. In most murder cases, I could tie it up with a bow and give it to the investigators and walk away a hero. I almost did that. I almost delivered the evidence in person. Then I thought about sending it in anonymously. But in surrendering the one piece of evidence, I'd be playing my entire hand."

"And it sounds like this guy knows exactly how to deal with evidence," Ross said.

She nodded. There was a blue wall around Vance Jordan. Nobody messed with him. "I feel like such a coward."

"Keeping yourself safe has to be the number one priority. If anything happens to you, then he *will* get away with murder—for good."

"You sound like Mel." Her heart constricted as she thought of Mel, lost in the shadows, his prognosis uncertain.

Ross held her as she cried. She told him how scared she was for Mel. She told him about the case worker involved in the hit-and-run accident, and how she was afraid that anyone she tried to tell would get hurt.

"You asked me once why I don't get involved with people," she said. "This is why. And you wondered how

I could stand doing this job, caring for people who are going to die on me. It's because dying is not the worst possible thing that can happen to a person. Failing to live—that's worse."

"Everything's going to change now," Ross assured her.

"How?"

"Just tell the truth."

"The way those boys did?"

"Ah, Claire. We'll figure this out together." He made a brief search of his wallet, extracting a business card.

He was a fixer. A rescuer. That was what he'd done in the army. Swooped and rescued people.

Twenty-Eight

Blurred vision was among the many symptoms of George's ailment. He found that if he held himself very still and blinked a few times, the world would come back into focus.

Sometimes, however, he was in no hurry for clarity to return. The genius painter, Claude Monet, had produced some of his best work while going blind. With lines softened by dappled light, the scene appeared before him in dreamlike splendor.

George was no painter, just an observer. He was seated in a cushioned Adirondack chair that was so big and imposing, it resembled a throne. The chair had been placed on the grassy lawn by the resort lodge, where a team from the resort staff was setting up for the family reunion.

The first annual Bellamy family reunion.

For George, it was bound to be the last. He hoped it would go well. He wished—dear God, he wished—his son Pierce could be here. He wished for that every day.

Jane had taken on most of the planning, in consultation with two of her granddaughters—Olivia and Dare.

From a distance, and seen through a haze of sunlight, Jane could easily be mistaken for a slender girl. She wore a sundress and a wide-brimmed straw hat with a yellow ribbon around its crown.

Ah, Jane, he thought. Jane.

As though summoned by his thoughts, she came toward him, still surrounded by a gauzy nimbus of light. "Olivia made a seating chart," she said. "Would you like to take a look at it?"

George smiled and shook his head. "I'm sure it's fine. Remind me again, which one is Olivia?"

"She's the daughter of our eldest son, Philip."

George wondered if there was the smallest bit of strain in her voice. He couldn't tell. Philip and his wife, Laura, had been away, so George hadn't met him yet. "And she's an only child?"

"She has a half sister, Jenny. Both girls have given me great-grandbabies, and I couldn't be happier. Can you imagine, George? I'm a great-grandmother."

To him, she would always be as young and fresh and beautiful as she'd been the last time he'd held her in his arms. He stayed silent. He had a searing headache now, but he ignored it.

"Philip was always quite a serious young man," she said, though George hadn't asked. "Laura is his second wife. His first marriage was… He didn't follow his heart. He married Pamela Lightsey, Sam and Gwen's daughter."

"I remember Samuel Lightsey from Yale," said George.

"Pamela is lovely, and for Olivia's sake, they worked hard to make a go of it. But…they had to try too hard. His heart was somewhere else. It was all a long time ago."

"Jane," said George, "there's something I've always

wondered." He didn't quite know how to ask. He took a small object from his pocket. "I have something that belongs to you." He handed her the earring.

"I don't recognize that."

"You left it in my dorm room in 1956."

She stood very still for a moment. Then she sat down in the chair next to him. "I can't believe you kept it all this time. I'm sure I threw away its mate decades ago. Thought it was a lost cause."

"I see."

She turned to him, leaning slightly forward. "Do you, George? Because I don't think you do."

"Then suppose you tell me," he said, not bothering to hide his irritation.

"I'm not making excuses, but those years after Stuart died were incredibly hard for me. My mother shut down. She wasn't there for any of us, and it was awful. My father did his best to raise me, but understandably, there were gaps. Vast ones. I was a vain and careless girl, plagued by insecurity. That night—" she indicated the earring "—I was tipsy, as well, as I recall. I was in a panic over a lovers' quarrel and flattered by your attention."

"It was more than attention, and you know it," he said. "I did love you, Jane, and the only reason I gave you to Charles was—"

"Let's be clear," she broke in. "You didn't *give* me to anyone, George. And Charles didn't take me. If that is what caused this rift then you're insane. I did a stupid, hurtful, impulsive thing, and I'm sorry for any pain that caused you. Please understand, I gave my love to one man and one man only, and it's been that way for fifty-five years, and it will be that way for the rest of our lives.

What you must understand is that *I* chose. I chose the life I've had, and it's a good one. It's been good beyond my wildest dreams. I can only hope you feel the same about your life."

"I could...up until I lost Pierce," he said. His heart was sore with unhealed grief. Perhaps, he thought, losing Pierce was the reason it had seemed so important to get to the bottom of the story behind Philip. Now George realized his curiosity was entirely wrong-headed. Passing on DNA didn't make a man a parent. *Parenting* made him a parent. Philip was Charles's son in every way that mattered.

Unlike Mrs. Gordon, George had not let himself neglect his other sons when Pierce died. However, that was when Jackie had changed, turning away from her husband, as though she couldn't bear their combined hurt. She had pursued her romantic adventures discreetly at first, but ultimately she ceased to care whose heart she broke. People grieved in different ways; George knew this. They loved in different ways, too.

Jane's hand covered his. "George. Oh, my dear sweet George." She got up and hugged him fiercely, and placed a kiss on his cheek. Then she went back to the preparations.

George's vision blurred again, the world melding into a sun-dappled Impressionist painting. A powerful feeling swept through him, and the image changed, coalescing into the face of his lost son. The wind sang strangely in his ears—*See you soon.*

Twenty-Nine

◦◦◦◦◦

"Good heavens, woman, I'm not dead yet," said George, giving Claire the once-over. "Don't you have a more cheery-looking frock than that?"

Claire plucked at the skirt of her gray dress. Like all her other dresses, it was decidedly plain, designed to help her fade into the background. "This is your day, George. Nobody cares what I wear."

"Balderdash. I'm calling Ivy." He grabbed his mobile phone.

Claire didn't argue. This *was* George's day. She had never planned to return to Avalon, yet she'd found herself aloft in Duke Elder's plane, flying northward over the Hudson, which formed a bright ribbon leading to the green-clad highlands of Ulster County. For the first time ever, she dared to believe there could be an end to her ordeal, that she could actually have a life that didn't involve a constant series of goodbyes.

Ross had contacted someone named Tyrone Kennedy with the state prosecutor's office. Mr. Kennedy put his best assistant on the case. Based on a retest of evidence—

the boys' clothing—there was enough forensic evidence for an arrest. Once he was charged, Claire would produce the missing piece of the puzzle—the bloodstained inner pocket. Mel Reno was put under guard, and was expected to make a full recovery.

And just like that, everything shifted. Claire didn't quite trust that the ordeal was finally over, though. She'd been let down by the system so many times.

This time would be different. Ross had promised.

Although still wary, she decided that at least for today, she'd put her worries aside. She was in her room in the cottage, scowling at the other four dresses hanging in the closet. Beige, brown, charcoal and black, her standard palette.

"Eeny, meeny, miney, moe," said Ivy, rapping at the door frame to her room. "Granddad said to help you figure out a dress for the reunion."

When Claire turned and saw Ivy, she gasped. "You look incredible."

In a floaty, colorful silk print dress, Ross's cousin flitted into the room, part girl, part butterfly. Her sandals were made of thin braids of colorful twine, and a rakish-looking clip held her hair in an informal updo. "You like?" she asked, twirling. "You think Granddad will like?"

"Of course. He didn't care for this one," she admitted, indicating the gray sleeveless sheath. "Which one of these, do you think?"

Ivy regarded the selections for about two seconds. "None of the above." She grabbed Claire's hand and marched her downstairs. She stopped to poke her head into her grandfather's room. "Are you all right in there?"

"I could use some help with my tie," said George.

His voice was thinner, a bit vague. Claire didn't say anything, though. She didn't want anyone to worry today.

"I don't know how to tie a tie," said Ivy.

"I do." Claire picked up the silky necktie. "Hold still, George." His coloring was slightly off. "Listen, if you need anything at all, you let me know."

"I'll be all right. Ivy, can you get my cuff links? In the top drawer of the bureau there."

She rifled around in the drawer. "Granddad, what's this box from Tiffany's?"

"That," he said, "is a very old ring, and it's part of a very long story."

"Wow, it's gorgeous. Must be worth a fortune. Did it belong to Grandma Jackie?"

He offered a slight smile. "I like to think it's still looking for its owner."

"Granddad. I never knew you were such a romantic." She helped him with his cuff links. The blast of a revving engine sounded outside. "Yikes, what's that?" she asked.

"That," said George, putting on his sport coat, "is my ride. Just a little something I've always wanted to do."

Connor Davis, Olivia's husband, had a Harley. He and George were going for a ride, and then they would arrive at the reunion in style. Ivy and Claire stood watching them go, the motorcycle a silver flash in the sunlight. George reached out both arms as if to embrace the very air around him. Over the low purr of the motor, they could hear his distinctive laughter.

"My granddad's so wonderful," Ivy said, her voice breaking.

"He is," Claire agreed.

"I'm scared. I don't want to lose him."

They watched together until the Harley rounded a curve in the path and disappeared. Ivy took Claire's hand. "And don't think you're off the hook." She brought her across the way to the rustic bunkhouse where the girl cousins and family friends were staying. Their shared accommodations were a throwback to Camp Kioga in its heyday as a summer camp. The walls were decked with authentic-looking handicrafts from times gone by—a painted wooden paddle, signed by campers in the 1970s, a crazy quilt from the sixties, collages made of found objects from the lake and the woods.

"Makeover time," Ivy announced, then turned to Claire. "Resistance is futile."

Claire blushed, though the idea intrigued her. She'd undergone makeovers in the past, but they were all designed to make herself even more nondescript and anonymous, which was clearly not the goal here. "I'm all yours."

Ivy and the others descended, choosing a sunflower-yellow sundress and heeled sandals with gleaming gold straps. "Love the dress," said Claire. "Not too sure about the sandals, though. I don't wear heels."

"You do today," Ivy said. "They're perfect. And they'll look incredible on the dance floor."

Claire examined the spike-sharp heels. "They're weapons of mass destruction."

"Hush, you'll be fine." Hair and makeup were next, and the pampering felt like pure indulgence. "I'm an artist by trade," Ivy explained, brandishing a wand of highlighter. "I do painting on ceramics."

"No offense," said another cousin, Gerard's daughter Nicole, "but that watch you're wearing is butt-ugly."

"No offense taken," Claire said easily, removing the

chunky watch and stuffing it in her pocket. She didn't explain why she had to keep it with her.

"Ross freaked out when you took off," said Ivy, brushing highlighter on Claire's brow.

"What do you mean, 'freaked out'?"

"He's head over heels in love with you."

The matter-of-fact statement gave her chills. "That's a bit of an exaggeration," Claire said.

"Nope," another cousin piped up. Her name was Bridget, and she was doing Claire's hair with a curling iron and a spritzing bottle. "Ivy's right. We've never seen Ross like this before. He's had girlfriends in the past, but with you, he's…different. We all thought he'd be so crushed about Granddad that he'd barely be able to function. But he's…okay. Not happy with the situation— none of us is. But he's found a kind of peace, and a lot of that is thanks to you."

Claire had no idea if they were right. She did know she loved him, even though she'd spent most of the summer trying not to. Like the most powerful of emotions, love had a will of its own, and would not be denied. She had no idea where it would lead, but for the first time in her life, she wasn't afraid of what waited for her around the next corner.

"Ready for the big reveal?" Nicole led her to a full-length mirror. "Check this out—ta-da!"

Claire regarded the girl in the mirror. The bright yellow look-at-me dress accentuated her figure. Her hair was no longer a mousy-brown pulled back with a clip, but a glossy brunette framing her face in flattering waves. The makeup accentuated her eyes and lips, and the color in her cheeks was a blush of pleasure. "Wow," she said. "I look…just, wow. You guys are miracle workers."

"It wasn't a huge stretch," said Nicole. "You're really pretty, Claire."

"You just need some practice in hair, makeup and wardrobe." Ivy handed her a pair of hoop earrings. "Try these."

They went together to the reunion party, chattering excitedly about meeting all the other Bellamys. This was to be the first official meeting of George and Charles's relatives together. Claire felt confident it would go well. These people were not perfect, but they all wanted the same thing—a joyous celebration.

"Who's that girl?" asked a familiar voice, stopping her as she made her way toward the buffet table to get something to drink.

She turned, a smile on her face. "What girl?"

Ross slipped his arm around her waist. "I don't recognize her."

Claire savored his expression, an irresistible mixture of pleasure and pride, tinged with unabashed lust and maybe even love. She thought the attention might feel like all too much, but not today. Today, she wanted to shine. "Your girl cousins gave me a makeover. And as a special bonus, the high heels can be used to aerate the lawn."

"You're a knockout." He turned to survey the arriving guests. "I hope one of Great Uncle Charles's relatives is a doctor, because I'm going to need CPR."

"Sophie's husband, Noah, is a vet."

"He might have to revive me. Seriously, Claire, you take my breath away."

"I hope that doesn't mean you're not going to dance with me," she said.

"The whole world is going to want to dance with you,

but I'm keeping you all to myself. Speaking of which, I wanted to ask you something, honey. How do you feel about a town like Avalon?"

"How do I feel? I—" She broke off, pondering his question. She'd never let herself get attached to a place before, yet here, the bond seemed to grow as naturally as the willows dipping their fronds into the lake. The beauty of nature and intimacy of small-town life, where everyone knew everyone else, had seemed daunting at first. She remembered feeling exposed and vulnerable, beginning with the day a cop had pulled her over. Over the summer, however, Avalon had come to represent a place of safety. "Why do you ask? And did you just call me 'honey'?"

"You got a problem with that? I hope not, because I'll probably be calling you honey from here on out. Dear. Sweetheart. She Who Must Be Obeyed."

"Ross—"

"I love you. I love you so much."

Despite the presence of the gathering crowd, she stood up on tiptoe and kissed him. "I love you, too. In the…the biggest sense of the word. If I could think of a bigger way to say it—"

"You just did."

She couldn't stop smiling. "I have a question for you, too. How does it feel, making another person's every dream come true?"

The blast of the Harley engine heralded George's arrival.

"To be continued," said Ross. "The guest of honor is here."

George was flushed but smiling as Ross helped him dismount from the cycle, and Connor drove it away to park. "Not quite as invigorating as skydiving," George said. "But nearly. How did you like my grand entrance?"

"Very impressive," said Claire.

George did a double take. "My, *my*. Look at you. This is much better. You are unbelievably beautiful, and I'm honored."

"Aw. Thanks, George. How are you feeling? A lot of people are here to see you today."

"Then let's get this party started."

She stayed close to George as the band—the local group Inner Child—warmed up and people gathered at the buffet tables. Philip Bellamy strode eagerly over to greet George. The eldest of all the various Bellamy cousins, he had been away, and he hadn't met George yet. Philip was tall and handsome, exuding personal charm and confidence. "I've been looking forward to meeting you," he said, taking George's hand.

George studied him for a long moment. His eyes, though faded in color, seemed to glow brighter as he regarded Philip. "It is," he said in an emotional voice, "a distinct honor."

Philip's mother, Jane, seemed tense and uncharacteristically quiet. Claire had come to think of her as the bubbly one. This was a solemn moment, though. The brothers had been estranged for the span of Philip's life. Meeting him now felt…significant.

George removed his hand from Philip's and gave him a long, tight hug. "Thank you for coming," he said.

"You bet," said Philip. He introduced his wife, Laura. "I'm just glad we got back from our trip in time for the reunion. And this," he added, indicating the swaddled infant in Laura's arms, "is my grandson, Ethan Bellamy Davis. He's Connor and Olivia's son."

Before George could protest, Laura placed the baby in George's arms. Claire, who had volunteered to take pictures of the day's festivities, caught a snapshot of his expression as he gazed with a look of wonder at the tiny face.

"I believe that makes you officially his…great-grand-uncle," said Philip.

George cleared his throat. "No, that makes me officially older than rock itself." He handed back the baby, offering congratulations to the parents. He studied Philip for several moments. "It's very, *very* good to meet you." Then George turned to Charles. "Your son's a fine man."

"Just like his father," Jane said softly.

"Go and get something to eat," George said with sudden briskness. "I'm told there's to be dancing later, so you'll need sustenance."

He watched them go, his eyes misty and thoughtful. Ross helped him take a seat in the wheelchair. He was so quiet, he scarcely seemed to be breathing. Claire observed him keenly; he could be in the grip of a seizure.

"George?" she softly prompted.

"I'm all right. Just…processing two different stories, one here, and one here." He touched his head and then his chest, and Claire knew he was still sorting through events of the past that had splintered the family apart long ago. She hoped today, the healing would be complete.

"A wise man once told me there's more wisdom in a single beat of the human heart than an entire board of experts," Ivy said.

"Your grandfather said that?" asked Claire. "George, you're brilliant, you know that?"

"No," said George, "I'm terribly flawed. The mistakes I've made in my life—"

"Look at this." She gestured at his family, everyone laughing and talking and eating. It was a beautiful scene, like a painting, with the lake and the forest in the background. "You and your brother did this. It's a monument to the life you lived. Be proud, George. Be happy for the times you've had."

"Now that," said Ross, "is why you're paying her the big bucks."

George chuckled. "You were the one who scolded me for finding her on the Internet." Then his humor faded. "Claire is right. I've been keeping my list, tallying things up, but what I've realized is that my greatest achievement is right here. This family. They are…proof that I was here. That I mattered."

Claire's throat heated with emotion. In the end, a human life amounted to the love he shared. She'd been so wrong, thinking she could go through life without it.

Ross reached down, pressing a hand to his grandfather's shoulder. She aimed the camera, liking the unstudied pose of the two of them. She got the shot, but the low-battery light blinked.

"I'll be back in a few minutes," she said. "I need to go grab the spare battery. There are a lot of shots I'll want to get today." As she made her way along the wooded path to the cottage, she found herself wishing she'd hired an event photographer, but it hadn't occurred to her or to anyone else. Apparently one of the Bellamys—Daisy— was a professional photographer, and the family usually relied on her for pictures. But she was away, so they would have to make do with Claire's snapshots.

She practically floated along the path. She felt flushed with love, her heart soaring. Did she want to stay in Avalon? Did she want to stay with Ross? It was all she could do to keep from climbing to the nearest rooftop and shouting *yes*. This was it, the leap of faith she'd always dreamed of, and now she was actually doing it. Because now she'd found a reason to take the risk.

Humming under her breath, she let herself into the cottage. The minute she stepped inside, she sensed that something was different. A faint, ineffable tension hung in the air, like a smell that was not quite a smell. A sound she couldn't identify, perhaps the creak of a floorboard or the intake of a soft breath.

An icy sense of danger flashed over her. She turned and ripped open the door, but it was already too late. Someone grabbed her from behind. Pinned her against the door, one hand on her throat, the other drilling the cool, smooth muzzle of a gun up into her jaw.

Thirty

"**D**id someone go see what's keeping Claire?" asked Ross. He thought she'd gone in search of another camera battery, but maybe he'd misheard. It had been more than an hour since he'd seen her.

A very busy hour. The Bellamy family reunion ballooned into a huge affair. Both brothers had big extended families, lots of grandkids and a few greats. Some of the kids were getting an early start on the fireworks, probably too impatient to wait for dark. He could hear them going off down by the lakeshore.

"I did." Ivy's voice sounded tense. "I went to find her."

"Well?"

"She's gone. And, um…Ross, I don't actually know how to say this. Granddad's antique Tiffany ring is missing from the cottage, too."

Ross took a step away from his cousin and Natalie. In the distance, the dancing went on. He could see his great-uncle Charles dancing with his wife, and nearby, Granddad with Miss Darrow. After all Granddad had said about the past, today could have been an emotional train wreck. But it hadn't. It had been a celebration of joy, all because Granddad and Jane and his brother chose to focus on the love in their hearts, not rivalry or bitterness, not the vanished past.

"Ross? What's going on?" asked his cousin.

"I have to go," he said hurriedly. "Tell Granddad—just tell him I'll be back as soon as I can."

"Y…you're supposed to be under arrest," Claire said through clenched teeth.

"And your friend the prosecutor's assistant is supposed to be alive and kicking," said Vance Jordan. He looked exactly the same—like a TV cop, handsome and strong.

God. Dear God. It was happening all over again. And it was all her fault.

"I'm disappointed in you, Clarissa," said Jordan. "You were smart for a long time, staying quiet the way you did. You kept our secret, not like those other two. Most people have trouble keeping secrets."

She hadn't had any trouble at all. It was easy for three kids to keep a secret when two of them were dead.

Everything she had come to believe about the terrible vulnerability of love turned out to be true. The moment Vance Jordan assured her that if she tried anything, the Bellamys would start to die, one by one, she shut down. There was not a doubt in her mind that he'd make good on his threat. She did everything he asked of her. Everything.

The small float plane bobbed at the side of the dock, tugging at its mooring line. Sounds bounced off the sheer rock walls that edged the lake. She could hear birdsong and the sighing of the wind, the lapping of the water against the pontoons of the plane.

She didn't ask what his plan was. He was going to force her to hand over the pocket with his blood on it, the one piece of physical evidence that tied him irrevocably to the murders. And the sad thing was, she would surrender it without a fight. Too much was at risk now. She'd entwined her life with Ross and his family, and that gave Vance the ultimate power over her.

That didn't mean she'd given up. She still had the transmitter in her pocket—the ugly watch she'd removed earlier.

The consummate police officer, Vance had bound her hands with zip ties, but not her feet, since he needed her mobile. He looked away for a few seconds while checking a portable GPS, and she used the heel of her sandal to loosen the mooring rope from the cleat. The line had been hastily tied, and slipped loose.

Vance himself had once told her that there was no such thing as the perfect crime. The bad guy, he'd explained, always managed to do at least one careless thing. Find that one thing, and you nail your guy.

Back when they'd had that conversation, she'd never imagined him as the bad guy. Now, everything she used to admire about him scared her—the strong, manly hands, the square jaw, the decisive attitude.

The sharp look of rage as the breeze blew the float plane away from the dock.

"Fuck," he said. "Grab that line. Do it *now.*"

Claire played dumb. "What? What line?"

The plane drifted farther. Jordan cast around, probably looking for a pole, but there was nothing. "Damn it.

You're going in after it." He clipped the plastic zip tie to free her hands, then shoved her off the dock.

The chilly water closed over her. A sound like none she'd ever heard before drilled through the water—the *zip* of a bullet. Every part of her recoiled, though she knew she wasn't hurt. He'd pulled off a shot to show her he meant business. If he'd meant to hit her, she would be dead.

She held her breath for as long as possible, stalling for time. This prompted him to fire another shot. Then, when she was on the verge of exploding, she surfaced.

"Grab the fucking rope," he said. "Do it."

She flailed, grabbed for it, missed on purpose, keeping his attention on her. It was crucial to keep him distracted, because she'd seen a shadow flicker in the trees along the shore. They weren't alone.

"I'm trying," she gasped. "Just...don't—"

He fired again. At the same time, Ross approached from behind, stooping low and grabbing Vance's ankles. He yanked back, and Vance fell flat on his face. Even through the echoes of the gun's report, Claire heard the air rush from his chest. The gun skittered across the wooden planks and fell in. Methodically, in a way that reminded her that Ross was a trained soldier, he delivered pitiless blows to Vance's eyes, neck, groin, with movements as fluid as a dancer's. Then he frisked Vance and took a second gun from an ankle holster.

Only seconds had passed. Claire was treading water, holding the mooring rope in her hand. Shaken to her core, she slowly swam to the dock, looping the rope around a cleat. She held the edge of a pontoon, and looked around, trying to decide how to get out of the chilly water.

Ross was using his belt to tie Vance's wrists behind his back.

"Claire—"

"Don't move," said another voice.

Claire froze. *"Teresa."* She could see Vance's wife reflected in the surface of the lake. Teresa had been waiting in the plane all along. Now she stood on the pontoon, holding a cable shroud in one hand and a gun in the other.

"Drop that, or I'll shoot her," said Teresa.

Without hesitation, Ross let go of the small handgun he'd taken from Vance. It dropped into the lake and sank out of sight.

Good move, thought Claire.

Teresa stepped from the pontoon onto the dock. "Get out of the water," she ordered Claire. "Make it quick." She turned to Ross. "And you—keep your distance."

Claire levered herself up between the pontoon and the dock. Her arms were shaking. She was shaking all over.

"Are you okay, baby?" Teresa asked her husband. "Please, tell me you're okay…"

Vance groaned. "Just stick with…the plan."

Claire's thoughts whirled. Teresa's involvement came as a surprise, yet it shouldn't have. She loved her husband to excess; it was one of the first things Claire had noticed about her. Claire remembered thinking Teresa would freak out if she found out about Vance's affair with Ava, his partner at work.

Claire had no idea whether or not the affair was still going on. She knew she might get herself shot if she opened her mouth—but she also might give Ross a chance to act.

"Ask him if Ava Snyder's part of that plan," Claire said.

Teresa's face froze, and Claire knew she was on the right track. "He and Ava are lovers," Claire explained. "They've been lovers for years. I'm surprised you didn't figure it out by now."

"Liar." Teresa pointed the gun at Claire's chest.

Claire felt as if her bones were about to melt with fear, but she kept talking. "He took a ring from Mr. Bellamy, a priceless antique Tiffany ring. He's planning to give it to Ava." She was speculating now, but sensed she was on the right track. "Check his pocket and see for yourself. He played you for a fool, living in your fancy house, spending your money—"

Teresa squeezed off a shot. Claire staggered back, and Ross lunged for Teresa. He stopped when the gun pointed at Claire again. As the sound of the shot echoed off the quarry walls, Claire said, "Ross! I'm all right."

Vance wasn't, though. His wife had shot him somewhere vital, judging by the dark blood spreading across the dock. Teresa stayed eerily calm. "I always have a plan B. Now I just need to decide on a setup. That's my specialty, remember?"

Claire looked at Ross, so deeply afraid, she couldn't think.

"Could be, the gallant boyfriend rushed in and executed his lover's captor," Teresa mused. "That's predictable, though. I love to keep people guessing. Now I'm thinking Clarissa will be the shooter. There's a peculiar poetic justice in having her murder her once-trusted foster father…."

There was a flash of sound and then a fleshy thud. Teresa's face lit with an expression of pure startlement; then she pitched forward.

"I have a better idea," said George Bellamy, lowering his bolt-action rifle. "How about none of the above?"

"Granddad? Holy crap," said Ross.

George looked pale but determined. "You'd better see if there's anything you can do, son."

Ross checked Vance's pulse. "Gone," he muttered, moving on to Teresa. "She's still with us, though," he said. And he did his duty, keeping her alive until the medics came.

"I didn't mean to ruin your party, George," said Claire. Clutching a thermal blanket around her, she leaned against Ross, unwilling to detach herself from him, even for a moment. The area swarmed with emergency vehicles as the medics and police took charge.

"Good heavens, you didn't ruin a thing," he said. "I'm just thankful you're all right."

"We're all thankful," added his brother, Charles.

She was still shaking as she thought about what she'd nearly brought to this innocent, happy family. Yet no one had hesitated to protect her, a stranger with a false identity. The extraordinary goodness of their actions shook her to her core.

Ross held her shoulders, and his touch was the only thing that soothed her. "Everything's okay now," he assured her. "The police will need a statement after you get into some dry clothes."

One of the police investigators was conferring with a colleague and gesturing at George Bellamy.

"Charles, I might find myself in need of a lawyer," George said to his brother.

"That's funny. I was about to offer my services."

"In that case, we're a perfect match."

Charles offered his arm for George to lean on. The two old men walked away together, surrounded by the deep jewel-toned twilight reflecting off Willow Lake.

Ross tightened his arms around Claire, holding on as if he'd never let her go. "Welcome back, Clarissa Tancredi," he whispered, pressing a kiss to her temple. "Welcome back."

Epilogue

Avalon, New York
Indian Summer

Ross stared at the altimeter of the plane, watching it climb toward ten thousand feet. Duke Elder had taken him up with his three uncles, not for skydiving but a more somber purpose. Except they weren't exactly somber. Trevor and Louis were passing a bottle of Rémy Martin back and forth between them, chuckling as they traded boyhood memories. Gerard was taking pictures. The hills were ablaze with the changing colors of the sugar maples, pink and amber and orange.

Over the headsets, they could be heard chattering about Granddad. It was agreed all around that George Bellamy had not led a perfect life, but it had been a life well-lived, and that was all anyone expected of a man. And if there was such a thing as a "good" death, then Granddad had had one. In the final days, Claire kept his pain to a minimum, and he'd spent time with everyone he loved, talking or playing some board game, sometimes just sitting together and saying nothing at all.

Granddad was proof of something Claire had once told him—that the dying can teach you to live. In just one summer, he'd shown Ross the importance of opening himself to a whole new life. He also, Ross had to allow, had succeeded in accomplishing his final mission— bringing Ross and Claire together. She had come to Avalon to lose herself; Ross had come to find himself, and in the process they'd found each other. Exactly as his grandfather had hoped for.

She'd kept the name Claire Turner, which she preferred. Clarissa Tancredi had endured things no child should ever have to face; Claire insisted on aiming for the future. Now every day with her was a gift. She had become a fixture in his dreams. He wanted to live with her in Avalon. He could picture them building a life that used to seem like an unreachable fantasy, but now lay within his grasp.

Granddad was gone, but his touch was indelible. He'd left Ross the Tiffany ring in its box, along with a note: *"Your move."*

Ross got the urn ready. The ceramic container had been made by Ivy, when she was about ten years old, for some unremembered purpose. But it was the right size and deemed appropriate for the occasion. The thing weighed a ton and was illustrated with fly-fishing lures and, in childish scrawl,

List of Ingredients:
clues
easy answers

facts of life
common sense
excuses
moot points
magic

Ross signaled to his uncles, then slid open the hatch. The wind screamed into the compartment. He made eye contact with the others. They watched in silence, each alone with his thoughts, all of them crying now. Ross carefully removed the lid, opened the plastic liner and tipped the urn so the ashes were sucked out in a thin stream, dispersing into nothingness. He recited the phrase his grandfather had written on a slip of paper the day they'd gone parachuting—a line from Plato's *Republic:* "'The soul takes flight to the world that is invisible, and thereupon arriving she is sure of bliss, and forever dwells in paradise.'"

Ross shut his eyes, remembering the fall through the sky with his grandfather, and all the other days of the summer, right up to the last. Shortly after the reunion, George had been playing a game of Parcheesi with Micah, Ross and Claire. Other members of the family had gathered nearby, enjoying the evening breeze. Someone was strumming a guitar, and the fireflies were coming out. Granddad had been ensconced on the lavish hanging bed that graced the front porch, declaring himself a sultan as he gleefully dominated his opponents in the game.

The last sound Ross heard from his grandfather was laughter.

* * * * *

$24.95 U.S./$27.95 CAN.

Limited time offer!

$2.⁰⁰ OFF

#1 *New York Times* bestselling author

SUSAN WIGGS

returns to sun-drenched Bella Vista,
where the land yields a rich harvest...
and long-buried secrets

*Available June 24, 2014,
wherever books are sold!*

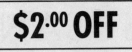

- ✂

$2.⁰⁰ OFF

the purchase price of
THE BEEKEEPEER'S BALL **by Susan Wiggs**

Offer valid from June 16, 2014, to July 14, 2014.
Redeemable at participating retail outlets. Limit one coupon per purchase.
Valid in the U.S.A. and Canada only.

52611432

5 65373 00082 3   (8100)0 11914

® and TM are trademarks owned and used by the trademark owner and/or its licensee.

© 2014 Harlequin Enterprises Limited

MSWI448CPN

An irresistible new installment in the
Swift River Valley series from
New York Times bestselling author

CARLA NEGGERS

**Unlikely partners bound by circumstance...
or by fate?**

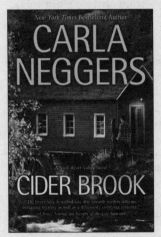

Rescued by a sexy bad-boy firefighter isn't how Samantha Bennett expected to start her stay in Knights Bridge, Massachusetts. Now she has everyone's attention—especially that of Justin Sloan, her rescuer, who wants to know why she was camped out in an abandoned New England cider mill.

Samantha is a treasure hunter, returned home to Knights Bridge to solve a three-hundred-year-old mystery. Justin may not trust her, but that doesn't mean he can resist her....

Available wherever books are sold.

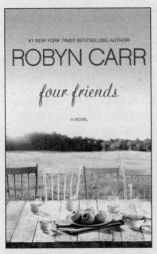

REQUEST YOUR
FREE BOOKS!

2 FREE NOVELS
FROM THE ROMANCE COLLECTION
PLUS 2 FREE GIFTS!

YES! Please send me 2 FREE novels from the Romance Collection and my 2 FREE gifts (gifts are worth about $10). After receiving them, if I don't wish to receive any more books, I can return the shipping statement marked "cancel." If I don't cancel, I will receive 4 brand-new novels every month and be billed just $6.24 per book in the U.S. or $6.74 per book in Canada. That's a savings of at least 22% off the cover price. It's quite a bargain! Shipping and handling is just 50¢ per book in the U.S. and 75¢ per book in Canada.* I understand that accepting the 2 free books and gifts places me under no obligation to buy anything. I can always return a shipment and cancel at any time. Even if I never buy another book, the two free books and gifts are mine to keep forever.

194/394 MDN F4XY

Name	(PLEASE PRINT)
Address	Apt. #
City	State/Prov. Zip/Postal Code

Signature (if under 18, a parent or guardian must sign)

Mail to the Harlequin® Reader Service:
IN U.S.A.: P.O. Box 1867, Buffalo, NY 14240-1867
IN CANADA: P.O. Box 609, Fort Erie, Ontario L2A 5X3

Want to try two free books from another line?
Call 1-800-873-8635 or visit www.ReaderService.com.

* Terms and prices subject to change without notice. Prices do not include applicable taxes. Sales tax applicable in N.Y. Canadian residents will be charged applicable taxes. Offer not valid in Quebec. This offer is limited to one order per household. Not valid for current subscribers to the Romance Collection or the Romance/Suspense Collection. All orders subject to credit approval. Credit or debit balances in a customer's account(s) may be offset by any other outstanding balance owed by or to the customer. Please allow 4 to 6 weeks for delivery. Offer available while quantities last.

ROM13R

SUSAN WIGGS